THE EAGLE'S PREY

Simon Scarrow

headline

First published in 2004
by HEADLINE BOOK PUBLISHING

2

Cataloguing in Publication Data is available
from the British Library

ISBN 0 7553 0115 3 (hardback)
ISBN 0 7553 0864 6 (trade paperback)

Typeset in Times by Avon DataSet Ltd,
Bidford-on-Avon, Warwickshire

Printed and bound in Great Britain by
Mackays of Chatham plc, Chatham, Kent

Headline's policy is to use papers that are natural, renewable and
recyclable products and made from wood grown in sustainable forests.
The logging and manufacturing processes are expected to conform to the
environmental regulations of the country of origin.

HEADLINE BOOK PUBLISHING
A division of Hodder Headline
338 Euston Road
London NW1 3BH

www.headline.co.uk
www.hodderheadline.com

THE EAGLE'S PREY

Also by Simon Scarrow

Under the Eagle
The Eagle's Conquest
When the Eagle Hunts
The Eagle and the Wolves

For my brothers Scott and Alex,
With love and thanks for all the good times.

THE ROMAN ARMY CHAIN OF COMMAND IN BRITAIN IN 44 AD

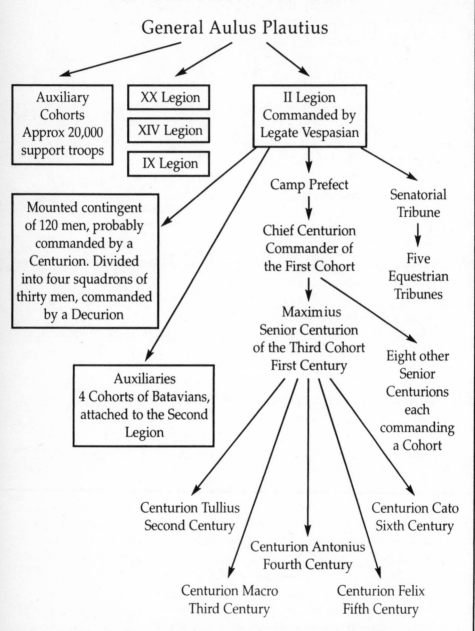

General Aulus Plautius

Auxiliary Cohorts Approx 20,000 support troops

XX Legion

XIV Legion

IX Legion

II Legion Commanded by Legate Vespasian

Camp Prefect

Senatorial Tribune

Mounted contingent of 120 men, probably commanded by a Centurion. Divided into four squadrons of thirty men, commanded by a Decurion

Chief Centurion Commander of the First Cohort

Five Equestrian Tribunes

Maximius Senior Centurion of the Third Cohort First Century

Auxiliaries 4 Cohorts of Batavians, attached to the Second Legion

Eight other Senior Centurions each commanding a Cohort

Centurion Tullius Second Century

Centurion Cato Sixth Century

Centurion Antonius Fourth Century

Centurion Macro Third Century

Centurion Felix Fifth Century

Each Century includes an Optio (second in command), a Standard Bearer and eighty Legionaries divided into ten sections of eight men

The Organisation of a Roman Legion

Centurions Macro and Cato are the main protagonists of *The Eagle's Prey*. In order to clarify the rank structure for readers unfamiliar with the Roman legions I have set out a basic guide to the ranks you will encounter in this novel. The Second Legion, the 'home' of Macro and Cato, comprised some five and a half thousand men. The basic unit was the century of eighty men led by a centurion with an optio acting as second in command. The century was divided into eight-man sections which shared a room together in barracks and a tent when on campaign. Six centuries made up a cohort, and ten cohorts made up a legion, with the first cohort being double-size. Each legion was accompanied by a mounted contingent of one hundred and twenty men, divided into four squadrons, who served as scouts and messengers. In descending order the main ranks of the legion were as follows:

The *legate* was a man from an aristocratic background. Typically in his mid-thirties, the legate would command the legion for up to five years and hope to make something of a reputation for himself in order to enhance his subsequent political career.

The *camp prefect* would be a grizzled veteran who would previously have been the chief centurion of the legion and was at the summit of a professional soldier's career. He would have vast experience and integrity, and to him would fall the command of the legion in the legate's absence.

Six *tribunes* served as staff officers. These would be men in their early twenties serving in the army for the first time to gain administrative experience before taking up junior posts in civil administration. The senior tribune was different. He came from a senatorial family and was destined for high political office and eventual command of a legion.

Sixty *centurions* provided the disciplinary and training backbone of the legion. They were hand-picked for their command qualities and a willingness to fight to the death. Accordingly their casualty rate far exceeded other ranks. The centurions were ranked by seniority based upon the date of their promotion. The most senior centurion commanded the First Century of the First Cohort and was a highly decorated and respected soldier.

The four *decurions* of the legion commanded the cavalry squadrons and hoped for promotion to the command of auxiliary cavalry units.

Each *centurion* was assisted by an *optio* who would act as an orderly, with minor command duties. Optios would be waiting for a vacancy in the centurionate.

The *legionaries* were men who had signed on for twenty-five years. In theory, a volunteer had to be a Roman citizen to qualify for enlistment, but recruits were increasingly drawn from provincial populations and given Roman citizenship on joining the legions.

Lower in status than the legionaries were the men of the *auxiliary cohorts*. They were recruited from the provinces and provided the Roman Empire with its cavalry, light infantry and other specialist arms. Roman citizenship was awarded on completion of twenty-five years of service, or as a reward for outstanding achievement in battle.

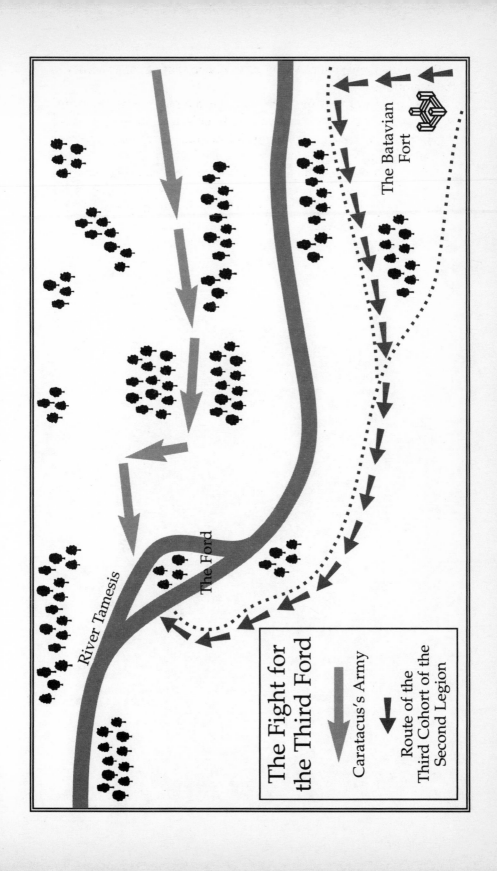

River Tamesis

The Ford

The Batavian Fort

The Fight for
the Third Ford

Caratacus's Army

Route of the
Third Cohort of the
Second Legion

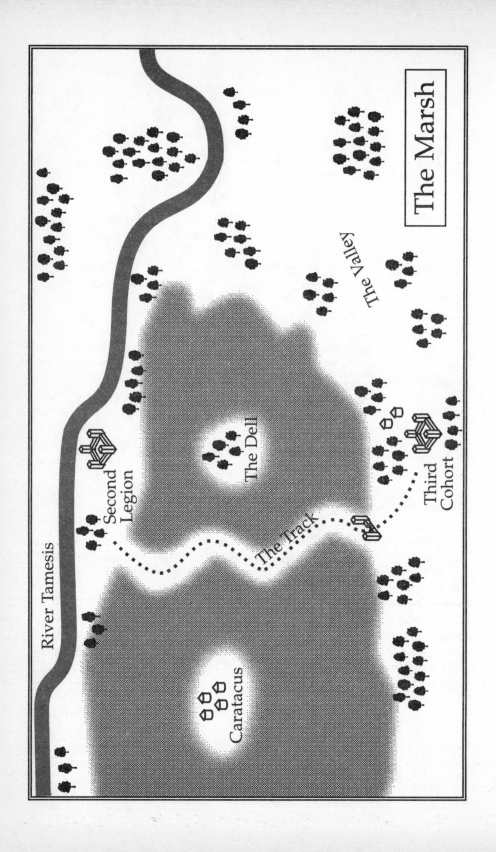

The Marsh

River Tamesis

Second
Legion

The Dell

The Track

The Valley

Third
Cohort

Caratacus

Chapter One

'How much further to the camp?' asked the Greek, looking back over his shoulder yet again. 'Will we reach it before dark?'

The decurion in charge of the small mounted escort spat out an apple seed and swallowed the sharp-tasting pulp before replying.

'We'll make it. Don't you worry, sir. Five or six miles, I reckon. That's all.'

'Can't we go faster?'

The man was still looking over his shoulder and the decurion could no longer resist the temptation also to glance back along the track. But there was nothing to see. The route was clear all the way to the saddle nestling between two densely wooded hills that shimmered in the heat. They were the only people on the road, and had been since leaving the fortified outpost at noon. Since then the decurion, the ten mounted men of the escort he commanded, and the Greek with his two bodyguards, had been following the road towards the massive forward camp of General Plautius. There, three legions and a dozen auxiliary units were concentrated in order to strike a final decisive blow against Caratacus and his army of Britons, drawn from the handful of tribes still openly at war with Rome.

Quite what business this Greek had with the general was a source of great curiosity for the decurion. At first light he had been ordered by the prefect of the Tungrian cavalry cohort to turn out the best men from his squadron and escort this Greek into the presence of the general. He did as he was told and asked no questions. But now, as he looked sidelong at the Greek, he was curious.

The man reeked of money and refinement, even though he wore a plain light cloak and a simple red tunic. His fingernails were carefully manicured, the decurion noted with distaste, and from the thinning dark hair and beard wafted the scent of an expensive citron pomade. There was no jewellery on his hands, but pale white bands showed that the Greek was accustomed to wearing a range of ostentatious rings. With a slight curl of his lip the decurion put the man down as one of those Greek freedmen who had wormed their way into the heart of the imperial bureaucracy. The fact that the man was now in Britain, and so obviously not trying to draw attention to himself, meant that he was on some

1

detached duty of such sensitivity that the imperial courier system could not be trusted with the delivery of the message to the general.

The decurion subtly shifted his gaze to the two bodyguards riding immediately behind the Greek. They were equally plainly dressed and under their cloaks they carried short swords hanging from army-pattern baldrics. These were not the ex-gladiators that the most wealthy men of Rome preferred to employ as bodyguards. The swords and their bearing were a dead giveaway and the decurion recognised them for what they were: Praetorian Guardsmen, attempting – and failing – to go undercover. And they were the final proof that the Greek was here on imperial business.

The palace official looked back once again.

'Missing somebody?' asked the decurion.

The Greek glanced round, then suppressed his anxious expression and forced a small smile on to his lips. 'Yes. At least I hope so.'

'Anybody I should be warned about?'

The Greek stared at him for a moment and then smiled again. 'No.'

The decurion waited for the man to elaborate but the Greek cut him dead and faced forward. Taking another bite of his apple the decurion shrugged and let his gaze wander across the surrounding countryside. To the south the upper reaches of the river Tamesis looped through the undulating landscape. Ancient woodlands hugged the tops of hills, while around them were dotted the small settlements and farms of the Dobunnian tribe – one of the first to pay homage to Rome when the legions had landed over a year earlier.

This would be a nice place to settle down, the decurion mused. Once he had served his twenty-five years and was awarded citizenship and a small gratuity, he would buy a farm on the edge of a veterans' colony and end his days in peace. He might even wed that native woman he had picked up in Camulodunum. Raise a few kids and drink himself silly.

The warm comfort of this reverie was interrupted as the Greek suddenly reined in and stared back down the track, brown eyes narrowed beneath his plucked brows. With a mouthed curse the decurion raised his arm to halt his men and then turned to his nervous charge.

'What now?'

'There!' The Greek pointed. 'Look there!'

The decurion wearily twisted on his saddle, the leather creaking under his riding breeches. For a moment he saw nothing; then as his gaze lifted to where the track disappeared over the hill he saw the dark silhouettes of horsemen flying from the shadows of the trees. Then they emerged into the sunlight, galloping straight towards the Greek and his escort.

'Who the hell are they?' the decurion muttered.

'I've no idea,' replied the Greek, 'but I think I know who sent them.'

The decurion glanced at him irritably. 'They're hostile?'

'Very.'

The decurion ran an experienced eye over their pursuers, now little more than a mile away: eight of them, their dark brown and black cloaks fluttering behind as they bent low over their mounts and urged them on. Eight against thirteen – not counting the Greek. Favourable odds, the decurion reflected.

'We've seen enough.' The Greek turned away from the distant horsemen and kicked his heels in. 'Let's go!'

'Forwards!' commanded the decurion, and the escort galloped after the Greek and his bodyguards.

The decurion was angry. There was no need to run like this. They had the advantage and could rest their mounts and wait for the pursuers to catch up, on blown horses. It would be over quickly enough. Then again, there was a vague chance that someone might get lucky and have a go at the Greek. The prefect's orders had been quite explicit: no harm must come to the Greek. His life must be protected at any cost. In that light, distasteful as it may be, the best thing to do was to stay out of harm's way, the decurion admitted. They had a mile's head start and would surely reach the general's camp long before the horsemen came within striking distance.

When he next looked over his shoulder the decurion was shocked to see how much closer the pursuers had come. They must be superbly mounted, he realised. His own horse, and those of his men, were as good as any in the cohort, but now they were wholly outclassed. And even then the pursuers would have to be fine riders to wring such performance out of them.

For the first time, the decurion was pricked by doubt. These were no mere brigands. Nor were they natives of this island, judging from their dark hair, swarthy complexions and flowing cloaks and tunics. Besides, Celtic tribesmen attacked Romans only when they heavily outnumbered them. Then again, the Greek seemed to know them. Even allowing for the timorousness of his race, the man's terror was palpable. Ahead of the decurion the Greek bounced up and down precariously on the back of his mount, while to each side his bodyguards rode their beasts with rather more style and confidence. The decurion's lips lifted in a wry grin around his gritted teeth. While the Greek might have acquitted himself well in the palace, he rode deplorably.

It wasn't long before the inevitable happened. With a sharp cry the Greek bounced too far to one side and despite a last desperate jerk of the reins his momentum hurled him from his saddle. Swearing, the decurion just managed to steer his beast to one side to avoid trampling the fallen man.

'Halt!'

With a chorus of curses and alarmed whinnying from the ponies, the escort drew up around the Greek, sprawled on his back.

'Bastard better not be dead,' the decurion grumbled as he swung himself down from the saddle. At once the two bodyguards were at his side, looming over the man whose life had been entrusted to them.

'Alive?' one muttered.

'Yes. He's breathing.'

The Greek's eyes flickered open, then he blinked them shut against the glare of the sun. 'What . . . what happened?' Then he slumped back, unconscious.

'Get him up!' the decurion snapped. 'Put him on his horse.'

The Praetorians heaved the Greek on his feet and slung him back into the saddle before remounting. One took the Greek's reins while the other steadied the man with a firm grasp on his shoulder.

The decurion pointed up the track. 'Get him out of here!'

As the three men spurred towards the safety of the general's camp, the decurion swung himself back on to his mount and turned towards their pursuers.

They were much closer now, no more than three hundred paces away, and fanning out into a loose chevron as they charged towards the halted escort. Light javelins were snatched from their holsters and raised overhead, ready to throw.

'Form skirmish line!' the decurion bellowed.

His men eased their snorting ponies apart and extended across the track to face their pursuers, each man drawing his shield up to cover his body while his spare hand lowered the tip of his lance towards the rapidly approaching horsemen. The decurion wished he had thought to order his men to bring javelins with them, but he had expected an uneventful day's ride to the general's camp. Now they would have to weather the volleys of light javelins before they could close to tackle this enemy hand to hand.

'Ready!' the decurion called out to his men, giving them warning of his intention to attack. 'On my order . . . charge!'

With savage cries and frantic urging of their mounts the auxiliaries rippled forward, quickly picking up speed as the two small lines rushed towards each other.

The enemy horsemen showed no signs of slowing as they pounded up towards the auxiliaries. For an instant the decurion was certain that they would simply smash into his men at full tilt, and he braced himself for the impact. The impulse to recoil shivered along the ranks of his men and the line slowed down.

The decurion quickly recovered his wits and bellowed to each side, 'Keep going! Keep going!'

Ahead, the individual expressions of their pursuers could be made out: intent, silent and utterly remorseless. The flowing folds of their tunics and cloaks gave no hint of any armour beneath and the decurion almost pitied them, given the one-sided nature of the imminent clash. Man to man they could not hope to prevail against the better-protected auxiliary cavalrymen, regardless of the quality of their mounts.

At the last moment, without the need for any order, the enemy suddenly jerked their horses round and rode across the face of the Roman charge. Their javelin arms swept back.

'Look out!' cried one of the decurion's men as the several javelins swept in a low trajectory towards the escort party. This was no frantic flurry of missiles – each man had carefully picked his target – and the iron javelin heads thudded home into the chests and flanks of the cavalry mounts. Only one had struck a cavalryman, taking him low in the stomach just above the saddle horn. The targeting of their horses was quite deliberate, the decurion realised at once. Some reared up, thrashing their hoofs at the wounds, while others shied to one side with shrill whinnies of terror. Riders were forced to abandon the charge as they struggled to regain control of their beasts, and two men were thrown, crashing headlong on to the dried earth of the track.

More javelins darted through the air. The decurion's mount convulsed as a dark shaft slammed into its right shoulder. Instinctively clamping his thighs tightly to the leather saddle the decurion swore at his horse as it stopped and swung its head from side to side, sparkling flecks of saliva flying into the sunlight. Around him the rest of the escort milled about in a chaos of wounded animals and unhorsed men scrabbling to get clear of the panicked beasts.

A short distance off, the enemy had exhausted their javelins and now each man drew his sword, the long-bladed spatha that was the standard issue for the cavalry of Rome. The odds had reversed and now the escort faced extinction.

'They're going to charge!' a terrified voice cried out close by the decurion. 'Run!'

'No! Stand together!' the decurion yelled, slipping off the back of his wounded mount. 'Run, and you're fucked! Close up! Close up on me.'

It was a futile order. With half his men on foot, some still dazed from their falls, and the rest struggling to control their mounts, a co-ordinated defence was impossible. It would be every man for himself. The decurion side-stepped into an open space to give himself room to wield his spear, and stared at the enemy trotting forward, swords levelled with deadly intent.

Then an order was shouted, in Latin. 'Leave them!'

The eight horsemen sheathed their blades and, with sharp tugs of the reins, they trotted round the wary circle of cavalrymen, then picked up speed and galloped down the track in the direction of the distant camp of the legions.

'Shit!' someone muttered with an explosive exhalation of relief. 'That was close. Thought they'd carve us up good and proper.'

The decurion instinctively shared the man's sentiment for a moment, before his guts turned to ice.

'The Greek . . . they're after the Greek.'

They'd catch him too. Despite the head start, his groggy condition would slow the Praetorians down, and long before they reached the safety of General Plautius and his army they would be overtaken and cut down.

The decurion cursed the Greek, and cursed his own bad fortune for having been charged with the man's protection. He snatched the reins of the horse belonging to the wounded soldier still struggling to draw the javelin out of his stomach.

'Get off!'

The man's face was clenched in agony and he seemed not to have heard the order, so the decurion thrust him from the saddle and swung himself up. There was a scream of agony as the wounded mad thudded heavily to the ground, the shaft of the javelin snapping.

'Anyone with a horse, follow me!' the decurion shouted, wheeling his mount and spurring it after their attackers. 'Follow me!'

He leaned low, the mane of the pony flicking back against his cheek as the animal snorted and strained every sinew to obey the savage commands of its rider. The decurion glanced round and saw that four men had broken free of the others and were galloping behind him. Five against eight. Not good. But at least there would be no more javelins, and his shield and spear would give him the edge over any man armed only with a sword. So the decurion gave chase, his heart filled with a cold desire to have his revenge on these strangers, even as his mind was filled with the need to save the Greek who had brought all this upon them.

The track dropped down a gentle slope and three hundred paces ahead galloped the enemy. A third of a mile beyond them rode the Greek and his Praetorian bodyguards who were still struggling to hold the Greek up on his horse.

'Come on!' the decurion yelled over his shoulder. 'Keep up!'

The three groups of horsemen crossed the bottom of the vale and started up the opposite slope. The earlier exertion of the pursuers' mounts began to make itself apparent as the gap between them and the decurion closed. With a growing thrill of triumph he dug his heels in and shouted encouragement into the horse's ear. 'Come on! Come on, girl! One last effort!'

The gap had halved by the time the enemy had crested the hill and momentarily disappeared from view. The decurion knew for certain that he and his men would catch them up before they could fall on the Greek and his Praetorians. He glanced back and his heart lifted to see his men close behind; he would not be riding into the enemy on his own.

As the track began to slope down, ahead, just over three miles away, the giant, sprawling square of the general's camp was visible. Intricate grids of minute tents filled the vast space bounded by the turf wall and ramparts. Three legions and several auxiliary cohorts, some twenty-five thousand men, were massing to advance, find and destroy the army of Caratacus and his British warriors. The spectacle had only a moment to impress itself upon the decurion before his view was filled with horsemen charging back along the track towards him. There was no time to rein in and let his men catch him up, and the decurion quickly raised his oval shield and lowered the tip of his spear, sighting it towards the centre of the nearest man's chest.

Then he was in amongst them, the shock of impact throwing his arm back, twisting his shoulder painfully. The shaft of the spear was ripped from his fingers and he heard the deep grunt of the man he had struck as the enemy passed by in a whirl of flowing capes and horse manes and tails. A sword blade thudded against his shield, clattering off the brass boss before it laid open his calf. Then the decurion was through them. He yanked the reins to one side and drew his sword. A sharp clatter of weapons and cries announced the arrival of the rest of his men.

Sword held high, the decurion charged into the mêlée. His men were fighting desperately, outnumbered two to one. As they fended off one attack they made themselves vulnerable to the next, and by the time their commander rejoined them, two were already down, bleeding on the ground beside the writhing form of the man the decurion had speared.

He sensed a movement to his left and ducked his helmet just as the edge of a sword cut through the metal rim of his shield. The decurion jerked his shield to the side, trying to tear the sword out of his opponent's hand, at the same time swinging his sword in a wide are as he twisted to face the man. The blade flashed, the man's eyes widened as he apprehended the danger and he threw his body back. The point ripped through his tunic, grazing his chest.

'Shit!' the decurion spat, nudging the flanks of his mount to edge closer to his foe for the backswing cut. The intent to finish the man blinded him to danger from another direction, and so he never saw the dismounted figure rush up to his side and thrust a sword towards his groin. He just sensed the blow, like a punch, and by the time he had turned back the man had leaped away, his sword stained crimson. The decurion realised at once that that was his blood, but there was no time to check the wound. A glimpse revealed that he was the only one of his men left. The others were already dead or dying, at a cost of only two of these strange, silent men who fought as if they were born to it.

Hands grabbed his shield arm, and the decurion was hauled savagely from his saddle and crashed down on to the hard earth of the track, the air driven from his lungs. As he lay on his back, winded and looking up into blue heavens, a dark silhouette came between him and the sun. The decurion knew this was the end, but refused to close his eyes.

His lips curled into a sneer. 'Go on then, you bastard!'

But there was no sword thrust. The man just whirled away and was gone. Then scuffling sounds, horses snorting, the pound of hoofs, which quickly receded, and the supernaturally serene sounds of a summer

7

afternoon. The shimmering drone of insects was punctuated only by the agonised groans of a man in the grass nearby. The decurion was shocked that he was still alive, that the man had spared him even as he lay defenceless on the ground. He struggled to draw breath, easing himself up into a sitting position.

The six surviving horsemen had renewed their pursuit of the Greek and a bitter rage welled up in the decurion. He had failed. Despite the sacrifice of the escort these strangers would still catch up with the Greek, and he could already imagine the harsh dressing-down he would receive when he, and what was left of the escort, limped back into the cohort's fort.

The decurion suddenly felt dizzy and nauseous, and he had to put a hand on the ground to steady himself. The earth felt warm and sticky and wet beneath his fingers. He looked down and saw that he was sitting in a puddle of blood. His blood, he dimly realised. Then he was aware of the wound in his groin again. A major artery had been severed and dark blood pulsed out in jets on to the grass between his splayed legs. At once he clamped a hand over the injury but the warm flow pressed urgently against the palm and squirted through the gaps between his fingers. He felt cold now, and with a sad smile he knew that there was no longer any danger of being bawled out by the prefect of the cohort. Not in this life, at least. The decurion looked up, and focused on the tiny figures of the Greek and his bodyguards fleeing for their lives.

The seriousness of their plight no longer affected him. They were mere shadows, dimly flickering across the edge of his dwindling senses. He slumped back on the grass and stared into the clear blue sky. All the sounds of the recent skirmish had faded; all that remained was the drowsy hubbub of insects. The decurion closed his eyes and let the warmth of the summer afternoon wash over him as his consciousness gradually ebbed away.

Chapter Two

'Wake up!' The Praetorian shook the Greek's shoulder. 'Narcissus! Come on, man!'

'You're wasting your time,' his companion said, on the other side of the Greek. 'He's out for the count.'

They both looked back up the track towards the skirmish on the brow of the hill.

'Bastard has to come round. We're all dead if he doesn't. I doubt our lads up there are going to last long.'

'They're not.' His companion squinted. 'It's over. Let's go.'

The Greek groaned and raised his head with a pained expression. 'What's . . . happening?'

'We're in trouble, sir. We have to move quickly.'

Narcissus shook his head to clear the dull fug clouding his mind. 'Where are the others?'

'Dead. Sir, we have to go.'

Narcissus nodded, took hold of his reins and urged his mount along the track. His horse suddenly lurched forward as the Praetorian behind him goaded the animal with a swift prod from his sword.

'Easy there!' Narcissus snapped.

'Sorry, sir. But there's no time to lose.'

'Now look here!' Narcissus turned round angrily to remind the Praetorian who he was speaking to. Then his eyes flickered back up the track just as their pursuers finished off the last of the escort and renewed the chase.

'Point taken,' he muttered. 'Let's be off.'

As the three of them spurred their horses on, Narcissus looked towards the distant camp and prayed that some of the more alert amongst the sentries would catch sight of the parties of horsemen and raise the alarm. Unless there was some help sent from the general's camp he might not reach it alive. The sunlight reflecting on the polished surfaces of arms and armour might as well have been the twinkle of distant stars, so cold and far off and unreachable did it seem.

Behind them, now no more than a quarter of a mile away, thundered the hoofs of their pursuers. Narcissus knew he could expect no mercy from those men. They were not interested in prisoners. They were simply

9

assassins, tasked with murdering the Imperial Secretary before he could reach General Aulus Plautius. The question of who had hired them plagued Narcissus. If the tables were turned and one of them should fall into his hands, he knew there were torturers on the general's staff who were adept at breaking the will of even the strongest men. But even then, the information, he suspected, would be of little use. The enemies of Narcissus and his master, Emperor Claudius, were shrewd enough to ensure that any killers were hired via anonymous and expendable middle men.

This was supposed to be a secret mission. As far as he knew, only the Emperor himself and a handful of Claudius' most trusted officials were privy to the knowledge that the Emperor's right-hand man had been sent to Britain to meet with General Plautius. The last time he had met the general, a year ago, Narcissus had been part of the imperial retinue when Claudius had joined the army just long enough to witness the defeat of the native army outside Camulodunum, and then claim the victory as his own. The imperial retinue had numbered thousands and no luxury or security had been spared for the Emperor and Narcissus. This time discretion was paramount and Narcissus, travelling in secret without any of his cherished adornments, had asked the prefect of the Praetorian Guard to lend him the two best men of this élite unit. So he had set out from a quiet backstreet exit of the palace in the company of Marcellus and Rufus.

But somehow the news had leaked out. Almost as soon as he was out of sight of Rome Narcissus suspected that they were being watched and followed. The road behind them had never been quite deserted – always some solitary figure dimly visible far down the road behind them. Of course, such figures might have been quite innocent, and his suspicions groundless, but Narcissus was haunted by fear of his enemies. Haunted enough to take every precaution he could, and he had lasted longer than most men in the perilous world of the imperial household. A man who played for high stakes, as Narcissus did, had to have eyes in the back of his head and see everything that happened around him: every action, every deed, every quiet tilt of the head amongst aristocrats as they exchanged whispers at palace banquets.

It often reminded him of the god Janus, the two-faced guardian of Rome, who watched for danger in both directions. Being part of the imperial household required wearing two faces: the first an eager servant willing to please his political master and social superiors; the second a fixer of utter ruthlessness and determination. The expression of his true thoughts was only permitted when confronting men he had had condemned to execution, when there was great satisfaction to be had in releasing his scorn and contempt for them.

Now, it seemed, it might well be his turn for extermination. Much as he was terrified of death, Narcissus was consumed with the need to know who, amongst the legions of his bitter enemies, wanted him dead. There had already been two attempts, the first at an inn in Noricum, where a fight had started over a few spilled drinks and quickly escalated into a general brawl. Narcissus and his bodyguards had been watching from a cubicle when a knife had flown across the room straight at him. Marcellus saw it coming and shoved the Imperial Secretary's head down into his bowl of stew, the blade thudding into the timber post behind Narcissus an instant later.

On the second occasion a party of horsemen had appeared on the road behind them as they headed towards the port of Gesoriacum. They had taken no chances and galloped ahead of the horsemen, arriving in the port on blown horses that had been pushed to the limits of their endurance. The quay was packed with shipping; supplies destined for Plautius' legions were being loaded on vessels bound for Britain, while ships returning from the island were busy unloading prisoners of war destined for slave markets across the Empire. Narcissus took berths on the first ship to leave for Britain. As the freighter pulled away from the chaotically busy quay Marcellus had gently touched his arm and nodded to a group of eight men silently watching the ship depart. The same men, no doubt, who were pursuing them now.

Narcissus glanced back and was shocked to see how much they had closed the gap. By contrast the camp seemed as far away as ever.

'They're catching us up,' he cried out to his bodyguards. 'Do something!'

Marcellus spared his Praetorian companion a quick glance and both men raised their eyes.

'What do you reckon?' Rufus called out. 'Save ourselves?'

'Why not? Damned if I'm going to die for some Greek.'

They hunkered down beside their horses' necks and spurred them on with wild shouts.

As they pulled ahead Narcissus cried out in panic, 'Don't leave me! Don't leave me!'

The Imperial Secretary kicked his heels in and his mount gradually caught the others up. As the acrid odour of horseflesh filled his nostrils and every jolt of the horse threatened to hurl him down on to the ground rushing past in a blur, Narcissus gritted his teeth in terror. He had never been so afraid in all his life, and vowed not to ride one of these animals ever again. From now he would travel in nothing faster, or less comfortable, than a litter. As he drew level with his bodyguards Marcellus tipped him a wink.

'That's more like it, sir . . . not so far now!'

The three of them pounded on, wind roaring in their ears, but every time that Narcissus or one of the bodyguards glanced back the horsemen were nearer. As the track drew closer to the camp the horses of prey and pursuer alike began to flag and the riders felt their mounts' chests expand and contract like huge bellows as the animals struggled for breath. The breakneck gallop subsided into an exhausted canter as the men became more savage in their attempts to wring every last effort out of their horses.

When the track reached the next bit of high ground Narcissus saw that they were no more than two miles from the safety of the camp and numerous parties of men were training or foraging in the open ground before the ramparts. Surely the approaching riders must have been seen by now? The alarm must have been raised and a force sent out to investigate. But the three men gazed down on a serene and undisturbed scene as they spurred their tired mounts on. And all the time the gap between them and their pursuers closed.

'They must be fucking blind!' Rufus called out bitterly, wildly waving an arm. 'Over here, you dozy bastards! Look over here!'

The track dipped down again, towards a brook that meandered along the edge of a small wood of ancient oak trees. The placid surface of the water exploded as Narcissus and his bodyguards splashed through the ford and emerged glistening on the far side. The horsemen were no more than two hundred paces behind as their prey galloped along the track winding through the oak trees. The path was well worn and deep wagon ruts forced them to the side to spare their mounts the risk of broken legs. There was gorse in the undergrowth and Narcissus felt it tear at his breeches as they raced on, heads lowered to avoid being knocked by projecting branches. The distant thrashing of water revealed that their pursuers had reached the ford.

'Nearly there!' Marcellus shouted. 'Keep going!'

The route wound through the trees, sunlight dappling the ground where it broke through the green canopy above the riders. Then the way opened out ahead of them and in the distance lay the fortified gate of the camp. Narcissus felt a surge of joy at the sight and the realisation that they might be spared after all.

The horses, dripping with water and perspiration, galloped out into the sunshine.

'You there!' a voice barked out. 'Halt! Halt!'

Narcissus saw a party of men resting in the shade of the trees at the fringe of the wood. Around them lay piles of freshly cut wood, and pack mules grazed contentedly. Javelins were stacked within easy reach and the men's shields were standing on their curved bases, ready to be snatched up at a moment's notice.

Marcellus jerked his reins in savagely and his horse slewed towards the firewood detachment. He drew a deep breath and shouted, 'To arms! To arms!'

The men reacted at once and jumped up and ran for their weapons as the three horsemen galloped towards them. The optio in charge of the detachment strode forwards, his sword raised warily.

'And who the hell do you think you are, sunshine?'

The three riders only slowed their mounts to a stop once they were in amongst the legionaries. Marcellus slipped from the back of his horse and thrust his arm back towards the track.

'Behind us! You must stop them!'

'Who's behind you?' the optio growled irritably. 'What are you talking about?'

'We're being pursued. They're trying to kill us.'

'You're not making sense! Calm down, man. Explain yourself. Who are you?'

Marcellus jerked his thumb at Narcissus, bent over his saddle as he struggled for breath. 'Special envoy from the Emperor. We've been attacked. The escort's been wiped out. They're just behind us.'

'Who is?' the optio demanded again.

'I don't know,' admitted Marcellus. 'But they'll be on us any moment. Form your men up!'

The optio glanced at him suspiciously and then shouted the order for his men to assemble. Most had already armed themselves and quickly fell into line, javelin in one hand and shield in the other. Their eyes fixed on the opening in the trees where the track emerged from the shadows and headed across the grassy plain towards the camp. A stillness fell over them as they waited for the horsemen to appear. But there was nothing. No sound of hoof-beats, no war cries, nothing. The oak trees stood still and silent and not a breath of life issued from the track that led into the wood. As the legionaries and the three others stood in tense expectation a pigeon made its throaty warble from the branch of a nearby tree.

The optio waited a moment before turning to the three strangers who had ruined his peaceful break from the rigours of woodcutting.

'Well?'

Narcissus tore his gaze away from the track, and shrugged. 'They must have withdrawn the moment they knew we were safe.'

'Assuming they were ever there in the first place.' The optio raised an eyebrow. 'Now then, would you please tell me what the hell is going on here?'

Chapter Three

'I don't think the beard suits you.'

Narcissus shrugged. 'It serves its purpose.'

'How was the journey?' General Plautius enquired politely.

'What? Aside from having to spend every night of the last month holed up in some flea-bitten inn. Aside from having to eat the indescribably awful slop that goes by the soubriquet of "food" amongst the poorer travelling classes. Aside from being hunted down by a gang of hired killers on your very doorstep . . .'

'Yes. Aside from all that,' the general smiled. 'How was the journey?'

'Quick.' Narcissus shrugged and took another sip of citron-scented water. The Imperial Secretary and the general were sitting under an awning that had been erected on top of a small knoll to one side of the sprawl of tents that made up army headquarters. A small marble-topped table squatted between their two chairs, and an ornate jug of the water and two glasses had been quietly set out by a slave by way of refreshment. Narcissus had shed his sweat-drenched riding clothes and sat in a light linen tunic. Perspiration pricked out of the skin of both men and the breathless air hung heavy as the late afternoon sun burned brilliantly in the clear sky.

Around them the camp stretched out on all sides. Narcissus, used to the smaller scale displays put on by the Praetorian Guard cohorts back in Rome, was impressed by the spectacle. Not that it was the first time he had seen the army of Britain massed for campaigning. He had been present when the four legions and the host of auxiliary units had crushed Caratacus a year earlier. There was something very comforting about the ordered lines of tents. Each one marked the presence of eight men, some of whom were drilling inside the camp. Others were busy grinding sharp edges on to the army's blades, or returning from foraging expeditions laden with baskets of grain, or driving farm animals they had seized from the lands nearby. It all smacked of order and the irresistible might of Rome. With such a huge, well-trained force taking the field it was hard to believe that anything might frustrate the Emperor's aim of adding this land and its tribes to the inventory of empire.

That thought was very much to the fore in Narcissus' mind, and was the reason why he had been sent in secret from the palace to this far-flung camp on the north bank of the river Tamesis.

'How long will you be staying with us?' asked the general.

'How long?' Narcissus looked amused. 'You haven't yet asked why I'm here.'

'I imagine it has something to do with enquiring about the progress of the campaign.'

'Partly that,' Narcissus admitted. 'So how are things going, General?'

'You should know well enough – you must read the dispatches I send back to the palace.'

'Ah, yes. Very informative and very detailed. You have a fine style, if I may say so. Somewhat reminiscent of Caesar's commentaries. Must be heady stuff, commanding so large an army . . .'

Plautius had known Narcissus long enough to become immune to the ingratiating flattery that was the Greek's stock in trade. He was also sufficiently familiar with the nuances of palace officials to recognise the threat implied in the Imperial Secretary's last remark.

'I am, of course, flattered by the comparison with the divine Julius. But I harbour none of his thirst for power.'

Narcissus smiled. 'Come now, General, surely a man in your position with such a large army at his disposal must have developed some small taste for ambition. Such a taste would not be unexpected or, indeed, unwelcome. Rome values ambition in its generals.'

'Rome might. I doubt the Emperor does.'

'Rome and the Emperor are as one,' Narcissus said mildly. 'Some people might regard it as faintly seditious to suggest anything else.'

'Seditious?' Plautius raised an eyebrow. 'You're not serious. Have things got that bad in Rome?'

Narcissus took another, long, sip. He watched the general closely over the rim of the glass before he set it down. 'The situation is worse than you can imagine, Plautius. How long is it since you were last in Rome?'

'Four years. And I haven't missed it a bit. Mind you, that was when Gaius Caligula was in the saddle. I've heard that Claudius is a much better proposition. I'm told things have got a lot better.'

Narcissus nodded. 'Better for most, I'll agree. Trouble is, the Emperor is tending to become over-reliant on the wrong sort of people.'

'Present company excepted, I assume.'

'Of course.' Narcissus frowned. 'And that's not even remotely funny, by the way. I have served the Emperor as loyally as any man. You might say I have dedicated myself to ensuring his success.'

'I understand, from my friends in Rome, that your finances have prospered quite remarkably in recent years . . .'

'So? Is it wrong for a man to be rewarded for his loyal service? But I'm not here to discuss my private finances.'

'Evidently not.'

'And I'll thank your friends to think long and hard before they make

15

such remarks again. That kind of talk has a way of rebounding on loose tongues, if you take my meaning . . . my warning.'

'I'll let them know.'

'Good. Now then, as I was saying, the Emperor's judgement has become misplaced in recent months. Especially since he slapped eyes, amongst other organs, on that little tart Messalina.'

'I've heard of her.'

'You should see her,' smiled Narcissus. 'Really you should. I've never known anyone quite like her. The moment she enters the room and makes those bloody eyes at men, they flop at her feet like puppies. Makes me sick. And Claudius is not so old that his head can't be turned by youth and beauty. Oh, and she's a smart one too. Jupiter knows how many lovers she is bedding, right there in the imperial palace, but as far as Claudius is concerned she is besotted with him and can do no wrong.'

'And is she doing wrong?'

'I'm not sure. Not intentionally, perhaps. Of course, the scandalous way Messalina is carrying on is damaging the Emperor's reputation and making him look like a fool. As to whether she has any more sinister designs . . . I have no proof as yet. Just suspicions. Then there's those bastards, the Liberators.'

'I thought you'd settled their account last year.'

'We bagged most of them following that mutiny in Gesoriacum. But there were still enough of them around to organise some arms shipments to the Britons last summer. My agents have picked up hints that they're planning something big. But they're powerless as long as the Praetorian Guard and the legions stay on side.'

'So you needed to assess my loyalty?' Plautius watched Narcissus closely.

'Why else do you think I'm here? Why else would I come so discreetly?'

'Won't you be missed?'

'Clearly someone's got wind of my mission. Just hope that the news doesn't get any wider circulation. The palace have put out word that I'm down in Capri, recovering from an illness. I hope to be back in Rome before any word of my presence here leaks out from any of the other side's spies on your staff.'

'Enemy spies on my staff?' Plautius affected a look of indignation. 'Whatever next? Imperial spies?'

'Your irony is duly noted, Plautius. But you should not resent my men. Their presence here is as much to do with your protection as it is to do with gathering intelligence on those who might pose a threat to the Emperor.'

'Who do I need to be protected against?'

Narcissus smiled. 'Why, yourself, my dear Plautius. Their presence will act as a reminder that those in the palace get to see and hear everything. Tends to curb the tongues and ambitions of some of our less politically acute commanders.'

'And you think I need discouraging?'

'I'm not sure.' Narcissus stroked his beard. 'Do you?'

The two men stared at each other in silence for a moment, before General Plautius let his gaze fall back to the glass he was turning round and round in his fingers. Narcissus laughed lightly.

'I thought not. Which leads me on to my next query. If you are not disloyal to the Emperor then why are you doing so much to undermine his cause?'

The general put his empty glass back on the table with a sharp rap and folded his arms. 'I don't know what you mean.'

'Let me put it another way, then; a less culpable form of words. Why are you doing so little to further his cause? As far as I can see, your army has done hardly more than consolidate the gains of last year. The only advances have been made in the south-west by Legate Vespasian and his Second Legion. You still haven't brought Caratacus to battle, despite having superior forces, and despite having half the tribes of this benighted land come over to us as allies. I can hardly think of any more propitious circumstances for pushing forward, defeating the enemy and ending this costly campaign.'

'So it's the cost you take exception to, then?' General Plautius sneered. 'There are some things in this world that don't have a price.'

'Wrong!' Narcissus snapped back before the patrician could launch into any high-flown rhetoric about Rome's manifest destiny and the need for each generation to extend the limits of the Empire's glory. 'There is nothing in this world that doesn't have a price. Nothing! Sometimes the price is paid in gold. Sometimes in blood, but it is always paid. The Emperor needs victory in Britain to make his position safe. That will cost Rome the lives of many thousand of its finest troops. That's regrettable. But we can rectify that. There will always be more men. What we can't afford to do is lose one more emperor. The murder of Caligula nearly brought the Empire to its knees. If Claudius' claim to the title hadn't been seized on by the Praetorian Guard we'd have had another civil war – power-mad generals tearing the legions to pieces in their pursuit of glory. In a short time the Empire would have become nothing more than a closed chapter in the histories of fallen powers. What sane man would wish that on the world?'

'Very nice. Very elegantly put,' said Plautius. 'But what's this got to do with me?'

Narcissus sighed patiently. 'Your slow progress is costing us dearly. It's costing the Emperor a loss of reputation. It's nearly a year now since he had a triumph to celebrate victory in Britain. And still I receive requests for more troops. More weapons. More supplies.'

'We're just mopping up.'

'No. Mopping up is what you do after you've beaten the enemy. What you're doing is soaking up resources. This island is like a sponge. It's continually sucking in men, money and political capital. How much longer is this going to go on, my dear General?'

'As I said in my reports, we're making progress. Slowly but steadily. We're forcing Caratacus back mile by mile. Very soon he will have to turn and fight us.'

'How soon, General? Another month? Another year? Longer than that?'

'A matter of days, as it happens.'

'Days?' Narcissus looked doubtful. 'Please explain.'

'Gladly. Caratacus and his army are camped less than ten miles away.' Plautius gestured to the west. 'He knows we're here, and knows that we're expecting him to fall back when we advance, as he has done every time. However, when we next push forward it's his plan to cross the Tamesis at a series of fords not far from here, march round behind us and lay waste to all those tribes we've subdued south of the Tamesis. He might even try to steal a large enough advance on us to storm the supply base at Londinium. It's a sound enough plan.'

'Indeed. And how did you come to know of it?'

'One of his senior chiefs is an agent of mine.'

'Really? First I've heard of it.'

'Some information is too sensitive to commit to written reports,' Plautius said smugly. 'You never know into whose hands it might fall. May I continue?'

'Please.'

'What Caratacus doesn't know is that the Second Legion has been moved up from Calleva to cover the crossing. Caratacus will be caught between this army and the river. There will be nowhere to run this time. He'll have to turn and fight, and when he does he'll be crushed. Then, Narcissus, you and the Emperor will have your victory in Britain. All that will remain are a few malcontents in the mountainous country to the west and those savages up in Caledonia. It may not be worth bringing them under our control, in which case some kind of barrier defence will be needed to keep them out of the province.'

'Barrier? What kind of barrier?'

'A ditch, a wall, maybe a canal.'

'Sounds horribly expensive.'

'Rebellion is more expensive. Anyway, that's work for the future. For now, we must concentrate out efforts on defeating Caratacus and breaking the tribes' will to resist. I trust you will want to be there to witness the battle?'

'Very much so. I'll look forward to it. Almost as much as I look forward to relating the event to the Emperor himself. You'll do well out of this, Plautius. We all will.'

'Then may I propose a toast?' Plautius refilled both their glasses and raised his own. 'To the frustration of the Emperor's enemies, and a . . . crushing victory over the barbarians!'

'To victory!' Narcissus smiled, and emptied his glass.

Chapter Four

The centurions of the Second Legion were seated on several rows of stools in the headquarters tent waiting for their legate to give his briefing. They had spent a long day preparing the legion for the rapid advance scheduled for the following morning. Quite where the unit was headed no one knew, except Vespasian, the legate, and he had not divulged any information to his headquarters staff. The sun had only just set and the air was alive with midges. They swarmed around the flickering yellow flares of the oil lamps and every so often there was a pop and crackle as an insect foolishly ventured into a flame. At the head of the tent a large hide map, depicting a section of the Tamesis, was suspended on a wooden frame.

Three rows from the front sat the six centurions of the Third Cohort. Tucked on to the end of the row sat a tall dark youth, who looked conspicuously out of place amongst the lined and weathered faces of the other centurions seated around him. Indeed, he looked barely old enough to qualify for service with the legions. Beneath a curly mop of dark hair, brown eyes gazed out of a lean-looking face. His thin frame was readily apparent beneath the tunic, chain-mail corselet and harness, and his bare arms and legs were not bulky with muscle, but slender and sinewy. In spite of the uniform and the two sets of untarnished medals fixed to his harness, he still looked like a boy, and the sidelong glances he darted about the tent revealed the self-consciousness he felt about his situation.

'Cato! For fuck's sake, stop fidgeting!' grumbled the centurion sitting next to him. 'You're like a flea on a hot plate.'

'Sorry, it's this heat. It's making me feel funny.'

'Well, you'll be the only one laughing. I don't know what's wrong with this bloody island. When it isn't wet and rainy it throws a blinder of a day at you. Wish it would make its mind up. I'm telling you, we should never have come to this dump. Why the hell are we here, anyway?'

'We're here because we're here, Macro.' His companion made a smile. 'I seem to remember you telling me that's always the answer.'

Macro spat on the ground between his boots. 'Try to help you out and all I ever get is backchat. Why do I bother?'

Cato smiled again, spontaneously this time. Only a few months earlier he had served as Macro's optio, second in command of the century Macro commanded. Much of what he had come to know of army ways over the last two years had been taught to him by Macro. Since Cato had been given his first legionary command ten days earlier he had felt terribly exposed to the onerous responsibilities of his new rank and had affected a hard and humourless countenance in front of the eighty men of his own century, and prayed that they did not see through the mask to the anxious and tormented soul beneath. Once that happened his authority to command would be lost, and Cato lived in dread of that moment. He had a very limited time to win their loyalty. No easy feat when he had barely come to know the names of the men under his command, still less the peculiarities of their character. He had drilled them hard, harder than most centurions did, but knew that until they had seen him perform in battle they would not fully accept him as their commander.

It was different for Macro, he reflected with a trace of bitterness. Macro had had more than ten years of service before being promoted, and he wore his rank like a second skin. Macro had nothing to prove and the scars that covered his body were testament to his courage in battle. Moreover, the older man was short and solidly built – the physical antithesis of his friend. A legionary only had to take one look at Macro to realise this centurion was not the sort of man you pissed off if you valued your teeth.

'When is this bloody briefing going to start?' Macro muttered, slapping at a mosquito that had landed on his knee.

'On your feet!' The camp prefect bawled out from the front of the tent. 'Legate present!'

The centurions instantly rose up and stood to attention as a side flap was held open by a sentry and the commander of the Second Legion entered the tent. Vespasian was powerfully built, with a broad, heavily lined face. While not handsome, there was, nevertheless, something about his face that put men at their ease. No haughty expression of social aloofness that was common amongst the senatorial class. But then his family had only recently been admitted from the equestrian tier of society, and his grandfather had been a centurion in the service of Pompey the Great. Vespasian was not so far removed from the background of the men he commanded. It was a feature that made his men warm to him to the extent that the Second Legion had fought well under his command and had won more than its share of the battle honours in this campaign.

'At ease, gentlemen. Please be seated.'

Vespasian waited until the tent was silent again. When all were still and the only sounds came from the camp beyond the leather walls of the tent, he positioned himself to one side of the map and cleared his throat.

'Gentlemen, we are within a day of concluding this campaign. The army of Caratacus is marching into a trap that will lead to its utter annihilation. With his army destroyed and Caratacus in the bag, the fight will be completely knocked out of those tribes still resisting us.'

21

'That'll be the day,' Macro whispered. 'How many times have I heard that one?'

'Shhh.' Cato nudged him.

The legate had seized the attention of his audience and raised a cane towards the suspended map. 'This is where we are camped, a short distance from the Tamesis. Our Atrebatan scouts tell us the area is called the three fords – for obvious reasons.' The legate raised his cane and indicated the land north of the fords. 'Caratacus is retreating in front of General Plautius' army and should have arrived at this point here, just above the fords. So far he has simply given ground every time the general and the other three legions advance on him. As far as Caratacus knows, we expect him to carry out the same manoeuvre again. Which is why he's planning to do something completely different this time. Instead of retreating, Caratacus will take his forces across these three fords and swing round behind us. That way he'll threaten our supply lines, and cut the legions off from the depot at Londinium. Even if he's successful it won't bring him victory, but it will cost us a few months to retrieve the situation.

'However, as the more observant of you will already have realised from the map, he's taking a big risk. The three fords are set in a wide loop of the Tamesis. If the fords are denied him and the general's force covers the open face of the loop he will be trapped with his back to the river. There will be no way out for him. He'll have to surrender or fight.

'At dawn tomorrow the Second Legion will advance to cover these three fords. We'll sow the riverbed with caltrops and wooden stakes and set up defence lines on our side of the fords. The main line of his advance will be towards these two crossings, here and here. They're quite broad and will need to be defended in strength. Accordingly, the First, Second, Fourth and Fifth Cohorts will be under my command at the downriver ford. The Sixth, Seventh, Eighth, Ninth and Tenth Cohorts, under the command of Camp Prefect Sextus, will defend the next ford upriver.'

Vespasian shifted along in front of the map and tapped it with his cane. 'The last ford is not likely to be used by Caratacus. It's too narrow and the current is quite swift at that point. Even so, he may try to push some of his lighter units across the river and we must prevent that. That's the job of the Third Cohort. Think your lads can handle it, Maximius?'

Heads turned towards the other end of the row Cato was sitting on, and the thin-faced centurion with a long nose, commanding Cato and Macro's cohort, pursed his lips and nodded.

'You can rely on the Third, sir. We won't let you down.'

'I'm counting on that,' Vespasian smiled. 'That's why you were picked for the job. It's nothing a former officer of the Praetorian Guard can't handle. Remember, not one of them must be permitted to cross the river. We must annihilate them utterly if we are to bring this campaign to a swift end . . . Now then, are there any questions?'

22

Cato looked round in the hope that someone else had raised an arm. When he saw that the rest of the centurions were sitting impassively, he swallowed nervously and raised his hand.

'Sir?'

'Yes, Centurion Cato.'

'What if the enemy force their way across one of the fords, sir? How will the other detachments know?'

'I've assigned two of our mounted squadrons to my command, and one each to Sextus and Maximius. If anything goes wrong we can alert the others and, if need be, the legion can fall back towards this position under cover of darkness. Let's just make sure it doesn't come to that. See to your defences and make sure your men give of their best. The advantage will be ours. We'll have the element of surprise and for the first time their confounded speed over the ground will work in our favour as they hurry towards these fords. If we do our job well the new province is as good as won, and all that remains is to clear up a few last nests of resistance. Then we can concentrate on dividing up the spoils.'

There was a murmur of approval at this last comment, and Cato saw the eyes of the men seated alongside him light up at the prospect of receiving their share of the booty. As centurions, they stood to make a tidy sum out of the money raised from the sale into slavery of the men they had taken prisoner over the last year. All the land seized fell into the hands of the imperial secretariat, whose agents stood to make vast fortunes from sales commissions. The system was a source of bitter contention amongst the men of the legions when they were drinking, and the unequal shares of legionaries and centurions ensured that the far greater inequality of fortunes between centurions and imperial land agents was generally overlooked.

'Any further questions?' asked Vespasian. There was a moment's stillness before the legate turned to his camp prefect. 'Very well. Sextus, you may dismiss them.'

The officers rose from their stools and snapped to attention. Once the legate had left the tent Sextus stood them down. The camp prefect reminded them to collect their written orders from the general's secretaries as they left headquarters. As the centurions of the Third Cohort stood up, Maximius raised a hand.

'Not so fast, lads. I want a word with you in my tent, soon as you've set the evening watch.'

Macro and Cato exchanged looks, which was instantly detected by Maximius. 'I'm sure my new centurions will be relieved to know that I won't be keeping them too long, and wasting their precious time.'

Cato coloured.

Maximius regarded the youth coldly for a moment before his face creased into a smile. 'Just make sure you're both in my tent before the first change of watch is sounded.'

'Yes, sir,' replied Cato and Macro.

Maximius gave a sharp nod, turned on his heel and strode stiffly from the briefing tent.

Macro's eyes followed their commander. 'Now what was all that about?'

The nearest of the centurions drew back, glancing warily at Maximius until the cohort commander had disappeared through the tent flaps. Then he spoke quietly to Macro and Cato.

'I'd play it carefully, if I were you two.'

'Carefully?' Macro frowned. 'What are you talking about, Tullius?'

Caius Tullius was the most senior of the centurions after Maximius; a veteran of over twenty years and several campaigns. Although he was reserved in manner, he had been the first to greet Macro and Cato when they had been appointed to the Third Cohort. The other two centurions, Caius Pollius Felix and Tiberius Antonius, had said no more than necessary to Cato as yet, and he sensed hostility in their attitude. Macro was more fortunate. They already knew him from the time before his promotion, and treated him in a cordial manner, as they must, given that Macro's appointment to the centurionate predated their own.

'Tullius?' Macro prompted.

For a moment Tullius hesitated, mouth open as he seemed to be on the verge of saying something. Then he just shook his head. 'It's nothing. Just try not to get on the wrong side of Maximius. Especially you, young 'un.'

Cato's lips compressed into a tight line, and Macro couldn't help laughing.

'Don't be so touchy, Cato. Centurion you may be, but you'll have to forgive people if they mistake you for a boy sometimes.'

'Boys don't get to wear these,' Cato snapped back, and tapped his medallions, instantly regretting the immature need to prove himself.

Macro raised both his hands with a placating smirk. 'All right! I'm sorry. But look around, Cato. See anyone else here that's within five or ten years of your age? I think you'll find that you're a bit of an exception.'

'Exception he may be,' Tullius added quietly, 'but he'd do well not to stand out, if he knows what's good for him.'

The veteran turned away and followed Felix and Antonius towards the entrance to the tent. Macro watched him go and scratched his chin.

'Wonder what he meant?'

'Can't you guess?' Cato muttered bitterly. 'Seems our cohort commander thinks I'm not up to the job.'

'Rubbish!' Macro punched him lightly on the shoulder. 'Everyone in the legion knows about you. You've got nothing to prove to anyone.'

'Tell Maximius that.'

'I might. One day. If he doesn't recognise it himself first.'

Cato shook his head. 'Maximius only joined the legion a few months back, in that batch of replacements that arrived while we were in hospital in Calleva. Chances are he knows next to nothing about me.'

Macro prodded one of Cato's medallions. 'These should tell him all he needs to know. Now come on, we've got to post our watches. Wouldn't want to be late for Maximius' briefing, would we?'

Chapter Five

Once Cato was satisfied that his optio had the watch organised, he marched through two rows of tents to Macro's century and stuck his head through the flap of the largest tent at the end of the line. Macro was sitting at a small trestle table, examining some tablets by the wan glow of an oil lamp.

'Ready?'

Macro looked up, and then pushed the wax tablets to one side. He rose from his chair and strode over to Cato. 'Yes. I've had enough of this. Bloody pay records. Sometimes I wish you were still my optio. Made the record-keeping side of things a lot easier. I could get on with the real job then.'

Cato nodded in sympathy. Life had indeed been easier before, for both of them. With Macro as his centurion Cato's introduction to army life had been unclouded by the need to take much responsibility on his own shoulders. There had been times when circumstances had forced command on him, and he had coped with such duties, but had always been relieved to hand the burden back to Macro afterwards. That was all gone, now that he was a centurion. Not only did Cato feel constantly judged by others, he sat in judgement of himself. Cato was not impressed by the image of the thin and boyish figure in a centurion's uniform he knew he presented.

'How's Figulus coping?' Macro asked as they made for the large square tent that marked the headquarters of the Third Cohort. 'Can't see why you chose him to be your optio. Outside of a straight fight the lad's a bloody nuisance.'

'He's coping well enough.'

'Oh, really?' Macro said with a trace of amusement. 'Handling the pay records on his own then? That, and all the other clerical crap?'

'I'm . . . instructing him at the moment.'

'Instructing him? As in showing him how to read and write, perhaps?'

Cato lowered his head to hide the dark expression on his face. Macro was right in his implication. Figulus was a poor choice for the job, in many respects – barely able to write his own name and completely out of his depth when required to calculate any sums larger than the small amount of savings he had scraped together in his first year of service with the legion. Yet Cato had offered the position to him immediately. Figulus was almost the same age and Cato desperately needed a familiar face amongst the men under his command. Most of the men he had known when he had first joined Macro's old century were dead, or discharged as invalids. The survivors had been distributed to the other centuries in the understrength cohort. So Figulus it had been.

He was not without redeeming features, Cato reflected in a self-justifying moment. Figulus was from Gallic stock; tall and broad, he was a match for any man in the legion, and any enemy outside it. Moreover, he was good with the men, with his easy-going and guileless nature. That made him a useful bridge between Cato and his century. And Figulus, like Cato himself, was anxious to prove himself worthy of his new rank. However, Cato's attempt to teach him the basics of record-keeping had quickly exhausted the centurion's patience. If things didn't improve soon it looked as if Cato would have to take on most of the optio's job as well.

'You could always replace him,' Macro suggested.

'No,' Cato replied obstinately. 'He'll do.'

'If you say so. It's your decision, lad.'

'Yes. It's my decision. And you're not my father, Macro. So please stop acting like it.'

'All right! All right!' Macro raised his hands in surrender. 'Won't mention it again.'

'Good . . .'

'So, er, what do you make of our man, Maximius?'

'Don't know him well enough to make a judgement yet. Seems competent enough. Bit harsh on the bullshit front.'

Macro nodded. 'He's from the old school: every buckle done up tightly, every blade polished until it dazzles and not a speck of mud allowed on parade. His kind are the backbone of the army.'

'What's his history?' Cato glanced at his companion. 'You speak to anyone about him yet?'

'Had a word with Antonius in the mess the other day. He came in with the same replacement column and got to know Maximius back in the depot at Gesoriacum.'

'And?'

'Not much to tell. He's been a centurion for the best part of ten years, and served right across the Empire. Before that he was in the Praetorian Guard. Served a few years and then transferred to the legions.' Macro shook his head. 'Beats me why he took a transfer. I'd have killed to serve in the Guard; better pay, better accommodation and the best fleshpots and cheapest dives that only Rome can provide.'

'Too much of a good thing, perhaps?'

'What?' Macro was astonished. 'What kind of bollocks is that? One of your stupid fucking philosophies, I bet. Look, lad, there's no such thing as enough of a good thing. Believe me.'

'Very epicurean of you, Macro.'

'Oh, piss off . . .'

They had reached Maximius' tent. A dull glow framed the flaps at the entrance, and as the sentries spied the two centurions approaching from the darkness, one stepped to one side and held a flap open. Macro led the way. They entered the thick, hot atmosphere inside the tent and saw Maximius seated beside his campaign table. In front of him were arranged five stools, three of which were already occupied by the other centurions of the Third Cohort.

'Thank you for joining us,' Maximius said curtly.

The signal for the change of watch was still not due for nearly half an hour, by Cato's calculation, but before he could even consider protesting Macro stepped in front of him.

'Sorry, sir.'

'Take your seats, gentlemen. Then we can get started.'

As they sat down Macro raised an eyebrow to Cato in warning. It dawned on Cato that this was how Maximius liked to run his cohort. He expected – no, demanded – that his subordinates exceed the requirements of his orders. It might lead to a certain amount of second-guessing, but it kept them on their toes. Cato had been aware of this style of command in other cohorts and disliked it intensely. A commander who adopted such an approach could never be certain that his orders would be carried out as he intended.

Once the last arrivals were seated Maximius cleared his throat and stiffened his spine before he began to address his officers. 'Now that we're all here . . . You saw the legate's map and understand our task. We hold the fords against Caratacus and he is beaten. We'll be the first cohort to march from camp tomorrow, before sunrise, as we've got the furthest to march. We'll be following a supply track that leads to the ford. There's an auxiliary post we should reach by noon. We'll rest there and draw from their rations. The ford's a mile or so further to the north and we can reach it and fortify it soon afterwards. We should arrive in plenty of time. Your men are to leave their packs here tomorrow. They're to be ready to fight and carry nothing else, apart from their canteens. We're marching to battle. There are to be no shirkers, no stragglers . . . and no surrender when we meet the enemy. Of course,' he grinned, 'if the enemy wants to surrender, then we must make every effort to accommodate his wishes. With a bit of luck we might just win the day, and a small fortune besides. You understand me?'

All but one of the centurions nodded solemnly. Maximius turned towards Macro.

'What's the matter?'

'Can we really afford to take prisoners, sir?'

'Can we afford not to?' Maximius laughed. 'You got something against being rich, Macro? Or do you want to be just a wretch when you retire?'

Macro smiled politely. 'I like money as much as the next man, sir. But we're one cohort, way out on the flank of the legion. If we have to start detaching men to guard prisoners it'll be a drain on our strength. And I'm not happy at the idea of having any sizeable body of Britons behind us as well as in front of us, whether they're armed or not. It's asking for trouble, sir.'

'Come now, Macro. I think you exaggerate the danger. What about you, young Cato? Wouldn't you agree?'

For a moment Cato was gripped by an instinctive panic as he struggled for a response to the direct question.

'I don't know, sir. Depends how many of them there are. If we can handle them then of course we should take prisoners. But, like Macro says, if they come at us in any kind of strength we'll need to face them with every man we have. In that event, any prisoners will pose a danger to us . . . sir.'

'I see.' Maximius nodded thoughtfully. 'You think we should err on the side of caution? You think that's what made us Romans the masters of the world?'

'I don't know about that, sir. I just think we should carry out our orders without taking any unnecessary risks.'

'So do I!' Maximius laughed loudly, and Felix and Antonius joined in. Tullius smiled. When Maximius had finished he leaned forward and clapped Cato on the shoulder. 'Don't worry. I'll not take any chances. You have my word. On the other hand, I'll not willingly pass up an opportunity to make some easy money. But you're right to be cautious. We'll see what the situation is tomorrow, and act on what we find. That should set your mind at rest, eh, lad?'

Cato nodded.

'Good. That's settled then.' Maximius took a step back to address his officers more formally. 'Following on from our orders, I wanted you to know that I am determined that the Third Cohort will prove itself worthy of the task the legate has assigned to us. I will tolerate nothing less than the best tomorrow, from both you and your men. I set high standards for the men under my command because I want us to be the hardest fighting cohort there is. Not just in this legion, but in any legion.' He paused to look round at his centurions' faces, scrutinising them for any unfavourable reaction. Cato returned the gaze without betraying any emotion.

'Now then, gentlemen, I know I have been commanding this cohort for a little more than a month, but I have watched the centuries being put through their paces and I'm certain that I have never served with a finer body of men . . . outside Rome, that is. I've also had the chance to assess the potential of Felix, Antonius and Tullius, and I'm pleased with what I've seen. You're good men. Which brings me to our recent appointments . . .' He turned fully towards Macro and Cato and made a brief smile. 'I've read through your records and I'm glad to have you both

29

serving under me. Macro, two years of service in the centurionate, with excellent reports and commendations from the legate and the general himself. I'm sure you will have every chance to build on that while you serve in my cohort.'

For a moment Macro felt a bitter twist of resentment in his guts. He had served with the Eagles for over fifteen years. Fifteen years of hard experience and some of the toughest fighting to be had. He doubted that anyone he had left behind in the small fishing village along the coast from Ostia would recognise him now. The thickset boy who had hitched a ride to Rome to join the legions was a distant memory, and Macro fumed at the patronising tone of his superior's welcome. But he bit back on the anger, and nodded stiffly. 'Thank you, sir.'

Maximius smiled, and turned his gaze to Cato. 'Of course, Centurion Cato, some records were quicker to read through than others. Despite your years you've racked up some impressive achievements, and you've even picked up some of the local lingo. That might come in useful,' he mused. 'It'll be interesting to see how you cope tomorrow.'

'I hope I won't disappoint you, sir,' Cato replied, tight-lipped as he bit back on his injured pride.

'You'd better not.' The smile faded from Maximius' face. 'There's a lot riding on this for all of us, from the general right down to the legionaries in the front rank. We carry it off and there'll be more than enough glory to go round. We fuck it up and you can be sure that the people back in Rome won't ever forgive us. Do I make myself clear?'

'Yes, sir,' Antonius and Felix answered at once.

'That's good. Now, gentlemen, if you'll join me in a toast . . .' Maximius reached under the table and lifted a small wine jar from the shadows. 'It ain't the best vintage, but think of it as a taster of the spoils to come. So I give you, the Emperor, Rome and her legions. Jupiter and Mars, bless them all, and grant bloody defeat and death to Caratacus and his barbarians!'

Maximius pulled the stopper out of the jar, grasped the handle and, letting the jar lie across his bent arm, he raised its rim to his lips and gulped down a couple of mouthfuls of wine. Cato watched as a red bead trickled from the corner of the cohort commander's lips and ran down his cheek. Maximius lowered the jar and passed it to Tullius, and one by one the centurions echoed the toast and sealed their oath by sharing the wine. When Macro's turn came, he took rather more mouthfuls than was required and then handed the jug to Cato as he wiped his lip on the back of his other hand.

As he lifted the jug and repeated the toast, Cato sensed every eye in the tent on him and he pursed his lips as the first trickle of wine came down the rough earthenware neck of the jar towards his mouth. As the liquid flowed over his tongue Cato resisted the impulse to gag at the sharp, burning vinegary taste. Even in the poorest quarters of Camulodunum

Cato had never tasted such a rancid wine. He forced himself to take another mouthful and then lowered the jar.

'There!' Maximius retrieved the jar, stopped it up and placed it back under the table. 'Tomorrow then, gentlemen. Tomorrow we show the rest of the army what a cohort can achieve.'

Chapter Six

It was still dark as the cohort prepared to move off. Two braziers either side of the gatehouse illuminated the head of the column, but the glow cast by the gently licking flames carried only as far down the Praetorian way as the First Century. The rest of the men were shrouded in the clammy air of the pre-dawn. Cato, standing with the other centurions by the gate, could hear only the muted exchanges and dull clunk and clatter of equipment of nearly five hundred men getting ready to march into battle. On the open ground, to one side of the gate, stood the mounted contingent that was to accompany the cohort – thirty men under the command of a decurion, lightly armed and trained for scouting and courier duties rather than battle. The horses waited expectantly, ears twitching and hoofs gently scraping the ground as their dismounted riders kept firm hands on the reins. From further off came the muffled sounds of other legionaries rousing; quiet curses amid the coughs and groans of men stretching sleep-stiffened bodies.

'Not long now, lads!' Centurion Maximius called out as he warmed his back against one of the braziers, and cast a huge wavering shadow across the nearest line of tents.

'He's up for it,' Macro remarked quietly.

Cato yawned. 'Wish I was.'

'Lose much sleep?'

'Had to finish the accounts before I turned in.'

'Accounts?' Centurion Felix shook his head in disbelief. 'On the eve of a battle? Are you mad?'

Cato shrugged and Felix turned to Macro. 'You've known him a while, haven't you?'

'Man and boy.'

'He always been like that?'

'Oh, yes! Bit of a perfectionist, our Cato. Never goes into a fight unless his records are sorted. Nothing worse than being killed with a bit of paperwork on your mind. Some peculiar religious thing he picked up from the palace officials. Something to do with his shadow being doomed to walk the earth until the accounts are completed, audited and filed. Only then can his spirit rest in peace.'

'Is that true?' Centurion Antonius asked, wide-eyed.

'Why do you ask?' Macro turned towards him with a horrified expression. 'You haven't gone and left your paperwork half done?'

Cato sighed. 'Just ignore him, Antonius. Taking the piss is Centurion Macro's stock in trade.'

Antonius glanced from Cato to Macro and narrowed his eyes. 'Fucking idiot . . .'

'Oh, yes? Had you going there for a moment, didn't I? So who's the idiot?'

'You were at the palace?' Felix said, turning to Cato. 'The imperial palace?'

Cato nodded.

'So what's the story, Cato?'

'Not much to say. I was born and raised in the palace. My father was a freedman on the general staff. He arranged most of the entertainments for Tiberius and Caligula. Never knew my mother. She didn't live long after giving birth to me. When my father died I was sent to join the legions, and here I am.'

'Must be a bit of a comedown, after the palace.'

'In some ways,' Cato admitted. 'But life in the palace could be every bit as dangerous as here in the legions.'

'Funny,' Felix smiled and nodded towards Maximius. 'That's just what he said.'

'Really?' Cato muttered. 'Can't seem to remember the Praetorian Guard ever having a hard time of it, Sejanus and his cronies excepted.'

'You were there then?' Felix's eyes lit up. 'Was it as bad as they say?'

'Worse.' Cato's expression hardened as he recalled the fall of Sejanus. 'Hundreds were slaughtered. Hundreds. Including his kids . . . They used to play with me when they visited the palace. The Praetorians took them away and butchered them. That's the kind of battle most of them get to fight.'

Macro frowned at the harsh tone in his friend's voice and nodded towards the cohort commander. 'Be fair, lad. He wasn't there when it happened.'

'No. I suppose not.'

'And the Guard did all right by us outside Camulodunum. That was a bloody tough fight.'

'Yes. All right. I won't mention it again.'

'You know,' Tullius spoke quietly, 'Maximius might have known your father. You should ask him some time. You might have something in common.'

Cato shrugged. He doubted that he and Maximius had anything in common. The cohort commander's disdain for the young centurion had become evident to Cato over the few days that they had served together. What was more painful was the thought that the other centurions of the cohort, apart from Macro, might share the sentiment.

An order barked out from the smothering darkness, commanding the men to stand to attention, and Cato recognised Figulus' voice. As iron-nailed boots stamped to the dry ground with a rippling thud like distant thunder, Maximius hurried over from the brazier to join his officers.

'Must be the legate! Stand to.'

Maximius strode two paces to the front and stiffened like a rod. Behind him the other centurions stood in a line, shoulders back, chins raised and arms held tightly to their sides. Then all was quiet, apart from the champing and stamping of the horses. The sounds of several marching men approaching reached the centurions at the gatehouse and moments later Vespasian and a handful of staff officers emerged from the gloom and into the orange glow of the braziers. The legate strode up to the centurions and returned their salute.

'Your men look well turned out, and keyed up for a fight, Maximius.'

'Yes, sir. They can't wait to get stuck in, sir.'

'Glad to hear it!' Vespasian stepped closer to the cohort commander and lowered his voice. 'You've got your orders, and you know the importance of your role in today's fight.'

'Yes, sir.'

'Any last questions?'

'None, sir.'

'Good man.' Vespasian reached out his hand and they clasped each other's forearms. 'One last battle. By the end of the day it should all be over. May the gods be with you today, Centurion.'

'And with you, sir.'

Vespasian smiled and then turned to face east, where the first hint of light was filtering up from the horizon. 'Time for you to get moving. I'll share a jar of wine with you and your men tonight.'

The legate stepped back and led his staff officers up the wooden steps on to the walkway above the gate.

Maximius turned to his centurions. 'Back to your units! Prepare to march.'

Cato and Macro saluted and trotted away from the gate, back down the column of silent men. Cato could pick out the highly polished shield bosses gleaming dully as he passed by; Maximius had given an order for the water-proofed leather shield covers to be left in the men's tents to reduce the burden they had to carry. It had better not rain, thought Cato, well remembering the awful weight of a water-logged shield.

Macro peeled off when they reached the Third Century and gave a quick parting nod to Cato as the youngster made his way to the rear of the column where Optio Figulus waited beside the standard of the Sixth Century. As yet the long staff carried only one decoration beside the unit's square identity pendant: a round disc with a profile of the Emperor Claudius stamped upon it, awarded to every century in the army of General Plautius following the defeat of Caratacus outside Camulodunum nearly a year ago.

Cato smiled bitterly to himself. A year ago. And here they were again, ready to do battle with Caratacus once more. For the last time. Even if there was a victorious outcome to the coming battle Cato was almost certain that the Roman legions would still not have heard the last of Caratacus. A year in this barbarous island had taught him one thing above all else: these Britons were too foolish to know the meaning of defeat. Every army they had sent against the Eagles had been bloodily defeated. And yet the Britons still fought on doggedly, no matter how many of them were cut down. For their sake, and the sake of their women and children, Cato hoped that the day's battle would finally break their will to resist.

Cato filled his lungs. 'Sixth Century will prepare to advance.'

There was a grating scrape in the darkness as his men lifted their shields from the ground and shouldered their javelins, a few grunts as they shuffled the weight around and then silence.

From the front of the column Cato heard the order given to open the gates and, with a protesting creak from the wooden hinges, the thick timbers were pulled inwards and a dark hole yawned beneath the illuminated gatehouse. Maximius bellowed out the order for the cohort to advance. The column rippled forward in a steady cadence as each century moved off after a short delay to leave a sufficient gap between units. Then Antonius shouted the order for the Fifth Century to march. As the rear rank stepped away before Cato he silently counted five paces and then called out.

'Sixth Century! Advance!'

Then he was leading his men forward, Figulus a pace to his side and a pace behind. Then came the century's standard and then the column of eighty men who were his first legionary command. Not one man on the sick list. Cato looked over his shoulder and for a moment his heart filled with pride. These were his men. This was his century. His eyes scanned the dim features of the front ranks and Cato felt that nothing in this life could be better than being centurion of the Sixth Century of the Third Cohort of the Second Legion Augusta.

As the cohort marched under the gatehouse, the legate unsheathed his sword and stabbed it into the thinning darkness of the sky.

'To victory! To victory! To Mars!'

'Draw swords!' Maximius bellowed from the front of the column, and with a rattling rasp of metal the wicked short stabbing swords of the legionaries flickered up and they returned the legate's cry with a full-throated roar as they invoked the blessing of the god of war. The cheers continued until the cohort had left the ramparts of the camp in the distance, silhouetted against the coming light of day.

Cato took one last look over his shoulder and then turned his gaze along the track to where Maximius led his men towards the battle that would seal the fate of Caratacus and his warriors once and for all.

Chapter Seven

With sunrise it was clear that the day would be breathless and hot. There was not even a hint of haze in the smooth cerulean heaven. The cohort trudged steadily along the supply track, the iron nails on the legionaries' boots kicking up the loose dust that covered the wagon ruts. Equipment jingled on harnesses and there was a steady, rhythmless rapping of javelin shafts and scabbards on the inside of the men's shields. A short distance to the right, the men of the cavalry squadron led their mounts parallel to the legionaries. The centurions marched at the head of the cohort, summoned there by Maximius.

'Keep 'em in step, at a nice steady pace,' he explained. 'No need to rush things. Don't want to exhaust the men.'

Macro silently disagreed. There was every reason to be in position as speedily as possible. The legate had made it quite clear that everyone must be ready in time to trap Caratacus. True, the Third Cohort should easily reach the ford just after noon, but if it had been his cohort Macro would have marched them hard, arrived early, immediately set up the defences, and only then stand the men down while they waited for the enemy to arrive. Sooner a wide margin for error than a narrow one, he decided. All those years of hard service with the Eagles had taught him that much at least. But then, it wasn't his cohort and it wasn't his job to question the order of his superior. So Macro kept his mouth shut and nodded with the other centurions in response to Maximius' last remark.

'Once we reach the auxiliary fort we'll pick up the entrenching tools and give the men a short rest.'

'Which unit do the auxiliaries belong to, sir?' Cato asked.

'The First Nervanians – Germans, born and bred. They're good lads.' Maximius smiled. 'And they're in good hands. Mate of mine commands them. Centurion Porcinus, ex-Praetorian Guardsman, like me.'

'First Nervanian?' Macro thought for a moment. 'Didn't they get a good pasting in the marshes on the Tamesis, last summer?'

'Yes . . .'

'Thought so.' Macro nodded, and jerked a thumb at Cato. 'We were there. Had to do some tidying up after them. Made a bit of a hash of it, chasing down some of the locals. Got lost in the marsh and pretty much cut to pieces. Ain't that right, Cato?'

'Er, yes. I suppose so.' Cato was watching Maximius carefully and saw the cohort commander frown. 'But they fought well enough.'

Macro turned to him with a surprised expression and Cato quickly shook his head.

'They did fight well,' Maximius growled. 'They were a credit to their commander. Lost over half their number and Porcinus still kept them at it. As I said, they're in good hands.'

'Well,' Macro sniffed. 'If he's a good commander, then why . . .?'

Cato was staring hard at his friend and finally Macro got the point. He paused, looked at Maximius quickly, and cleared his throat.

'Why what?' Maximius prompted him in a harsh tone.

'Er, why . . . why didn't the general honour him?'

'You know the score, Macro. Some centurions just happen to get on the wrong side of our generals and legates. While some others –' Maximius glanced towards Cato – 'just seem to get everything handed to them on a plate. That's the way of the world. Wouldn't you agree, Centurion Cato?'

'Yes, sir.' Cato forced himself to smile. 'Just one of the profession's iniquities.'

'Iniquities?' Maximius repeated in a mocking tone. 'Now there's a fine word. Know any more like that, son?'

'Sir?'

'You got any other smart words you want to use on me?'

'Sir, I didn't mean—'

'Rest easy!' Maximius grinned, too widely, and raised his hand. 'No harm done, lad, and no offence taken, eh? You can't help it if you've spent most of your life with your nose stuck in a book, instead of doing proper soldiering, can you?'

Cato looked down to hide the anger flushing through his face. 'No, sir. And I aim to make up for it.'

'Of course you do, lad.' Maximius winked at Antonius and Felix. 'A boy's got to learn, after all.'

'After all what, sir?' Cato looked round at his commander. Maximius smiled at the determined glint in the young officer's eyes. He slapped Cato on the shoulder.

'Figure of speech, son. That's all it was.'

'Fair enough, sir.' Cato gave a small nod. 'Might I get back to my men now?'

'No need to sulk, Cato.'

There was a tense beat as Cato tried to control a new flush of anger. He realised well enough that Maximius was baiting him, trying to force him into some kind of petulant display in front of the other centurions. It was so tempting to bite back, to defend his achievements, to point out the medallions he wore on his harness. Unfortunately, Maximius, Macro and Tullius each carried more sets than he did. Antonius and Felix had yet to win any decorations for bravery and Cato would merely offend them as the other three centurions laughed at his bratish arrogance. Any attempt at a put-down would be taken as insubordination and only make the situation worse. Yet to do nothing would make him look like a weakling, and merely invite further lacerating remarks from Maximius. Bullying was a prerogative of rank, and Cato realised it was something he would just have to put up with. Unfair as it was, few of his fellow centurions would side with him. A man had to pay his dues and put up with all the petty slights and cruel taunts, with no possibility of being able to respond. Any man who succumbed to that temptation was as good as broken. All Cato could do was weather the torment and accept the . . . iniquity – he smiled bitterly to himself – of the situation.

With a flash of insight he realised that was just another way the army had of toughening up its men. The discomforts of army life were as much mental as physical, and he'd better get used to it, because if he didn't then men like Maximius would break Cato as surely as night follows day. Very well, if he couldn't afford to outwit his commander, and couldn't bear to be the butt of his humour then Cato must keep as far away from Maximius as possible.

Cato glanced over his shoulder, back down the line of men towards his century bringing up the rear of the column. He frowned.

'Sir, I think my century's falling behind. Can I go back and chivvy them along?'

Maximius looked back and then turned his gaze on Cato with a shrewd narrowing of the eyes. For a moment Cato feared that his request would be denied. Then Maximius nodded.

'Very well. Make sure they keep up.'

'Yes, sir.' Cato saluted, quickly turned away and strode back down the column of sweating legionaries, under the watchful eye of Maximius.

'Macro?'

'Sir?'

'How well do you know that boy?'

'Well enough, I suppose, sir,' Macro replied guardedly. 'At least I've known him ever since he joined the Second Legion as a recruit.'

'As long as that?' Maximius arched his eyebrows. 'That must be, almost, let me see . . . two years. My, that is a long time.'

Even Macro could pick up the heavy helping of sarcasm. He immediately decided that Cato had to be defended, before Maximius settled on a mistaken judgement of the young centurion. First impressions were hard to shake, and the last thing Macro wanted to see was Cato handicapped by some veteran's prejudice as he made a go of his first legionary command. The legionaries of the Sixth Century, he knew, were still bridling over the appointment of a centurion who was younger than all but a handful of the men. The situation was not helped by Cato's choice of Figulus for optio. Figulus was only a few months older than his centurion, but at least he had the kind of physique that deters those in the ranks from insubordination.

Figulus was safe enough, Macro realised. It was Cato who would be pressured to justify his rapid promotion. Macro knew that Cato, cursed by lack of self-confidence and by driving ambition in equal measure, would do anything to prove he deserved his advancement. Macro had seen the lad's desperate courage on many occasions. Given half a chance Cato would prove Maximius wrong or die in the attempt. Unless Maximius knew that, and backed off from his snide treatment of his subordinate, then Cato would be a danger to himself.

Then Macro paused, mid-thought, as something more disturbing occurred to him. What if Maximius recognised that same flaw in Cato and decided to exploit it cruelly?

Macro cleared his throat, and spoke in what he hoped sounded like a light-hearted tone. 'Sure he's young, sir. But he's learned the trade fast. And he's got guts.'

'Young!' Maximius snorted. 'I'll say.'

The other centurions laughed and Macro forced himself to smile along with them as he steeled himself for another attempt to steer Maximius towards a more sensitive treatment of the cohort's most junior centurion.

'He's just a bit touchy, sir.' Macro smiled. 'You know what it was like at that age.'

'Yes I do. That's precisely why boys should not be placed in command of men. They lack the necessary temperament, wouldn't you agree?'

'In most cases, yes, sir.'

'In your case?'

Macro thought about this a moment and then nodded. 'I suppose so. I could never have been a centurion at Cato's age.'

'Me neither,' Maximius chuckled. 'That's why I'm not convinced by our young centurion.'

'But Cato's different.'

Maximius shrugged and turned his gaze along the track ahead of them. 'We'll see soon enough.'

The dust at the end of the column hung in the air and made the men's mouths feel dry and gritty. That was why Cato's men had slowly dropped back from the rear of the Fifth Century. He immediately ordered them forward and then kept them in the correct formation with the rest of the cohort, despite the undercurrent of muttered protest that greeted his command.

'Silence!' Cato shouted. 'Silence in the ranks there! Optio, take the name of the next man who opens his mouth out of turn.'

'Yes, sir!' Figulus saluted.

Cato stepped away from the track and stood and watched the men closely as his century marched past. His eye was practised enough to distinguish between the good and the bad legionaries, between the veterans and the recruits, between those in good physical condition and those who were in poor health. There was no question that they were all fit; the merciless regime of perpetual training and route marches saw to that. Cato's eyes glanced over the men's kit, mentally noting those who had taken every effort to maintain their armour and weapons to the highest standards. He noted the faces of those men whose armour was heavily tarnished; he would have Figulus see to them later. A few days of fatigues might sort them out. If that didn't work he'd slap some fines on them.

As the tail of the century tramped by, Cato waited a moment longer, making sure that the lines of his men were even, then he fell in on the track and double-paced to catch up. He was pleased enough with what he had seen so far. There was a handful of obvious bad characters, but the majority looked like good men, conscientious and hardy enough. The only thing that bothered Cato was that he still lacked a firm understanding of their collective spirit. The faces he had scrutinised from the side of the track were largely expressionless, and since he had ordered them to be silent there was little tangible sense of their feelings, only, perhaps, a sullen resentment over the order. Cato thought about changing his mind and letting them talk, which would allow him to gauge their mood a little more readily. But to countermand an order so recently given would only make him look indecisive and irresolute. He'd have to let them resent him for the moment then. That might even help foster his preferred image as a stern disciplinarian who would not brook the slightest hint of insubordination from the men under his command. He'd show that bastard Maximius . . .

Which was why he was being so harsh on the men, Cato realised. He was taking out his anger on them, and with that thought he was awash with guilt and self-contempt. There was really no difference between Maximius' bullying of Cato and Cato's taking it out on the men of his century. Maximius – it pained him to admit it – was right. He was sulking, and now over eighty good men were suffering the consequences. Unless he grew out of his sensitivity he would be a perpetual burden to his men. Men who must trust him implicitly if they were to overcome the savage ferocity of Caratacus and his horde.

Not long after noon the track curved towards a small hillock. On its crest stood the raw dark earth of a recently erected rampart. A wooden barricade ran along the top of the earthworks with solid timber towers constructed above the two gates and at each corner of the fort. The distant detail of the structure was lost in the shimmering heat, but beyond the hill there was the glint of the Tamesis, looking cool and inviting to the eyes of sweating legionaries. Cato felt that he had not seen a more serene and peaceful view for months, but sight of the river brought the prospect of the coming battle sharply to mind. Soon enough those quiet waters would be stained with men's blood and their corpses would lay strewn about under the harsh glare of the sun.

As the cohort approached, there was no sign of movement behind the rampart, almost as if the sentries had decided to find some shelter from the sun to enjoy an afternoon nap. Above the fort Cato could see tiny black dots slowly swirling: carrion birds of some kind, he decided. Apart from a few solitary swifts darting high and low, they were the only birds in the clear sky. When the cohort was less than a mile from the fort and there was still no sign of life, Centurion Maximius halted his men and bellowed out an order for the scouts to mount and move ahead to investigate. With a soft thrumming of hoofs the scouts trotted forwards and started up the gentle incline towards the gatehouse.

'Officers to the front!'

Cato ran forward, his harness jingling loudly as he passed by the silent ranks of each century. He joined the other officers breathing heavily and mopped the perspiration from his brow.

'Something's wrong,' muttered Felix.

Maximius slowly turned towards him. 'Really? Do you think so?'

Felix looked surprised. 'Well, yes, sir. That or they have the worst sentries I've ever encountered. In which case someone's in for a roasting.'

Maximius nodded. 'Well, thank you for your concise appraisal of the situation. Most instructive . . . you idiot! Of course something's wrong.'

Felix began to stammer something, and then shut his mouth and gazed down at his boots as he scraped one foot across the loose soil. The other centurions turned their gaze on the fort and silently watched the scouts ride up towards the entrance. One of the gates began to swing open slowly.

'Sir!'

'I see it, Antonius.'

A dark shape flitted out of the shadows under the gatehouse into the sunlight. A large dog, one of the hunting beasts the Nervanians insisted on taking with them on campaign. It glanced quickly at the approaching horsemen and then turned and bolted down the slope in the opposite direction. For a moment the officers watched it run, sleek back bobbing up and down as it disappeared round the flank of the hill.

'Sir, what's that?' asked Cato, and raised an arm to point at the gatehouse.

The gate had continued to inch open and was now swinging out from the shadows. Something had been fixed to the inside of the gate.

'Oh, shit,' Centurion Felix whispered.

No one replied. They could see it clearly now and for a moment no one spoke. It was the body of a man, nailed to the timbers with a spike through both his palms. He was stripped and had been disembowelled, and his guts hung down over his legs, red and grey and glistening.

Chapter Eight

Centurion Maximius swung round. 'Cohort! Form up. Close order!'

As the men shuffled together and raised their shields Maximius ordered his centurions to rejoin their units. Up by the fort the scouts had spread out across the track and the decurion took three of his men and slowly approached the gate. They paused by the corpse for a moment and had disappeared inside by the time Cato ran up to Figulus at the head of the Sixth Century.

'What's happening, sir?'

'You've got eyes, Optio,' Cato snapped back at him. 'See for yourself.'

While Figulus shaded his brow with his hand and squinted towards the gateway, Cato became aware of several muted exchanges from the men behind him. He shot an angry look over his shoulder.

'Shut your mouths!'

Cato saw one man mutter something to his neighbour and turned round and strode over to him, pointing.

'You! Yes, you! You're on a charge. What's your name?'

'Titus Velius, sir!'

'What the fuck are you doing, talking after I've told you to be silent?' Cato stopped in front of him and leaned forward, glaring into the legionary's face. Velius was a little shorter than Cato, several years older and much more heavily built. He stared over the shoulder of his centurion, expressionless.

'Well?'

'Just saying we're in trouble, sir.' He met Cato's eyes briefly. 'That's all.' Then his gaze reverted to a fixed forward stare.

Cato's nostrils flared as he exhaled angrily. 'Optio!'

'Sir?' Figulus trotted over towards him.

'Put Velius on a charge. Ten days' latrines.'

'Yes, sir.'

Cato stepped back and looked round at his men. 'Next loudmouth I catch speaking out of turn pulls twenty days in the shit!'

He turned away and scanned the fort once again. The gate had fetched up against the wall of the gatehouse and the man hung motionless. There was no sign of any life beyond the gate and only the slowly wheeling crows broke the awful stillness that hung over the silent ramparts.

42

Cato scanned the surrounding landscape, but not a soul moved in any direction. No enemies, no auxiliary troops and none of the local natives.

At length the decurion of the scouts emerged from the shadows of the gatehouse and trotted his horse down towards Centurion Maximius, who had advanced a short distance in front of his cohort, impatient to discover what had happened to the garrison of the fort.

'Well?'

The decurion looked badly shaken. 'They're all dead, sir.'

'All? The entire unit?'

'I suppose so, sir. Didn't count 'em but there must be over a hundred of them in there . . . dead. Most don't look like they died quickly.'

Maximius looked towards the fort for a moment before he gave his orders to the decurion. 'Take your men. Find the tracks of whoever did this. Find out where they went and report back to me at once.'

The decurion saluted, wheeled his horse about and trotted back towards his men, ordering them to form up. Maximius marched steadily towards the gate and entered the fort.

Once the scouts had galloped off to the north, on the trail of the enemy, the men of the cohort waited quietly in the baking sunshine, watching anxiously for the cohort commander to reappear. A long time passed, maybe a quarter of an hour, by Cato's estimate, and at length he slapped his thigh in frustration.

'Think something's happened to him, sir?' Figulus asked quietly.

'I hope not. But he'd better get out of there soon. We can't afford to be delayed. He's got his orders.'

'Shouldn't someone go and check on him?'

Cato looked along the column, picking out the other centurions. Macro was looking his way and raised his hands in a gesture of frustration.

'You're right,' Cato replied. 'Someone has to find him. Stay here.'

Cato trotted forward. Felix and Antonius eyed him with surprised expressions as he passed by. He stopped when he reached Macro.

'Taking his bloody time!' Macro grumbled.

'I know. We have to get moving.'

'We need the trenching tools from the fort.'

'Then we should be getting them and moving on to the ford. Someone has to go up there . . .'

While Macro scratched his chin and considered the situation, they were joined by Centurion Tullius, an anxious expression on his weathered features.

'What do you think we should do?'

Macro looked at Tullius in surprise. As the senior officer present Tullius should be making decisions, not asking for advice, or worse still, opinions. The old centurion looked hopefully at the other two officers, waiting for them to say something.

43

'Someone has to go up there,' Cato said, at length.

'He told us to stay with our centuries.'

'Look,' said Macro, 'we can't fuck about here all day. We've got to get to that ford. Someone has to fetch Maximius. Right now.'

'Yes. But who?'

'Who cares?' Macro replied. 'You go.'

'Me?' Tullius looked frightened by the idea. He shook his head. 'No. I'd better stay with the cohort. If it's a trap I'll be needed here. You go, Cato. You'd better double up there right away.'

Cato didn't wait to show an expression of distaste, but turned towards the fort and began to run up the slope. Almost at once a figure emerged from the gate and Maximius came striding down the track. He saw the gathering of centurions at once and started towards them angrily. The three centurions steeled themselves for his wrath.

'What the hell is this? Who told you to leave your units?'

'Sir,' Cato protested, 'we were concerned for your safety.'

'And we're running behind schedule,' added Macro. 'We should be heading for the ford by now, sir.'

Maximius instantly rounded on him and stabbed a finger at his chest. 'Don't you dare presume to tell me my duty, Centurion!'

'Sir, I only meant to remind—'

'Shut up!' Maximius screamed down into Macro's face. For a moment the two officers glared at each other, as the men surrounding them looked on in astonishment.

Cato coughed. 'Sir?'

'What?'

'Were there any survivors?'

'None.'

'Any sign of Centurion Porcinus?'

Maximius winced at the mention of his friend's name. 'Oh, I found him all right. In fact I kept finding him.'

'I don't understand.'

'Want me to draw you a fucking picture? If I ever catch the bastards who did this, I swear on my family name they'll spend all day dying.'

The distant pounding of hoofs drew the men's attention to the slope below the fort; one of the scouts was galloping towards them. He reined in a short distance from the officers and his mount sprayed them with clods of earth. The scout dropped to the ground at once and breathlessly saluted Maximius.

'Make your report!'

'Sir, we've found them!' The scout jabbed his thumb over his shoulder, north towards the Tamesis. 'Infantry. Heading west along the river, two miles away.'

'How many?' Cato asked.

'Three, maybe four hundred, sir.'

Maximius shot Cato a withering glance before he addressed the scout. 'You're reporting to me, boy.'

'Yes, sir.' The scout was flustered. 'Of course. Sorry, sir.'

The cohort commander nodded sternly. 'Right. Let's have them. Get back to your decurion. I want them followed. Any change of direction, he's to let me know at once. Understand?'

'Yes, sir.'

'Then go.' Maximius waved him away and turned back to the other officers. As the scout threw himself back over the saddlecloth of his mount and spurred it away with wild shouts of command, Maximius briefly collected his thoughts. 'It's most likely to be a raiding party.'

'Raiding party?' Cato wondered.

'What else?'

Cato was surprised. 'Well, it's obvious.'

Macro winced at his friend's unusually blunt response.

'Is it? Well, Centurion, do please share your tactical insight with us mere mortals.'

'They must be scouting ahead of Caratacus' army. He's sent them to check the fords.'

'Why attack the fort?'

'Because they might have spotted the scouting force. Maybe Caratacus didn't want anyone left alive to make any report on his movements.'

'Why kill them like they did? Why did they do that then?'

'They're barbarians,' Cato shrugged. 'They can't help themselves.'

'Bollocks! They're murderers . . . butchers! That's all. And now they'll pay for it.'

'Sir,' Macro intervened, 'what about our orders?'

Maximius ignored him and turned towards the column, filling his lungs. 'Cohort! Prepare to advance!'

'If we leave the ford uncovered and Caratacus makes for it—'

Maximius turned to him with a forced smile. 'Macro, there's time enough to deal with our friends and then secure the ford. Trust me.'

'But the trenching tools are in the fort, sir.'

'We can return for those afterwards . . .'

'If we have to come back for them—'

'Damn you, Macro!' Maximius shouted, hands balling into fists. 'Take your century, then. Get the bloody tools and I'll see you at the ford.'

'Yes, sir.'

'Cohort!' Maximius raised his arm and then swept it forward. 'Advance!'

'Third Century!' Macro shouted. 'Fall out of line!'

Macro's men shuffled off the track and the rest of the cohort followed Centurion Maximius as he quick marched across the slope towards the Tamesis. With a brief glance at the back of the cohort commander Macro grasped Cato by the arm.

'Look here. Things are turning to shit. Maximius has lost it. If he tries anything that puts you and the rest of the lads in any danger . . .'

Cato nodded slowly. 'I'll do what I have to, if it comes to that. See you at the ford.'

'Right. Watch yourself, lad.'

'I always do.' Cato made himself smile, then turned towards his men.

Macro watched his friend drop into line alongside Figulus, then the Sixth Century tramped by and as the rear of the last rank moved off round the hill Macro ordered his men up the slope. Apart from the steady chink and jingle of the men's equipment the only sound was the raw grating cry of the crows fighting over the fresh corpses in the fort.

Chapter Nine

Nearly an hour later the cohort caught up with the Britons. A compact mass of infantry was marching quickly upriver, towards the ford that the cohort had been ordered to defend. From the outset it was clear that they would not reach the ford first, but their leader was a game individual who would at least give it a try and drove his men on as the Romans remorselessly closed in at a tangent. Then the Britons changed their minds and abruptly reversed their direction, heading away from the ford as they made a last desperate bid to escape their pursuers. Maximius gave orders to the decurion in charge of the scouts to skirmish ahead of the enemy column and slow it down.

So the scouts started to dart in, throwing a few of their light javelins at the leading ranks of the Britons, and then galloping back to safety. When this minor distraction failed to have much effect on the enemy's pace the decurion drew up his men and feigned a few charges, forcing the Britons to halt momentarily to brace themselves for the impact. It did not take long for the enemy to see through the feint and they ignored the third charge, forcing the scouts to quickly break off and scurry away to safety. Even so, some time had been bought for Maximius and his men. A little more than an hour after the cohort had left the fort behind them the Britons turned to face their pursuers.

'Cohort . . . halt!' Maximius bellowed. 'Deploy into line!'

While the five centuries moved quietly into position the Britons formed up into a crude wedge, two hundred paces away, with their backs to the broad sweep of the river. At once they began to beat their weapons against their shields and raised their voices in a cacophony of jeers, contempt and challenges as they worked themselves up into a frenzy. Most of the legionaries had seen this performance many times in the last year and yet the din and the mad capering of their enemies still worked on their nerves as the Romans braced themselves for the 'Celtic rush' that seemed to be the tribes' only tactical manoeuvre.

Cato walked slowly along in front of his men. The Sixth Century was on the left of the Roman line. Some of the younger faces, and a few of the veterans, wore eloquent expressions of doubt and fear, and needed some form of distraction. Cato stopped and turned his back to the enemy.

'I wouldn't worry about that lot!' He had to shout to be heard clearly above the rising roar of the enemy's battle cries. 'In a moment they'll charge us. All we have to do is stand firm, give 'em six inches of the short sword and they'll break in no time. Most of us have been here before and know the form. For the rest of you, once it's all over, you'll wonder what you were ever worried about.' Cato grinned. 'Trust me, I'm a centurion!'

A few men laughed, and Cato was glad to see a release of the nervous tension he had marked in some of those faces an instant before.

'You tell 'em, *boy*!' a voice cried out from somewhere amongst the rear ranks.

Figulus spun round. 'Who said that? Who the fuck said that?' The optio thrust his way through the front line. 'Which one of you pricks just signed his own death warrant?'

'Optio!' Cato called out. 'Get back to your post!'

'Yes, sir!' Figulus glowered at the men around him before shoving back through the broad shields to take his place alongside the century's standard bearer. Cato met his eyes and gave him a slight nod of approval; the optio's intervention had forestalled any wider breach of discipline. Very well, if some of the men didn't want his encouragement they could wait for the charge in silence.

Fortunately patience was not numbered among the Celtic virtues, and with a sudden great roar the natives rippled forward and charged across the open ground towards the still, red line of Roman shields, above which polished helmets glinted in the harsh sunlight. Cato made himself turn round slowly to face the enemy. His keen eyesight took in the myriad details of lime-washed hair, tattoos and swirling patterns painted on to bare, glistening flesh, brilliant reflections shimmering off swords and helmets. Spears jabbed the air and every face amongst them was twisted and strained with savage expressions of rage and bloodlust that were the stuff of nightmares.

Cato was terrified, and for an instant the urge to turn and run seized his limbs. Then the horror of showing his fear in front of his men rescued him and he welcomed the cold chill of fright that pulsed through him and keyed up every muscle, and every one of his senses, in readiness for the imminent need to kill and to live. He made himself stand still a few heartbeats longer and face the howling mob racing across the grass towards the Roman line. Then he turned and walked towards the front rank of his century.

'Standard to the rear!' Cato thought he heard a tremor in his voice and concentrated on steadying it for the next order. 'Keep your shields up!'

As he assumed his position in the middle of the front rank Cato took a firm grasp on the handle of the shield Figulus held ready for him, and drew his sword.

At the far end of the cohort, Maximius cupped a hand to his mouth and roared out an order, only just audible above the din of the charging tribesmen. 'Front rank . . . ready javelins!'

The front rank rippled forward as the men advanced two paces and halted.

'Prepare!'

The men twisted at the waist and reached back with their right arms, angling the shafts of their javelins up towards the sky. Then they tensed, waiting for the final order. Maximius faced the enemy, gauging the gap between the Britons and his cohort. He let them come on, sprinting across the rich green tufts of grass. When they were no more than thirty paces away he swung back to his men.

'Release!'

There was a deep grunt from the front rank as their arms shot the javelins forward and a slender veil of dark shafts curved up, slowing as they reached the peak of their trajectory, then dipped, picking up speed, and clattered and thudded into the ranks of the enemy. The range was short, and scores of the Britons were struck down – pierced through by the heavy iron heads of the Roman javelins.

'Rear ranks, down javelins and move forward!' Maximius yelled, and the rest of the cohort stepped into position behind the men of the front rank, who quickly drew their swords and braced themselves for the impact of the charge. An instant later the Britons hurled themselves upon the Roman line, hacking and thrusting at the wide curved shields with their long swords and spears. Some, more powerfully built than their comrades, burst through the gaps between the shields, and straight on to the points of the swords of the men in the rank behind. Cato, tall and thin, was thrust back by a body piling into the surface of his shield. He gave ground, but as the enemy warrior plunged into the Sixth Century, he was cut down by the frenzied thrusts of the man to the left of Cato. The centurion briefly nodded his thanks to Velius and thrust his way back into line.

Once the immediate impact of the charge had been absorbed the Roman line quickly re-formed and the Britons were whittled down as they vented their rage and frustration on the red shields. Cato blocked the blows of the enemies in front of him, and thrust his blade out between his shield and that of the man next to him whenever a Briton dared to come within range. When he could, Cato glanced to each side to try to snatch some overview of how the fight was progressing. Despite the initial ferocity of their charge, the Britons were outnumbered and outfought, and the Roman line was never in danger of being broken.

Above the clash and thud and cries of battle Cato heard a command being passed along the cohort, and saw, away to his right, the First Century edge forward. Then he heard Centurion Felix's voice, nearby, bellow an order.

'Advance!'

As the Fifth began to press forward Cato repeated the order to his men and the legionaries leaned into the curve of their shields and pressed into the loose ranks of the enemy. With the Roman line thrusting forwards, the tribesmen had even less space to wield their longer blades and the exultant battle cries of a moment earlier died in their throats as each man sought to get away from the vicious blades of the short swords that stabbed out from between the broad shields. As it was only a skirmish there was no mass of bodies behind them to pin them in place and the Britons began to back away. Cato, watching over the metal rim of his shield, saw the men in front of him give ground, then there was a clear gap between the two sides. The legionaries continued to tramp forwards in close formation, then they passed over the line of those struck down by the javelin volley. They killed the injured as they passed by and moved steadily on. There was no pretence of further resistance now, and the Britons broke and fled.

Ahead lay the river, and as soon as they realised the danger of being caught in between the iron and the water the Britons started to run towards the flanks of the cohort, hoping to escape round them while they still could. But the decurion and his men lay in wait with a half-squadron at each end of the Roman line. They spurred their horses on and cut down the fleeing warriors without mercy. Denied any escape on the flanks the Britons turned once more towards the river and, with the current gliding peacefully at their backs they made ready to die. Cato estimated that there were more than a hundred of them left, and many had lost or abandoned their weapons and stood with clenched fists and bared teeth, wild-eyed with terror. They were finished, he realised. All that was left to them now was death or surrender. Cato drew a deep breath and called out in Celtic.

'Drop your weapons! Drop them, or die!'

The warriors' eyes turned towards him, some filled with defiance, some with hope. Still the legionaries closed in on them, and the warriors retreated, splashing into the shallows of the Tamesis, then wading out until water reached their waists.

'Throw your weapons down!' Cato ordered. 'Do it!'

At once one of the warriors turned and tossed his sword out into deeper waters. Another followed suit, and then the rest threw down their weapons and stood in the slow current watching the Romans anxiously.

Cato turned down the line of the cohort, cupping a hand to his mouth. 'Halt! Halt!'

The centuries slowed and then stood still, a few paces short of the river bank. Cato saw the cohort commander break away from the end of the first cohort and come trotting down the line towards him.

'What do you think you're doing?' Maximius barked as he reached Cato.

'I told them to surrender, sir.'

'Surrender?' Maximius raised his eyebrows in frank astonishment. 'Who said anything about taking prisoners?'

Cato frowned. 'But, sir, I thought you wanted prisoners . . .'

'After what they did? What the hell were you thinking?'

'I was trying to save lives, sir. Ours as well as theirs.'

'I see.' Maximius glanced round at the Sixth Century and leaned closer to their centurion before he continued quietly. 'This is no time for noble sentiments, young Cato. We can't afford to burden ourselves with prisoners. Besides, you didn't see what they did to the men back in the fort. My friend Porcinus . . . They have to die.'

'Sir, they're unarmed. They've surrendered. It wouldn't be right. Not now.'

'Wouldn't be right?' Maximius laughed and shook his head. 'This isn't a game. There aren't any rules here, Cato.'

There was no mercy in the commander's eyes, and Cato desperately tried another tack.

'Sir, they might have valuable intelligence. If we send them to the rear for interrogation—'

'No. I can't afford to detach men for guard duties.' Maximius drew his lips back in a faint smile. He turned round to Cato's men. 'Get them out of there! Get 'em out and bind their hands. Use strips from their clothing.'

The men of the Sixth Century lay their shields down and started dragging the Britons out of the river. The prisoners were thrown face first on to the ground, their arms pinned to their backs as the legionaries bound them securely. When the last of them had been dealt with, Maximius stood over them with a look of bitter satisfaction. Cato stood to one side, relieved that they had been spared.

'That's them sorted, sir. Won't be giving us any more problems today.'

'No.'

'And we can come back for them later, sir.'

'Yes.'

'I suppose they might try to escape, but they won't get far.'

'No, they won't. Not after we've dealt with them.'

'Sir?' Cato felt a chill ripple up through the hairs on the back of his neck.

Maximius ignored him, and turned to the men of the Sixth Century. 'Blind them.'

Figulus frowned, not sure that he had heard right.

'I said blind them. Put their eyes out. Use your daggers.'

Cato opened his mouth to protest, but was too horrified to find the right words. While he paused the cohort commander sprang towards Figulus, snatched the optio's dagger from its scabbard and leaned over the nearest prisoner.

'Here, like this . . .'

There was a piercing shriek of the purest terror and agony that Cato had ever heard and he felt his stomach knot, as if he would throw up. The cohort commander worked his sword arm about, and then slowly stood up, a bitter look etched on his face as he turned round. At his side his arm hung loose, blood dripping from the dagger that was tightly clenched in his fist. Behind him the Briton writhed on the ground, still screaming as blood gushed from his eye sockets and spattered the grass around his head.

'There!' Maximius handed the dagger back to Figulus. 'That's how it's done. Now get on with it.'

Figulus regarded him with horror, then looked to Cato pleadingly.

Maximius glared at the optio. 'Why, you—'

'Optio!' Cato shouted. 'You have your orders. Carry them out!'

'Yes . . .' Figulus nodded. 'Yes, sir.' He turned to the nearest men. 'Get the blades out. You heard the centurion!'

As the men started on their bloody work and the hot afternoon was pierced by terrible screams, Maximius nodded his satisfaction.

'We're done here then. Soon as your lot have finished the cohort moves on to the ford.'

'Yes, sir,' Cato replied. 'Best move quickly then.'

'Yes. We had.' Maximius suddenly looked worried, and spun round and strode off towards his men. The last of the prisoners was quickly dealt with and the men of the Sixth Century cleaned their blades and retrieved their shields and javelins before forming up at the end of the small Roman column. The cohort had suffered only seven dead, and a handful of men had been injured. Their wounds were bound and they headed back towards the shelter of the fort. The rest of the cohort waited for Maximius to give the order to march, and then they tramped forward, along the bank towards the ford.

Behind them the pitiful cries and screams of the prisoners faded slowly, accompanied by the shrill calls of the crows who were already wheeling above the battleground as they sought out fresh pickings amongst the dead and dying that littered the bright green grass below.

Chapter Ten

The ford was situated at a point where the Tamesis narrowed to less than half its usual width. In the middle of the river was a small island with a handful of willows growing either side of the track. The end of their long branches dipped down into the current and provided a green glimmering shade. Centurion Macro looked longingly at the shade as he mopped the sweat from his brow with the back of his hairy forearm. In a fleeting moment of fancy Macro imagined himself resting on his back under the willow, boots off and feet trailing in the cool water of the Tamesis. It was tempting . . . too tempting. He frowned and strode across the tiny island towards the north bank of the river. There was a shallow stretch of shingle over which the current swept, its disturbed surface glittering in the sunlight.

As soon as the Third Century had reached the ford, Macro had waded across to test the depth. The water came up to his waist when he reached the deepest part between the small island and each bank. Although his footing was firm enough the current was strong and might easily sweep away anyone who was careless as they crossed. Macro posted one section on the far bank to keep watch for the enemy and immediately set about preparing his defences. It was, perhaps, a hundred paces to the far bank and the width of the ford was no more than ten paces. Either side of the shingle bar the depth increased quickly and the riverbed was soft and covered with long reeds that slowly waved like hair beneath the surface of the river.

Macro had ordered half of his century to seed the ford with small sharpened stakes, and the men had hacked lengths of wood from the trees growing on the river banks and were busy driving them into the shingle, struggling against the pull of the current as they thrust the stakes in, angled towards the enemy shore. If the Britons were forced to use this ford the stakes would not stop them crossing, but might at least injure a few and slow down the rest.

Macro's next line of defence was the small island, on which twenty men toiled to construct a rough barricade at the water's edge. A dense tangle of branches and gorse had been dragged across from the south bank and piled up across the track in a line that extended either side of the shallows. Stout timbers had been pounded into the earth to brace the tangle, and other branches had been trimmed and sharpened and thrust in amongst the gorse to deter any attackers. It wasn't much to look at, Macro decided, but it was the best they could do with the time and materials available.

He had not discovered many trenching tools back in the sacked auxiliary fort. The Britons had been almost as thorough in their destruction of material as they had been of the garrison. A smouldering pyre of shields, slings, javelins and other equipment had been discovered inside the headquarters courtyard. Some of the tools at the periphery of the fire were salvageable, and a quick search through the timber barrack blocks had revealed some more picks and shovels, but Macro had come away with barely enough to equip half his century, let alone the rest of the cohort. Macro hoped that the cohort commander's thirst for revenge had been quickly satisfied. The Third Century would not be able to defend the crossing alone should the enemy appear in force.

Besides, Macro thought angrily, Maximius had no bloody business chasing the small raiding party down in the first place. It was not in his orders. The protection of the ford should have been his priority. The cohort needed to be in position shortly after noon, yet three hours later still only Macro and his century were preparing to defend the crossing. The enemy might appear at any moment, and if they did then the crossing must fall into their hands.

Macro glanced back over his shoulder, scanning the southern bank for any sign of Maximius and the rest of the cohort.

'Come on . . . come on, you bastard.' Macro slapped his hand against his thigh. 'Where the fuck are you?'

A faint shout from the northern bank drew his attention and Macro turned round. One of the men carrying a bundle of freshly cut stakes was waving to attract his attention.

'What is it?'

'There, sir. Up there!' The man pointed behind him. On the far side of the river the track rose up from the edge of the ford and disappeared over the crest of a small hill. Standing on the crest was a small figure, waving his javelin to and fro – the signal that the enemy had been sighted.

At once Macro brushed through the gap that had been left in the barricade and splashed down into the ford. He kept to the right, still unseeded with stakes to allow the defenders access to the crossing. The water closed around him, dragging at his legs as Macro thrust his way across to the far bank, throwing up sparkling cascades of spray as he emerged. A number of his men paused in their work, distracted by the alarm.

'Get back to work!' Macro shouted. 'You keep at it until I tell you otherwise!'

He didn't pause but ran on, puffing up the slope to where his lookout was watching the landscape to the north. By the time that he had reached the man the centurion was exhausted and was fighting for breath as he followed the direction of the lookout's javelin.

'There, sir.'

Macro squinted. Just over two miles away the track led into the dense greenery of a forest. Emerging from the trees was a screen of mounted scouts, and a few chariots. They were fanning out ahead of the line of march and galloping for the high ground to scan the way ahead. A moment later a dense column of infantry began to flow down the track out of the forest.

'Is that Caratacus then, sir?'

Macro glanced at the legionary, recalling that the young man was one of the raw recruits who had only just been posted to the legion. He looked tense and excited. Perhaps too excited, Macro thought.

'Too early to say for certain, lad.'

'Should we get back to the others, sir?'

'It's Lentulus, isn't it?'

'Yes, sir.' The legionary seemed surprised that his centurion knew his name and was mildly flattered to be individually addressed by someone as august as a centurion.

'Keep a cool head, Lentulus. You're supposed to observe and keep track of events, not worry yourself about them. A lookout has to be calm. That's why I picked you for this duty.' It was a bald lie. Macro could have chosen anyone for the job, but the recruit was green enough to take it at face value, seemed to take a firm grip on his nerves and drew himself up.

'Yes, sir. Thank you, sir.'

'Just do your job, lad.'

Lentulus nodded and then turned back to keep watch on the enemy. They stood in silence for a while and Macro raised a hand to shade his eyes. More and more men spilled out of the forest. At length he was satisfied that this had to be the main column of the enemy.

'Looks like you're right,' Macro said quietly. 'Looks like Caratacus is making a run for our crossing.'

'Oh, shit . . .'

'And we're shortly going to be right up to our necks in it.' Macro lowered his hand and punched the recruit on the shoulder. 'Bet you didn't think it would ever be as exciting as this!'

'Well, no, sir.'

'I want you to stay here for as long as it's safe. I'm assuming the enemy will come straight down the track towards us. But if he doesn't, if he turns off and heads away, I want to know at once. And keep an eye out for any sign of General Plautius following them up. Understand?'

'Yes, sir.'

'Right. Then keep watching them. Stay low; there's no point in attracting attention to yourself.' Macro pointed a finger at him. 'And no heroics. Give yourself plenty of time to get back to the century.'

Lentulus nodded and squatted down, keeping his eyes on the approaching enemy. The centurion turned and walked a few paces back down towards the ford, and stopped to scan the south bank of the Tamesis. There was no sign of life close to the track on the far side and nothing to be seen as he scanned left along the bank. Then a far-off glint caught his eye and Macro stared hard in that direction. He made out a faint shimmering glitter against the green and brown landscape, and a slight haze hanging in the air about it. That had to be the Third Cohort, still a good three miles from the ford.

Caratacus was going to reach the crossing first.

Lentulus was still in earshot and Macro gritted his teeth to avoid any explosive outpouring of expletives as he silently invoked every curse in his repertoire and directed it at the distant – too distant – column of the cohort crawling across the hot shimmering landscape towards the ford. He took a last longing look, and then trotted back down the slope towards the Tamesis.

As he approached the ford Macro slowed down to catch his breath. No sense in making the lads even more anxious, he decided. Best to try to keep a veneer of calmness and confidence.

'That's enough work!' he called out to the men still embedding the stakes in the shingle. 'Get back to the island and kit up! We've got company.'

The legionaries abandoned the remaining stakes and let them flow downriver with the current as they splashed along the safe path towards the gap in the barricade.

'Don't run!' Macro bellowed angrily. 'If anyone gets caught on one of the stakes I'll leave them there for the Britons.'

With a great effort of will, bolstered by fear of their centurion's wrath, the legionaries slowed down.

Macro followed them at a more measured pace, keeping a wary eye out for the tips of the stakes they had planted. Glancing ahead he could see more of his men forming up behind the barricade, hurriedly strapping on helmets and hefting their shields and javelins from where they had been left beside the worn and rutted track that crossed over the back of the little island. As Macro emerged dripping from the river, he glanced round at his men and then fixed his gaze on a tall, wiry legionary.

'Fabius!'

'Sir!' The man snapped to attention as Macro strode up to him.

'Get your armour off. I need a runner.'

'Yes, sir.' Fabius quickly undid the leather ties of his segmented armour as Macro explained.

'Centurion Maximius is approaching along the south bank. He's nearly three miles away. You run to him as fast as you can. You tell him that Caratacus is making for this ford. Tell him to send a rider to the legate at once to let him know what's happening. No, wait . . .' Macro could visualise how that part of the message would be received by the touchy cohort commander. 'Tell him, I respectfully suggest that he sends a rider to the legate. Finally, tell him that Caratacus is closer to the ford than he is and that he must get the cohort here as quick as possible. Quicker!'

'Yes, sir.' Fabius grinned as he struggled out of the armour and laid it down on the track.

'Well, what're you waiting for?' Macro growled. 'Move yourself!'

Fabius turned and ran down to the river, plunging into the ford. Macro watched him for a moment before turning back to the rest of his men. Most had finished arming and stood ready for orders. He waited until the last man had tied his chinstraps; no easy feat under the impatient gaze of all his comrades and commanding officer. At last the legionary looked up with a guilty expression and pulled himself up into a stiff posture of readiness. Macro cleared his throat.

'Stand to!'

'The legionaries grounded their shields and spears and gathered in a compact line across the track and under the willows.

'In less than an hour Caratacus and his army are going to come pouring down the track towards the ford. Right behind them should be General Plautius, with his sword right in their backside.'

A few of the men chuckled at the crude image and Macro indulged it a moment before continuing.

'The rest of the cohort is on the way. I saw it from the top of the hill there. I've sent Fabius to hurry them along and they should reach us before the enemy gives us much grief. Not that we're going to need 'em, of course! The Third Century can hold its own with the best of them. It's only a few days that we've served together, but I've lived with the Eagles long enough to know quality when I see it. You'll do. It's those poor bastards on the other side I feel sorry for! They can only attack us on a narrow front, and only then after they've impaled themselves on our stakes and the barricade. If they're really lucky, and I'm feeling generous, I might just spare them a little more bloodshed and accept Caratacus' surrender.'

Macro smiled, and to his relief his men smiled back.

'However, the Britons are a mad lot, and might not see sense. If they really want to cross the river, they will. We can only buy time. I'm not in the business of creating martyrs, so if we've done our bit and it looks like they're going to break through I'll give the order to fall back. If I do, I don't want any heroics. You get over to our side of the ford as fast as you can, then you head downriver towards the cohort. Understand?'

Some of the men nodded.

'I can't fucking hear you!' Macro shouted.

'YES, SIR!'

'That's better. Now form up facing the river!'

His men turned round and shuffled forward until they lined the makeshift defences facing the north bank of the Tamesis. Macro ran his eyes over his small command in their tarnished armour and dusty and stained red tunics. The men were formed up in three lines that stretched along the length of the small island. Eighty men against twenty, maybe thirty thousand barbarians. Macro, like most soldiers, was a gambler, but never had he known such unfavourable odds. Despite his attempt to bolster the confidence of his men he knew that they were as good as dead. If only Maximius had arrived at the ford in time to defend it properly, things might have been different.

The afternoon dragged on. Macro allowed his men to sit on the ground. Now that all activity had ceased across the ford the scene looked quite idyllic. Macro smiled. Cato would have loved this; it would have touched the lad's poetic sensibility. To Macro's left the sun was long past its zenith and bathed the scene in an angled glare that intensified the colours of the landscape and flashed brilliantly off the surface of the river. But despite the serenity of nature, a tension stretched through the air like the torsion ropes of a catapult, and Macro was aware that his senses were straining to catch any sight or sound of the enemy.

Perhaps half an hour had passed when a small figure came pelting down the track towards the ford. Before Lentulus had reached the river's edge a party of horsemen burst over the crest of the hill behind and charged down the near slope. Lentulus looked over his shoulder as he ran into the shallows.

'Keep to your left!' Macro shouted. 'Keep to the left!'

If Lentulus heard him, he gave no sign of it, and plunged into the river. He charged headlong, kicking up sheets of spray, and then suddenly pitched forward with a shrill cry. A groan rippled through the men on the island as Lentulus struggled to his feet, blood gushing from his thigh. The legionary looked down at his injury in horror. Then the splashing of the enemy horsemen behind him made him glance back as he staggered towards his comrades. The Britons picked their way forward towards the legionary thrashing through the waist-deep water. Lentulus' wound must have cut a major blood vessel, Macro realised, for he seemed quickly to become faint. Then slowly he collapsed to his knees, head bowed forward so that only his torso was above the water. The horsemen hung back, watching the Roman for a moment. Then they turned round carefully and returned to the far bank.

For a while both sides watched Lentulus in silence as his head rolled from side to side. A thin red slick flowed downstream from his body. At last he collapsed sideways, and disappeared, his body dragged down by the weight of his armour.

'Poor sod,' someone muttered.

'Silence in the ranks!' Macro shouted. 'Silence!'

The awful tension became evermore taut and strained for the legionaries as they waited for the main body of the enemy to arrive, though they did not have to wait long. At first there was the sound of a faint rumbling that grew steadily louder and more distinct. Then a haze thickened over the crest of the hill where the track disappeared from sight. At last the silhouettes of standards, spears, then helmets and the bodies of men came into sight, all along the top of the hill.

Macro's eyes ran along the vanguard of Caratacus' army, taking in the sight of thousands of men pouring down the slope towards the ford. Then he turned to the opposite bank and looked for any sign of Maximius and the rest of the cohort. But across the placid surface of the Tamesis all was quite still.

Chapter Eleven

'Are you certain Macro said it was the main enemy force?'

'Yes, sir,' the runner replied.

'Right, get over to the decurion.' Maximius pointed out the column of mounted men out to their left flank. 'Tell him to send word of the enemy column to Vespasian, at once. Go!'

As the runner saluted and made off towards the scouts Maximius summoned his centurions. Immediately they came trotting up along the halted column and he waited until Cato, who had furthest to run, had joined them before he told them the news.

'Caratacus is making for our ford. He's got a head start. Look over there.' The cohort commander pointed to the far side of the river. A faint haze that Cato had not noticed before stretched out low over the far bank of the Tamesis.

'Where's Macro?' asked Tullius.

'He's at the ford, preparing his defences.'

'Defences? He's going to make a stand?' Tullius raised his eyebrows in disbelief.

'Those were the orders given to the cohort.'

'Yes, but, sir, it's suicide.'

'Let's hope not, since we're going to join him.'

Antonius and Felix exchanged a look of surprise.

Cato edged forward. 'We'd better get moving, sir.'

'Indeed, Cato. All of you, get-back to your units. We'll move at double time. No stopping for stragglers.'

The centurions were running back to their men as Maximius bellowed the order for the cohort to advance at quick pace. The column rolled forward with a fast-paced rhythm of tramping boots. Glancing to his side Maximius saw the runner Macro had sent him trotting back from the mounted scouts. Beyond him was a small plume of dust swirling round the figure of a man bent low over his horse. As the runner fell into step beside him to wait for orders Maximius glanced round, appraising his condition.

'You ready to run back to Macro?'

'Of course, sir,' the runner replied, his chest heaving as he strained for breath.

The cohort commander lowered his voice. 'If he's still there when you get back to the ford tell him we're on our way as fast we can go. And, if he's not there, you come straight back and warn us. Understand?'

'Not there?' the runner said softly. 'Sir, do you mean—'

'You know what I mean,' Maximius snapped. 'Now go!'

The runner saluted and ran off along the track towards the ford. Maximius glanced over his shoulder and saw that the five centuries had all gathered speed and were moving steadily. He filled his lungs and then shouted the order to increase the pace to a slow run. The men had drilled for this many times and could keep it up for an hour at a time. By then they should have reached Macro. If there was time Maximius must let them catch their breath before throwing them into the fight if they were to perform well enough to make a difference.

Towards the rear of the column, Centurion Cato and his men followed the pace set by the century in front. Their equipment jingled and chinked as they ran along the track, accompanied by the laboured breathing drawn by men who were heavily weighed down by their weapons and equipment. Now and then a centurion or an optio somewhere along the column barked out an order for their men to keep up, and followed it up with a stream of abuse and threats of dire punishment to spur the men on. Cato swerved out to the side and slowed down until he was level with the middle of his century.

'Keep it up, lads! Macro's depending on us. Keep going!'

As he resumed running alongside, Cato kept glancing towards the far bank of the river. The dust cloud from Caratacus' army was more pronounced now, and although the barbarian host that had kicked it up was out of sight Cato realised the cohort would be facing odds of fifty to one. If Macro had to face them alone then the odds were more like three hundred to one, and as his mind did the calculations Cato knew they were doomed the instant the enemy gained the south bank of the river. And that would surely happen.

The heat and the effort of carrying his chain-mail vest, shield, helmet and weapons soon caused Cato's blood to pound in his ears. His breathing became fast and laboured. His lungs felt as if someone had fastened an iron strap around his chest, which was slowly being tightened. Soon every sinew of his body was screaming in torment. The desire to stop, to stop and vomit and gasp for breath, was almost impossible to resist. Had it not been for fear of the shame of being seen as weak in front of the men, and the fact that Macro was in danger, Cato would have dropped to the ground. As it was, he forced himself through the pain, one step at a time, with the same iron determination to fight on that had thrust him through every challenge he had faced since he had joined the legion.

So it was that in between bouts of harsh internal resolve, and strained cries of encouragement to his men, Cato looked up from the ground ahead and saw that Figulus had fallen back and was running in step beside him.

'Why are you out . . . of position?' Cato panted hoarsely.

'Did you hear it, sir?'

'Hear what?'

'Thought I heard horns, sir. British war horns. Just now.'

Cato thought back a moment, but could remember hearing nothing beyond the sounds of the column running. 'You sure?'

Figulus looked uncertain for a moment, shamefaced at the thought that he had allowed his imagination to take hold of his senses. Then his face suddenly lightened.

'There, sir! You hear it?'

'Shut up!' Cato stopped and listened. There was the blood pulsing through his ears, his own panting and then . . . yes, a faint braying. A strident note from an overlapping chorus of war horns. 'I hear it. Get back in position.'

Cato ran forward, back alongside his century, as Figulus sprinted ahead. They must be close to the ford now, no more than a mile away. Cato stared ahead. The river was bending to the north, lined with scattered copses on either side. A small vista opened out on the north bank and between two small hillocks, half a mile off, he saw a dense mass of infantry marching parallel to the cohort.

'Keep going!' Cato called to his men. 'Not much further! Keep going!'

He steeled himself and drove every thought out of his head save the need to reach the ford in time to stop Caratacus and his army escaping – and to save Macro and his eighty men from being annihilated.

Macro turned back to the north bank of the Tamesis as a fresh chorus of blasts sounded from the horns. With a roar the Britons swept down the track and into the ford, sending up a foaming white chaos of spray as they burst through the gleaming surface of the river.

'Close ranks!' Macro shouted above the din. 'Shields up!'

Either side of him the legionaries shuffled closer together and raised their shields to present a continuous line of defence to the enemy. The Romans shifted the grip on their javelin shafts as they waited for the order to loose a volley on the enemy thrashing through the current towards them.

'Easy now!' Macro called out. 'They'll reach the stakes any moment now . . .'

Nearly eighty paces away the Britons charged forward, cheered on by the deep-throated roar of their comrades lining the river bank behind them. Suddenly, several of the men at the front of the charge jerked to a stop and doubled up. The men behind them surged on regardless and those that managed to avoid their stricken companions were impaled on the next set of obstacles. More men thrust on from behind until the charge broke down in a heaving tangle of bodies. Those at the front cried out in agony and fear, while those behind shouted in frustration and anger, not aware of the reason for the abrupt halt to their charge. All the time more men were pressing forward into the ford and crushing those at the front.

'A fine tangle!' Macro cried out gleefully. 'Couldn't be better.'

Either side of him the legionaries shouted out crude taunts and whoops of joy at the confusion opposite the island. For a moment the neat orderliness of the Roman line was disrupted, but Macro decided to let it go this time. Let his men have their moment of triumph – they would need every boost to morale they could get for the next enemy assault.

At length the enemy war horns cut across the confusion in the ford and sounded three flat notes. Slowly the Britons began to retreat, swelling up along the bank each side of the track. Those caught towards the front of the charge struggled to disentangle themselves, and limped back. A score of warriors were left behind: pinned on to the stakes, or crushed by the weight of men behind them. A few had stumbled, and had drowned under the crush of bodies above them. Almost all those left behind were dead, and the few wounded struggled feebly in the current that carried a thin red stain downriver.

'Round one to us!' Macro shouted to his men, and they gave him a gleeful cheer in return. While the cheering died away Macro glanced over his shoulder and compressed his lips into a thin line when he saw there was still no sign of the cohort. If the runner Macro had sent did not find them in time to reinforce the Third Century then very soon Macro would have to choose between making a run for it or fighting it out to the last man. If he chose the latter then his sacrifice would buy only a little time for the Roman army pursuing Caratacus. Macro did not fool himself that his defence of the island would last long enough for General Plautius to close in for the kill. But if he ordered his men to fall back and make for safety he would be accused of letting the enemy escape the trap. That kind of dereliction of duty could lead to only one punishment. Either way he was a dead man.

He shrugged and made a small, bitter smile. It was so typical of the army way of life. How often had he been forced into a dilemma where every choice it afforded was equally unpleasant? If there was one thing Macro hoped for in the afterlife, it was that he would never again have such choices forced on him.

On the far side of the river the enemy was on the move again and Macro instantly dismissed all thought of the future.

'Form up!' he ordered.

A small party of enemy warriors approached the ford. This time there was no wild cheering and no mad charge towards the Romans on the island. Instead the Britons advanced cautiously, weapons sheathed, and crouching low they groped their way forward. It was what Macro had expected, and he was content to let them waste time clearing away the obstacles his men had placed across the ford. Besides, he had another trick to play.

'Make ready slingshot!'

Macro had posted those men who had been issued with slings from the fort on the flanks of his century, and small piles of rounded pebbles plucked from the riverbed lay close to hand. The legionaries laid down their shields and javelins, moved back to give themselves room, and prepared the leather pouches at the end of the long thongs. Pebbles were fitted and the air was filled with whirring as the legionaries swung the slings round above their heads, waiting for Macro's order.

'Loose slingshot!'

There was a chorus of whipping sounds and tiny dark pellets zipped across the ford towards the enemy warriors. Some cracked against the surface of shields, or splashed harmlessly into the water, but several struck home and cracked skulls or shattered other bones.

'Well done!' Macro called out. 'Loose at will!'

Soon the whirring sounds of slings being worked up to speed and the faint zipping of shots flying through the air was constant. But though the enemy warriors were whittled down, the onslaught served only to slow the speed at which the obstacles were being discovered and wrenched up from the riverbed. Every man who was struck by slingshot was quickly replaced from the host that lined the river bank. As the mass of Britons sat on the north bank, silent in the glare of the late afternoon sun, all the time more men, cavalry and chariots arrived and swelled their numbers, waiting for the river crossing to be cleared.

Macro watched the progress of the men in the ford, and when they came within javelin range he considered the impact that a volley of the deadly iron-tipped shafts might have. But they were too dispersed for him to be sure of maximising the effect and he decided to save the javelins for the attack that would follow the Britons' clearing of the riverbed. Besides, as the range decreased so the effectiveness of the slingshot became more pronounced and the rate at which men were being struck down by the Romans delighted Macro. So far, he estimated, his century must have inflicted well over a hundred casualties, with poor Lentulus being the only Roman killed.

Despite their losses the Britons pressed forward, methodically finding and removing every one of the stakes. It was taking them far less time to clear the obstacles away than Macro's men had spent planting them. A little more than quarter of an hour after they had begun the task, the enemy had almost reached the tangle of cut and sharpened wood that formed the barricade along the bank of the island. A few of the Romans leaned forward and thrust the points of their javelins towards the warriors.

'Get back in line!' Macro bawled at them. 'You don't do a thing until I tell you to!'

Their dangerous work done, the Britons in the river slowly backed away, keeping low behind their shields as the slingshot continued to splash into the water all around them. Behind them the native chieftains were already marshalling their men for the assault. Macro noted that the initial wave was made up of well-equipped men: nearly all had helmets and chain-mail vests. Caratacus must be in a hurry to get his forces across the river if he was prepared to throw his finest warriors in first. Beyond the three hundred or so men pressed close together at the edge of the river was a dense mass of slingers and bowmen. The latter were of little concern to Macro; their short bows might be an irritant to skirmishers, but they would never penetrate a legionary shield. The slingers, though, could inflict terrible punishment.

'This is going to be rough, lads! Keep your shields up until I give the order. We'll use the rear rank javelins only; we'll need to use the rest as spears The javelins will have to go in quick, so I'll only give the order to loose. Throw it in and get down again until that lot reach the barricade.' He looked round at his men. 'Understand?'

The nearest men nodded, and a few men mumbled their acknowledgement.

'Bullshit! I can't hear you! Do you bastards understand me?'

'Yes, sir!' every man in his century roared back.

Macro smiled. 'Good! Once they get close enough to go hand to hand, I want you to give them a fucking good kicking. They'll not forget the Third Century in a hurry!'

'Here they come!' someone shouted out, and all eyes turned towards the far bank. The native warriors lurched forward, down the track and then splashed into the river. As they came on the Britons screamed out their battle cries, accompanying their challenges with a deafening clatter of weapons being struck against the metal rims of their shields. There were no horns to urge them on – they were making enough noise to drown out any encouragement from their own side. They were close enough for the Romans to make out the cold determined expressions on the faces beneath the helmets. These were not the usual run of wild woad-stained barbarians with lime-washed hair; they knew their business and would be formidable opponents.

Macro glanced beyond the front rank of the enemy surging through the water and saw the slingers begin to whirl their thongs over their heads.

'Get down!'

The Romans dropped behind their shields as the air was filled with the zipping sound of slingshot hurtling towards them. The volley was well aimed and only a handful of shots cracked through the branches overhead. The rest struck the Roman shields in a rattling cacophony of thuds. The bombardment continued remorselessly and Macro had to take the risk of being struck each time he glimpsed round his shield to check the progress of Caratacus' assault wave. The enemy waded steadily across the ford, no longer slowed down by the underwater obstacles. This was no wild charge, and the warriors advanced with deadly intent, not needing the cheap morale boost of a frenzied Celtic rush towards the thin Roman line.

The slingshot barrage abruptly slackened and then stopped and Macro peered cautiously over the rim of his shield. The enemy was no more than twenty paces away, thigh-deep in foaming spray, and the slingers no longer dared to loose their missiles at the Romans for fear of striking their own men.

'Hit 'em back!' Macro called out. 'Javelins! Slingers, loose!'

There was no parade-ground finesse in the way the legionaries rose up with a shout ripping from each man's throat as those in the rear rank swung their javelin arms back, took a line on the enemy massed before them, and hurled their weapons. On the flanks the Roman slingers let loose a fusillade of shot against the exposed sides of the enemy column, and a few of the warriors fell, sprawling and splashing into the river. The rest recovered quickly from the javelin volley and picked their way through their dead and injured comrades, then closed on the barricade. Macro had hoped that they would rush the last distance in the usual reckless manner but these men were superbly self-controlled, and as some raised their shields towards the waiting Romans their comrades hacked at the tangle of branches and wrenched pieces free.

'Get stuck in!' Macro shouted, grabbing a javelin from the nearest legionary. He flicked it round into an overhand grip and pushed his shield forward, crushing up against the barricade until he was within reach of the enemy. An arm stretched out between the shields and grasped a length of branch. Macro thrust the point of the javelin into the flesh just below the elbow and heard a voice cry out in pain. As he ripped the iron head back there was a sharp clang and heavy impact on his shield boss. He glanced round and saw that a number of the enemy warriors were armed with long, heavy spears and were trying to keep the Romans pinned back, away from the barricade.

'Watch the spears!' Macro yelled.

He searched for a new target and saw eyes glaring at him over the rim of a kite shield. Macro feinted and as the shield shot up he switched the aim and thrust at the man's thigh. At the limit of his reach, the iron tip ripped through the warrior's woven trousers and only grazed the flesh beneath. The centurion grunted in frustration and then carefully stepped back from the barricade, nodding to a legionary in the rear rank to take his place.

Macro looked around at his century. The men were holding their own. The slingers, distanced from the fight along the barricade, had been targeted by the enemy and an unequal exchange was being fought out between the slingers of both sides. The Romans crouched low as they worked their slings up to speed and then rose quickly to release the shot before ducking down again. Their foes enjoyed no such shelter, and Macro noted, with satisfaction, that a number of almost submerged bodies were slowly spiralling downstream from the bloodstained ford. But enough of that, he decided. The slingers' attention was needed elsewhere. He

66

bellowed his next order above the clash and thud of weapons and cries of men.

'Slingers! Target the infantry! The infantry!'

The men on the wings looked towards him, understanding. One fool quickly rose up to have a last shot at the enemy slingers and was instantly struck in the face. His head snapped back and blood sprayed into the air, splattering his comrades on either side. The man collapsed in an inert bundle on the ground. Macro ground his teeth in anger. He had few enough men already, without anyone throwing his life away in such a careless fashion. A soldier's first duty was to his comrades, and he served them best by staying alive and fighting at their side. Such reckless acts of courage or battle rage were criminally selfish, in his view, and he cursed the man. But he was not the first to die. Already there were three other Roman dead: one sprawled on the ground inside the barricade, the others hanging over the tangle of branches, blood pouring from their wounds on to the muddy river bank below.

'Look at that!' a legionary called out nearby, and Macro followed the direction of the man's gaze across the ford. As the slingshot from the Roman flanks lashed into the sides of the enemy column an older warrior was bellowing out orders. The men around him steadily closed up and offered their shields up in an unbroken line to either side and overhead. Macro was astonished by the manoeuvre, which the enemy had clearly adapted from the example of the legions. Now the shot was rattling harmlessly off the shields, protecting the men within.

'Bugger me,' Macro said softly. 'The Britons can be taught.'

A cry of alarm instantly drew his attention back to the struggle along the barricade. At the centre of the line the enemy had succeeded in taking hold of one of the rough-hewn stakes that Macro's men had driven in to hold it all together. Several hands grasped the stake, working it furiously to pull it free, and even as Macro glanced in their direction, the stake lurched a small way towards the enemy, dragging a section of the barricade with it.

'Shit!' Macro hissed, thrusting his way through his men towards the threatened area. 'Stop them! Get those bastards now!'

The legionaries turned their attention on the men grasping the stake, desperately thrusting at their exposed arms. The warriors charged with defending these men were equally determined and shoved forward into the barricade, stabbing the broad iron spearheads at the defenders. The intensity of the struggle was such that both sides fought in teeth-gritting silence, straining with the effort to push the enemy back. Suddenly there came the sharp cracking of wood and with a lurch the stake came free, sending half a dozen of the warriors flying back into the ford. Around them the Britons roared with triumph and pressed forward into the gap.

'Hold them back!' Macro cried out, hurriedly throwing his javelin into the enemy ranks. 'Hold them back!'

He snatched his sword from its scabbard, crouched low and threw his weight behind his shield as he rushed forward to meet the enemy, the nearest legionaries piling in on either side, and behind him. The two sides crunched together, shield to shield, close enough to hear the panted breath of the enemy and the sound of straining in their throats. Crushed inside the curve of his shield Macro worked his sword arm free and stabbed it at any expanse of barbarian cloth, or flesh that came within range. The spears and long swords of the Britons were now useless in the kind of fight the shorter blades of the legions had been expressly designed for. In the press of bodies more and more of the enemy were cut down. Unable to pull back through their ranks, or even collapse, they suffered on their feet or simply bled to death, heads lolling beside the desperate expressions of their still-living comrades.

The Romans had the advantage of height on the river bank, and more solid footing, and managed to hold off the greater weight of enemy numbers. Macro had no idea how long the contest lasted. His mind was simply fixed on defying his enemy, to hold his ground. All around were the grunts and cries of men, the splashing of the red-hued river and the glitter and glare of the harsh sunlight reflecting off raised sword blades and polished helmets, now spattered with gore and mud.

He never heard the harsh bray of the enemy war horns. He became aware only that the Britons were pulling back when the pressure against his shield abruptly eased and he had space to work his sword forward again.

'They're going!' someone shouted with disbelief. A ragged chorus of elated cheers from the Romans echoed across the ford as the Britons withdrew. Macro kept silent, quickly taking the chance to glance around and appraise the situation. One of his men brushed past him, dropping down into the current and taking a pace towards the retreating enemy.

'YOU!' Macro bellowed, and the man glanced back, afraid. 'You are on a fucking charge, my son. Get back up here!'

The legionary backstepped and climbed up the bank to his furious centurion.

'What the hell are you thinking? Going to take on the whole of bloody Caratacus' army on your own, were you?'

'Sorry, sir. I—'

'You're sorry, all right! As sorry an excuse for a bloody legionary as I've ever met. Do that again and I'll ram this sword right up your arse. Understand me, boy?'

'Yes, sir.'

'Get back in line.'

The man backed away, merging into the ranks as his comrades mocked him with shakes of the head and muttered tutting noises.

Macro ignored them as he stared across the ford to see what the enemy would try next. Most likely they would simply regroup and attempt to force the gap in the barricade in a more ordered fashion. A movement at his feet drew Macro's eyes and he saw an enemy warrior trying to rise up from the river bank. All along the edge of the ford the enemy dead and injured were piled on the churned-up shore and in the pebbled shallows. With hardly a thought Macro leaned down to the man and thrust the point of his sword into the warrior's neck. With a gasp the Briton slumped back down amongst the bodies of his comrades, blood pumping from the wound. His eyes fixed on Macro, wild and desperate. Then they glazed over and he was dead. Macro shook his head and looked up. One down, another twenty-nine thousand to go.

On the far side of the ford the chieftain in charge of the diminished assault group was re-forming his men into a crude testudo, a bristling hedge of spears to the front. As soon as he was satisfied with the formation he shouted an order and the warriors splashed back into the ford.

'I thought we'd taught the bastards a lesson,' muttered a soldier close to Macro.

The centurion made a wry smile. 'I think we've taught them one lesson too many.'

This time the enemy had a clear route to the Roman defenders. The testudo would rise up from the river, push through the gap in the barricade and crush the men behind. This was the moment of decision, Macro realised. He strode back up the small hump of the island and looked toward the south bank of the river, searching for sign of Maximius. Nothing. Then he saw a flash, and another, half a mile away, downriver. Macro squinted and made out a tiny silvered mass, like a slender centipede, crawling towards him. For an instant his heart lifted. Then he realised they were still too far off to render any help in time. The decision remained. He could obey his orders and stay and fight, even though there was no hope of keeping the enemy at bay, or he would have to stomach the order to withdraw and try to save his men, even at the cost of his reputation.

Macro turned round and looked towards the enemy shield wall, already a third of the way across the ford, and they were still retaining the formation. It was obvious what he must do. There was simply nothing else for it now and he walked briskly back to his exhausted men leaning on their shields.

Chapter Twelve

As his men marched along in the dust kicked up by those ahead, Centurion Cato was continually scanning the far bank of the Tamesis. The approaches to the ford were choked with men, horses and chariots as the enemy sought to escape the Roman army pursuing them. The trap should have been closed by the Second Legion at the two main crossing points, but it was now clear that General Plautius had failed to catch the Britons between the jaws of his legions and the main blocking forces of Vespasian. Somehow Caratacus had managed to slip out from between them and make for the third crossing, defended by the small covering force of the Third Cohort.

Only the cohort wasn't in position. The crossing was being held by the eighty men of Macro's command. Despite all the careful preparation and concentration of forces, the plan was failing. Although he had thirty thousand soldiers under his command, General Plautius would have the issue decided by the actions of a mere eighty. On their shoulders lay the responsibility for the success or failure of the general's grand scheme to end organised native resistance once and for all. If Caratacus could be crushed before the day was ended then countless lives would be saved in the long run – Roman lives at least.

With a sickening dread Cato feared that Macro would see it the same way and be determined to do everything he could to stop the Britons crossing the river, even if that meant the death of himself and every man in his century. His sacrifice might just delay the Britons long enough for Plautius to fall upon them from behind, and maybe even for Maximius to stall them on the south bank and deny them any escape route.

As he marched beside his men Cato tried to put himself in Macro's position and as he quickly weighed up the options he realised that he would have accepted the need to stay and fight it out. The stakes were too great to do anything else. He turned to his men.

'Keep moving! Keep moving, damn you!'

Some of the legionaries in the Sixth Century exchanged surprised looks at this needless outburst and a bitter voice called out, 'We're going as fast as we fucking well can!'

Figulus jumped to one side of the column and turned on the men. 'Shut your mouths! I'll personally take the head off the next bastard to breathe a word! Save it for the Celts.'

Cato turned his eyes back to the enemy. The far bank was almost covered with men and horses now. They must be close to the ford. Ahead, the river curved away from him and appeared to narrow abruptly. Then, as the gleaming river seemed to cut into the north bank, Cato realised that he was seeing the island that lay in the middle of the ford. His pulse quickened as he squinted his eyes to catch the distant details. The far side of the island was a mass of tiny figures. Sunlight flashed off polished equipment and the spray in the water at the men's feet. The trees on the small island hid Macro's legionaries from view and there was no telling how the defenders fared.

As Cato watched, the enemy in the ford began to pull back, scurrying antlike towards their comrades massing on the far bank. His spirits rose as he knew that Macro and his men had repulsed the attack and still lived. Only half a mile now separated the cohort from Macro's century, and from the front of the column Maximius could be heard bellowing at his men, urging them on with every vile imprecation available to him.

The width of the river was in full view now and Cato could see the enemy forming up for another assault on the island defences. But this time there was something altogether more organised about the attempt to force the crossing. Instead of the shapeless mob rushing towards the Roman lines, Cato saw a dense mass moving across the ford at a steady pace. By the time the enemy reached the far side of the island the cohort was no more than a few hundred yards from the entrance to the ford and Maximius sent the mounted scouts ahead to reinforce Centurion Macro.

They urged their horses on and pounded into the shallows with a great shower of white, sparkling spray. But before they were a third of the way across a legionary burst into sight from between the willows that lined the banks of the island. More men appeared, thrashing through the water. As they caught sight of the scouts they paused a moment, then continued fleeing towards the south bank. This was no rout, Cato realised as he saw that every man still carried his cumbersome shield and bronze and iron helmet. The scouts paused midstream and Cato could see the decurion angrily addressing the legionaries and stabbing his hand towards the island. They ignored him, filing between the flanks of the horses before rushing back towards the near bank. From the island a small tight knot of men emerged and plunged down into the crossing, keeping their shields towards the enemy. A short distance behind them, a handful of Britons followed the Romans into the ford, then more and more joined them, surging after the tiny rearguard covering the retreat of their comrades in the Third Century.

Maximius threw his arm forward along the track and shouted the order to advance. The sweating and panting legionaries broke into a run behind him, boots thudding down on the baked earth. Ahead, Macro's rearguard and the scouts fought a desperate withdrawal back across the ford, pursued all the way by growing numbers of the enemy. The men who had already reached the near bank were forming up, two deep, across the entrance to the ford. Even so, that thin scarlet line would not hold the bloodthirsty flood of Britons back for more than a brief moment.

The men of the cohort streamed along the track towards their comrades and soon the fittest and fastest of them began to join the Third Century, bolstering their small formation. Cato was close enough to the ford to make out more details of the unequal struggle being fought out midstream, and his heart rose at the sight of the transverse red crest of a centurion's helmet bobbing about above the heaving figures locked in bloody conflict. Macro still lived then. Even in the face of almost certain annihilation that thought was of some comfort to Cato as he charged down the last slope towards the legionaries hastily being thrust into position at the edge of the ford. Massively outnumbered as they were, they still enjoyed the tactical advantage of occupying a position that could only be assaulted on a narrow front. There was some hope, Cato told himself. Some hope that they might hold Caratacus back.

'Sixth Century!' Cato called out. 'Form up to the right of the line!'

His shattered men shuffled into place at the end of the cohort and could barely stand, coughing and gasping for breath as they leaned on their grounded shields. There was not much fight left in them, and wouldn't be until they recovered from the forced march under a blistering sun. But the enemy was almost upon them and in a moment they would be fighting for their lives.

The survivors of Macro's rearguard and the squadron of scouts fought their way back into the shallows, shields locked together as they thrust their short swords at any enemy body or limb that tried to force a gap through the Roman line. Maximius turned to men waiting on the river bank.

'Fourth Century! Give way!'

A gap opened up in the cohort behind Macro to allow him passage into the line and he bellowed an order to the decurion. 'Scouts first! Go!'

The mounted men disengaged and urged their horses towards the narrow gap. One rider was too slow, and as his horse struggled round a figure leaped up, grabbed him by the arm and wrenched him to the side. Attacker and scout crashed down into the water together and in an instant the enemy warriors closed round the scout with cries of triumph. A gurgling scream rent the air, then it was cut short as spears and swords thrust into the man's chest, driving the air from his lungs under the crushing impact of so many weapons. The brief distraction allowed Macro and his men to pull back safely into the ranks of the cohort, soaked by the spray from the river and spattered with the blood of comrades and enemies.

Maximius, standing behind the centre of the cohort, met Macro's wild-eyed gaze with a look of intense and bitter hatred. 'You've lost the ford.' There was no time for any exchange of words, and Macro turned round and formed up with his men, facing the endless tide of barbarians surging across the ford towards the cohort. They piled into the shields lining the edge of the ford and hacked and thrust at the Romans behind.

At first the legionaries held their ground, exhausted as they were. The relentless years of training paid off in the steady one-two rhythm of punching the shield boss forward, then withdrawing it as the short sword stabbed at the enemy; a pause for the counterstroke and then the sequence was repeated. As long as the line held. If it broke then all the advantages of tight formation and strict training that made them so ruthlessly effective in battle would be lost in an artless test of strength and violent savagery.

As the weight of enemy numbers increased the cohort began to give ground. It was almost imperceptible, but Cato, positioned on the end of the line and not yet engaged, saw the Roman centre begin to bulge backwards. Maximius saw it too and turned to the decurion and the handful of survivors of his squadron.

'Find the legate and report the situation to him. Go!'

The decurion saluted and turned his horse downriver, ordering his men to follow. He glanced back over his shoulder one last time at his comrades. 'Good luck, lads!'

Then he was gone, the pounding of hoofs lost against the clatter of weapons and wild shouts of men locked in the desperate struggle.

'Hold the line!' Maximius roared, thrusting his sword in the air towards the enemy. 'Hold the line, you bastards! Don't give them an inch!'

The violence of his words was no match for the violent efforts of the enemy, and still the Romans gave ground, forced back step by step. Now some of the legionaries, mostly newer men not yet hardened to the savage reality of battle, began to look nervously over their shoulders. Even as Cato glanced towards the rear of the Roman line he saw a figure take a step back, out of formation. The cohort commander saw it too and ran down to the man, swiping at his head with the flat of his blade.

'Get back in line!' Maximius screamed. 'Move again and I'll take your fucking head off!'

The legionary jumped forward, the fear of his cohort commander briefly overcoming his terror of the enemy. But he was far from alone in his dread of being butchered by the Britons. As the Romans were steadily thrust back, more and more heads turned to look for a passage to safety.

At the opposite end of the line Cato saw one of the men from Maximius' own century suddenly throw down his shield, turn and run. Maximius caught the rapid movement and snapped his head round.

'Get back in line!'

The man turned towards the voice, then snatched at the thongs tying his helmet in place, fumbling to undo them. Then they came free and he wrenched the helmet from his head, threw it to one side and ran towards a small thicket of gorse and stunted trees a short way off.

Maximius slapped the flat of his sword against the side of his silvered greave in rage. He screamed after the fleeing figure. 'All right then, you scum! You coward! RUN! I've got your number! When this is over I'll fucking stone you to death myself!'

The damage had been done, Cato realised. Other men began to shuffle back, with guilty glances at their companions. The Roman line began to lose more ground and the Britons pressed home their advantage. They forced their enemies back from the ford, all the time broadening the bridgehead so that they could feed more and more men into the fight. Soon the wings of the cohort would be pushed away from the ford and once that happened the legionaries would be enveloped and annihilated.

Maximius saw the building danger and knew that he must act swiftly to save his command. It would require some adroit handling of the cohort; only the First and Sixth Centuries were not engaged in the fight.

'First Century! Refuse the left flank!'

As his unit folded back to form a right angle with Tullius' century Maximius turned to the other end of the line and bellowed towards Cato, 'Sixth Century! Form up on the left!'

'Come on!' Cato called to his men. 'At the double!'

They ran across the rear of the cohort and took position at the end of Maximius' century, also at a right angle, parallel with the men still fighting the Britons. When all was ready Maximius cast a last eye over the situation and then took the decisive step.

'Cohort! Disengage to the right!'

Step by step the cohort shifted its ground downriver, the men facing the Britons now concentrating on keeping tight formation rather than killing their enemies. As the Fifth Century moved out of the enemy's reach it began to wheel round and joined with the end of Cato's men. But now the cohort had shifted along the bank far enough to open a gap on the left flank and the Britons quickly rolled round it and began to engage the men of the First Century. As more and more of them poured out from the ford and flowed round the Roman formation Maximius glanced towards the right, anxious to complete the transformation of his cohort from line to rectangle. At last the Fourth Century cleared the ford and at once wheeled round to form the last face of the defensive formation. Slowly, with shields facing out on all sides the cohort edged away from the ford and back down the track towards the rest of the legion, their only chance of salvation now.

More and more of the enemy had crossed the river and fell at once on the retreating Romans. Cato, in the front rank of his century, kept his shield aligned with the men on either side of him and slowly sidestepped as blows landed continuously on the curved surface. He kept glimpsing the enemy, and repeatedly thrust his sword out to keep them at bay. Now and then his blade struck a man and there would be a cry of pain, or shout of rage. As the cohort crept away from the ford it too suffered casualties. The wounded men dropped out of line, and the spaces they left were quickly filled by men from the next rank. Those injured who could still walk were shoved through to the centre of the formation, the others were left where they fell, to be butchered the moment their comrades had passed by. Once, this had seemed cold-blooded to Cato. Now he accepted it as a grim necessity of war. Much as he dreaded a disabling wound that would leave him helpless on the ground, Cato knew he could not expect others to sacrifice their lives to save his. That was the harsh code of the legions.

A sharp cry of agony sounded close to his left. Cato did not even glance round, not daring to risk tearing his intent gaze away from the enemy. Yet he was aware of someone on the ground as he sidestepped along with the rest.

'Don't leave me!' a voice called out, shrill with terror. 'For pity's sake, don't leave me!'

A hand suddenly grasped Cato's ankle. 'Sir!'

Cato had to look down quickly. One of his men, a young recruit not much older than Cato himself, lay on the ground, propped up on one elbow. A sword cut had shattered his knee and severed the tendons and muscles attached to his thigh, felling him at once.

'Sir!' the legionary pleaded, tightening his grip. 'Save me!'

'Let go!' Cato snarled at him. 'Let go of me, or so help me, I'll kill you!'

The man stared back in shock, mouth hanging open. Cato was aware that the man to his left had taken a small pace to the left and a gap opened between them.

'Let go!' Cato shouted.

For a brief moment the grip slackened, then tightened again with renewed panic. 'Please!' the man wailed.

Cato had no choice. If he paused a moment longer, one of the enemy warriors was bound to leap into the gap between the centurion and the next man. Gritting his teeth Cato slashed down with his short sword and cut deep into the injured man's forearm, just above the wrist. The fingers loosened and Cato tore his foot away and sidestepped quickly to link up with the next legionary. He heard the injured man scream in agony.

'You bastards!' he choked as his comrades stepped over him. 'You murdering bastards!'

When Cato next looked round at the cohort he saw that they had left the ford behind and were halfway up the gentle slope on which the track followed the course of the Tamesis. The enemy were still swarming around the formation, intent on obliterating the Romans, but now they were no longer reinforced by those who continued to pour across from the far bank. They were already marching past and swinging upriver, making good their chance to escape the pursuing legions of General

Plautius. As the cohort clawed up the slope the enemy warriors gradually broke off their attack and stood leaning on their weapons, panting for breath. The track from the ford was scattered with bodies, Britons and Romans, bloody and mutilated by the cuts and thrusts of sword and spear.

At last the cohort was free of the enemy, and Maximius led it up to the top of the rise before he ordered his men to halt. Three hundred paces away the army of Caratacus marched steadily past, making no attempt to close with the cohort. If Caratacus had a mind to wipe them out it could be done in short order, but the native commander could spare them no time.

'Lower shields!' Maximius called out, and all around the exhausted legionaries let their shields rest on the flattened grass as they leaned on them for support and struggled to catch their breath. Down the slope the Britons who had forced Macro and his men back across the ford and then dislodged the rest of the cohort, also rested on their shields. Both sides eyed each other warily for any sign of a renewed will to continue the fight. Neither was willing.

While there was a pause Cato crossed the interior of the formation to find Macro. The veteran centurion was holding out an arm to his optio. Blood welled up from a slash across the bulk of muscle on his forearm and dripped steadily on to the ground.

'Not too serious,' the optio was saying. He reached into his haversack, pulled out a roll of linen and began binding the wound as Macro looked up.

'Ah, Cato!' he grinned. 'Seems I have another scar to tell tall tales about in retirement.'

'Should you get so old.' Cato grasped Macro's spare hand. 'Good to see you. I was afraid you'd be overwhelmed back at the crossing.'

'We were,' Macro said quietly. 'If there'd been more of us there, we'd have held on.'

Cato glanced round, but Maximius had his back to them and was out of earshot. 'Quite,' he muttered, with a brief nod towards the cohort commander.

Macro leaned closer. 'There's going to be trouble over this. Watch yourself.'

'Officers to me!' Maximius called out.

They came walking over to Maximius, too weary to run. Besides Macro, Tullius and Felix were also wounded, the latter with a deep wound to the face. He was stanching the flow of blood with a bundle of linen that was already drenched. Cato saw the strained look on the cohort commander's face and could guess at the inner turmoil that tormented the man. He had failed in his duty, and further down the slope the proof of his failure was marching right by him. Nothing short of a miracle could save his career from abject ruin now. Maximius cleared his throat

'We're safe for the moment. Suggestions?' His voice was harsh and grating.

There was an embarrassed silence and only Macro was prepared to meet his eye.

'Centurion?'

'Yes, sir?'

'Anything you want to say to me?'

'No, sir.' Macro shrugged. 'It can wait.'

Cato looked down towards the ford. 'We shouldn't let them get away, sir.'

Maximius rounded on him angrily. 'What do you propose? We charge down there and get stuck into them? Look at the state we're in. How long do you think we'd last?'

'Maybe long enough to make a difference, sir.' Cato stiffened.

'Whatever the cost?' Maximius sneered, but Cato saw a trace of desperation in his expression.

'That's for others to say, afterwards, sir.'

'And easy for you to say now!'

Cato refused to respond. Instead he stared past the cohort commander and watched Caratacus' men march across the ford. His eye travelled back over the enemy forces to the far bank and the dark masses waiting beyond. The sun was low in the sky and the distorted shadows of the enemy made them seem more numerous and frightening. As he watched, the flat blasts of war horns carried across the river and all eyes turned towards the far bank. Men were streaming away from the ford and forming up into a line across a low ridge a third of a mile beyond. Several thousand infantry, with cavalry and chariots on each wing.

'Sir!' Centurion Antonius raised his arm and pointed downstream. 'Look there!'

The officers turned their heads and followed his direction. On the far bank, a mile to the right the head of a dense column of men had appeared.

Macro squinted. 'Ours?'

'Who else?' Cato replied. 'And there's the Second on our side of the river.'

The officers looked back along the track. Sure enough another column of Roman infantry was marching towards them. For an instant Cato felt the blood burn in his veins and he faced the cohort commander.

'Sir, there's still time for us to do something. All you have to do is give the order.'

'No.' Maximius shook his head sadly. 'It's too late for that now. We stay here.'

Cato opened his mouth to protest but the cohort commander raised his hand to stop him. 'That's my decision, Centurion. There's no more to be said.'

That was it then, Cato realised. The matter was decided. The failure of the Third Cohort was complete and its men and officers humiliated. If they were very fortunate, humiliation would be the least of their worries.

The forces of General Plautius arrived at the ford in three columns and immediately deployed and attacked the enemy. From the far side of the river the men of the Third Cohort watched as the Britons on the ridge charged forward, disappearing from view. All that could be heard were the muffled calls of war horns and trumpets and the faint sounds of battle. Then a scattering of figures appeared over the ridge, running towards the ford. More men followed them, and then it was clear that the Britons had broken as the slope was covered with the tiny figures of men.

A flash drew Cato's eyes to the crest of the ridge and in the warm orange glow of the sun, low on the horizon, Roman cavalry burst upon the fleeing enemy, cutting them down as they raced towards the river. The ford could take no more than fifteen men across its width, and in a short time there was a huge tangle of men, horses and chariots desperately trying to cross the river and get away from the merciless pursuit of the Roman cavalry. Some of the Britons cast down their weapons and swam for it; scores of them thrashing across the wide expanse of the Tamesis. Some, too weak or too weighed down by their clothes and equipment, began to struggle, thrashed the water briefly and then drowned.

The first of the Roman legionaries crested the ridge and marched down the slope in well ordered lines. As the men of the Third Cohort watched by the glow of the setting sun a great groan of despair swept through the packed mass of enemy warriors. Some still had enough wits about them to realise that even though they were dead men they could still take some Romans with them, and maybe win some time for the men still crossing the river. But they were too few to make a difference and were cut down as the glittering red ranks closed in around the ford.

The sun had disappeared over the horizon and the light began to fail so that it was impossible to tell the sides apart on the far bank. Only the din of thousands of men screaming in agony and shrieking for mercy told of the massacre taking place, and Cato felt relieved of the burden of seeing the terrible slaughter.

Down the slope, on the near side of the ford, the numbers of the enemy slipping past began to diminish, and they scattered in every direction, trusting to the coming night to conceal their escape. There were Roman voices from the direction of the ford, and out of the gloom behind the men of the Third Cohort came the sound of hoofs pounding along the track.

'Cohort stand to!' Maximius yelled, and the legionaries, still in box formation, hurriedly snatched up their shields and closed ranks as the centurions ran back to their units. A column of horsemen emerged from the dusk and drew up a short distance away, horses champing at their bits and pawing the ground as their riders sat silently.

'Who goes there?' Maximius bellowed. 'Give the password!'

'Pollux!'

'Approach friend.'

An order was given and a large body of mounted men trotted past the cohort, heading down towards the ford to hunt down any enemy stragglers. Out of the shadows a small party of horsemen made for the Third Cohort.

'It's the bloody legate himself!' someone close to Cato muttered.

'Silence there!' Cato shouted.

The horsemen stopped a short distance from the legionaries and dismounted. Vespasian strode forward and the men moved aside to let him past. As he passed Cato the centurion could see the dark look of fury in his clenched features. Maximius went to meet him and saluted. Vespasian stared at him silently for a moment.

'Centurion . . .' he began in a cold, barely controlled voice. 'I don't exactly know what happened here today, but if it reflects badly on me and the rest of the Second Legion I swear that I will break you, and every man in this cohort.'

Chapter Thirteen

The inside of the general's tent was stifling after the cool wash of the moonlit air. Vespasian felt the clammy prickle of sweat on his brow and cuffed it away quickly. He had no desire to let the general think he was nervous. That would imply he had something to be nervous about; like carrying the blame for the failure of the general's plan. It might be the fault of his subordinates that Caratacus and a large number of his men had managed to escape the trap, but that would not matter a great deal to Aulus Plautius. Vespasian was responsible for the performance of the men under his command – that was the way it was in the army – and he must suffer the consequences. How he subsequently disciplined his men was his own affair.

The legate was kept waiting at the entrance, standing just inside the tent flaps, as the clerk pushed through a linen curtain into the section reserved for Plautius and his staff. A number of lamps glowed through the fine material and the distorted shapes of men flitted across its uneven surface. The entrance was lit by a single lamp hanging by a chain from the tent pole and the dull yellow flame guttered at every waft of air. Outside the entrance, between the squad of bodyguards that lined the approach to the tent, the ground sloped down to the river, gliding serenely by under the moonlight. Down at the ford it twinkled as the current raced over the shallow pebbles and round the dark heaps of bodies that still choked the passage. On the far bank, in the pale silvery light of the moon, he could clearly see the ramparts of the Second Legion's marching camp. Within its dark outline tiny fires glinted brightly, like fallen stars.

Vespasian had left the camp and ridden across the ford a short while earlier, in response to the terse summons he had received from the general. Every step of the way his horse had had to pick a path through the dead that were strewn on the ground. Some men still lived amongst the corpses, moaning softly to themselves, or still possessed of enough strength to scream out in agony and cause the horse to start nervously. The sickly stench of blood drenched the air and made it seem hotter than it was. There had been no end to the bodies as the legate splashed through the ford and reached the small island in the middle of the Tamesis. More dead men lay along the track and were heaped in front of the remains of Centurion Macro's rough barricade. But the very worst was saved for last as Vespasian's horse emerged from the crossing and picked its way up towards the low ridge on which the general had set up his camp.

Bodies had been dragged clear of the track leading down to the ford, and the corpses were piled on either side, a shadowy tangle of torsos and limbs, stiffening as the sultry night dragged on. Beyond the nearest corpses the legate saw a field of bodies stretching out across the moonlit landscape, thousands of them. He shuddered at the thought of all the spirits of the dead that must be wreathing the air about him, lingering a while before beginning the journey to the land of endless shadows where the dead eked out their dreary existence for eternity. He knew well enough that these barbarians believed in an afterlife of endless drunken revelry, but the grim austerity of death made it hard for him to accept such a vision. The awfulness of the scale of human destruction all around him was the most oppressive sensation Vespasian had ever felt. Surely, he thought, next to a battle lost there is nothing so dreadful as a battle won.

'The general will see you now, sir.'

Vespasian turned towards the clerk, forcing himself to withdraw from thoughts of death that hung like a black mantle across the world outside the tent. He turned and ducked through the gap in the linen curtain the clerk held open for him. Inside, a few clerks still worked at their desks, even though it was the middle of the night. They did not look up as Vespasian was led towards another flap at the rear of the tent, and he wondered if they already knew something about his fate. He was cross with himself for entertaining such thoughts. These men were just busy, that was all. Nothing could have been decided yet. It was too early. The clerk pulled back the curtain and Vespasian stepped into another, smaller, section of the tent. In the far corner, dimly lit, there was a camp bed and a few chests. In the centre stood a large table on which rested an ornate lamp-stand with several lights issuing flickering yellow flames as a huge Nubian slave slowly wafted a vast feather fan to cool the two men seated there.

'Vespasian!' Narcissus smiled warmly. 'It's good to see you again, my dear Legate.'

There was something dismissive about the tone in which Narcissus uttered the last word, and Vespasian recognised the customary attempt to put him in his place. Legate he may be, and from a senatorial family as well. Yet Narcissus, a mere freedman – lower in social status than the meanest Roman citizen – was the right hand of Emperor Claudius himself. His power was very real, and before it all the prestige and haughtiness of the senatorial class was as nothing.

'Narcissus.' Vespasian bowed his head politely, as if greeting an equal. He turned to General Plautius and saluted formally. 'You asked for me, sir.'

'I did. Take a seat. I've sent for some wine.'

'Thank you, sir.' Vespasian eased himself down into a seat opposite the others, and found some small relief from the gentle current of air that emanated from the slave's fan.

There was a brief silence before Narcissus spoke again. 'The problem, as far as a mere bureaucrat can understand the military situation, is that the campaign is not quite over.' Narcissus turned towards the general. 'I believe I have that right. Now that Caratacus has slipped from our grasp . . . once again.'

General Plautius nodded. 'It's true, as far as we know. A few thousand men did cross the river before we brought Caratacus to battle.'

Vespasian's eyebrows rose briefly in surprise. There had been no battle, just a pitiless massacre. Then he realised that the general's description had been for the benefit of the Imperial Secretary, who, no doubt, would write a report to his Emperor the moment he reached his own quarters. A battle would win more plaudits than a massacre.

'Caratacus,' Plautius continued, 'may well be amongst those who escaped across the ford. It is of little consequence. There's not much he can do with a handful of men.'

Narcissus frowned. 'I hate to split hairs, General, but to me a handful of men implies a somewhat smaller number than several thousand.'

'Maybe,' Plautius conceded with a shrug, 'but on our scale of operations it will not cause us any concern.'

'So I can report to the Emperor that the campaign is over?'

Plautius did not answer, and glanced quickly at the legate, a warning look. Before the conversation could continue a slave arrived with the wine and carefully and quietly set the bronze tray down on the table. He poured a honey-coloured liquid from an elegant decanter into the three silver goblets and, setting the decanter down, he turned and backed out through the entrance. Vespasian waited for the others to take their goblets before he reached for the last one. The silver was cool to his touch and when he held it under his nose a rich aroma filled his nostrils.

'It has been chilled,' Plautius explained. 'In the river. I thought that after the heat of the day's battle some soothing refreshment was well deserved. A toast then.' He raised his goblet. 'To victory!'

'To victory,' said Vespasian.

'To victory . . . when it comes.'

The general and the legate stared at the Imperial Secretary as he slowly downed his drink and set the goblet lightly upon the table.

'A fine refreshment indeed! I shall have to get the recipe before I return to Rome.'

'How soon will you go?' Plautius asked bluntly.

'When the campaign is over. The moment I can report to the Emperor that we have ended organised resistance to Rome in the heartland of this island. When that is achieved the Emperor will be able to face his enemies in the senate knowing that *they* know that victory has been achieved. We cannot afford to have any tongues whispering that the war is still unresolved here in Britain. I have spies in your legions, and so do the Emperor's enemies. It is up to you to make sure they have nothing to report that can be used against Claudius.'

Narcissus looked directly at the general, who nodded slowly. 'I understand.'

'Good. Then it's time we were honest with each other. Tell me, how do things stand after today's . . . battle? Assuming Caratacus still lives.'

'If he has escaped then he will need to retire and lick his wounds. I imagine he'll head for some fortification we haven't discovered yet. He'll let his men recover, pick up any stragglers and rearm his forces. He'll also try and recruit more men, and send envoys to the other tribes to win more allies.'

'I see.' Some of the condensation had run off the bottom of Narcissus' cup and he arranged it into a pattern with the tip of his finger. 'Is he likely to win more allies?'

'I doubt it. The man is quite a shrewd political operator, but the record stands against him. We have beaten him time and again. These native warriors are no match for us.'

'So what will he do now?'

'Caratacus will have to adapt his strategy. He can afford only small engagements now, and will limit himself to picking off small garrisons, foraging columns, patrols and so on.'

'All of which will no doubt be a drain on your manpower, and prolong the campaign indefinitely, I suppose?'

'There is that possibility.'

'Not very satisfactory then, my dear General.'

'No.' Plautius reached for the decanter and refilled Narcissus' goblet.

'So, the question is, how did you come to let him escape? You had led me to believe that this battle would be the end of it all. That Caratacus would be dead, or our prisoner by the end of the day. Instead, it seems that he will continue to plague us for months to come. Nothing has changed. The Emperor will not be pleased, to put it mildly. You both have family in Rome?'

It was not really a question, but a statement, a threat, and both the general and the legate stared at him with naked hatred and fear.

'What are you suggesting?' Vespasian asked quietly.

Narcissus leaned back in his chair and interweaved his long elegant fingers. 'You have failed here today. There is a price for failure and it must be paid. The Emperor expects it and I must report to him that you have taken the appropriate steps. If you fail to do so here then the price will have to be paid back in Rome. It's not much of a choice really. So, gentlemen, who fouled up today? Who is to blame for the escape of Caratacus?' The Imperial Secretary looked from man to man. His face was impassive as he waited patiently for a response.

At last the general shrugged. 'It's obvious. He escaped across a ford that should have been better guarded. My plan depended on that.' Plautius looked across the table at his subordinate. 'The fault is with the Second Legion.'

Vespasian pressed his lips into a thin line and returned the look with contempt. At the same time his mind raced for a response. He realised at once that his reputation, his career, maybe even his life and those of his family were in danger. The same, of course, applied to the general. Yet Vespasian was wise enough to know that in such circumstances the powerful men who ran Rome would always close ranks and pass the blame on to a more junior figure: someone high enough in rank to serve as a salutary reminder of the cost of failure, but junior enough to be expendable. Someone like Vespasian himself.

For a moment he considered taking the blame and showing that he had more pride and dignity than this general, with his long noble lineage. There was satisfaction to be gained in that. A highly selfish satisfaction, he reflected. In any case, the only real achievement of his sacrifice would be the saving of Plautius' reputation. When it came down to it Vespasian felt that he had more to offer Rome in the long run than this aged and worn out general. Then, in a moment of clarity he was aware that, however one dressed it up, the real issue was self-preservation. It always was. He'd be damned before he let a bunch of smug aristocrats throw him to the dogs to preserve one of their own. He cleared his throat and made sure that his tone was free of any emotion that would betray his bitterness, or fear.

'The enemy was never supposed to have reached this ford. The plan – the general's plan, as I understood it – was that the other three legions and auxiliary cohorts were to close with the enemy quickly enough to force Caratacus against the main crossings, where I would be waiting with the main strength of my legion. The third ford was an afterthought. It was only supposed to be defended against those of the enemy who escaped the battle in front of the first two crossings. It was never expected that they would bear the full weight of Caratacus and his army.'

'It was always a marginal possibility,' Plautius cut in. 'The orders were clear enough. Your men were told to hold the crossings in all circumstances.'

'That was in my orders?' Vespasian raised his eyebrows.

'I'm sure it will be,' Narcissus muttered. 'Legate, I take it that you are inferring that the general failed to move with sufficient speed to close the trap?'

'Yes.'

Plautius leaned forward angrily. 'We marched as fast as we could, damn it! Our heavy infantry cannot be expected to outpace native troops. The speed of our troops is not the issue. We had them in a trap and if the Second Legion had done its job properly the trap would have worked perfectly. Vespasian should have made sure that the ford was adequately protected. One cohort was not enough. Any fool could see that.'

'One cohort was ample, for the job it was *actually* given,' Vespasian snapped back.'

For a moment the two senior officers glared at each other, eyes glinting with the wavering reflection of the lamp flames. Then the general eased himself back in his seat and turned to Narcissus.

'I want this man out of my army. He is not competent to command a legion in the field and his insubordination cannot be tolerated.' He turned back towards the legate. 'Vespasian, I want your resignation. I want you out of here, on the first ship back to Gaul.'

'I bet you do,' Vespasian replied coldly. 'If I'm not around to defend myself against any charges you bring, it doesn't take a genius to work out the consequences. I refuse to resign my command, and I'll put that in writing.'

Before Plautius could respond Narcissus coughed. 'Gentlemen! That's enough of this. I'm sure the fault is not wholly on one side or the other.'

Both officers turned on him angrily to protest but the Imperial Secretary quickly raised a hand and continued speaking before they could interrupt him. 'Since you are both adamant that the blame lies with the other I fear your testimonies in front of the senate would only serve to destroy you both. Therefore, it seems to me that the best solution is to have an immediate inquiry and find some culpable character lower down the chain of command. If you can make a swift decision and deliver a suitably draconian punishment then I'm sure we can satisfy those back in Rome who demand action in response to your failure.'

Plautius visibly winced at the last word but immediately accepted the lifeline being handed to him and the legate.

'Very well.' Plautius nodded. 'A court of inquiry, then. The legate and I will act as presiding magistrates. At least you'll agree to that, Vespasian?'

'Yes, sir.'

'Then I'll issue the orders at first light. Statements will be taken by all the relevant officers at once. If we move quickly the matter can be solved in a few days. Will that satisfy the Emperor?'

'It will,' Narcissus smiled. 'Trust me. Now, I think we have settled the issue satisfactorily. Neither of you need lose any sleep over this matter. The blame will rest on other shoulders, in place of their heads.' He chuckled at the quip. 'Have your inquiry. Find some plausible men to blame and as soon as judgement has been made I can return to Rome and make my report. Are we in agreement, gentlemen?'

Plautius nodded, and a moment later, his stomach twisted by cold, bitter contempt for the other men, but mostly for himself, Vespasian lowered his head, stared at the silver decanter on the tray, and nodded slowly.

Chapter Fourteen

The men of the Second Legion had spent the night in the open, curled up by their equipment. They slept deeply, exhausted by the rapid marching of the day before, and by the construction of the marching camp. Since their trenching equipment had been left with the baggage train the men had dug the ditches with their swords and piled up the inner rampart by hand. Roughly cut wooden stakes projected from the outer face of the rampart, and sentries patrolled along each side of the camp.

The men of the Third Cohort were the most exhausted of them all, having had to fight a battle on top of everything else. Yet a handful of them were denied sleep and tossed restlessly on the flattened grass. Some because they could not forget the terrible sights and sensations that had been etched into their minds, others mourned the loss of close friends, cut down in front of their eyes. But for Cato the cause of sleeplessness was anxiety about the days to come, rather than the eventful day that had passed.

The escape of a significant number of the enemy practically guaranteed that the exhausting struggle would continue. Even if Caratacus was not amongst them, then one of his lieutenants was bound to swear the survivors to further resistance to Rome, spurred on by the need to exact revenge for the loss of so many of their comrades. They would ensure that more blood was spilled, and Cato wondered how much more the soil of this land could absorb before it sank into a sea of gore. The image was fanciful and he smiled mirthlessly and turned over, pulling his cloak round his shoulders and resting his head on his greaves.

But worse than the escape of the enemy was the failure of the cohort to do its duty. Centurion Maximius had fouled up badly. He should never have diverted from his mission to chase down the small band that had sacked the supply fort and slaughtered its garrison. He should have made straight for the ford.

Maximius well knew that he would be called to account for this costly error in judgement, and before the cohort had bedded down for the night he had summoned his officers for a quiet meeting, out of earshot of the men.

'There'll be questions asked about today's events,' he had begun, staring intently into the moonlit faces of his centurions. 'I'm counting on you to stick together on this. I'll speak for us, and take whatever blame the legate tries to pin on the Third Cohort.'

His expression had been sincere and Cato had felt a simultaneous wave of relief that the blame would not attach to him, and then a shameful sense of empathy for the cohort commander who could expect to be harshly disciplined. Maximius' career was over. He would be lucky if he was only broken back to the ranks. That in itself was a bad fall from grace. His pay, pension and the privileges due to his present post would all be lost and the men who had suffered punishment at his hands would be seeking to exact a painful revenge when he became their equal.

'I'm sorry I led you to this,' Maximius had continued. 'You're fine men, and you lead fine men. You deserved better.'

There'd been a painful silence before Felix leaned forward and clasped the cohort commander's arm. 'It's been an honour to serve with you, sir.'

'Thank you, lad. I knew I could count on your loyalty. And the loyalty of the rest of you, eh?'

The centurions had murmured their agreement, all except Macro, who stood stiffly and refused to make a sound. If Maximius noticed, he'd made no mention of it as he clasped the arms of his officers and bid them good night.

'Remember, I'll speak for us all . . .'

Before sunrise the trumpets sounded and all across the marching camp men stirred, muscles stiff. Those with injuries winced at the aching and throbbing from under their dressings. Cato, who had finally fallen asleep only a few hours earlier, did not stir with the others and his men let him sleep on, partly out of kindness but mostly because the longer he slept the longer it would be before his orders stirred them into the daily routine. So it was that Macro came to find him after the sun had risen, tutting as he discovered his lanky friend still asleep under his cape, mouth hanging open and an arm stretched out above the shock of dark curls on his head. Macro shoved his boot into Cato's side and rolled him over.

'Come on! Wakey, wakey! Sun's burning your eyes out.'

'Ohhh . . .' Cato groaned, squinting up at the clear sky. His gaze drifted across to the grizzled features of his friend and he sat up with a guilty start. 'Shit!'

'You fully awake now?' Macro asked quietly as he glanced around.

Cato nodded, and stretched his shoulders. 'What's up?'

'Plenty. There's a rumour going round that the general has ordered an inquiry into yesterday's cock-up.'

'An inquiry?'

'Shhh! Not so loud. There's also talk that they're going to make an example of whoever is held responsible.'

Cato looked up at him. 'Where'd you hear all this?'

'One of the legate's clerks told me. He had it from someone on the general's staff.'

'Oh, it must be true then,' Cato muttered.

Macro ignored his sarcastic tone. 'Sounds plausible enough to me. They're going to need someone to blame, and it happened on our patch. So watch your back.'

'Maximius went through that last night. He's carrying the responsibility.'

'That's what he said . . .'

'You don't believe him?'

Macro shrugged. 'I don't trust him.'

'There's a difference?'

'For now. Come on, you'd better get up.'

'The legion's on the march again?' Cato hoped not. His muscles ached terribly, and the prospect of another day's tramping across the land under a blistering hot sun was almost unbearable.

'No. General's sent some mounted cohorts after the enemy. We're to rest here and wait for the baggage trains to come up.'

'Good.' Cato threw back his cape, struggled to his feet and stretched his neck.

Macro nodded over his shoulder. 'Maximius' slave has got breakfast on the go. He's brought some provisions with him. See you over there.'

The centurions of the Third Cohort sat around a small fire over which the slave was frying several thick sausages in olive oil. A jar of warmed mulsum rested close to the fire and a honeyed scent curled up from the spout. The slave had arrived at sunrise and set straight to work, having walked through the night to catch up with his master. The air was filled with the aroma of meat as the pan sizzled and spat. The nearest legionaries looked over with twitching nostrils, knowing that they had several hours to wait before the baggage train arrived with their food.

'Jupiter's balls!' Centurion Tullius growled. 'Will you hurry up with those sausages? I'll start chewing my bloody boot leather if I have to wait much longer.'

'It's nearly ready, master,' the slave replied quietly, well used to the impatience of centurions.

While they waited Cato looked across the river. The far bank was covered with bodies, washed in the rosy glow of sunrise. Above them wheeled a swirling cloud of carrion birds, drawn to the ripe stench of death. Scores of them had already settled to plucking shreds of flesh from the bodies. But even that failed to ruin Cato's appetite when the slave handed him his mess tin, filled with steaming sliced sausage and hunks of bread. The centurions set to the meal and soon the warm food in their bellies had revived their spirits and, mouths full, they began to talk about the battle.

'How was it on the island, Macro?' asked Felix. 'How long did you hold them for?'

Macro thought about it, trying to recall the detail. 'An hour or so.'

'You fought them off for an hour?' Felix's jaw dropped in amazement. 'The whole bloody army?'

'Not the whole army, you twat!' Macro jabbed a finger towards the ford. 'They could only take us on a few at a time. And then only after they cleared away the little surprises we'd prepared for them. I doubt we were in contact for a fraction of that time. And that was more than enough.'

Maximius was watching him closely. 'Why did you give way?'

'Once they'd opened a gap in the barricade what else could we do? And I'll tell you something else,' Macro waved a length of sausage at him to emphasise the point. 'Those bastards are starting to pick up a few tricks from us now.'

'What do you mean?' asked Tullius.

'They only went and formed a testudo when they came in for the second attack!'

'A testudo?' Tullius shook his head. 'I don't believe it.'

'It's true! Ask any of my men. That's why we had to fall back. We had no way of stopping that. If we'd stayed they'd have cut us to pieces in short order.'

'Same as the rest of us on the river bank,' Maximius said thoughtfully. 'We had to give ground or fall where we stood. Wouldn't have taken 'em long to carve us up.'

The other centurions glanced at each other warily, and ate their food in silence until Antonius looked up.

'Oi! Slave!'

'Yes, master?'

'Any more sausage there?'

'Yes, master. There's one left.' He looked to Maximius, waiting for instruction. 'Master Maximius . . . sir?'

'What?' Maximius looked round irritably. 'What is it?'

'The sausage, sir.' The slave nodded towards Centurion Antonius, who was holding out his mess tin.

Maximius smiled and nodded his assent. 'Let him have it. He's a growing boy and needs his food.'

'Thank you, sir.' Antonius beamed, eyes greedily fixed on the skillet the slave swung towards him. He thrust his mess tin forwards, caught the edge of the pan and the sausage jumped over the rim into the fire.

'Fucking shit!' Antonius glared at the sausage spitting in the heart of the fire and everyone else laughed.

'Consider that a sacrifice!' Maximius grinned. 'An offering to . . . which god shall we honour?'

'Fortuna,' Macro said seriously. 'We need all the luck we can get. Right now.'

He nodded over Maximius' shoulder and the centurions turned to look at a squad of soldiers marching down the sleeping lines of the men of the Third Cohort.

'Provosts!' Felix spat into the fire. 'Trust them to go and ruin a decent breakfast.'

They fell silent as the squad marched up, led by an optio from the legate's personal bodyguard. They halted a short distance from the group sitting round the fire. The optio stepped forward.

'Centurion Maximius, sir.'

'Yes.'

'You're to come with us. The general wants to question you.'

'I see.' Maximius bowed his head for a moment, as if composing himself, then he nodded. 'All right . . . All right, then. Let's go.'

He set his mess tin down and rose to his feet, brushing the crumbs from his soiled and bloodied tunic. He forced a smile on to his face. 'I'll see you lads a bit later. Tullius?'

'Sir?'

'Get the cohort up for me. Ready for duty. I'll do an inspection as soon as I get back.'

'Yes, sir.'

The optio nodded towards the small collection of tents in the centre of the camp.

'I'm coming,' Maximius responded with a trace of irritation at the optio's manner.

The centurions silently watched as their cohort commander was marched away between the double file of provosts. Maximius stiffened his back and strode forward as if he was on the parade ground.

'Poor bastard,' Cato said softly enough that only Macro heard him. 'This is the end of the road for him, isn't it?'

'Yes,' Macro muttered. 'If there's any justice.'

Chapter Fifteen

The optio and the provosts returned with Maximius just over an hour later. Tullius had carried out his orders and the legionaries were formed up ready for inspection. In the short time that they had been allowed, the men had struggled to make the best of their appearance. As Tullius caught sight of their commander approaching he bellowed out the order to call them to attention and the men stamped their feet together and stiffened their backs, staring fixedly ahead. The centurions stood to the front of their men, and to each side of them stood their optio and standard-bearer. As Maximius and his escort approached, Cato could see that he looked strained and shaken by his questioning. He acknowledged Tullius' formal greeting with a nod and then, without even looking at the men, he quietly ordered Tullius to dismiss them.

'Cohort! Fall out!'

The men turned and filed back towards their sleeping lines and Cato noted their discontented expressions and the faint grumblings of resentment at being roused and rushed into preparing for an inspection. That was the army way, he knew. Moments of frenzied activity, often for no better reason than to keep the men on their toes, ready to respond to any demand on the instant. But right now they were still tired and hungry, and their resentment was understandable. Even so . . .

Cato raised his vine cane towards a pair of soldiers whose complaints had reached his ears. 'Quiet there!'

The men, tough-looking veterans, fell silent, but briefly eyed their centurion with contempt before turning away. For a moment Cato was filled with cold, bitter rage and was tempted to call them back and punish them for their impudence. Legionaries must always respect the rank, if not the man, and no infraction could be overlooked. But by then the two men had merged with the rest of the century walking away from him and it was too late for Cato to act. He slapped his cane hard into the palm of his left hand, wincing at the pain of this self-inflicted punishment for his hopeless indecision. Macro would have had them by the balls in an instant.

Cato turned and saw that the other centurions were making their way towards Maximius, while behind him the provost escort stood and waited. Cato strolled over to join them, the self-contempt of a moment earlier turning to anxious curiosity. The centurions gathered in a rough semi-circle about their cohort commander. Maximius was still wearing only his tunic and clearly felt uncomfortable about addressing his fully dressed and armed officers.

'The legate has taken my deposition. Now he wants to speak to the rest of you individually. The optio here will call for us in order of seniority. None of you is to discuss the evidence you give with anyone. Is that understood?'

'Yes, sir,' the centurions replied quietly. Tullius raised his hand.

'Yes?'

'What about the men, sir?'

'What about them?'

'Will any of them be required today?'

'No. Stand them down. Pass the word that it's going to be a make-and-mend day.'

Tullius nodded unhappily. Make and mend was a rarely granted privilege when the legionaries were permitted time to maintain their equipment, or fashion some trinket, or simply rest and talk or gamble. Much as the men delighted in make and mend, the centurions resented it, grumbling that it softened them and too much of it made the men slack. It did, of course, win a small measure of popularity and good will for the officer who gave the order.

'Make and mend,' Tullius nodded. 'Yes, sir. Shall I tell them now?'

'No, you're to go with the optio. I'll tell them.'

'Yes, sir.' Tullius switched his gaze to the impassive faces of the provosts. Maximius noted his concerned expression and spoke quietly to his officers.

'It's all right. I did as I said I would earlier. None of you has anything to worry about. Just tell the truth.'

'Centurion Tullius?' the optio called out, extending his arm towards the provosts. 'If you please, sir?'

Tullius swallowed nervously. 'Yes, of course.'

Tullius fumbled with his helmet ties as he strode towards the escort. Then, flanked on either side, he was marched off, crested helmet tucked under his arm. When the escort was out of earshot Centurion Antonius stepped close to his cohort commander.

'What happened, sir?'

Maximius stared at him, his blank expression giving nothing away. 'What happened to me is . . . nothing to do with you. Understand?'

Antonius looked down. 'Sorry, sir. I just . . . it's just that I'm worried. Never experienced anything like this before.'

Maximius' lips relaxed into a slight smile. 'Me neither. Just answer the questions the legate asks you as straight as you can, and remember you're a centurion of the finest bloody legion in the empire. The only things in life that should worry a centurion are barbarians, plagues, wine droughts and insanely jealous women with access to cutlery. Questions –' he shook his head – 'questions will never hurt you.'

Antonius smiled. So did the others, even Cato, who as a child had lived in the imperial palace long enough to know that the wrong answer to a question could kill a man just as surely as the strongest barbarian warrior.

All morning and into the afternoon, the centurions waited by the smouldering remains of the fire the slave had built to cook their food. When he returned from his interrogation Macro had taken the whetstone out of his leather haversack and busied himself in sharpening the edges of his short sword. He spoke to no one, not even Cato, and refused to meet the eyes of the other centurions as he concentrated on rasping the stone along the bright shining length of his blade.

While Antonius was being questioned Tullius and Felix played at dice, and the luck seemed to be going Felix's way to an extent that outraged the laws of probability. The fact that he owned the dice began to feed the suspicion growing in the mind of the normally trustful Tullius. Cato watched them with amusement for a while. He never bet on games of chance, and thought it weak-minded of men who did. When he had lived in Rome, the tiny sums of money he had bet as a boy had always been on the races in the Circus Maximus, and then only after exhaustive study of form.

A little apart from the others, Maximius sat with his back to his men and his officers, staring down towards the ford and the field of corpses beyond. Cato felt sorry for him, in spite of the harsh way the cohort commander had treated him in the short time they had served together. A ruined soldier, especially one as respected as a senior centurion, was indeed a pitiful sight, and if the inquiry did ruin Maximius he would be too old to achieve anything else in his life. In a few years he would take the meagre pension of a legionary and eke out his days in some veterans' colony, drinking and reminiscing. A centurion's retirement, by contrast, offered a chance for further service and advancement as a magistrate. At the moment Maximius had little prospect of such a future.

He shifted his gaze from the cohort commander, and looked down towards the inviting water of the river. Antonius was still being questioned, and once he was done it would be Felix's turn.. So there was time for Cato to have a swim. He stripped down to his tunic and turned to Macro.

'Going for a swim. You coming?'

Macro paused in his work and looked up with an amused expression. 'You, swim?'

'Well, I'm getting better at it.'

'Better at it? As opposed to not totally useless at it?'

Cato frowned. 'Are you coming, or not?'

Macro carefully sheathed his sword. 'I think I'd better come. Make sure you don't get out of your depth.'

'Ha – fucking – ha.'

As they set off towards the camp entrance nearest the river, Maximius called after them, 'Make sure you're not too long.'

Cato nodded and as he turned back Macro glanced at him and raised his eyebrows with a weary expression. 'I sometimes wish we were back with those native lads in Calleva. That was nice simple soldiering with no bloody superiors looking over your shoulder the whole time.'

'I seem to remember you saying you couldn't wait to get back to serving with the legion?'

'That was before this cock-up. Trust our bloody luck to get saddled with Maximius. I wouldn't put him in charge of a soup kitchen.'

'He seems competent enough to me. Harsh, too harsh sometimes. But he seems to know what he's doing.'

'What do you know about it?' Macro shook his head. 'Couple of months in the job and you still can't tell what's right from what's shite. And look at the others. Tullius is getting on. Don't know how he managed to keep up with you yesterday – guess he must be tougher than he looks,' Macro conceded. 'But Felix and Antonius are too young, too inexperienced for the job.'

'Five and ten years older than me,' Cato pointed out.

'True. And it shows sometimes. But at least you've got brains and a good eye for the ground. If we hadn't had so many casualties in the last year there'd be better men available for promotion than those two jokers.'

Macro stopped talking as they passed by the gate guards, standing to attention in the hot sunshine. The two centurions were passed through on their own authority and then they began strolling down the slight slope towards the river. The summer grass was long and dry, and rustled against their legs as they headed to a spot a few hundred paces upriver of the ford and away from the bodies that still choked the river. Unfortunately the fluky breeze was billowing from the other direction and, every so often, as the nearby willows tossed their long locks of leaves, the sickening stench of dead men wafted over them.

The two centurions found a place where the bank sloped gently into the water and stripped off their tunics and untied their boots. Macro charged into the water and threw himself forward in a dive, sending a sheet of spray into the air. He surfaced almost at once, shaking the drops from his dark cropped hair.

'Shit, that's cold!' He turned and swam a few powerful strokes into the river. Cato waited for him to get clear of the bank and then waded a few paces out. In contrast to the exhausting heat of the summer's day the water felt icy and he tentatively tiptoed out towards Macro, arms raised and wincing as the current lapped across his stomach. Further out Macro turned round, treading water, and laughed.

'You bloody old woman! Come on in!'

Cato gritted his teeth and relaxed his knees, dropping to the surface.

There was a moment of shock, a gasp at the cold water that clenched his chest, then he struck out towards his friend. The strokes were clumsy and he struggled to keep his face out of the water as he floundered towards Macro.

'Just as well I decided to come!' Macro smiled as Cato stopped and trod water close by. 'You need more than a bit of practice.'

'And when do I ever get the chance?'

'Come on, I'll show you.'

Macro tried his best to teach his friend the rudiments of a good style, and Cato tried to make the most of it, handicapped by the fear of having the water close over his head for even an instant. At length Macro gave up and they sat in the shallows, the river flowing around their midriffs as the sun warmed their backs.

'I could get used to this,' Cato murmured.

'I wouldn't . . .'

Cato turned towards his friend. 'Why? Did someone say anything I should know about?'

'No. It's just that the legate seemed to be in a hurry. I think he's keen to get this inquiry sorted out as soon as possible and get after Caratacus. He's got a reputation to save.'

'Surely not? It wasn't his fault that the cohort wasn't in position in time to stop Caratacus crossing.'

'True, but the cohort is from his legion. Some of the mud's going to stick to the legate. You can be sure of that. It's too good an opportunity for his rivals to waste.'

'Rivals?'

'Oh, come on, Cato! Don't be so bloody thick. Vespasian's made praetor, and it hasn't been an easy route to reach that rank. Someone told me he got passed over the first time he went up for one of the aedile posts. Every step of the way there are more senators chasing fewer posts. That lot would stab their children in the eyes if it would help their chances of climbing the next rung. If someone on the general's staff doesn't try and pin this mess on the legate it'll be a miracle. Which means –' Macro looked sadly at Cato – 'which means that Vespasian will look for any way he can find to fix the blame on someone else.'

'Our cohort?'

'Who else?'

'Poor old Maximius.'

'Maximius?' Macro laughed bitterly. 'What makes you think he'll get the blame?'

Cato was surprised. 'He said he would. He said it was his responsibility.'

'And you believe him?'

'Yes,' Cato said seriously. 'If he hadn't gone after those raiders, he—'

'No, you idiot. Do you believe that he would take the responsibility for it?'

Cato considered the situation for a moment. 'He said he would. He seemed to be straight enough about that.'

'And what makes you think that he won't operate on the same basis as the legate? There's a lot at stake for Maximius too, even though he's not running for high office. He's a senior centurion, right?'

Cato nodded.

'Same thing applies to him as Vespasian. The next grade up for Maximius is an appointment to the First Cohort of the legion. Five jobs and nine applicants. Doesn't take a genius to work out that there's going to be a spot of competition from the other cohort commanders. If Maximius falls by the wayside, they'll not shed too many tears. So, Maximius will be doing his level best to pass the blame on to someone else. And who do you think that'll be?'

'You?'

'Spot on,' Macro said gloomily. 'The problem is, that's where the chain of command ends. I don't get the chance to pass the blame on. Unless, of course, I try and pin it on Caratacus, who shouldn't have bloody well been there in the first place.'

'You could try—'

'Shut up, Cato. There's a good lad.' Macro rose out of the river and splashed back towards his tunic, spread on the bank. 'Let's get back to the camp. It'll be your turn for questioning soon.'

'Yes,' Cato replied, following him on to the river bank. 'Better figure out what I'm going to say.'

'Don't try anything clever, for my sake, eh? Just play it straight.'

Cato shrugged. 'As you wish.'

Chapter Sixteen

'At ease,' Vespasian commanded, and Cato planted his feet apart, in line with his shoulders, and gripped his hands behind his back. He was standing inside the legate's personal quarters, at the heart of the small network of tents that made up the Second Legion's field headquarters. The side panels had been drawn up to admit the afternoon breeze and the ends of Vespasian's thinning hair occasionally stirred as he reclined in his chair. At his side, on a stool, sat a clerk with several thin waxed slates resting on his knees.

'Just to make sure you understand the situation,' the legate began brusquely, 'the general is conducting an inquiry into the events of yesterday. It is his contention that his orders were not obeyed and that as a consequence of this the enemy was permitted to escape the field with, between two and three thousand warriors including, as far as we know, Caratacus himself. Had the enemy been held at the ford then the entire army would have been forced to surrender and we would have been spared the butchery that occurred as they tried to escape. As a result, the campaign against Caratacus has been unnecessarily prolonged and the Empire has lost captives to the value of several million sesterces. Do you understand the gravity of the situation, Centurion Gaius Licinius Cato?'

He paused, and from the toneless delivery of the short speech Cato realised he must have said exactly the same thing to the other five centurions he had interviewed. Cato understood the situation well enough but the formality with which he had been greeted and addressed by the legate had added a sense of menace to proceedings. He coughed to clear his throat.

'Yes, sir. I understand.'

'Good. Now, Centurion, I require you to describe, to the best of your understanding, the movements and actions of the Third Cohort yesterday. Try to keep it paced so that the clerk can keep up. It is vital that his record is as accurate as possible.'

'Yes, sir.'

Cato concentrated his mind and began a detailed account of the march of the cohort towards the supply fort, the scene they found there, the orders for Macro's century to find what tools they could from the fort and then head to the ford and start preparing defences while they waited for the rest of the cohort to arrive, once they had finished chasing down and destroying the raiders. He did not flinch from describing Maximius' orders to blind the prisoners. He broke off his account to ask a question.

'Has anyone been sent to find the prisoners, sir?'

'Yes. A squadron of scouts went out this morning to find them and put them out of their misery.'

'Oh . . .'

'Please continue.'

Cato described how the cohort had marched as fast as they could towards the ford, and that they had broken into a run once they spied the enemy assaulting Macro's century; how they had seen Macro's cohort falling back, and then quickly outlined the attempt made to hold the near side of the crossing before they were driven back and desperately fought their way to safety in the direction of the rest of the Second Legion.

When he had finished Vespasian nodded and reached down to the clerk to read back over Cato's evidence. He paused a few times to check it against other slates that Cato realised must be the results of the previous interviews. At length Vespasian took up a blank slate and a stylus and carefully made some notes before he looked up at Cato again.

'Just a few questions, Centurion. Then you can go.'

'Yes, sir.'

'At the fort, when Centurion Maximius gave the order to pursue the raiders, did you or any other officer point out that this was a breach of the orders your cohort had been given?'

'Not me, sir. It's not for me to question the word of a cohort commander. The others clearly felt the same, sir. Except Macro. He tried to point out that our orders required us to move to the ford by a specified time, and we were already behind schedule.'

Vespasian raised an eyebrow. 'But you'd left the marching camp in plenty of time. Why the delay?'

'Troops seemed to be marching slower than I'd have liked, sir.'

'Did anyone else notice?'

'Someone might have made a comment. I can't recall.'

'Did Maximius notice?'

'I don't know, sir.'

'Very well.' The legate scribbled a note and ran his finger down the slate to his next question. 'Did Maximius give any reasons for his order to go after the raiders?'

'He didn't have to, sir. He's the cohort commander.'

'Very well. In your view, why did the cohort commander ignore Centurion Macro and go after the raiders?'

Cato knew that he was stepping on to much more sensitive ground now and would have to think carefully about his responses before he put them into words for the legate.

'I suppose he was upset by the massacre of the fort's garrison.'

'He must have seen dead men before?'

'Yes, but one – the commander of the fort – was a friend – a good one, it seemed.'

'Are you saying that he disobeyed his orders on emotional grounds?'

Cato froze. If he answered yes then his evidence might be damning. 'I don't know, sir. It's possible that Centurion Maximius was concerned that the raiders might have posed a danger to the cohort if they moved against us while we attempted to defend the ford. He might have wanted to remove that threat.'

'He might have,' Vespasian repeated. 'But you couldn't know that if he never said anything about such a danger.'

'No, sir.'

Vespasian sniffed. 'Just keep to what you know as fact from now on.'

'Sorry, sir.'

'Next . . . when you came in sight of the ford and saw the enemy moving to take the island, would you say that Macro's century offered the enemy much resistance?'

'Much resistance, sir?'

'All right then. For how long did they attempt to defend the crossing once they had caught sight of the rest of the cohort approaching?'

Cato could see the implication of the question immediately, and for the first time began to fear for his friend. 'It's hard for me to say, sir. I was at the rear of the column.'

Vespasian sighed and tapped his stylus against the slate. 'Was he defending the crossing when you came in sight of it?'

'No, sir. Some of the men were falling back. They were being covered by Macro and his rearguard. He had to fight his way back to the cohort.'

'Could you see the fight from where you were on the far bank?'

'Not quite, sir.'

'Not quite?'

'There were trees in the way, sir.'

'So you had no way of knowing if Macro was forced back, or whether he simply abandoned his position?'

Cato did not reply for a moment. He couldn't. Even though a denial would not condemn his friend it would not save him either.

'Sir, you know Macro. You know his quality. He'd never give way to an enemy until the last instant, and even then—'

'That's irrelevant, Centurion Cato,' Vespasian responded curtly. 'I'm still waiting for an answer to my question.'

Cato stared at his legate helplessly, before he finally spoke. 'No . . . I couldn't see the fighting on the island.'

Vespasian made a note, and then looked up and stared searchingly at Cato. Here it comes, the centurion thought. He's saved the toughest question until last. Cato focused his mind.

'Just one more issue I need to clear up, then you can go. When the Third Cohort reached the ford there was an attempt to hold the enemy back, I understand.'

'Yes, sir.'

'How effectively, in your opinion, was this defence prosecuted?'

Images of the desperate fight shimmered in and out his memory before Cato forced himself to reflect more objectively on the conduct of the cohort.

'We were outnumbered, sir. We were forced to give ground.'

'Forced to?'

'Yes, sir. Once they had pushed us back from the ford they threatened to outflank us. We had to pull back or be wiped out.'

'Has it occurred to you that if the Third Cohort had been a little more resolute and held their ground then the battle would have been a complete success?'

'Of course it has, sir. But, with respect, you weren't there . . .'

The clerk sucked in his breath nervously and risked a glance at his legate. Vespasian looked furious at having been spoken to in such a manner by the most junior centurion in his legion. For a while he continued to glare at Cato and then he clicked his fingers at the clerk. 'Delete that last remark from the record.'

While the clerk reversed his stylus and used the flat end to erase the offending statement Vespasian addressed the centurion quietly.

'In view of your previous service record I'll let that one pass. Next time you won't find me so forgiving. I want you and the others to remain in camp. No more swimming. You may be called on without notice. Dismissed!'

'Yes, sir.' Cato stood to attention, saluted, turned smartly and marched out of the tent. He walked slowly back towards the Third Cohort's station. The baggage train had arrived earlier in the afternoon, and after a quick meal the legionaries had erected their tents. Instead of the long lines of kit there were now hundreds of goatskin tents ranged in ordered lines stretching out on both sides of the Praetorian Way, and the men had stowed their equipment inside and now slept in the shade or chatted quietly in small groups outside in the sunshine.

Back amongst his men, Cato found his own tent and saw that a camp bed had been set up for him. He slumped down on it and started to unfasten his harness. A shadow partially blocked the light streaming in through the tent flaps, he looked up and there was Macro.

'I saw you coming back. How did it go?'

'Badly. Everything I said seemed to go the wrong way.'

'I know,' Macro smiled bitterly. 'But you're not usually at a loss for words.'

'No. But nothing I said seemed to make a difference. I think the legate's already made his mind up about what happened.' Cato stopped fiddling with his buckles and looked down at the ground. 'I think we're in trouble . . . deep trouble.'

Chapter Seventeen

Shortly before dusk Vespasian headed across the Tamesis to report to General Plautius in the main camp. He carried the results of his interviews in a large pannier bag hanging across the horse's back behind his saddle. The auxiliary units had been busy during the day, digging huge pits a short distance away from the crossing. The bodies of the Britons massacred the previous evening were still being dragged away and the crushed grass where they had been heaped was dark with their dried blood. Vespasian's horse wrinkled its nostrils nervously at the smell hanging in the air and he urged it on, anxious to reach the ridge and leave the unsettling scene behind him.

Inside the camp the legate dismounted outside the general's head-quarters and signalled to one of the guards to carry his pannier bags. A clerk ushered him into Plautius' tents as the last glimmer of the sun set on the horizon. Inside the headquarters the general's staff were busy with the administrative consequences of the previous day's battle. There were after-action reports that needed collating for the official history: logging of unit strength returns; compiling weapons and supplies inventories; recording the numbers of the enemy dead and preparing orders for the next stage of the campaign. It was nearly September, Vespasian reflected, and Plautius had hoped to be firmly entrenched on the banks of the Sabrina by autumn when the rain and mud would bog the legions down.

Now that Caratacus' army had been all but eliminated, the enemy would be limited to small operations – at least until large numbers of fresh tribal levies could be raised, armed and given some basic training. The warrior caste that had formed the backbone of his army had been whittled away over the last year and only a small cadre remained. Amongst them, in all likelihood, Caratacus himself. And while he lived the spirit of resistance would still smoulder in the hearts of the Britons, threatening all the while to flare up in the faces of the Roman invaders.

Vespasian frowned. That bloody man had far more than his fair share of luck. Far more, at least, than the thousands of natives being buried down by the river.

General Plautius was examining a large map spread across a table when Vespasian was ushered into his presence. The other legates and senior tribunes stood round him. Vespasian caught the eye of his older brother, Sabinus, and nodded a greeting. Seated to one side of the table, and looking thoroughly bored, was Narcissus, painstakingly peeling a pear with an ornate dagger.

The general glanced up. 'Vespasian, you've joined us at an interesting moment. We've just had the reports in from the mounted units.'

Vespasian nodded to the soldier who had carried the bags and he set them down beside one of the leather sides of the tent, and then withdrew. Vespasian joined the others at the table.

The map was made up from finely cured hides upon which the general's staff continually added new geographical features. The disposition of Roman forces was marked by red painted blocks of wood with unit identifiers cut into the top surface. There was no sign of any enemy markers on the map.

The general cleared his throat with a small cough. 'We know that a number of the enemy escaped us yesterday, perhaps as many as five thousand. I ordered our cavalry to pursue them and cut them down. So far they claim to have killed at least another two thousand, before they came up against a vast expanse of wetlands . . . here.'

Plautius leaned forward and tapped the map some ten to fifteen miles south and west of the crossing. 'The downs quickly give way to a marsh. That's where the survivors gave our cavalry the slip. But only after they turned on our cavalry and started to fight back. We began to lose men so the cavalry withdrew and now they're screening the approaches to the marsh. So, we're faced with a pretty little conundrum, gentlemen. We could ignore these survivors for the moment. After all, there can't be too many left. Certainly not enough to significantly threaten our operations. On the other hand, they will undoubtedly recover their nerve fairly quickly and make a nuisance of themselves. As such they will act as an inspiration to any tribes still thinking of opposing Rome. Our immediate goal, then, is to finish the job and destroy whatever's left of Caratacus' army, and, of course, Caratacus himself, assuming he survived yesterday's battle.

'We need to make the most of the situation while Caratacus is licking his wounds. Since there's no significant enemy force left to oppose us we can at last afford to disperse our forces and consolidate our gains. If we move swiftly we can lay down a network of forts and roads across the heartlands of Britain. Once that's done the tribes will not be able to move without us knowing about it. Should be a simple policing operation from then on. To that end . . .'

Plautius reached for one of the markers and placed it away to the east, in position just outside the boundary of the lands the map ascribed to the Iceni, a tribe that had declared itself for Rome the previous year. The general then turned towards an older officer, Hosidius Geta – legate of the Ninth Legion.

'. . . the Ninth will move there, establish a base and start probing north with auxiliary troops, establishing small forts along your lines of advance.

The tribes in that area are nominally allied to us. That's fine, but I want a display of strength, understand? You make it clear to them that Rome is here to stay. No marching camps. I want permanent structures, and I want them to look imposing.'

'Yes, sir.' Geta smiled eagerly. 'Trust me, sir. I'll sort them out.'

'No!' Plautius stabbed a finger towards him. 'That's precisely what I want to avoid. We'll be thinly spread and I want no man here giving the natives an easy excuse to rise up. Once your forces are in place I want you to go out of your way to cultivate good relations with local chieftains. Go hunting with them. Get your engineers to build them bridges, baths, comfortable villas – whatever it takes to get them on our side and make them appreciate the benefits of joining the Empire. I want these bog-hopping barbarian bastards Romanised as soon as possible. Once that's done we can think about extending the province west and north.'

He gestured towards the lands of the Silurians and the Brigantians, and the officers registered surprise at the scope of his ambitions. Plautius observed their reactions and smiled. 'That's work for the future, gentlemen. All in good time . . . The Twentieth will continue to advance north of the Tamesis, then cut across to the river Sabrina and establish its base there. I'll be marching with the Twentieth, so Legate Sulpicius Piso will have to double the guard on his fine collection of wines.'

The officers laughed politely and then the general turned to Sabinus. 'You'll have the strongest column. I want you to move directly north. To here.' Plautius pushed the Fourteenth Legion's marker across the map to a point between the Twentieth and the Ninth. 'I want you to start construction of a road to link all three legions. That way we can concentrate our forces quickly, should we ever need to. Gentlemen, the end is in sight. Rome can at last consider these lands to be part of the Empire. In a few more years Britain will be a fully functioning province, paying taxes into the imperial treasury.'

'I rather think that the people back in Rome already regard this vile land as part of the Empire . . .'

The officers' heads turned towards Narcissus, who had started peeling another pear as he spoke and did not return their gaze.

'After all, the Emperor had his triumph through the streets of the capital at the end of last year. You fellows are just doing the mopping-up. I'd remember that if I were you. To imply that the Emperor had somehow fallen short in his conquest of the Britons might smack of treason to some people.' Narcissus lowered his dagger, popped a dripping slice of fruit into his mouth and smiled. 'A word of advice on how to phrase your official reports, that's all. No offence intended. Please continue, my dear General.'

Plautius nodded curtly, and turned his attention back to the map. 'Vespasian, you will remain in the south. Your first task is to complete the pacification of the south-west. I want that done as swiftly as possible. By the end of this campaign season, if you can. Find and eliminate what is left of Caratacus' army. If you come upon Caratacus, try and take him alive. His life is to be spared.'

'Spared, sir? Surely we want him out of the way permanently.'

'He will be out of the way. The Imperial Secretary wants him shipped back to Rome in chains, as a souvenir for Emperor Claudius, to remind him of his brilliant campaign to conquer and subdue the Britons.'

'Don't overegg it, General,' Narcissus said quietly.

Plautius pretended to ignore the remark as he continued to brief Vespasian. 'According to our intelligence the marsh covers a vast area, all the way to the river Sabrina. It's crossed by a multitude of tracks. Parts of it are slightly elevated and support a few small settlements. There are stretches of open water and some narrow creeks, but they're too small to navigate with anything larger than a raft. It is rumoured that Caratacus has established a fortified camp somewhere in the flats, but so far we've not been able to get any of the prisoners to tell us the location. I appreciate it's difficult ground to work with, Vespasian, but I must have the enemy survivors found and destroyed. If there is a camp, I want it razed. If you can take Caratacus alive, do it.' Plautius paused, and smiled. 'But if not, then we'll just have to present the Emperor with some other souvenir of his trip to Britain.'

'That would be wise,' added Narcissus.

Vespasian was looking at the map. The area occupied by the flats was huge. The map simply marked its boundaries, with one or two known features, culled from natives or traders. The only area that had any amount of detail was a valley that ran alongside the marshland, following the course of the river that fed into the marshes and fens. A few tracks had been drawn in tentatively, and as Vespasian ran his finger along one of the lines, it smudged, and he realised it was only chalked on to the map. The general saw the gesture and frowned irritably at the smudge mark.

'As soon as we've updated the map, I'll ensure that you have a copy. There aren't many of the enemy left, Legate. Shouldn't be too difficult to find them and finish them off. Once you've crushed Caratacus and his surviving forces, that should be the end of resistance to us in the south.'

The general looked up brightly. 'That's that, gentlemen. Any questions? . . . No? That's good. Your written orders will be with you shortly and you're to begin preparations to break camp the day after tomorrow.'

Sabinus looked uncomfortable. 'Only one day to prepare, sir?'

'That's what I said. We've already lost enough time this year. We need to move fast to catch up. Now, unless there's anything else, you may return to your legions and get your staffs to work.'

As the officers filed out, Vespasian waited for a moment and then approached his commander. 'Sir, I've questioned the officers of my Third Cohort and taken their statements, which I've brought with me.' He indicated the bag over by the side of the tent.

'Good. I'll send for my chief clerk. He can make preparations for the inquiry. If we move quickly we can settle the matter in the next few days.'

'No.' Narcissus interrupted him. 'Now.'

General Plautius turned towards the freedman, and Vespasian saw his jaw stiffen with suppressed anger. 'I beg your pardon, Narcissus. Did you have anything to contribute to the disciplinary procedures of my legions?'

'You mean the Emperor's legions, of course.'

'Of course.'

Narcissus smiled. 'I'm afraid I must rush you on this matter. You know I'm leaving at first light to report back to Rome.'

'Yes . . . a great shame.'

'Quite. Anyway, I will, naturally, have to mention yesterday's missed opportunity to crush Caratacus completely.'

'Oh, naturally.'

'The Emperor and the senate will want to know that those responsible for the mistake have paid a price commensurate with the scale of their failure. So I'm afraid we can't wait for a proper inquiry. We need to act now.'

'Now?' The general frowned.

'Tonight,' Narcissus replied firmly. 'The inquiry must be held tonight, and those found responsible must be sentenced before I leave in the morning.'

'That's absurd!' Plautius blustered. 'It's impossible.'

'No it's not. And I'll tell you what is possible. It's possible that Rome will take a dim view of your failure to eliminate Caratacus and his army. Unless I can persuade them that you have won a decisive victory. The escape of Caratacus can be presented as a minor detail, provided that those responsible for letting him slip away are identified and punished swiftly and decisively. Vespasian's Third Cohort should fit the bill nicely.'

'We haven't had the inquiry yet,' the General pointed out. 'They might not be found at fault.'

'You'd better make sure that they are. In the end, it's you or them, my dear General.' Narcissus paused to let the threat sink in, then he spoke again, in his quiet, polite, unflustered manner. 'So, might I suggest that you give the necessary orders?'

General Plautius glared at the man, visions of bloody torture and revenge flooding into his mind in rapid succession. The freedman's impudence was breathtaking, but the gulf in social status between a senator and a freedman, who had been a slave of Claudius only a few years ago, was erased by the fact that Narcissus was the Emperor's most trusted and closest advisor. The Emperor ruled Rome, but the Emperor, Plautius had heard it said, was ruled by his freedman. Only now, the freedman had a rival in Messalina, Claudius's scheming young wife, and that made Narcissus an even more desperate and dangerous man to cross.

'I'll give the orders.'

106

'Thank you, General.' Narcissus resumed his concentration on the skinless pear on the silver plate on his lap, slicing it as finely as possible with the glinting blade of his dagger. 'Send me word when all is ready. I'll wait here.'

Plautius could not stomach remaining in the same tent as the freedman and, grasping the pannier bags, he clapped a hand on to Vespasian's shoulder and led him out of the tent. Outside, in the clerks' tent, and out of the Imperial Secretary's hearing, Plautius spoke softly to his subordinate.

'You'd better get back to your legion. I want your Third Cohort stood to, unarmed, in tunics only and under guard.'

'Why, sir? Why shame them so?'

'Because they need shaming. They need to know that every man in the cohort is held to account, whatever their rank. It'll serve as a warning to the other cohorts.'

'But, sir—' Vespasian's exhausted mind was reeling with the way that the inquiry was being rushed through at this mad speed. 'Think of the men's morale. This will bring shame to the whole legion and all the spirit we've built up on the campaign will be pissed away.'

Plautius stopped walking, and turned towards him with raised eyebrows. 'Pissed away? That's an awfully common expression. I think you've been spending rather too long in the company of the lower orders . . . Perhaps you should return to Rome before you forget who you are.'

'I know who I am,' Vespasian replied coolly. 'And I know what's right and what's wrong. I'm telling you, this inquiry is a mistake. Nothing good can come of it . . . sir.'

Plautius stared back at him. 'I think you forget yourself, Legate. I've given you an order. Get back to your legion and have everything ready for the hearing. As soon as I've discussed these statements with my clerks I'll ride over and join you and we'll start immediately. If the preparations are not complete by then, I may have to widen the scope of the inquiry beyond the officers of your Third Cohort. Do I make myself clear?'

'Yes, sir.'

'Then go.'

Chapter Eighteen

Senior Tribune Plinius filled his lungs and shouted the order. 'Centurions . . . to the front!'

Outside the headquarters tents of the Second Legion the men of Maximius' cohort stood in well-ordered ranks. They were made visible in the night by the wavering glare of scores of torches held aloft by the legionaries of the First Cohort assigned to guard them. Unlike their comrades Maximius' men were not armed, they were not even permitted to wear their armour, only plain tunics. They were under judgement, and as such might soon be cast out of the camp as a punishment for their failure to hold the ford the day before. Some of the men looked terrified. As well they might, thought Cato as he marched over towards the senior tribune. They would be without shelter from the elements and without weapons to defend themselves against any enemy patrols that might want to take a few easy heads from the Roman invaders. For however long the punishment lasted.

Cato fell into line with the other centurions behind the tribune, and the escort formed up on either side.

'Forward!' called the tribune, and the party marched towards the entrance to the largest tent. The flaps were tied back and an orange-hued light spilled out from the oil-lamp stands inside. Through the flaps Cato could see that the clerks' desks had been rearranged so that a long table was set against the rear of the tent, leaving an open space in front of it. A smaller arrangement of tables ran down one side and a number of clerks were already seated there, preparing their writing materials for keeping a record of the inquiry.

Tribune Plinius marched the centurions and their escort inside the tent and indicated that they were to stand in a line in front of the empty table. The escort formed up behind them, hands resting on the pommels of their swords. The clerks sat beside their tablets, styluses to hand, ready to begin. Then all was still and silent as they waited in the stuffy heat for the presiding officers to appear. Cato, who had never witnessed such an event before, was terrified but determined not to let it show as he stood stiff as his vine cane and stared directly ahead. As they waited, he let his glance slip to the side and saw that Felix's fingers were clenching and unclenching into a fist, over and over again. He suddenly turned his head slightly and caught Cato's eyes. Cato's gaze flickered down momentarily and he gave a slight nod. Felix followed the direction indicated and looked surprised when he saw his hand moving, almost as if it belonged to another. He abruptly stopped the nervous tic and winked his gratitude to Cato before facing forward again. For his part, Cato was relieved to find someone who felt as nervous as he did.

A side flap was thrust open and the camp prefect entered the tent. He stepped smartly to one side and bellowed, 'Senior officers present! All rise!'

The clerks immediately stood up and snapped to attention along with the other men in the room as the legate and the general entered the tent and walked briskly to their seats. There was a brief pause before Narcissus followed them inside and sat beside the general. As soon as he had taken his seat the camp prefect called out, 'At ease!'

General Plautius began proceedings at once. 'Before the inquiry commences I want it entered in the record that the exigencies of the situation require the circumventing of normal procedure in order that the inquiry is completed as swiftly as possible. To that end, I require that sentencing take place directly upon completion of the inquiry process, and that execution of any sentence be carried out as soon as possible.'

The officers of the Third Cohort glanced at each other anxiously at this curtailment of their rights. Any hearing in a settled garrison fortress would be far more protracted, but here in the field it was necessary for justice to take a more direct route. However, this flouting of even the most basic procedures stunned the centurions.

Before anyone could protest the general continued, 'This inquiry has been called to determine whether the performance of the officers and men of the Third Cohort, Second Legion conforms to the standards required of those who serve in the name of Emperor Claudius and the senate and people of Rome. The charges laid before the inquiry are that on the ides of August last, the commander of the cohort, Gaius Norbanus Maximius, failed to obey orders and by such dereliction of duty permitted the escape of some five thousand enemy soldiers. Furthermore, it is charged by Centurion Maximius that Centurion Lucius Cornelius Macro failed to carry the battle to the enemy with sufficient determination in defending the island in the middle of the ford. It is also charged by Centurion Maximius that the Third Cohort failed to engage the enemy with sufficient vigour and determination in its subsequent defence of the near bank of the ford. However, it is my view, after carefully considering the evidence submitted to me, that the Third Cohort and all its officers are equally culpable in regard to all the charges specified. Before judgement is passed, does any officer wish the opportunity to answer the charges?'

General Plautius looked up and waited for one of the centurions to respond. Macro's jaw was clenched with bitter anger as he took in his betrayal by Centurion Maximius. He could not trust himself to speak, nor to turn to his right and look past Tullius to the man who had lied so completely to his officers in an effort to escape the blame for his failure to do his duty. Even more unforgivable was his attempt to spread the blame even further by accusing the cohort as a whole of cowardice.

'Sir, if I may?'

Every pair of eyes turned towards Vespasian.

'You may speak, Legate. As long as you keep it brief, and to the point.'

'Yes, sir, I will. I wish to have it entered on the record that I oppose all the charges specified.'

Plautius' eyes widened in surprise at this show of open revolt against his judgement. He swallowed nervously before he responded. 'On what grounds?'

Vespasian weighed his words with care. 'On the grounds that the charges are too narrow in scope. While I do not deny that the Third Cohort failed to act with sufficient speed or valour in carrying out their duties, the fact is that they were only ever required to defend the crossing against fugitives of the main battle. A battle that should have been fought in front of either of the other two fords. It was never anticipated that Maximius and his men would face the entire enemy army.' Vespasian paused and took a deep breath before getting to the meat of his accusation. 'The question I would like entered on the official record is, what reason can be given for the failure of the army of General Plautius to force the enemy to give battle before the two major crossings, as the general had planned?'

This time the shock and surprise of those in the tent was so profound that there was a long silence while the men glanced from general to legate, and back to their general as they waited for his response to Vespasian's open attack. Cato could sense the tension in the tent like the air that precedes a violent storm. Plautius stared at the legate for a moment and then glanced at Narcissus. The Imperial Secretary gave a slight shake of the head. Plautius turned back to the other men arranged around the tent.

'That question is outside the scope of this inquiry, and therefore irrelevant.' He glanced towards the clerks. 'It will not be entered into the official record.'

'That's not acceptable, sir.'

'It is acceptable, Legate. On my authority.'

'Sir, you cannot condemn men on the basis that they failed to hold the line in the face of vastly superior forces.'

Plautius smiled. 'There is a precedent for heroic sacrifice in every army.'

'It happens,' Vespasian conceded. 'But when such a situation was forced upon the Third Cohort by the failure of others to press home their attack, surely a double standard is being applied? You would condemn these men and their legionaries on the basis that they failed in their duty. Yet you would not condemn those men, under your direct command, who failed to attack swiftly enough to close the trap you originally conceived. It is by *their* failure to carry out *their* orders that the enemy managed to evade the trap, and fall upon the Third Cohort in overwhelming numbers.'

The Legate had overdone it, thought Cato, glancing around the room. The shock on the faces of the officers in the tent was eloquent expression of just how far Vespasian had breached the accepted protocols for such an inquiry. The general glared at his subordinate, so consumed with anger and surprise that he did not know how to proceed for a moment. Then he cleared his throat and turned to the clerks.

'Make a note for the records. The legate has registered an objection to the conduct of the inquiry. At a future date, to be determined, a subsequent inquiry will be held to investigate his claims of impropriety. Now, we must deal with the matter of the present inquiry. Charge by charge. Centurion Maximius.'

'Yes, sir?'

'Do you deny disobeying your orders?'

'Yes, sir.'

'Yes?'

'We marched towards the ford as quickly as we could, sir. On reaching the fort I decided that it would be dangerous to proceed while an enemy column threatened our flank. We closed with and destroyed the raiders and then continued to the ford, sir. In accordance with our orders.'

'Was your decision to destroy the raiders immediately determined by tactical considerations alone?'

'Of course, sir,' Maximius replied without the slightest hesitation.

'And did any of your officers try to dissuade you?'

'I recall that there was some disagreement, sir. There was too little time to explain the situation to the individual concerned. Besides, when a senior centurion gives an order, that should be the end of the discussion.'

'Quite so.' Plautius nodded and then turned his gaze on Macro. 'On the matter of the second charge, Centurion Macro, why was the ford not adequately defended before the enemy arrived?'

Macro tore his eyes away from Maximius, recomposed his livid expression and cleared his throat noisily. 'Because there weren't as many men there as there should have been, sir. That, and the fact that we found only a handful of usable trenching tools at the depot. The raiders had burned the rest. When I reached the ford, we didn't have enough tools, nor enough time to prepare a ditch and rampart. The best defence I could make was to erect a barrier on the island and place some sharpened stakes into the crossing. We had only a handful of axes and most had to cut wood with their swords.'

'Fair enough. I accept there was little chance to prepare anything better. But why did you fall back before the rest of the cohort could reach the ford? Had you received many casualties?'

'No, sir.'

111

'Were you outflanked?'

'No, sir.'

'Then why break off contact and retreat? I assume you had a good reason.'

Macro looked surprised. 'Why, of course, sir.'

'Go on.'

'The enemy's second attack had cleared away a section of our defences and they were preparing a fresh assault on our line. They were using heavy infantry, formed into a testudo, sir. Soon as I saw that I knew we'd have to give ground, link up with Centurion Maximius and try to hold the bank on our side of the river.'

'A testudo?' Plautius smiled faintly. 'You claim they formed a testudo?'

'Yes, sir. Made quite a decent job of it too.'

'Oh, I'm sure they did, Centurion. Decent enough to send you running.'

'I didn't run, sir,' Macro growled. 'Never have and never will.'

'What did you do, then?'

'I think you'll find it referred to as a fighting withdrawal in the manuals, sir.'

'We'll see about that . . .' General Plautius looked down at his notes. 'On to the last charge. Centurion Maximius, would you say that your men prosecuted the defence of the ford as effectively as they might have done?'

'Frankly, sir, no. No, I don't. The lads were tired, sir. We'd run the last mile or so to the ford and gone straight into the fight with no time to recover. The men were exhausted and, well, as soon as they saw how many of the enemy there were on the far side waiting to come across and fight us . . .'

'Yes?'

Maximius looked down at his boots. 'I think they got scared, sir. Fight went right out of them. So we pulled back and waited for support. I had no choice. No sense in throwing the cohort away if it wasn't prepared to fight.' He looked up defiantly. 'On any other day—'

'Centurion!' Plautius snapped. 'There's never another day. Just the one you're in. You, and your men, have failed to live up to the standards required of legionaries.'

The general paused before passing his judgement. He intended more than a cheap theatrical effect. The men must have some moments to anticipate their fate with a growing sense of dread.

'The Third Cohort will be denied shelter for six months. They will be denied the shelter of barracks. Their standards will be stripped of any decorations. Pay will be suspended and their rations restricted to barley and water. Sentence effective immediately.'

Despite the prospect of half a year of unremitting discomfort, Cato felt more shame than anything else. Every unit in the army would know that he, and the other officers and men of the cohort, had failed in their duty. Their bare standards would be badges of dishonour everywhere they marched. He knew that the shadow of this evening's judgement would linger over him longer than six months; men's memory of the crime always outlived the duration of the punishment.

The general slapped his slate notebook closed and was about to rise when the Imperial Secretary leaned towards him and placed a hand on his shoulder.

'A moment, if you please, General.'

'What is it?'

Narcissus leaned closer and spoke in a low voice so that only Plautius would hear. The silence in the tent was unnatural as everyone else kept quite still and strained to catch any of the words passing between the two men. Plautius listened a moment, before a look of horror flitted over his face, and he shook his head. Narcissus spoke intently, stabbing his finger in the general's direction to emphasise his points. At length the general appeared to give way, and nodded solemnly. He turned to Vespasian and whispered something. Vespasian stared ahead, at the officers of his Third Cohort, lips compressed tightly.

General Plautius leaned back and folded his hands together before he addressed the other men in the tent. 'In view of the seriousness of the Third Cohort's dereliction of duty, and in order to set an example to the rest of the army serving in this province and beyond, the sentence has been revised to include decimation. Lots to be drawn by centuries immediately. Executions will take place at dawn, the day after next, before an assembly of units representing each of the legions. Tribune! Take the officers out to join their men.'

As the centurions filed out of the headquarters tent Cato watched their expressions as they passed. Maximius looked down, refusing to meet anyone's eyes. Tullius looked ashen-faced. Macro was still angry and communicated his bitter resentment to Cato with a slight shake of the head as he marched stiffly by. Felix and Antonius appeared stunned. Then Cato turned and joined the end of the line as the escort marched them outside. He felt numb, and the hard reality of the world around him seemed somehow distant and vague.

Decimation. He'd only ever read of it: the most dreadful of the field punishments that could be imposed upon the men of the legions. One man in ten, selected by lot, would be beaten to death by his comrades. The odds made him feel sick with fear.

The centurions were returned to their places in front of their centuries and then all were made to wait in silence, in the wavering glare of the reed torches, until six clerks emerged from the headquarters tent. Each carried a plain Samian ware jar. They spread out, one heading towards each of the centuries of the Third Cohort. When they were in position, Tribune Plinius stepped forward.

113

'Every man in each century is to draw a corn tally from the jar in front of them. If you draw a white tally you will return to your unit. Any man who draws a black tally will be escorted to one side.'

A groan of despair welled up from the Third Cohort as they realised the nature of their punishment.

'Silence!' screamed the senior tribune. 'You will be silent when a senior officer addresses you!'

He glowered at the terrified men on parade in front of him. 'Begin!'

The legionaries approached the clerks by sections to draw their lots. Beside each clerk stood two men from the First Cohort, one holding a torch above the jar to ensure that each man's tally was clearly visible when it emerged and the other to escort the unlucky ones away. Cato turned towards his men.

'First section! To the front!'

The eight men marched up to the clerk. He raised the pot above eyelevel so that the men could not see inside, and then the first man reached in. There was a dull rattling noise as his fingers probed the tallies.

'Draw it quickly!' the legionary holding the torch growled.

The man withdrew his hand and showed the tally to the clerk – a wooden disc, the size of a denarius.

'White!' the clerk called out and the first man turned round and walked quickly away, hurrying back towards the rest of the century, hands trembling with relief.

'White!' cried the clerk for the next man.

'Black!'

The third man stared into the palm of his hand, frozen in place, staring as if at any moment the disc would turn white in front of his eyes.

'Come on, you!' The legionary grabbed him by the arm and thrust him towards the squad of guards waiting behind the senior tribune. 'Over there. Let's go!'

The man stumbled as he was half dragged away from his comrades. He glanced back over his shoulder and caught Cato's eye. The appeal for help was as clear as it could be, but there was nothing Cato could do, and he shook his head helplessly, and looked away.

So it continued, and a steady trickle of victims was separated from the rest of the cohort. Cato saw Maximius take his turn, draw a white tally and turn away, clutching it like a lucky talisman. Maybe that was an omen for him too, he decided, and he turned to his optio.

'Come on, Figulus. We'll draw ours with the next section.'

Two of the eight men ahead of them drew black tallies, and Cato quickly calculated that only one could still be in the jar. One black and twenty-six white. Good odds. Even as his spirits rose at the thought he felt ashamed that those odds had been improved at the cost of the lives of some of the men whom he had let go ahead of him.

It was Figulus' turn, and the huge Gaul hesitated in front of the jar.

114

'Go on, son,' the legionary with the torch whispered. 'Don't let 'em see you're afraid.'

'I'm not,' Figulus hissed back. 'I'm not, you bastard!'

He stepped forward, plunged his hand into the jar, snatched the first tally that fell into his grasp and drew it out.

'White!' cried the clerk, then turned to Cato.

His heart was beating fast and he could feel the blood pounding in his ears. Yet he felt cold, the night air icy on his skin, even though he knew it was warm. The clerk gestured towards him with the jar.

'Sir?'

'Yes, of course.' The quiet words came from his lips like another man's voice and even though Cato wanted more than anything to back away from that jar he found himself rooted in front of it. His hand rose up, over the rim and began to dip down inside. Cato noticed a hairline fracture that ran, in a fine black line, down from a tiny chip on the rim of the jar, and wondered what accident had caused that to happen. Then the tips of his fingers brushed against the small pile of tallies remaining in the bottom of the jar. For an instant his hand recoiled. Then he gritted his teeth, and closed his hand round one of the wooden discs, drawing it out of the jar. Cato stared at the face of the clerk as he opened his fist. The clerk's eyes dropped down and there was a flicker of pity in his expression as he opened his mouth.

'Black!'

Chapter Nineteen

The Imperial Secretary left the army just after dawn, accompanied by his two bodyguards and four full squadrons of auxiliary cavalry. After the earlier attempt on his life Narcissus was not prepared to take any more chances. He had delivered the Emperor's motivational threat to the general and would be the bearer of some good news on the way home. Caratacus' army had been smashed and all that remained was to mop up the survivors. The commander of the native forces had used up the goodwill of the lowland tribes and would find little sympathy for any further struggle from that quarter. A generation of young warriors had been sacrificed for the cause, and across the land families wept bitter tears for their sons, lying dead and buried in fields far from home. It was only a matter of time, Narcissus comforted himself, before Caratacus was killed or captured. Barring a few druid troublemakers, peddling their bizarre philosophies and religious practices from the safety of obscure sanctuaries, the province was as good as conquered. That should keep the Emperor's critics quiet for a while.

The column of horses splashed across the ford, shattering the calm surface of the river. On either side a thin milky white mist rose up along the river and spilled over on to the banks. The horsemen emerged from the crossing and climbed the track that led towards Calleva. The Atrebatan capital would be a safe place to spend the night now that the tribe had been incorporated into the kingdom of the Regenses, ruled by the sycophantically loyal Cogidubnus.

Narcissus smiled. There would never be any trouble from Cogidubnus. That man had been bought body and soul, and aped the ways of his Roman masters with a rare enthusiasm. All it had taken was some vague promise of building him a palace as soon as funds allowed.

As Narcissus rode past the side of the Second Legion's marching camp, he saw, a short way off, hundreds of men labouring to erect a stockade. That would be the Third Cohort, he mused with a faint smile of satisfaction. The harsh judgement meted out to those men would act as a fine example to their comrades in the four legions gathered about the crossing. Better still, it would satisfy the armchair generals of the senate back in Rome, who would be pleased to know that the legions still cleaved to the harsh and hardening traditions that had won them an empire that stretched around the limits of the known world.

A small party of men sat to one side, under guard, hands tied behind them. They looked up as the horsemen trotted by. Narcissus realised they were the condemned men, due to be beaten to death by the men of their cohort the following day. Most looked vacant; some were sullen. Then Narcissus started as he found himself looking into a face he had once known well back in the halls and corridors of the imperial palace. He flicked his reins and steered his horse off the track, waving at his escort to keep moving. The bodyguards, silently fell into position on either side and slightly behind the Imperial Secretary.

'Cato . . .' Narcissus began to smile, but the young centurion just glared back at him, eyes filled with a pitiless fury. 'You're to be executed?'

Cato was still for a moment before he nodded, once. Narcissus, so used to deciding the fates of men who were rarely ever more than names or numbers on a writing tablet, was uncomfortable to be confronted with this man he had watched grow from an infant into a gangly youth. The son of a man he had once called friend. Now Cato would die in order to maintain belief in the uncompromising discipline of the legions. In that respect, Narcissus consoled himself, the lad would be dying a martyr's death. Most unfortunate, but necessary.

Narcissus felt he must say something, some kind of valediction that would comfort the young man so that he would understand. But all that came to mind were empty platitudes that would demean both of them.

'I'm sorry, Cato. It had to be done.'

'Why?' Cato replied through clenched teeth. 'We did our duty. You must tell the general. Tell him to change his mind.'

Narcissus shook his head. 'No. That's impossible. I'm sorry, my hands are tied.'

Cato stared at him a moment, then laughed bitterly as he raised his hands to reveal the rope that bound his wrists. Narcissus coloured but could not think of anything further to say. Nothing to comfort this youth, nor to justify the need for his death. Greater destinies than his were at stake, and much as Narcissus had once been genuinely fond of the boy, nothing must come between the Imperial Secretary and his duty to protect and further the Emperor's interests. So Cato must die. Narcissus clicked his tongue and firmly tugged on the reins. The horse snorted and turned back towards the track.

Cato watched him go, a twisted expression of distaste curling his lips. He had hated to beg for a reprieve in front of the others. But it was for them that he made the attempt, he tried to convince himself. Narcissus represented the last chance of an appeal over the general's head. Now he was gone, already lost from sight in the column of horsemen that trotted up the track towards Calleva, kicking up a haze of dust in their wake.

When they were out of sight Cato slumped to the ground and stared at the grass between his bare feet. This time tomorrow, he and the forty other men condemned to death would be led into a loose circle of their comrades and friends from the Third Cohort. They would be carrying heavy wooden clubs, and when the signal was given they would close in and beat the prisoners to death, one by one. Cursed with a vivid imagination, Cato projected the scene inside his head, clear in every terrible detail. The blur of clubs sweeping down, the dull thud and crack of wood on flesh and bone, and the winded gasps and cries of bound men, curled into balls on the blood-drenched ground. Some of the men would soil themselves, to the jeers of their executioners, and when Cato's time came he would have to kneel amid their blood, piss and excrement while he waited for his death to come.

It was shaming, humiliating, and Cato hoped that he would have the strength of spirit to die without a whimper, silently staring his defiance back at his killers. But he knew it would not be like that. He would be dragged, shivering and filthy to the killing ground. He might not beg for mercy, but he would cry out at the first blow, and scream at the rest. Cato prayed that a badly aimed blow struck him on the head early on, so that he was unconscious when his beaten, broken body eventually released his spirit.

That was wishful thinking, he sneered at himself. The executioners would be carefully briefed to make sure that his arms and legs were shattered before they were permitted to break his ribs. Only then would they be allowed to take their clubs to his skull, and end the torment. He felt sick, and bile simmered uneasily in his stomach, so that he was glad that he had not eaten since early the previous day. Memory of the food cooked by Maximius' slave caused him to retch and Cato raised his bound hands to cover his mouth until the impulse to vomit passed.

A hand rested gently on his shoulder. 'You all right, lad?'

Cato quickly swallowed the bitter fluid in his mouth and looked round to see Macro looming over him with an uncertain smile on his creased face. A quick glance showed that the rest of the condemned men were too preoccupied to spare him any curious attention. He quickly shook his head.

'Not surprised.' Macro's fingers squeezed his shoulder as the older centurion squatted down beside Cato. 'It's a bad business. We've been well and truly shafted. You and this lot most of all . . . Look here, Cato. I don't know what to say about this. It stinks. I wish there was something I could do to change it. I really do. But . . .'

'But there's nothing that can be done. I know.' Cato forced himself to smile. 'We're here because we're here. Isn't that what the old hands say?'

Macro nodded. 'That's right. But it only applies when the situation's out of our control. This could've been prevented – should have been.

Bloody general's screwed up and he wants someone else to carry the blame. Bastard.'

'Yes,' Cato replied softly. 'He's a real bastard, all right . . . You ever seen a decimation carried out before?'

'Twice. Both units deserved it,' Macro recalled. 'Ran, and left the rest of us in the shit. Nothing like this.'

'Don't suppose a decimation has ever been cancelled?' Cato looked up, trying to keep his face expressionless. 'I mean, have you ever heard of one being called off?'

For a moment Macro was tempted to lie. Any shred of comfort he could offer Cato might make the time he had left more bearable. But Macro knew he was a bad liar; he didn't have the skill for such deception. Besides, he owed Cato the truth. That burden was what made friendships count. 'No. Never.'

'I see.' Cato looked down. 'You might have lied to me.'

Macro laughed, and patted Cato on the back. 'Not to you, Cato. Not to you. Ask me for anything else, but not that.'

'All right, then. Get me out of here.'

'I can't.' Macro looked away, towards the river. 'Sorry. Want me to find you some decent food? Wine?'

'I'm not hungry.'

'Eat something. It'll settle your guts.'

'I'm not fucking hungry!' Cato snapped and regretted it at once, knowing that Macro had only meant to offer him some comfort before the next dawn. It wasn't Macro's fault, and in a moment of intuitive under-standing he realised that Macro would have had to screw up his moral courage to come and speak to his condemned friend. It was never going to be an easy discussion. Cato looked up. 'Could use a flask of good wine, though.'

'That's the spirit!' Macro clapped him on the back, and rose wearily to his feet. 'I'll see what I can do.'

Macro started to stride away from the condemned men.

'Macro!' Cato called after him, and the veteran looked back over his shoulder. Cato stared at him briefly, his tormented mind churning with dreadful fears. 'Thanks.'

Macro frowned and then nodded before he turned away and marched off. Cato watched him for a moment and then cast his eyes around, taking in the change of guards at the entrance to the Second Legion's camp. The daily routine of army life continued as before, a routine that had locked him in its harsh embrace for nearly two years now and made him a man. Now that same army had cast him out and, at dawn tomorrow, it would kill him. The sentries changed over and the watch-keeping slate was passed to the centurion coming on duty. Cato envied them the endless routine that would keep them occupied throughout the day, while he simply sat on the ground, a prisoner to his thoughts, waiting for it all to end.

The guards on the gate suddenly snapped to attention as a mounted figure emerged from inside the camp. As the horseman emerged into the bright orange glow of the rising sun, Cato saw that it was the legate. He rode down the side of the camp towards the men of the Third Cohort, who were toiling to excavate their defences. Vespasian glanced at them as he passed by. Then, as he reached the huddled forms of the condemned men, under the guard of two legionaries, the legate fixed his gaze straight ahead and spurred his horse into a trot. A few of the condemned men propped themselves up to watch their commander. They were no longer bound by military discipline now that the legion had disowned them. Yesterday they would have jumped to their feet and stood to attention, saluting as he passed. Today they were criminals, as good as dead, and any display of respect towards the legate would simply be insulting to him.

That's the difference a day makes, Cato thought wryly. For the condemned men at least. Vespasian was free to live his privileged life out to the end, and a few days from now no doubt would have forgotten that Cato and his companions had ever existed. For a moment Cato indulged himself in a wave of bitter contempt for Vespasian, a man he had served loyally and come to admire. So this was how his good service was rewarded. Vespasian, it seemed, was not so very different from the rest of the self-serving class of aristocrats who led the legions. After a show of opposition to Plautius last night he had caved in at the merest hint of a threat to himself, and meekly gone along with the decimation of his men.

Sickened by the sight of the man, Cato spat on the ground. He stared hard at the back of the legate as he rode down the track towards the crossing, heading towards the camp of the general on the far side of the Tamesis.

'Well, Legate, what can I do for you?' Aulus Plautius looked up from his desk and greeted him with a smile. With Narcissus no longer shadowing him the general felt a burden had been lifted from his shoulders. He was free to continue with the campaign, and in a few more months these lands and their unruly tribesmen would be under his control. The army could then take time to consolidate the territory wrested from Caratacus and his dwindling band of allies. The legions could rest and re-equip over the winter, and be ready for a much easier expansion of the province in the following campaign season. The future looked bright for the first time in weeks, and it was going to be a sunny day with a light, cooling breeze. What more could a man ask for? As a result, the general was feeling well disposed towards the world, and the smile stayed on his face as Vespasian saluted then eased himself down into the proffered seat on the other side of the general's desk.

'Can we talk in private, sir?'

The smile quickly faded from Plautius' lips. 'Is it important?'

'I think so.'

'Very well.' Plautius clicked his fingers, and the clerks working at small tables to one side of the tent looked round. The general nodded towards the entrance. 'Leave us. I'll send for you when I've finished with the legate.'

As soon as the last of the clerks had left the tent, Plautius leaned back in his chair and rested his chin on the knuckles of one hand. 'Well? What do you want?'

Vespasian had not been able to sleep the previous night and feared that his mind might be too dull for what lay ahead. He rubbed his chin as he quickly collected his thoughts.

'Sir, we can't execute those men.'

'Why not?'

'It isn't right. You know that as well as I do. They're not the only ones who didn't perform as well as they might during the battle.'

'You're implying what, exactly?'

'It didn't work out as you planned. Caratacus got away from you, and me. We were damn lucky to catch up with him before he could get the rest of his army over the river. Some people might say that we should be thanking my men for stalling them long enough to make that possible.'

'Really?' Plautius replied coolly. 'Some men might say that I let them off too lightly after they failed to hold their ground. Some might say that such a narrow front as they had to defend could have been held by a handful of men, provided they had the guts to do it.'

'My men aren't cowards,' Vespasian replied quietly.

'That's not what Maximius said.'

Vespasian paused. He had to be careful now. Maximius was a senior centurion, a man with a long service record, much of which he had spent in the Praetorian Guard. Such men were bound to have powerful friends and patrons in Rome, who would bear a grudge on his behalf. But whatever the risk for his future career, Vespasian felt compelled to act on his principles.

'Maximius may have exaggerated their lack of grit.'

'And why would he do that?'

'For the same reason that we want to go along with his version of events.'

'The reason being?'

'Self-preservation.' Vespasian mentally braced himself for a sharp retort, but the general remained still and silent, waiting for Vespasian to continue. 'Maximius was responsible for the failure of his cohort to reach the crossing in time to defend it properly. We both know that, sir.'

'Yes. And that's why he shares in their punishment. He could just as easily have been selected for decimation as any of his men.'

'True,' Vespasian acknowledged. 'But why should they share the blame for his mistake? If anyone has to be disciplined, let it be him alone. We can't let his men be punished for his failings. What kind of example does that set?'

'The kind of example that reminds the rest of the rabble that failure will not be tolerated in the legions under my command.' Plautius spoke with a quiet intensity. 'Whenever it is encountered I will act in a swift and merciless manner. You know the saying: "Let them hate, so long as they fear." In some ways, the fact that innocent men are going to their deaths makes the disciplinary lesson even more effective, don't you think?'

Vespasian stared back, feeling contempt well up inside. The general's attitude disgusted him. What had happened to Plautius? A year ago, Vespasian's appeal on moral grounds would have had its effect. Plautius had been hard, but had played fair with his officers and men. But now . . .?

'This is insupportable, and you know it,' Vespasian said firmly. 'Those men are being used as scapegoats.'

'Amongst other things, yes.'

'And you're prepared to use them in that way? To let them die to save your reputation?' Another line of argument suddenly occurred to Vespasian. 'One of the condemned men is Centurion Cato. Do you realise that?'

'I know,' the General nodded. 'I know that well enough. But it doesn't make any difference.'

'Doesn't make any difference?' Vespasian could not hide his astonishment, or his anger. 'You know his record well enough. We can't afford to throw away men of his calibre.'

'Then what would you have me do?' Plautius looked up. 'What if I spared him now? What if he was allowed to live while his men were executed? Just think how that would look to the rest. One rule for them, another for centurions. We've had a mutiny in this army already. How many officers lost their lives in that one? Do you really think we'd survive another? If the rankers die, then Cato must die with them.'

'So spare them all!'

'And look like a squeamish weakling?' Plautius shook his head. 'I think not, Vespasian. You must see that. If I condemn men one day and pardon them the next it'll be the first step down the road to completely losing our authority over our soldiers. And not just them – the plebs as well. Fear is what holds them all in check, and what better way of focusing their minds on blind obedience than fear of punishment, even if they are quite blameless? That's how it works, Vespasian. That's how it has always worked. That's why our class rules Rome . . . But I forgot,' Plautius smiled. 'You're one of the new men. You and your brother. In time, when you've grown used to wearing the broad stripe, you'll fully understand what I mean.'

'I understand it well enough right now,' Vespasian replied, 'and it disgusts me.'

'It goes with the rank. Get used to it.'

'Rank?' Vespasian chuckled bitterly. 'Oh, it's rank all right.'

He felt a weariness that went beyond tired muscles, a weariness that sapped his very soul. He had been raised by a father for whom Rome and everything it stood for represented the best of all worlds. It was his father's legacy to inspire the same devotion to duty and service to Rome in his two sons. Ever since Vespasian had embarked on a political career, little by little that faith had been chipped away, as a sculptor strikes away shards of stone. But what remained was no proud monument, merely a shrine to selfishness, steeped in the blood of those who were sacrificed, not for the greater good, but for the narrow self-interest of a select circle of cynical cold-blooded aristocrats.

'Enough!' Plautius slapped a hand down on the desk, making the slates jump and rattle. 'You forget yourself, Legate! Now hear me.'

For an instant both men stared across the table at each other with an implacable sense of estrangement, and Vespasian knew he had lost. Not only the attempt to save the lives of his men, but also any admission to the higher reaches of society in Rome. He lacked the necessary ruthlessness. The general's brow creased with anger as he addressed his subordinate.

'Hear me. There will be no pardon. The men will die, and by their deaths they will serve as an example to their comrades. That is an end to it. I will not tolerate any further discussion of the matter. Never mention this to me again. Do I make myself clear?'

'Yes, sir.'

'Then the execution will take place at dawn tomorrow. In front of the First Cohorts of all four legions. Find out who amongst your men are the closest friends and companions of the condemned. They will be the executioners. If any one of them demurs or protests in any way then they will be crucified, the moment the executions have concluded.' Plautius eased himself back and took a deep breath through his nose. 'Now, you have your orders, Legate. You are dismissed.'

Vespasian rose stiffly to his feet and saluted. Before he turned away from the general, he was tempted to try one last time – one final appeal to justice and reason, despite everything that had been said. Then he saw the deathly cold glint of iron resolve in Plautius' eyes and he knew that, worse than a waste of time, it would be positively dangerous to breathe another word.

So he turned and marched out of the tent, into the fresh air, as fast as the decorum of his ill-fitting rank allowed.

Chapter Twenty

There was a cool shaded patch of grass under one of the willow trees growing along the river bank, and Macro rustled through the thin flowing branches and sat down heavily. He had left his optio, Publius Sentius, to oversee the men as they set up their tents. Centurion Felix had suggested that the officers go for a swim in the river, but despite the glaring heat of the day neither Macro nor any of the others had felt it appropriate with their condemned comrades sitting in full view. Maximius had busied himself with every aspect of setting up a separate camp; anything to give the impression of a stoic professional continuing with his duties, whatever the circumstances. But whatever efforts he had driven the men to since dawn, they still moved with a heavy lethargy that made no secret of their mood. The Third Cohort was in the depths of gloom and the silent and still presence of those men awaiting execution loomed over them. Particularly those who had been detailed to carry out the execution: twenty men, under the command of Centurion Macro.

When the legate had given the orders, Macro had immediately refused, horrified by the prospect of clubbing his friend Cato to death.

'It's an order, Centurion,' the legate had said firmly. 'You can't refuse. That's not an option.'

'Why me, sir?'

'Orders.' Vespasian looked up sadly. 'Just make sure he doesn't suffer for too long . . . understand?'

Macro nodded. A sharp heavy blow to the head should render Cato unconscious and save him the agonies of having his bones shattered and crushed. The very thought of it made Macro's stomach tighten uncomfortably.

'And the rest of the lads, sir?'

'No. Just Cato. We go easy on the men and the general will simply stop it and get someone else to finish the job.'

'I see.' Macro nodded. If there was any real chance of being merciful to all of the condemned men he would have taken it without hesitation. But the legate was right: they could get away with only one small act of mercy.

'It's a bad situation, Centurion. For all of us. But at least this way Cato is spared the worst.'

'Yes, sir.'

'Now go and select the men for the execution party.'

Macro had saluted quickly and bowed out of the tent, glad to get back outside and breathe the clean, pure air into his lungs. He had never before been asked to do anything that so revolted against his notions of what was right and wrong. An image of Cato, bound and kneeling at his feet, flashed through Macro's mind. The lad raised his eyes to meet his friend's as Macro raised his club . . . His blood chilled at the thought, and Macro slapped his fist against his thigh and marched back to the camp of the Third Cohort.

The men he selected were mostly from Cato's century, burly veterans who could be counted on not to flinch from the dreadful duty they had been ordered to perform. Even now they were busy preparing the pick handles they would use. The wood had to be of the right length and weight to ensure that the blows could be delivered with sufficient force to do mortal damage. The men went about their work pragmatically enough and Macro, veteran as he was, could not help wondering at the casual way they bent to the task as if it were no different to any other duty asked of them. He had been hanging around Cato for too long, he decided with a grim smile. Before the lad had turned up Macro had never questioned any aspect of army life. But now he was beginning to see things with fresh eyes and it discomforted him. Perhaps, after Cato was dead and cremated, he could get on with life. Slip back into the easy oblivion of carrying out duties and ducking the bigger questions in life.

Dead and cremated . . .

Someone as sharp and lively as Cato? It wasn't right, thought Macro. It just wasn't right. The legate must be mad to carry this through. Mad, perhaps, and cowardly, insofar as he had off-loaded the dirty work on to Macro, and Macro would never forgive him for that.

'Shit!' he muttered. He was angry at the legate, and angry with himself for ever befriending Cato in the first place. Macro snapped off a length of branch, and methodically began to strip the leaves away from the slender stem of willow. On the far side of the Tamesis a party of men from the other legions were stripping off their tunics and wading into the water. The brown tan of their faces, arms and legs contrasted sharply with the gleaming whiteness of torsos and thighs. Their cries of shock at the coldness of the water, and the whooping and laughter of horseplay as they splashed each other, carried flatly across the surface of the water. It made Macro angrier still, and he glanced over them to where the men of the auxiliary cohorts were filling in the last of the funeral pits, piled high with the heat-ripened dead. The cold and dead existing side by side with the vital lives of the young and carefree. Macro tore off another strip of willow branch and shredded its leaves furiously.

Then he was aware of someone walking down to the river bank about fifty paces upstream. The huge frame of Figulus squatted down in the grass, a length of straw tilting from the Gaul's lips as he gazed into the river. Figulus slowly looked round and then fixed on the centurion sitting beneath the willow, and he rose to his feet, hesitated a moment and then walked towards Macro.

'Shit,' the centurion whispered to himself.

Macro was tempted to tell Figulus to get lost. He had come down to the river to get some time to think things through alone, and the prospect of talking to the optio made his heart feel leaden. Then he realised that Figulus too must be dreading Cato's fate. Macro relented and made himself smile as Figulus approached him. The optio stiffened and saluted.

'It's all right, lad. We're off duty for the moment. You can drop the bullshit.'

'Yes, sir.' Figulus hovered back, a few paces outside the thin curtain of leafy tendrils.

Macro sighed. 'You got something you want to say to me?'

The optio lowered his head a little and nodded.

'Out with it then.'

'Yes, sir.'

'And do sit down in the shade, before the sun boils your tiny brain.'

'Yes, sir.'

Figulus raised a thickly muscled arm and swept the leaves aside, blotting out the sun as he towered over Macro for an instant, and then squatted down, keeping a respectful pace away from his superior.

'Well?'

Figulus looked up sharply, his straw eyebrows coming together in a frustrated expression. 'It's Centurion Cato, sir. They've no right to do this to him. It ain't fucking fair. Pardon my language, sir.'

Macro looked at him sidelong. 'Yes, you want to watch that. Doesn't become an officer at all.'

'Sorry, sir.' Figulus nodded seriously. 'Won't happen again.'

'See that it fucking doesn't, then.'

Figulus looked startled for a moment, then Macro relaxed his stern expression and grinned. 'Just taking the piss, lad.'

'Oh, right . . .'

Macro's smile faded. 'As far as Cato goes, I'm afraid there's nothing we can do. Nothing. Orders is orders. You'll have to get used to that now that you're acting centurion. How's it going?'

Figulus shrugged unhappily, and reached out for one of the strands of willow before he realised that Macro was idly stripping a branch. His hand froze, and then dropped back to his side as he decided that it would be bad form to be seen to be aping his superior so openly. So his fingers scrabbled for one of the pebbles that lay in the loose, dry earth where the bank crumbled into the slow current. He tossed it in his hand and then threw the stone out over the river, where a small explosion in the glassy surface marked its fall. He watched the ripples fade before he spoke again without turning to Macro.

126

'There must be something we can do about it, sir.'

'Like what?'

'We go and see the legate.'

Macro shook his head. 'I'm telling you, he won't change his mind.'

'The general then.'

'He definitely won't listen. Plautius would probably throw us in with them if we so much as breathed a word of protest in his hearing. Besides,' Macro shrugged, 'what could we say? That it's not fair? That's not going to work. Our unit fucked up, and in a way that looked awfully like we didn't have the balls to do the job. Nobody's going to let the Third Cohort off the hook.'

'But we didn't run. Maximius ordered us to fall back. He's the reason we never made it to the ford in time in the first place. He should be taking the blame, not Cato and all the rest, sir.'

Macro twisted towards the optio. 'You think I don't know that? You think I don't give a shit about them? I'm telling you, Figulus, the whole bloody legion knows the score. I'd be surprised if the whole army didn't. But someone has to pay the price for this almightly balls-up and fate has gone and picked on Cato. It ain't fair, you're right there. It's just bad luck. Sticks in my gut just as much as yours.'

Both men turned to watch the figures swimming on the far side of the river, then Macro idly started to doodle in the dust with the end of the length of branch he had stripped. He cleared his throat. 'But you're right. Someone should do something about it . . .'

As a cool dusk settled over the land Cato found himself shivering. His head ached badly. He and the others had been forced to sit in the blazing sun all through the day and now the exposed parts of his skin felt tight and tingled painfully. Only as the day had ended had the sky become overcast and the air filled with a clammy closeness that threatened rain. Cato took this as a further sign that the gods had wholly abandoned him: tormented by the sun during the day and cold and wet by night.

One of the camp slaves had brought a few canteens of water up from the river and each man had been permitted a few mouthfuls to wet their dried throats. But there had been no food. When rations were in short supply condemned men were the first to go without. It made sense, Cato told himself. It was the logical thing to do.

About the only logical thing to be happening in the present circumstances. The fact that he had done nothing to merit tomorrow's punishment was tormenting him more than any other thought. He had faced the enemy in battle, when a moment's carelessness would have seen him dead. He had undertaken a perilous quest to find and snatch the general's family from the heart of a druid stronghold. He had risked being burned alive to save Macro in that village in Germania nearly two years ago. Every one of those actions had been fraught with terrible risks, and he had entered into them knowing and accepting the danger. To have been killed at any of those times would have been a reasonable consequence of the dangers he had exposed himself to. That was the price paid by men of his profession.

But this? This cold-blooded execution designed to act as an example to the other legionaries? An example of what, precisely? An example of what happens to cowards. But he was no coward. To be sure he had been afraid more times than he would care to admit – terrified, even. That he had continued to fight on, despite such terror, was a kind of courage, he reflected earnestly. Courage, yes.

The fight at the crossing had been no exception. He had fought with the same will, driven by the same desire to be seen in the front rank, fighting alongside the rest of his men. No shirking behind the rear of the line, bellowing out weasel words of encouragement, and savage threats to those whose flinching cowardice was not protected by rank. To be singled out for execution, for a crime he had no part in, by something as blind and heedless of his virtues as a lottery, was the worst fate he could imagine.

The first raindrops pricked lightly at his skin and then pattered on the grass around him. A chill breeze stirred the long grass, and rustled the leafy boughs of the trees along the river bank. The young centurion eased himself over on to his side and curled into a ball to try to keep warm. The leather thongs binding his wrists and ankles had rubbed the flesh raw so that every movement was painful. He tried to keep still, and closed his eyes, even though this was his last night in this world. Cato had often thought that imminent death would make him want to be aware of even the smallest detail around him, to seize each last measure of delight in life.

'Seize the day,' he muttered, and then gave a small bitter laugh. 'Bollocks.'

There was no poignant appreciation of the world on his senses, no thrill of life, just a smouldering anger at the injustice of it all, and a hatred for Centurion Maximius so intense that he could feel it burning through his veins. Maximius would live on, free to redeem himself eventually for his failure at the river crossing, while Cato would be ferried across an altogether different river, never to return, never to prove himself innocent of the charge for which he was being executed.

As night fell, and the rhythms of rain and wind continued unabated, Cato lay on the ground, shivering miserably as he succumbed to wave upon wave of depressing thoughts and images. Around him, most of the other prisoners were equally silent. A few others talked in quiet, subdued tones, and one man suffered occasional states of tearful delirium after the sun had got to work on his shredded nerves during the afternoon. Every so often he would call out for his mother, and slowly subside in a choking babble. Further off Cato could detect that the rest of the Third Cohort was subdued, quietly sheltering in their tents. The only sounds of happiness drifted over the rampart of the Second Legion's camp; the odd cries of triumph or disappointment from men playing dice, some faint chorused refrains from songs, and the shouted challenges from men on sentry duty. A hundred paces, and a world away.

Overhead, through a break in the clouds, the stars pricked out of a velvet moonless sky, reminding him of his paltry insignificance when measured against the scale of the world about him. He had almost come to some kind of acceptance of his fate when the first watch was changed. A quick blast of trumpets from the legion's camp marked the passing of the second hour of the night and the two legionaries assigned to guard the condemned men waited impatiently to be relieved. The rain pattered off their helmets as they pulled greased cloaks tightly about their shoulders.

'They're late,' one of them growled. 'Who's it supposed to be again?'

'Fabius Afer and Nipius Kaeso, new boys.'

'Fucking recruits,' the first man spat on the ground. 'Can't move for recruits these days. Bastards don't know their arses from their elbows.'

'Right enough, Vassus. Someone should give 'em a good kicking. Wasn't for them pansies the bloody cohort wouldn't be in this mess.'

'Yeah, a good kicking's what they need. Look, here they come.'

Two figures emerged from the darkness and the sound of their boots swishing through the grass could just be heard above the wind and rain.

'What the fuck kept you?'

'The shits!' a voice cried back, and there was a short laugh from his companion as they strode up to relieve their comrades.

'Hang on,' Vassus muttered, squinting at the looming shapes. 'There's no way that big one's Kaeso or Afer. Who's that?'

'Change of detail!'

'Who is it?'

Vassus was leaning his helmet forward to inspect the new arrivals when a fist shot out of the darkness and connected with his jaw with a loud crack. There was a blinding flash of light in his skull and then he collapsed to the ground, unconscious.

'What the . . .? It's Fig—' His friend's hand instantly dropped to grasp the handle of his sword, but before it had rasped more than a hand's breadth from its scabbard he too was felled, thudding to the ground with a grunt of exhaled air.

'Ouch!' Figulus whispered as he shook his hand. 'Bugger's got a jaw like a rock.'

'Certainly dropped like one.' Macro set down a large sack, and there was a dull clatter of metal from within. 'I'd hate to be on the receiving end of your fist.'

Figulus chuckled. 'Just like those shits we dropped outside the quartermaster's tent.'

'Right. Very funny. But this one recognised you. You know what that means?'

'I know, sir. Can we get on with it?'

129

'Yes . . . Cato!' Macro called out softly. 'Cato! Where are you?'

Several of the prone figures on the ground had wriggled upright as they realised something out of the ordinary was going on. A ripple of nervous excitement spread through the prisoners, voices muttered anxiously.

'Quiet there!' Macro whispered as loud as he dared. 'That's better . . . Cato!'

'Here! Over here!'

'Keep it down, lad!' Macro picked his way over towards the voice and squinted his eyes to see the unmistakably tall and thin frame of his friend. 'Want the whole bloody world to hear? Provosts will be down on us like a shot.'

'What are you doing here?' Cato sounded astonished.

'Can't you guess? You and the rest of this lot are going to escape. With Figulus.'

'Figulus?'

'He was seen by the sentries. He has to go with you. You're going to make a run for it. You and any others who want to get out of here.'

'Make a run for it?' Cato whispered. 'Are you mad?'

'As a March hare. But then so are the twats who put you here. So we're quits.' Macro drew his dagger. 'Get your hands up where I can reach 'em. Don't want to go and cut your wrist.'

Cato at once raised his arms, paused, then lowered them again. 'No.'

'What?' Macro replied loudly, provoking an angry hiss from Figulus, who was bent over another of the prisoners, carefully sawing through their bonds. Desperate figures clustered round the optio, tied arms raised up to him.

Cato shook his head. 'I said no. You can't do this, Macro. What if they find out you helped us escape?'

'Helped? I did a little more than that, I think.'

'You'll never get away with it.'

'Just give me your hands.'

'No. Think about it. Where would we go? What happens to you if we get recaptured, and they make someone talk? They'd kill you too. Leave us, while you've got a chance.'

Macro shook his head. 'Too late for that. Now get your hands up.'

Cato reluctantly did as he was told, and Macro grabbed his wrists, fingers groping for the thongs. He found them, carefully slipped the tip of the blade underneath and began to saw at it. Moments later the thongs parted and Cato rubbed his wrists.

'Here. Take the knife and get busy cutting the others loose. You've got to get out of here.'

'And go where?'

'As far from here as possible. Somewhere you can't be found.'

'And then?'

'Fuck knows.'

130

'How far do you think a handful of unarmed men are going to get?'

'Not unarmed.' Macro shook the sack. 'I've got you some blades. Enough to go round.'

Cato looked up from cutting the bonds around his ankles. 'That's your plan?'

'You got a better one? It's that or you stay here and die in the morning.'

'Some choice.' Cato shook his head. Execution tomorrow, or inevitable death at the hands of search parties, or the enemy? The situation had not got much better in the last few moments, and now Figulus would join the list of the condemned. Macro too, if his part in this was discovered. The thongs around his ankles parted and Cato rubbed his skin vigorously.

'What now?'

'Head west. To the marshes. It's your only chance.'

Chapter Twenty-One

Macro told the men to stay down and keep still while he and Figulus cut their bonds. The legionaries rubbed their ankles and wrists, painfully flexing limbs as they waited. All the time they glanced round anxiously for any sign that their escape attempt had been discovered. The centurion handed each man a sword or dagger from the sack of weapons, until he had run out. The man who had been raving just lay on the ground after he had been cut loose. He refused to accept the sword Macro offered him.

'Take it!' Macro whispered fiercely. 'Pick the bloody thing up! You'll need it.'

The legionary turned away, curled into a ball, and started moaning, rising to a shrill keening sound. Macro quickly looked over his shoulder towards the glistening lines of tents, but there was no movement there. He turned back to the man on the ground and savagely swung his boot between the legionary's shoulder blades. The man stiffened and cried out. At once Macro kneeled over him, snatching up the sword that lay on the muddy ground. He pressed the tip into the flesh under the man's chin.

'Shut it! One more sound and it'll be the last thing you do.'

The legionary jerked his head back, eyes wide with panic as his hands scrabbled for purchase on the ground as he tried to get away from Macro.

'Keep still, you little shit!' the centurion hissed furiously. 'Keep still!'

'Leave him, sir!' Cato whispered. 'Just leave him.'

Macro glared at the man for a moment and then eased himself up into a standing position, turning towards Cato. 'He can't be left behind. He might tell them that I was involved. You'll have to take him.'

Cato nodded, and Macro quietly sheathed his sword. 'Get him up then.'

'Sir, you'd better get out of here.'

'As soon as you're away. Come on, let's head for the palisade.'

'But that'll bring us out opposite the main camp.'

'Better than having to pick your way across our tent lines. You're bound to be noticed, especially with this worthless piece of shit.' Macro jabbed his toe into the man whimpering at their feet. Cato looked down and for a moment took pity on the man racked by terror. He reached over and gently shook the legionary's shoulder.

'What's your name, soldier?'

The man turned his head towards the voice and Cato caught a dim glimpse of jagged teeth in a coarsely shaped mouth. 'Proculus . . . Proculus Secundus.'

'You call me "sir" when we talk, Proculus. Understand?'

'Y-yes, sir.'

'You have to get on your feet.' Cato spoke in a low voice, trying to inject as much iron into his words as possible. 'We're not leaving anyone behind to die. Now, up.'

He firmly pulled the man's forearm and helped him to his feet, handing Proculus the sword Macro had dropped by his side a moment ago. 'There. Now hold it steady . . . Better?'

'Yes, sir. I guess so.'

'Good.' Cato patted the heavily muscled shoulder. 'Now let's go.'

The newly liberated men rose up from the ground and followed Macro as the centurion padded over the ground towards the rampart. Cato glanced left and right, but saw no sign of anyone along the length of the small rampart. He tapped Macro and whispered. 'Where's—'

'Out for the count. There.' Macro pointed out a small bundle lying close to the base of the rampart. 'You should be able to get over the palisade and ditch without anyone noticing. Anyone in this camp, at least.'

They crept up the inner slope and when they reached the short wooden stakes driven into the top of the earth rampart Macro turned and waved his hand down. There was a short, almost silent commotion as the men stumbled into each other, then Macro turned back to the palisade. Grasping one of the stakes in both hands, he worked it forward and backwards, while the veins bulged on his neck. At last, with a soft tearing sound, he ripped the stake out of the compacted turf. The second stake came out quickly and was gently lowered to the ground alongside the first. Cato glanced round anxiously, wiping the rain from his brow as he scanned the lines of tents for any sign of alarm. But the legionaries of the Third Cohort slept on, quite oblivious to the escape attempt of the condemned men. The next stake came out and there was a gap large enough for a man to squeeze through. Cato turned and sought out the looming hulk of Figulus.

'Optio, you first. Get down into the ditch and head towards the corner of the camp. Stay low.'

Figulus nodded, and then eased himself through the gap, dropping at once on to his stomach and crawling down the steep incline into the defence ditch. Cato thrust the next man forward, and one by one they crept through and down, and then spread out along the ditch. Cato was the last man to leave. He turned towards Macro and they clasped hands clumsily. Cato realised that there was every chance that he would not live to see his friend again, and the thought of not having the reassuringly powerful and weathered figure of Macro at his side filled him with anxiety. But he had to be strong. Whatever future this small band of fugitives had, they would

133

be depending upon him. Cato forced himself to smile at the dark, glistening features squatting opposite.

'Thank you, sir.'

Macro nodded, and then gently thrust Cato into the gap. 'Get going. You must be as far away from here as possible before they discover you've escaped.'

'Right.'

Cato slithered down the muddy slope. He glanced back at the palisade, but Macro had gone. Cato eased himself forward and crawled along the line of men lying in the ditch, smeared with mud. All around them the rain hissed into the grass and drops struck the water pooling in the ditch with tiny explosions. At length Cato drew up alongside Figulus and pointed towards the corner of the cohort's fortifications. With the centurion in the lead the condemned men slithered along. When Cato reached the corner he slowly raised his head and looked around carefully, straining his eyes to pick up any signs of the sentries on the walls of the main camp. A few indistinct shapes moved slowly along the ramparts, but he felt sure that it was dark enough that they would not be detected if they moved slowly and carefully. The only danger was Proculus. The man might well panic and give his comrades away. Cato glanced over his shoulder at Figulus.

'We'll head out this way. The grass is long enough to give us some cover. Pass the word for everyone to follow me and stay low.'

'Yes, sir.'

'I want you to stick with Proculus.' Cato lowered his voice so that there was no chance the other men would hear him. 'If he panics, silence him.'

'Silence him?'

'Do whatever you have to. Understand?'

'Yes, sir.'

Cato turned away, took a last look along the ramparts, then fixed his gaze on the large copse of oak trees he had noticed earlier in the day when foraging parties had set out to find firewood. Then he eased himself forward into the grass and slowly advanced on hands and knees, ears and eyes straining for any sign of danger. Behind him, the first of the legionaries emerged from the ditch and crept after him. One by one the condemned men followed on as stealthily as possible, hearts pounding. Figulus brought up the rear, thrusting Proculus ahead of him. The latter was terrified and stopped at the slightest threatening sound, dropping down to hug the earth in his trembling embrace before a swift prod from Figulus' swordpoint started him forward again.

Cato had covered nearly two-thirds of the distance to the copse when he paused and raised his head to look back towards the camp of the Second Legion. Still no alarm. He was about to move forward again when he sensed a vibration beneath his splayed fingers.

'Stop!' he hissed. 'Get down!'

The men stilled as the order was passed back and then Cato strained his ears to discover the source of the vibrations, growing ever stronger. Around him the rain pattered down steadily and the low wind made a faint roar in his ears as it ruffled the tips of the long blades of grass. Then a dark shape appeared around the edge of the copse they were making for. Another joined it, quickly followed by a steady stream of other shapes. The sound of a horse whinnying carried across the plain towards the men hiding in the grass. Cato eased himself down as he strained his eyes to pick out any detail. The horsemen suddenly altered course, seemingly heading directly towards Cato.

'Shit!' he hissed, hand instantly going to the handle of the sword he had stuck in his belt. Then he realised they couldn't have been spotted by the horsemen. It was far too dark for that. Nevertheless . . . 'Stay down! Pass it on. Stay down, but have your swords ready to hand. No one makes a move before I do.'

The legionaries flattened, hugging the earth, as the order was hurriedly whispered back down the thin column. Cato turned back towards the horsemen, no more than two hundred paces away. At least two squadrons of scouts, he calculated. More than enough to wipe them out. And still they came on, heading for the camp, wholly unaware of the presence of the escaped prisoners – for the next few moments at least, Cato thought bitterly, as he pressed himself down, his cheek juddering from the growing vibration as horses' hoofs pounded closer.

At the rear of the column Figulus thrust his hand forwards and grabbed a fold of Proculus' tunic.

'For fuck's sake! Stay down!'

'No! No. We must run. Run for it!'

Proculus started to rise up from the grass, kicking out at the arm that grasped his tunic. 'Let go!'

Figulus glanced at the approaching horsemen, and instinctively rose up behind Proculus. He threw himself forward, smothering the man as the two of them crashed back to the ground. The optio slammed the pommel of his sword into the side of the legionary's head and Proculus went limp at once. Figulus took no chances and lay across the inert body, sword poised at the man's throat as the horsemen rumbled towards them.

Almost at the last moment the column edged fractionally away from the men in the grass and began to pass down the side of the prone figures, no more than twenty feet away. Cato's head was turned to the side and he hardly breathed as he stared at the dark shapes of men huddled inside their cloaks as they urged their mounts back towards the promise of a dry tent and shelter from the rain and wind. The column pounded along, quite oblivious to the legionaries, yet it seemed to Cato that the last of the horsemen would never pass them. Just when he felt an almost over-whelming urge to rise up and throw himself upon the mounted scouts, the tail of the column galloped by. Cato watched the back of the last horseman,

135

watched him ride on towards the camp, and he drew a deep breath and released some of the tension that had wound his muscles up as tight as a quartermaster's purse. He waited until the end of the scout column was far enough away that he could not make out any details before he passed the word for his men to continue towards the copse.

It took the best part of an hour before Figulus joined the others crouching in the dark shadows beneath the dripping boughs of the oak trees. Proculus was conscious again, but groggy, and he made no protest as the optio thrust him towards the others. Cato looked back towards the fortress, but there was no sign that the alarm had been raised yet. By his reckoning they had no more than four hours under the cover of night: enough to put perhaps as much as ten miles between themselves and the first of the pursuers. The fringe of the marsh, as far as he could recall, was at least fifteen miles away. It would be a close thing.

And then what?

The perils and uncertainties of the future weighed down on Cato's heart like a sack of rocks. If they were caught by their own side, execution would follow swiftly, and a stoning, or being beaten to death would be the least of the agonies an angry General Plautius would visit on them. A slow, agonising death by crucifixion was more than likely. And if the enemy got to them first the Romans would be sure to suffer some barbaric torment: burning alive, flaying or being thrown to the dogs. And if they managed to evade both sides, then they would hide in the marshes, reduced to eating anything they could find or steal. A lingering starvation then, until winter killed them off.

For a moment Cato was tempted to turn round and accept the least terrible of these fates. But then he cursed himself for being a weak-minded fool. He was alive, and that was all that mattered. And he would cling on to life for all he was worth; for even the worst of lives was better than the endless oblivion of death. Cato had little faith in the afterlife vouchsafed by Mithras, the mysterious god from the east who had found so much secret favour with the men of the legions. Death was final and absolute, and the only thing that mattered was to defy its cold embrace until the very last breath whispered from his lungs.

Cato shrugged off his morbid reflections and stood up, his wet body trembling as the keen breeze bit into his flesh.

'On your feet!' he called out, and without waiting for the others to obey his order, the centurion turned away from the camp and struck out towards the gloomy haven of the marshes to the west.

Chapter Twenty-Two

Macro was wide awake when the alarm was sounded. He had not been able to sleep since he returned to his tent. That was something of a first for Macro, who, like most veterans, usually dropped into a deep sleep the moment his head hit the bolster. But the situation was far from usual. Cato was out there, with the most slender chance of survival, and Macro himself was in considerable danger. The moment the quartermaster's assistants were discovered bound and gagged in the equipment tent it would be clear that someone had aided the prisoners' escape. If they discovered his involvement then he would be standing in for the those who had been facing execution. There was little doubt in his mind about that. Rank and exemplary battle record notwithstanding, Macro would be killed.

Now the first faint tinge of light washed the sky a dull grey through the gap in his tent flaps. It was still raining, not as heavily as during the night, but still a steady tapping on the leather over his head and a wet rustling sound from outside. A shout sounded in the distance, calling the duty century to arms. A squad of men ran past his tent, dark silhouettes against the strengthening light, feet slithering and squelching in the mud.

Macro decided that he had better get outside and be seen to be responding to the alarm. His survival depended on him acting as if he was as surprised as the rest. He swung his feet over the side of the camp bed and reached for his boots. As his fingers closed on the well-seasoned leather he paused, let go of them and quickly ducked out of the tent.

'You!' He pointed to one of the men running past. 'What's all the bloody racket about?'

The legionary stopped, stood to attention, breathing heavily. 'The prisoners, sir.'

'What about 'em?'

'They've gone, sir. Escaped.'

'Bollocks! How could they?'

The legionary shrugged helplessly. He had no idea, and couldn't be expected to know the details.

Macro nodded. 'Very well then. Carry on.'

'Sir!' The legionary saluted, then turned back towards his standard, slowly being waved from side to side in the distance, above the ridges of the line of tents. Macro watched him go, noting the difficulty the man had

137

in making any speedy process over the glutinous mud that surrounded the tents. That was good. Anything that might slow down the pursuit of Cato and his men. Ducking back inside his tent Macro hurriedly laced on his boots and swept up his heavy cape. The folds of wool had only recently been greased and would keep most of the water out. Cato's men had no such comfort and would be shivering in the sodden tunics, he realised with a momentary pang of conscience. But there had been no time to grab anything more than the weapons, and that had been a big enough risk for him and Figulus to take. Cato would have to make do and be thankful that he was alive at least, Macro reflected as he strode off to join the men gathering around the standard.

Centurion Maximius came trotting up to join his officers, his cloak bundled under his arm.

'What's the alarm?'

Tullius, commanding the duty century, stiffened his back and stepped forward. 'Prisoners have escaped, sir.'

'Escaped?' Maximius was astonished. 'That's not possible. Show me.'

Tullius turned towards the open area where the prisoners had been held, and his men stumbled back to clear a path for the officers. They marched up to the holding area and approached the two sentries that Figulus had knocked out. They were sitting on the ground, drinking from the canteens of the men who had set them free.

'What the hell are you doing?' Maximius bawled out. 'On your bloody feet!'

The two men clambered up stiffly and stood to attention with the other legionaries as the officers strode up to them. The cohort commander ignored them at first, casting his gaze on the flattened grass where the prisoners had been held. He took three quick paces, bent down and snatched up some severed lengths of leather from the ground, then glanced at them closely before holding them up for the other officers to see.

'These have been cut.'

Macro swallowed and nodded. 'Someone must have given them a hand.'

'So it would seem.' Maximius turned back towards the two sentries. 'Vassus, what happened here?'

The older legionary stared straight ahead, not meeting the cohort commander's gaze.

'Well?' Maximius said quietly. 'Out with it.'

'Sir, me and the lad here, we were surprised. They jumped us out of the darkness, like.'

'They? How many were there?'

'Two, sir!' The younger sentry piped up. 'Bloody big they were too, sir.'

'Did you recognise them?'

'It was dark, sir . . .' the older man replied. 'Couldn't say for sure.'

His companion's eyes widened. 'We recognised one of them, sir. Figulus.'

'Optio Figulus?' The cohort commander scratched his jaw. 'Cato's optio. That makes some sort of sense. What about the other man?'

Macro forced himself to keep quite still as he waited for the veteran to reply.

'Didn't get a good look at him, sir. He was shorter than Figulus, but then most men are, sir.'

'I see.' Maximius looked round at Macro. 'I want a strength return for the entire cohort. Find out who else is missing. Now!'

Macro turned away and began to look for the cohort's trumpeter. As he expected, the man had joined the standard of the duty century and the broad arc of his bronze instrument was held ready in his grip. Macro strode up to him.

'Sound the assembly!'

As the deep notes blasted across the rows of tents, the remaining men of the cohort started to pile out into the daylight, and scrambled across the mud to join the ranks mustering along the inside of the rampart. The centurions formed up in front of their men while their optios carried out a quick head count. Macro took charge of Cato's century now that it had lost both its centurion and now its acting centurion.

A short time later the officers reported back to Maximius.

'Only Figulus missing? But the sentries said there were two.'

'Seeing double, perhaps?' Macro smiled. 'Under the influence.'

'Didn't look drunk to me,' Centurion Tullius muttered.

'No,' agreed Maximius. 'They weren't. So it looks as if one of the men who helped the prisoners escape stayed behind. He's still here.'

'Maybe not, sir,' said Macro. 'Could've been one of the slaves.'

'Yes . . . that's true. Send someone to do a head count of the slaves.'

While they waited Macro noticed that his superior was eyeing the coming dawn with an anxious expression. Then he realised why, and quickly glanced towards the main camp.

'Won't be long until the legate arrives.'

Maximius snorted and let out a bitter little laugh. 'The legate, the general and the first cohorts of each of the legions. We're going to be a laughing stock.'

'I doubt the legate will be laughing,' Centurion Tullius added. 'He's going to have our balls for breakfast.'

Macro nodded. 'If we're lucky.'

Just then the trumpets sounded from across the river, announcing the change of watch that marked the official opening of the day. An instant later a louder blast rang out from the Second Legion's trumpeters. Maximius and his officers exchanged nervous looks; the cohorts selected to witness punishment would be hurriedly pulling on their tunics and wriggling into their armour. Allowing time for them to form up and cross

139

the river and then take position on the open ground outside the ramparts of the Second Legion, Maximius and his men had little more than half an hour before the truth was out. Then the wrath of the senior officers in the army would crash down on them like an avalanche of granite.

'Legate approaching!' the optio on the main gate called out. 'Honour guard, stand to!'

Maximius' shoulders sagged. No reprieve then: he would have to face Vespasian now. For a moment Macro felt sorry for him, and a little bit ashamed for engineering the escape. But then he recalled that the cohort commander bore the sole responsibility for their disgrace and the condemning of Cato and the others to an undeserved death. Macro's expression hardened as a bitter contempt for the senior centurion clenched round his heart.

The optio on the gate shouted an order for it to be opened and then hurried down to take up position in front of the section that lined the route into the small camp. The timbers creaked as the gates were hauled inwards, and the legate and a few of his staff were visible as they rode up the muddy approach to the camp.

Maximius wiped his fringe to one side and blinked away some raindrops. 'Better get it over with. Come on.'

The centurions of the Third Cohort steadily picked their way over towards the gate, weighed down by a palpable sense of dread over the legate's reaction to the news of the condemned men's escape. Around them the rain fell in a desultory manner; just enough to make them miserably uncomfortable, complementing the gloomy mood nicely.

Vespasian ran a quick eye over the honour guard and nodded his satisfaction at the turnout. One or two spots of mud above their mud-caked boots, but that was acceptable. He turned to the optio.

'Very good. You can dismiss them now.'

'Sir!' The optio saluted, turned smartly towards his men and bawled out the order as if he was on the parade ground and not standing within easy earshot. The men stamped to attention and as soon as the formalities were completed they hurried away to find shelter.

The legate swung himself down from the saddle and landed softly. The five centurions pulled themselves up and pushed their shoulders back.

'Good morning, gentlemen. I trust all the preparations have been made.'

'Well, yes, sir . . .'

Vespasian sensed the man's hesitation at once. 'But?'

Macro glanced sidelong and saw Centurion Maximius roll his head helplessly. 'Sir, I regret to report that the prisoners have escaped.'

For a moment the legate froze, a frown etched on his broad forehead, then the horse turned its head and jerked the reins still held in his hand, breaking the spell.

'Escaped? How many?'

'All of them, sir,' Maximius replied with a flinch.

'All? That's bullshit, Centurion. How could all of them have escaped? They were under guard, weren't they?'

'Of course, sir.'

'So?'

'The guards were overpowered by some accomplices, sir. They tied 'em up, set the prisoners free and slipped out through the ramparts.'

'You've sent some men after them, I trust?'

Maximius shook his head faintly. 'Only just discovered it, sir. The alarm was raised at first light.'

The legate clenched a fist at his side. He shut his eyes tightly for an instant as he fought down the rage that had been provoked by the cohort commander's confession. Then: 'Don't you think it might be wise to send some men to look for them right now?'

'Yes, sir. At once, sir. Tullius, see to it immediately.'

As the centurion trotted off to carry out the order Vespasian clicked his fingers and beckoned to his senior tribune. The officer immediately slid down from his saddle and trotted over.

'Plinius, did that scout patrol have anything unusual to report?'

Tribune Plinius thought for a moment and then shook his head. 'No, sir. Nothing out of the ordinary.'

'Right, well, I want you to return to the camp and get them all back into the saddle. They're to sweep south, west and east of the river. If they find any of the deserters they must make every effort to bring them back alive to face punishment. If they resist, the scouts have my permission to kill them on the spot. Understand?'

'Yes, sir.'

'Then go and see to it.'

The tribune ran back to his horse, threw himself across its back and yanked the reins round, spurring his mount towards the main camp. The hoofs flung back thick gouts of mud at the legate and the centurions of the Third Cohort, and Macro flinched as a clod splattered on his cheek.

'Pardon me, sir.'

Macro glanced round and saw the man he had detailed to report on the number of men in the cohort's camp.

'Yes?'

'There's only one man unaccounted for. That's Optio Figulus. All the rest of the legionaries and slaves are here in the camp.'

'You're sure?' Macro raised his dark eyebrows.

'Yes, sir. That's not all. We found some of the quartermaster's assistants tied up in the equipment tent. Some weapons are missing, sir.'

'Very well, you can go.'

Macro swapped a quick look of dismay with Centurion Maximius.

'Problem, Centurion Macro?' asked Vespasian. 'That is to say, yet one more problem to add to the catalogue of cock-ups for this morning?'

Macro nodded. 'Yes, sir. It appears that only Figulus has deserted with the others. But our sentries claim that they were jumped by two men. Seems that the second man is still in the camp.'

'He'd better be found then,' Vespasian said quietly. 'I think that General Plautius will want someone's head in compensation. Rather this accomplice than one of your heads, wouldn't you agree, gentlemen?'

There was no reply to that and the centurions faced their legate with drained and despairing expressions. Behind them Tullius was leading a squad of men through the gap that had been torn in the palisade, and fully armed they slithered in an ungainly fashion down into the ditch on the far side and followed the marks left by the prisoners that led towards the corner of the camp.

Vespasian shook his head. 'This is a sorry state of affairs, Centurion Maximius. Not only are you in the deepest shit for this complete and utter balls-up, you've dragged me into it as well . . . Thanks.'

There was nothing Maximius could say. What use was an apology, and to even utter one would worsen the burden of shame that lay on his shoulders. So he stared mutely back at his legate until the latter wearily turned round and mounted his horse. Vespasian looked down at the centurions with a sneer on his lips.

'I'm going to break the news to the general, before he can march the cohorts from the other legions across the river to witness punishment. I somehow doubt that Aulus Plautius is going to take the bad news in his stride. You'd better make sure your affairs are in order.'

Vespasian swung his horse away, and urged it back through the gate and down the muddy track towards the main camp. His escort of staff officers set off after him. As they rounded the corner of the legion's camp a squadron of the mounted scouts came galloping the other way. They slewed round and rode along the gap between the two camps, towards the place where Tullius and his men were following the passage of the men through the long grass towards the copse of oak trees. A distant movement on a slight rise visible beyond the main camp drew Macro's eye and he saw the dark shapes of another squadron galloping up the slope, fanning out as they scouted the land to the west.

'We'd better hope they find Cato and the others quickly,' Centurion Felix muttered. 'Which direction do you think they've gone?'

'West,' Antonius said with certainty. 'Or south-west. It's the only direction that makes sense.'

'Right into the heart of enemy territory?' Felix shook his head. 'Are you mad?'

'Where else can they go? If they go east they'll be picked up by our lads at some point. If not, they'll be seen and reported by our allied tribes. West is their only chance. Besides, there's that bloody great marsh in that direction. Best place to hide out.'

'Bollocks! They'd be throwing themselves right into the hands of Caratacus, and you know what that lot do to any Romans they capture.'

'I still say it's their best chance,' Antonius said firmly, then turned to Macro. 'What do you reckon?'

Macro stared at him in silence, then made himself look casually towards the horsemen disappearing over the crest of the hill beyond the main camp. He cleared his throat, so as not to give away the terrible anxiety that gnawed away at him from inside. 'West. Like you say, it's their best chance. Their only chance.'

Felix sniffed his contempt at this judgement, and turned towards Maximius. 'What about you, sir. What do you think?'

'Think?' Maximius looked round with a distant expression, and frowned. 'What do I think? I think that it doesn't bloody matter what direction they've gone. The damage is done and we've all had it. Every officer in this cohort will have this on their record like a scar. That's what I think.'

He glared at the three centurions with a bitter curl of his lips. His eyes fixed on Macro last of all. 'I tell you what else I think. If I ever find out who helped those bastards to escape, then I'll have the cunt skinned alive. In fact, I'll do it myself.'

Chapter Twenty-Three

'We'll have to leave him,' Cato said quietly.

Figulus shook his head. 'We can't. If they catch him, they'll make him talk. And then they'll execute him.'

The optio paused and looked over his shoulder at the legionary sitting on a rock beside the stream, nursing his ankle. It was the same rock the man had fallen off a short while before; glistening and slippery in the rain. A too-hurried step and the exhausted soldier had tumbled over. The landing had wrenched his ankle so badly he had cried out in agony the moment he had attempted to put any weight back on the joint. There was no question of him continuing on foot. Daylight had found them little more than eight miles from the camp, by Cato's calculation, with the edge of the marsh still as much as six miles away. The legate would be sure to send out the scouts to hunt them down the instant there was enough light to track them by. They would have to run for it if they were to make good their escape. There was no way the injured man could be carried, not without slowing them down, at the risk of all their lives.

Cato fixed the optio with his eyes. 'We're not taking him with us. We can't afford to. He has to look after himself now, understand?'

'It's not right, sir,' Figulus replied. 'I'll not be party to his death.'

'He was dead anyway. You and Macro bought him a few more hours of life. I've made my decision, Optio. Now don't question my orders again.'

Figulus returned his gaze in silence for a moment. 'Orders? We're not soldiers any more, sir. We're deserters. What makes you think I have to obey—'

'Shut your mouth!' Cato snapped back at him. 'You'll do as I say, Optio! Whatever happens I'm still the ranking officer here. Don't you forget it, or I'll kill you where you stand.'

Figulus stared at him in astonishment, before he nodded. 'Yes, sir. Of course.'

Cato realised that his heart was beating wildly and his fists were clenched. He must look like a complete fool, he chided himself. Exhaustion and the dread of being caught and dragged back to the camp and executed had worn his nerves to shreds. He had to be strong if he was going to survive this ordeal, and bring these men through it with him. He already had a plan half formed in his mind, albeit one that was wildly ambitious and optimistic. But then men clinging on to life, as if from a precipitous cliff, are wont to embrace even the most unrealistic chance of salvation. The metaphor had jumped into Cato's mind and the idea that the hand of a god would pluck them all to safety almost made him laugh at himself with scorn. The temptation was almost irresistible and in that temptation he recognised the danger of a paralysing hysteria that would kill them all if he surrendered to it.

Cato rubbed his eyes and then squeezed his optio's shoulder. 'I'm sorry, Figulus. I owe my life to you and Macro. We all do. I'm sorry you've been dragged into this mess. You don't deserve it.'

'It's all right, sir. I understand,' Figulus smiled weakly. 'Truth is, I'm having a hard time coming to terms with it myself. If I'd known it'd work out like this . . . What are we going to do about him?'

'We'll leave him. He's a dead man, and he knows it. We just have to be certain he goes down fighting, or makes sure he isn't captured alive.' Cato straightened up, clearing his throat. 'You take the others on. I'll have a word with him and follow you.'

'A word?' Figulus looked at him sharply. 'Just a word, mind.'

'You don't trust me?'

'Trust a centurion? After ending up in this situation? Don't push your luck, sir.'

Cato smiled. 'I've been pushing it ever since I joined the legion. Fortune hasn't let me down yet.'

'There's a first time for everything, sir.'

'Maybe. Now get 'em moving. And keep up the pace.'

Figulus nodded. 'Same direction?'

Cato thought a moment and looked round at the landscape. 'No. Start heading south, towards that crest there. Once the last man is over it, and out of sight, turn back to the original direction. I'll explain later. Get going.'

While the optio rounded up the exhausted men sitting scattered in the long grass beside the stream, Cato went over to the injured man.

'You're one of Tullius' men, aren't you?'

The legionary looked up. His face was weathered, like old leather, and fringed with thinning grey curls. Cato guessed he must have been only a few years short of completing his enlistment. It was a harsh play of fate to have picked such a man out for execution.

'Yes, sir. Vibius Pollius.' The man saluted. He glanced round at the others, on their feet and already moving off. 'You're going to leave me behind, aren't you?'

Cato nodded slowly. 'Sorry. We can't afford to be slowed down. If there was any other way . . .'

'There ain't. I understand that, sir. No hard feelings.'

Cato squatted down on a nearby slab of rock that rose proud of the rushing stream.

'Look here, Pollius. There's no sign of any pursuit yet. If you go to ground and nurse that ankle, you might be able to find us later. You look like the kind of man I could use. Just keep out of sight until that leg's better. Then head south-west.'

'Thought we were going to hide in the marshes, sir.'

Cato shook his head. 'No. It's not safe. If we get caught by Caratacus' men they'll make the prospect of a quick execution look like a lucky break.'

They shared a quick smile before Cato continued, 'Figulus reckons our chances might be better if we look to the Dumnonians. Seems that some of them are related to Figulus' tribe back in Gaul. He knows a bit of their tongue and might talk 'em into taking us in. Just make sure that you mention his name if you come across any of their tribesmen.'

'I'll do that, sir. Soon as this leg gets better.' Pollius slapped his thigh.

Cato nodded thoughtfully. 'If it doesn't get better . . .'

'Then I'll have to join you next time round. Don't worry, sir. I won't let them take me alive. You have my word.'

'That's good enough for me, Pollius.' Cato slapped him on the shoulder, burning inside with shame at having deceived the unfortunate veteran. 'Just be sure that if they do take you alive, you don't breathe one word about where we're headed. Or Macro's part in this.'

Pollius drew the sword from his belt. 'This'll keep 'em off for a bit. If it doesn't, then I'll be sure to use it so they don't get a chance to make me talk, sir.'

Given that the man was facing an almost certain death, one way or another, Cato weighed his next words carefully. 'By all means defend yourself. But remember, the men who'll be sent to hunt us down will only be soldiers obeying orders. They're not the ones who forced us into this. Do you see what I mean?'

Pollius looked down at his sword, and nodded sadly. 'Never thought I'd ever have to turn this on myself. I always thought falling on your sword was a hobby of your senators and the like.'

'You must be going up in the world.'

'Not from where I'm sitting.'

'Right . . . I have to go now, Pollius.' Cato grasped the man's spare hand and squeezed it firmly. 'I'm sure I'll see you later. A few days from now.'

'Not if I see you first, sir.'

Cato laughed, then stood up and without another word he broke into a run, following Figulus and the others, already a short distance away. He glanced back once, just before the place they had crossed the stream disappeared from view behind a fold in the ground. Pollius had hauled himself up on to the bank above the stream and sat with the point of the sword stuck in the ground between his open legs. He rested both hands on the pommel, and then lowered his chin on to his hands and sat looking back the way they had come. Cato realised at that moment that his attempt

146

at deception had been unnecessary. Pollius was ready to die, and was determined to ensure that happened before he breathed one word that might betray his companions. Even so, Cato refused to deny the need for the extra insurance. Even the most honourable of men, with the most honourable of intentions, were sometimes caught unaware. Cato had seen enough of the handiwork of the Second Legion's torturers to know that only the most exceptional of men could deny them the information they sought. And Pollius was only a man at the end of the day.

The rain gradually subsided into a light drizzle as the morning wore on, but the gloomy overcast remained in place and denied the fugitives any warming ray of sunshine. Cato and Figulus drove them on, alternately running and then walking, mile by mile towards the distant marshes that offered the best chance of evading the inevitable patrols sent to hunt them down. The rain had washed off most of the mud from the night before but the men were still streaked with grime and reduced to shivering as the sweat chilled on them when they slowed to a walk. With no canteens the only chance to slake their thirst had been at the stream where they had left Pollius behind, and Cato found that his tongue felt increasingly big and tacky as the relentless pace continued. Despite their weariness, not one of the other men dropped out of line. There were no stragglers, since every man knew that death would be waiting on any who dropped out of the line of march. Cato was relieved at this, since he was certain that no amount of cajoling or physical punishment could lift a man who had reached the end of his endurance.

As he trotted on, breathing heavily, and fighting the stitch that stabbed at his side, Cato tried to keep some sense of the passing time. With no sun crossing the sky to mark the passage of the hours he could only roughly estimate their progess, so that it might have been close to noon when they crossed over a low ridge and beheld, barely a mile ahead, the fringe of the vast area of flat land that sprawled towards the distant horizon. The poor light lent the dismal vista an even more gloomy aspect, and the fugitives gazed down on the endless mix of reeds, narrow waterways and scattered hummocks of land, with their stunted trees and thick growths of hawthorn and gorse.

'Not very homely,' Figulus grunted.

Cato had to breathe deeply and compose himself before he could respond. 'No . . . but it's all we've got. We're going to have to get used to it for a while yet.'

'What then, sir?'

'Then?' Cato chuckled bitterly before he replied in an undertone, 'There probably won't be a then, Figulus. We'll be living from moment to moment, always in danger of being discovered by either side and ending up dead . . . unless we can win a reprieve.'

'Reprieve?' Figulus snorted. 'How's that going to happen, sir?'

'I'm not sure,' admitted Cato. 'Best not build the men's hopes up too soon. I'll tell you when I've had a chance to think things through in detail. Let's keep moving.'

Ahead on the slope the track forked, one arm bending left, round the edge of the marsh and quickly lost to view in the haze that hung over everything and merged with the patchwork of mist still clinging to the dampest dips and folds in the ground. The other fork followed a track less rutted and worn that led straight into the heart of the marsh.

'Keep to the right-hand path!' Cato shouted out as he dropped out of line and turned towards Figulus. 'Keep 'em moving. Don't let them rest until you are at least a quarter of a mile inside the marsh.'

'Yes, sir. Where are you going?'

'Just checking back over the hill; make sure we're not being followed. Keep a good look out for me. I don't fancy being lost in that marsh all on my own.'

Figulus smiled. 'See you later then, sir.'

They parted company, Figulus leading the bedraggled fugitives west towards the unwelcoming sprawl of the wetlands, Cato turning back towards the ridge they had just crossed. He was not sure why he felt he had to go back for one last look. Perhaps he was driven by the need to stop and think, to plan the next step. Perhaps he just needed a rest and one last look at the world before he was plunged into a life of concealment and terrible deprivation. Whatever the motive, he walked slowly back up the slope, heart heavy with the hopelessness of his situation. What if there was no hope of redemption? What if he was doomed to spend what remained of his life running in fear of his discovery and capture by his own people? Was such a life worth living? Even if they managed to survive being caught between what was left of Caratacus' army and the legions in the immediate future, the legions were bound to take control of the southern part of the island before the year was out. Then they would have ample time to search out and destroy any last settlements that dared to defy the rule of Rome. At some point the surviving fugitives were bound to be discovered and hauled off to a place of execution – however dimly the military authorities would recall their crime.

If that was to be his fate then Cato decided he would rather risk everything now in an attempt to win back the favour of General Plautius and Legate Vespasian, and the rescinding of his death sentence. The alternative was too awful to contemplate at any length, and he hoped that he would make the others realise that when the time came to outline his plan. He would call only for volunteers, since he no longer had the authority of the army to enforce his orders. Faith in his ability to command was all the authority Cato possessed now. Figulus had seen that at once, but at least the optio had the presence of mind to realise that some kind of order must be maintained if the small band of men were to survive, and that Cato was the best man to provide that order . . . for the present at least.

His mind was so preoccupied by thought of the future that Cato had reached the crest of the hill before he was aware of it, and found himself looking back across the drizzle-shrouded landscape they had hurriedly crossed shortly before.

He saw the scattered screen of cavalry at once, perhaps twenty men, stretched across the landscape with a gap of fifty paces between each horse. They were no more than two miles away, and heading at a tangent across the direction Cato and his band had taken. Cato dropped to the ground, heart beating with renewed pace as he waited to see if he had been spotted. He cursed himself for not approaching the skyline of the ridge in a far more cautious manner. Exhaustion was no excuse when it endangered the lives of his companions.

'Fool!' he muttered through clenched teeth. 'Bloody fool . . .'

As he watched there was no sign that the scouts had seen the distant figure of their prey. They must have been intent on scouring the ground directly in front of them for any sign of the fugitives' passage. Their progress was unhurried and they walked their horses across the gently rolling grassland, pausing only to search through each copse they encountered. On their current course Cato calculated that they would miss him by a wide margin and his strained nerves began to relax a little. He wondered if these men had encountered Pollius. Had the veteran raised a sword to his pursuers after all? Or had he heeded Cato's call to turn his weapon on himself rather than lash out at his former comrades? Perhaps he had decided to try to find some place of concealment and had been passed by. Cato found himself hoping that the man had been found and forced to divulge the false trail Cato had set for Pollius to pass on. The horsemen were certainly heading in that general direction.

When the nearest rider was no more than a mile away from him Cato saw a sudden flurry of movement halfway along the line of mounted men. One had dropped to the ground and was beckoning to his comrades. As word was passed each way along the line the men wheeled their mounts in and trotted towards the growing cluster of men and animals. Cato strained his eyes to try to see more clearly what was happening below him. Most of the men had dismounted and their officer was conferring with the man who had made the discovery. As he stared at them, Cato realised that these men were not legionary scouts. The cut of their capes and the kite shields slung across their backs showed that they were from an auxiliary cohort and a cold chill of realisation burst through Cato's veins as he picked out the dull gleam of a bear's head standard.

'Batavians . . .'

The ruthless Germanic tribe had provided General Plautius with a number of hard-fighting but reckless cohorts of cavalry. The Batavians had won a fearsome reputation at the crossing of the Mead Way a year earlier, and had promptly cut down every prisoner that came their way in a fit of bloodlust – one of several such fits, Cato recalled with a growing sense of dread. They would show no mercy to their prey if they came upon Cato and his men. The tensions between the men of the legions and the Batavians went way beyond the usual inter-unit rivalry that was to be found in most armies. Men had died when bands of off-duty Romans and Germans had clashed in Camulodunum.

The leader of the patrol strode clear of his men. He braced his shoulders and rubbed his stiff backside as he scanned the surrounding landscape. Cato instinctively pressed himself down as the man's face turned fully towards his position on the ridge. It was absurd, he reassured himself; no one could have seen him in that poor light and at that distance. The Batavian leader swung round and waved his arms. The men on the ground quickly mounted and formed a loose column as they waited for orders. Their leader swung himself across the back of his horse and pulled on the reins. With a wave of his arm the small column edged forwards and then broke into a steady trot. A moment later it was clear to Cato that they were heading almost directly towards him. He had no idea what they could have seen lying on the ground, but whatever it was the Batavians had correctly deduced the direction the fugitives had taken.

Cato scrambled back from the crest and as soon as he was sure it was safe he rose to his feet and turned to run back along the track towards the marsh. A half-mile ahead of him he could see the small figures of his comrades entering the faint mist that had begun to lie across the track. As he ran he frequently glanced down to make sure of his footing, and every so often he saw the unmistakable outline of a legionary boot imprinted in the mud. Those footprints would lead the Batavians straight to them – they were already doing so, Cato realised with a sickening feeling.

As if this bloody rain hadn't made life miserable enough for the Roman fugitives, it was now conspiring to point them out to the Batavians, and when the pursuers inevitably caught up with their prey they would butcher them without mercy.

Chapter Twenty-Four

General Plautius walked slowly across the area where the prisoners had been held, under the anxious gaze of his officers. Not only were the centurions of the Third Cohort present, but also Legate Vespasian, his senior tribunes, the Second's camp prefect, and the senior staff of the other three legions who had been expecting to attend an execution this morning. Only a few of them talked, in tones so muted that they were only just audible above the steady patter of raindrops. The rest watched the army's commander with fixed expressions as they huddled under the shelter of their cloaks. The heat from their bodies was making the fat used to waterproof the coats give off a thick musty smell that Vespasian had always found quite sickening. It reminded him of the mule tannery owned by his uncle in Reate. Vespasian recalled both the foul oily stench that hung over the steaming workshops and the oath he had taken never to enter into any business that had anything to do with the wretched animals.

Focusing his mind back on the present Vespasian glanced towards Maximius and the other officers of the Third Cohort. It was hard not to feel sorry for them – the other centurions. They had been poorly led and the harsh punishments that had befallen them had not been deserved. Maximius, despite his years of experience, just lacked the necessary moral fibre and cool-headedness required of a cohort commander. A classic example of overpromotion and the consequences that follow from the dangerous elevation of a man who was simply not up to the job. Vespasian bitterly regretted ever having accepted him into the Second Legion, and he wondered how many of the officers that stood beside the cohort commander would have their careers blighted by the events of the last few days. There were some good men there, the legate mused. Tullius was old and would complete his term of service in two years' time. But he had experience and a steady enough nerve, and would never let his comrades down. Centurion Macro was as dependable as they came, and was, in so many ways, the ideal centurion: brave, resourceful and tough as old leather. Unimaginative perhaps, but in a centurion that was a positive virtue. The other two Vespasian was less certain about. Only recently promoted, Antonius and Felix had excellent records and were highly commended for promotion to the centurionate by the Second's camp prefect. Remembering their stumbling performance in the disciplinary hearing Vespasian

151

wondered if Sextus had been bribed to recommend them. They had proved themselves as legionaries, but were they ready to prove themselves as centurions?

The missing officer, Centurion Cato, was the last of Maximius' men that Vespasian considered. He had deliberately put off thinking about the young man in the hope that General Plautius would have finished his inspection of the ground before Vespasian got round to thinking about Cato. Cato's career was over, and soon – very soon – his life would be over as well. That thought troubled Vespasian deeply, for he had quickly come to realise that there were few men of Cato's calibre in his legion, or indeed in any other legion. In the two years since the youngster had joined the Second, Vespasian had watched him mature into an officer with outstanding courage and intelligence. He made mistakes, for sure, but he learned from them every time, and knew how to get the best out of the men he commanded. Men like Cato, provided they lived long enough, were the brains and backbone of the professional army, and could expect to end their careers in one of the top jobs: chief centurion, camp prefect or, if they were truly exceptional, the prefecture of the legions in Egypt – the highest military post available to men outside the exclusive senatorial class in Rome.

Provided they weren't snuffed out by the fortunes of war, or the exigencies of Emperor Claudius' reputation-building first.

Vespasian caught a movement over by the rampart and looked up with a start. He had been so lost in thought that he had momentarily lost track of the general's movements and was surprised to see that he had reached the gap in the palisade. The legate told himself he would have to watch that. Letting his attention wander in the presence of superiors was a dangerous habit.

General Plautius bent down to look at the gap for a moment, then straightened up and leaned carefully over the palisade to inspect the ditch on the far side. At length he turned round slowly and paced back towards his officers.

Sextus leaned closer to his legate and growled in a low voice, 'Now we're for it.'

The general stopped several paces from the silent officers and let his eyes wander over them until they came to rest on Vespasian.

'Every single one?'

'Yes, sir.'

'And no sign of them?'

'Not yet, sir. But I've sent all my scouts and my Batavian mounted cohort out to look for the prisoners. They'll report as soon as they find anything.'

'I'd imagine they would,' Plautius replied with scything sarcasm. 'Otherwise there's not much point them being out in this weather, is there?'

'Er, no, sir.' Vespasian made himself steady his gaze, fighting off the temptation to glance down, or away from his commander. 'Not much.'

'So, forty-odd men just happened to escape without anyone in this camp, or the Second Legion's main camp, noticing. Strikes me as rather unlikely. Which implies two possibilities. Either your lookouts are as blind as Tiresias, or . . . the prisoners were permitted to escape. Either way, your men are responsible for this situation, Legate.'

Vespasian bowed his head a fraction. Plautius was being unfair. It had been a dark and rainy night and the men of his camp might well have missed movement from the rampart of the Third Cohort. That would sound like an excuse and Vespasian could well imagine the quiet sneers and sidelong glances that would greet such an explanation. He kept his mouth shut and met his general's gaze steadily.

'If my men are to be held to account, then since I am their commander, any fault is mine as much as theirs . . . sir.'

The general nodded. 'That's right, Legate. The question is, what am I to do about it? What would be a suitable punishment for you and your legion?'

Vespasian flushed with anger. He could see the direction Plautius was taking this and needed to act swiftly if he was to limit the damage to his legion. If the general wanted more blood then the morale of the Second would receive yet another blow. The disgrace of decimation already weighed heavily on their minds, but the fact that the punishment had been levied on the Third Cohort alone had allowed the rest of the legion to escape any significant damage to their hard-won reputation. A reputation that had been bought with the blood of their comrades, and a reputation that had been built on some spectacular feats of arms. As their commander, it was natural that Vespasian should bask in the reflected glow of his men's achievements. Yet his first thought was for his men – for how shamed they would feel to be the target of the general's wrath yet again. All thanks to the failures of Maximius and the Third Cohort. If Vespasian was to preserve what remained of his men's battle spirit then he would need to make a sacrifice.

'My legion does not deserve to be held accountable for the deeds of a disgraced cohort, sir. The Second has put in an outstanding performance on this campaign. They have fought like lions. You said it yourself, sir, only a few months back. Like lions. If any unit is to be punished, then let it be the cohort who permitted the prisoners to escape. Let the Third be held to blame, sir.'

General Plautius did not reply immediately, as he weighed up the legate's offer. At length the general nodded. 'Very well then, those who permitted their comrades to escape punishment will have to provide a replacement for each condemned man.'

Vespasian felt his heart begin to race as he listened. Surely he did not mean another round of decimation? What would the enemy make of that,

Vespasian wondered. Leave the Romans alone long enough and they would surely decimate themselves into oblivion and save everyone else the job.

'Sir,' Vespasian spoke as calmly as he could manage, 'we dare not decimate the Third Cohort again. They'd be finished as a fighting unit.'

'Maybe they should be finished,' Plautius replied. 'In which case a ruthless execution might encourage the others to fight on when the time comes, and not just turn and run away, like those scum. Perhaps after we've executed the next batch they might just provide the example I wanted for the rest of the army. Legate, this cohort has cost us the final victory over Caratacus. Their failure will cost us dear in coming months. Now this? How much more damage will they do to my army, and the reputation of your legion? Another decimation is the least they deserve.'

'Maybe not.' Vespasian's mind was racing ahead. It would be inhuman to subject these men to further punishment. Besides, they might yet serve some useful function. But they had to be seen to be punished, and punished harshly. He looked at his general with a sharp glint in his eyes. 'Maybe we can use them to lure the Britons out of that marsh. Use them as bait. It's dangerous, but then, as you said yourself, sir, they must be punished.'

'Bait?' General Plautius looked sceptical.

'Yes, sir.' Vespasian nodded eagerly, then realised that he would need to do more than enthusiastically offer up the obliteration of his Third Cohort in order to persuade Plautius to agree to the scheme he was only just starting to sketch out in his mind.

'Sir, will you come back to my headquarters so that we can discuss my plan in detail? I'll need to show you a map.'

'Plan?' Plautius replied suspiciously. 'If I didn't know better, I'd say that you were in on this escape. Better not be one of your hare-brained ideas, Legate.'

'No, sir. Not at all. I think you'll find it'll serve all our needs.'

Plautius thought for a moment, and Vespasian stood waiting, trying hard not to show any signs of the excitement and frustration that filled every muscle of his body with an unbearable tension.

'There you are, sir,' said Vespasian as he unrolled the sheepskin map across his campaign desk.

'Very nice,' Plautius replied coolly as he glanced down, and then looked up at the legate. 'Now would you explain what is so very interesting about this map?'

'Here.' Vespasian leaned forward and tapped his finger on an area to one side of the sprawling, virtually unmapped marsh.

'Yes . . . and that is?'

'It's a valley, sir. A small valley. A trader, one of our agents, came across it and sent a report back. I've had the scouts check on it, and the valley's there all right. There's a small village, scores of farms, and a track that leads through it before cutting right across the heart of the marsh.'

'All very interesting,' Plautius mused. 'But of what use is this to me? And what bearing does it have on the disposal of your Third Cohort?'

The legate paused. It all seemed quite obvious to him, but clearly the opportunity that had struck him so clearly had been missed by the general. His plan would have to be set out very tactfully so as not to cause any offence to Plautius.

'We're still after Caratacus, I presume, sir.'

'Of course.'

'And he's hiding out in that marsh. Probably has some kind of forward base concealed there.'

'Yes, we know all that, Vespasian. What of it?'

'Well, sir, we're not going to find that base very easily, if at all. Look at the mess we got into in the marshes by the Tamesis last summer, sir.'

Plautius frowned at the memory. The legions had been forced to break formation and enter the marshes in small units. Unfamiliar with the tracework of paths that weaved through the tangled and boggy undergrowth, several detachments had been roughly handled by the enemy, losing scores of men. It was an experience no one was keen to repeat.

'Nevertheless, we must dig Caratacus out of there,' said the general. 'He must not be given the time or space to regroup.'

'Precisely, sir. That's why we must send forces into the marsh to root him out.' Vespasian paused to allow his small audience of staff officers to exchange despairing looks. He could hardly contain a smile as they played into his hands. 'Or, we tempt Caratacus out of the marsh.'

'And how do we do that?'

'We use some bait.'

'Bait? You mean the Third Cohort?'

'Yes, sir. You implied that they were expendable.'

'And they are. How do you intend to use them?'

Vespasian leaned back over the map and indicated the valley once again. 'We send them into the valley to establish a fort a short distance from the marsh. Maximius is ordered to beat the place up, treat the locals as harshly as possible. Pretty soon they'll be making advances to Caratacus to come and save them from their Roman oppressors. He won't be able to resist their call for two very good reasons.

'First, it will be a chance to win over more allies. If he comes to the rescue of the people of this valley, he'll be sure to milk it for all its worth. This kind of minor success always breeds a renewed desire for resistance in the natives. The example might be contagious. Secondly, our scout was able to add one very useful piece of information to the picture.' Vespasian's eyes swept round the faces before him and came to rest on that of Plautius. The legate smiled openly and ignored the growing sense of frustration etched into the face of his superior.

'Well, bloody well get on with it,' said Plautius.

'Yes, sir. It turns out that the nobleman who owns this valley is distantly related to Caratacus. I doubt that he would stand by and watch his kin put to the sword. Chances are that he'll try and strike back at us. Anything to destabilise our control of the area. When he does strike we'll be ready for him. If we can tempt him out of his lair then there's a good chance my legion can finish him off.'

Plautius shook his head. 'You make it sound easy. What if Caratacus refuses to take the bait?'

'Then let's make sure he comes out to fight us, sir.'

'How?'

'He can't have more than two or three thousand men left – and there'll be a steady flow of deserters until he can give them another victory. Caratacus will need to pick a fight; the sooner the better as far as he's concerned. So let's make things even more difficult for him. See how the marsh curves round on its northern edge?'

Plautius examined the map and nodded.

'I should be able to cover it, sir. If you permit me to post some blocking forces on every track and trail leading into the marsh from the north, with the Third Cohort blocking the south we should be able to strangle Caratacus' supply lines eventually. With no food coming in, and no foraging parties able to get out, Caratacus and his men are soon going to get hungry. Then, either they starve, or they fight. They'll fight, of course. And when they come out and face us, we'll be ready. Assuming they take the bait.'

'And what if they do take the bait and you're too late to save the Third Cohort?'

Vespasian shrugged. 'Then let's hope they'll have served their purpose.'

And, he thought, buried the shame that would otherwise have attached itself to the Second Legion, and its commander. Vespasian was stabbed by a shard of guilt at this casual reflection that implied the deaths of nearly four hundred men. But they might survive, and win back some honour for themselves. There was a slight chance that most of the damage Maximius had caused might be repaired by a hard-fought battle and a glorious conclusion to the campaign.

One of the general's staff officers raised a hand.

'What is it, Tribune?'

'Even if Caratacus does emerge from the swamp to attack the Third Cohort, we'll probably fail to catch him. He'll simply throw a rearguard at us, to buy time for the rest of his men to slip back into hiding. Then we're back where we started, minus one cohort, of course.'

'Yes, that's a possibility,' Vespasian nodded thoughtfully. 'If that's the case, we'll just have to starve him out. Either way, if we act now, he's had it. The virtue of forcing him into a battle is that we can finish him off as soon as possible, and stop him trying to whip up any more support from the tribes who are still outside of our control.' Vespasian turned back to the general. 'And it gives Maximius and his men something useful to do, while they're being punished.'

The general frowned. 'Punished?'

'Yes, sir. I don't expect they will survive when Caratacus comes for them. Not after what they will have done to his people.'

'I see.' General Plautius scratched his cheek as he weighed up the legate's plan. 'Make sure he understands the need to be as cruel as possible.'

Vespasian smiled. 'Given the mood he and his men are in, I doubt I'll have much persuading to do. I should think he'll be only too keen to take it out on the natives.'

'Very well then.' Plautius stood back from the table and stretched his back. 'I'll have my staff draft the orders immediately.'

Chapter Twenty-Five

'Batavians?' Figulus looked towards the crest of the ridge, as if expecting their pursuers to ride into sight at any moment. He turned back to his breathless centurion. 'How many of them did you see, sir?'

Cato gulped for air before he could reply. 'No more . . . no more than a squadron . . . less . . . coming this way. Get the men under cover.'

Figulus took a last glance back up the track and then turned to issue the orders, calling out to the legionaries in a low voice, as if the Batavians might hear him even now. The men hurried from the track, scattering a small distance into the long grass and stunted bushes that grew on either side. Crouching down, they drew their swords and daggers and held them in clenched fists. On the track only Cato and Figulus remained, the centurion bent over as he fought to catch his breath.

'Are we going to take them on?' asked Figulus.

Cato glanced up at the optio as if the man were mad. 'No! Not unless we have to. It's not worth the risk.'

'We outnumber them, sir.'

'They're better armed, and they're mounted. We wouldn't stand a chance.'

Figulus shrugged. 'We might, if we caught them on this track. And we could use those horses to carry some of the men.'

'They'd be more trouble than they're worth in these marshes.'

'In that case, sir,' Figulus smiled, 'we could always eat them.'

Cato shook his head in despair. Here they were, on the verge of being found and hunted down, and his optio was thinking about food. He drew a last deep breath and straightened up.

'We'll avoid a fight if we can. Understand?'

'Yes, sir.'

'I'll go with the men on this side of the track. You're on the other. You keep 'em down and keep 'em silent until you hear from me.'

'And if we're spotted, sir?'

'You do nothing unless I give the order. Nothing at all.'

Figulus nodded, turned away and ran over to his men, rustling through the long blades of grass and scattering drops of beaded rainwater in his wake. Cato glanced quickly after him, and saw that his men had trampled some of the undergrowth down in their bid to find a hiding place. It was too late to do anything about that now and Cato ran to join the men on the other side of the track. Only the shaking of a tall clump of bulrushes showed where some men were still adjusting their positions.

'Keep still, damn you!' Cato called out.

The brown heads of the bulrushes quickly ceased moving as Cato found himself a spot between two of his men and dropped down on one knee. He cupped a hand to his mouth. 'Figulus!'

A head popped up thirty paces away on the opposite side of the track. 'Sir?'

'Remember what I said. Remember!'

'Right!' Figulus ducked back down, leaving Cato to run a last glance over his band of fugitives. Nearby he could see a handful of his men, lying flat, clearly straining to hear the first sounds of the approaching Batavians. Cato too cocked his head and waited, and found himself praying that the horsemen had lost their tracks and were even now starting to search in a new direction. As he waited his heart beat as fast as ever, and the rhythmic pounding in his ears made it hard to listen. As the drizzle continued to patter down softly on the surrounding foliage everything remained still in the gloomy haze that hid the sky from view. Time passed slowly and the tension increased.

Then, just when Cato had begun to believe that the Batavians had passed them by, he heard the faint chink of riding tackle and loose equipment. Then, the dull thump and thud of hoofs on the track. Glancing round at his men, Cato was furious to see that a handful had raised their heads to look for the source of the sound.

'Down!' he whispered furiously, and they dropped out of sight. Cato was the last to go to ground, and he pressed himself into the soft, peaty earth and waited, sword gripped tightly, head turned towards the track, and heart beating with renewed anxiety. So great was the tension in his muscles that Cato felt a tremor shaking his leg and there was nothing he could do to still the limb. Muffled, but harsh, guttural voices drifted through the damp air until a sharp word of command stilled the Batavians' tongues. Then there was quiet, broken only by the faint champing of the horses, and Cato realised that the commander of the squadron had paused to listen for any signs of his prey.

For a while there were only the sounds of nature in the clammy air and Cato, who would have normally relished the gentle rhythm of the rain, felt strained beyond all endurance. He was horribly tempted to jump to his feet and give the order to charge, rather than endure any more waiting, but instead he gritted his teeth and clenched his hand into a fist, letting the nails bite painfully into his palms. He hoped that Figulus was made of stronger stuff and would not be so badly tempted. It was in the nature of the optio to fight, and Cato was not sure how far he could trust Figulus to control his fierce Celtic blood.

159

At last the Batavian commander barked an order and his patrol trotted forward along the track, no more than ten paces from where Cato lay motionless, breathing as softly as he could. From the sound of the hoofs it was clear that two or three men had been sent ahead to scout the trail, then the main body entered the marsh at a steady pace. If the goddess Fortuna smiled kindly on them today, the Batavians might march right through them and be none the wiser. Cato offered a quick prayer to the goddess and promised her a votive javelin if he ever survived this nightmare.

The rumble of hoofs slowly passed by. There was a chorus of shouts. Cato tensed every muscle, ready to spring up and throw himself upon the Batavians at the first sign their ruse had been discovered. Then it dawned on him that of course their pathetic attempt at evasion had been detected. The same tracks that had led the horsemen here would have disappeared further down the track and that could only mean one thing to the Batavians.

Any moment now . . .

Cato glimpsed a shadowy presence to his left and turned his head. One of the horsemen was walking a short distance off the track, his back angled towards Cato, no more than six feet away, as he lifted his tunic and slackened the cord that held his leggings up. The man grunted and a deeper spatter could be heard above the gentle rain. Suddenly the noise stopped. Cato saw the man quickly lean forward and then he spun round, a cry of alarm already on his lips.

'Get 'em!' Cato screamed as he jumped up. 'Get up and get 'em!'

The man nearest him continued to turn, one hand wrenching at the handle of his sword, the other still holding his penis. Cato threw himself into the man, his blade thrusting into his stomach an instant before Cato crashed into him and sent the Batavian sprawling back into the long grass. All around, the grimy forms of the legionaries rose up and sprinted towards the wheeling confusion of men and horses. Beyond them Cato glimpsed Figulus and his men racing in from the far side of the track. The commander of the Batavians recovered from the surprise like a true professional and had his sword in his hand even as he bellowed his orders. But there was no time for orders; all was chaos, a seething mêlée of mud-stained furies, and the large-framed bodies of the horsemen struggling to control their panicked horses while they fought for their lives. Even though they had the advantage of numbers and surprise the legionaries carried only an assortment of blades, while their foes had shields, helmets and chain-mail vests. They also had long-bladed cavalry swords, which they now swept through the air in swooshing deadly arcs at the unprotected bodies of the men rushing amongst them.

Cato glimpsed a glint of light to his side and ducked down just as a blade cut through the air where his head had been a moment before and he felt the rush of air through the top of his scalp as the sword flashed over him. The sharp musty stench of horses filled his nostrils as he glanced up at the man who had tried to kill him. The momentum of the blade had

160

twisted him round in his saddle. Before he could reverse the swing Cato hacked at his elbow, shattering the joint with a dull crack. The Batavian screamed and his nerveless fingers released the sword. Hands grabbed at his cloak and he was dragged down into the mud and killed under a hail of sword-blows and the stamping hoofs of his own horse.

'Kill them!' Figulus roared above the din of clashing weapons, the harsh cries of fighting men and the shrill whinnying of the horses. 'Kill 'em all!'

One of the legionaries, just in front of Cato, could not get round his comrades to reach the rider and was thrusting his dagger into the neck of the rider's mount instead. Jets of blood sprayed out from the glossy black flesh below the bedraggled mane. There was a roar of anguish and rage as the rider saw what was being done to his horse and his sword slashed forward, cutting through the legionary's throat and spine in an instant and sending the head leaping from the man's shoulders in a hot explosion of blood.

'Don't let any get away!' Cato called out, as he quickly glanced round to find a new target. Several of the Batavians were down, one pinned beneath his horse as its hoofs lashed at the air. It tried to fight its way back on to its feet, oblivious to the screams of agony that were coming from beneath it. Cato worked his way round the animal, and then, to one side, the black-crested helmet of the Batavian commander rose up in front of him. The man's eyes narrowed as he caught sight of Cato and he threw back his arm to cut the centurion down. As the blade began to slash down the Batavian's horse stumbled to one side and the blow missed. The Batavian shouted at his animal and yanked the reins to bring it round towards Cato. For an instant his back was to the Roman, and Cato jumped forward, grabbed the hem of the man's tunic and tried to wrench him from the saddle. For a moment the Batavian commander held his balance, clenching his thighs against the high saddle horns. Then another Roman grabbed his left arm and pulled him away from Cato. The instant he had recovered his balance, the Batavian hacked through the legionary's arm. As his comrade screamed Cato gritted his teeth and slammed his sword low into the Batavian's back, cutting through the chain mail and into his spine. Instantly, his legs spasmed and went limp, and he slid helplessly off his horse, arms flailing, as he thudded down on to the track. Cato stepped forward and cut the man's throat, then crouching low he forced a way along the track, towards the edge of the marsh.

'You!' He grabbed a man by the arm, and turned to look for some more. 'And you two! With me.'

The small party backed out of the fight and Cato led them round the fringe until they reached the track leading out of the marsh.

'Spread across the track. Don't let any of them get past!'

The men nodded, and held their blades ready. Further down the track the fight was coming to an end, and the legionaries had had the better of it. Only six of the Batavians still lived, clustered together, and still mounted as they warded off the lightly armed men who danced warily around them, short blades thrusting at any horse or human flesh that came within reach. Cato could see the danger at once. As soon as these men realised that their only chance lay in flight, they would pack together and charge the legionaries, trusting to the weight and impetus of their mounts to carry them through.

'Don't just stand there!' he shouted. 'Figulus! Get stuck in!'

An instant later one of the Batavians screamed out his battle cry, and it was taken up at once by the other five. They raised their swords high, kicked in their heels and their mounts surged forward. The legionaries nearest to them scattered, diving for safety rather than risk being trampled. Those further back moved aside more deliberately and poised for a strike as the horsemen galloped past. The Batavians ignored the men who posed no danger. They were intent on escape, not going down in a desperate fight in some far-flung marsh at the ends of the earth. So they covered their bodies with their large oval shields, hunched down and spurred their horses on.

The narrow width of the track meant that only two horses could gallop side by side and the Batavians slowed down as they jostled for position. At once, the more daring amongst the legionaries dodged forward and thrust their blades into the sides of the horses, or aimed at the bare legs between the leather breeches and the boots of the horsemen. A horse, stabbed in the flank, swerved round across the track and blocked the three horses immediately behind it. They crashed into the wounded animal and it stumbled back and rolled on to its side. At the last moment the rider threw himself clear and landed heavily at the feet of a group of legionaries. They hacked him to death at once. The other three desperately regained control of their mounts and tried to pick a path round the injured beast, but it was already too late. Their momentum had gone, and the surrounding legionaries rushed in, plucked them from their saddles and butchered them on the ground.

All this Cato saw in a blur of motion; then his eyes fixed on the two Batavians who had led the charge, and still came on, teeth-bared and eyes wide with desperation as they spurred their mounts forward. Cato saw a cavalry sword on the ground close by and snatched it up, the blade's weight and balance unfamiliar in a hand used to the feel of a short sword. On either side of him he sensed his men shrinking back from the horses pounding down the track towards them.

'Hold still! Don't let them escape!'

A moment before the Batavians were upon him, Cato raised the sword and sighted along its length to the glistening chest of the nearest horse, and braced himself. The horse galloped on to the point, which ripped through its hide, tore through its muscle and pierced the heart. Cato had thrown his weight behind the sword and the shock of the impact now hurled him to one side. He landed heavily in the long grass beside the track, the wind driven from his lungs.

The blinding white that had exploded through his head when he struck the ground faded into a cloud of swirling white sparks. Then it cleared and Cato was staring straight up, the grey sky fringed with dark blades of grass. He couldn't breathe and his mouth opened, lungs straining for air. There was a ringing sound in his ears, and when Figulus leaned over him, with a concerned expression, Cato could not comprehend what the optio was saying to him at first. Then the words quickly became audible as the ringing died away.

'Sir? Sir? Can you hear me? Sir?'

'Stop . . .' Cato wheezed, and tried to draw another breath.

'Stop? Stop what, sir?'

'Stop . . . bloody shouting . . . in my face.'

Figulus smiled, then reached an arm round Cato's shoulders and eased the centurion up into a sitting position. Scattered along the track were bodies and splashes of blood. Several horses were down, some still writhing feebly. The others had run off, riderless. Only one remained on its feet, nuzzling the body of the Batavian commander.

'The last one?' Cato turned back to Figulus.

'He got away. He'll be heading back to the legion as fast as Mercury himself.'

'Shit . . . how many did we lose?'

Figulus' smile faded. 'A third, maybe a half of the men. Killed and wounded. Some of the wounded will die, or we'll have to leave them. Comes to the same thing.'

'Oh . . .' Cato suddenly felt very cold, as the post-battle shock gripped his body, as it always did, and he trembled.

'Come on, sir,' said Figulus. 'On your feet. We'll sort this lot out and find somewhere safe to rest, until it gets dark.'

'And then?' Cato wondered aloud.

Figulus grinned. 'Then we'll roast some horse-meat!'

Chapter Twenty-Six

The army of General Plautius broke camp the next day. Vespasian watched the activity from the watch-tower on the Second Legion's ramparts south of the Tamesis. He had risen early and leaned on the wooden rail, looking on as a multitude of tiny figures packed away their tents in the vast fortified camp that sprawled across the landscape on the far side of the river. Already a haze of disturbed dust had blended with the dispersed smoke of the campfires and hung over the scene, bathed in the diffuse glow of first light. Small detachments were busy removing the palisade and collecting the spiked iron caltrops from the ditch at the foot of the rampart. Once they had finished, other men laid into the rampart with their picks and shovelled the earth into the ditch. In the space of a few hours the marching camp would have been completely dismantled and would leave nothing behind that could serve the interests of the enemy.

Vespasian had seen it all before, on many occasions, but was still filled with satisfaction and pride by the sight. There was something almost miraculous about the way nearly thirty thousand men could build something on the scale of a small city in so short a time, and then level it and move on before the sun had even begun to warm the earth. Of course, he reminded himself, there was no miracle involved, only long years of hard training to ensure the efficiency with which the whole job was carried out. It was the Roman way of war, and upon it rested the future of the greatest empire the world had seen.

On the far side of the camp a dense column of men was marching out through a gap in the ramparts where the gate-house had already been torn down. Vespasian squinted to make out the detail as tiny twinkles of light flickered up and down the column from sunlight reflecting off polished helmets. As the soldiers tramped along, they quickly kicked up a dusty haze that swallowed up the main body of legionaries.

The Ninth Legion, with two regiments of cavalry and four cohorts of auxiliary infantry, turned away from the Tamesis and marched east to crush any last pockets of resistance amongst the Icenians and the Trinovantians. Once that had been achieved Legate Hosidius Geta was tasked with constructing a network of small forts to police the rolling expanse of rich farmland, trailing off into vast impenetrable marshes on the northern fringe of the Icenian kingdom. An army, much larger than the pitiful remnants that still clung to Caratacus, could easily hide themselves away in these marshes and never be discovered by Roman patrols.

Now that the Britons had been defeated on the battlefield, Plautius was free to disperse his forces and begin the process of turning the war-ravaged south of the island into a new province. There were colonies to be established, towns to build and a network of roads to be laid down to link them all. Then there was the need to build up a parallel network of administrators and clerks to run the province and make sure that it began to pay its way at the earliest possible date.

Even now, with Caratacus defeated scant days before, the general had received instructions to appoint local officials to prepare the groundwork for the tax farmers who had won the contracts for the new province. A full inventory was to be taken of the kingdoms of the tribes who had already passed completely into Roman rule. A number of client kingdoms were also to be approached to determine the appropriate level of tribute that they would be expected to pay into the imperial treasury.

This was a delicate task, since some client kingdoms were more important, strategically, than others. While there was no chance of the Cantians affecting the outcome of the current campaign, the Icenians – a large and war-like tribe – bordered the right flank of the Roman advance, and needed to be treated with careful respect, until sufficient force could be brought to bear on them and put them in their place. Further north, much further north, lay the kingdom of the Brigantians, ruled by Cartimandua, a young queen of formidable will, who had decided that there was more to be gained from appeasing rather than opposing Rome. For now at least. But in time, these client kingdoms would be remorselessly drawn into the Empire and subjected to its rule. The presence of a legion camped on their doorstep was usually enough to quell any temptation to rebel against the new order. And if they did resist then they would be taught a swift and bloody lesson in the realities of the new order. The dispatching of Hosidius Geta's column to the east was merely the first step in adding the lands of the Icenians to the new province.

Meanwhile General Plautius would take the Twentieth and the Four-teenth legions, and most of the auxiliary cohorts and push forward north of the Tamesis to establish the other end of the new province's frontier, and begin the task of constructing military roads to link up the forces dispersing across the width of the island.

The third column, under Vespasian, consisted of his legion, the Second, four cohorts of Batavian horse, two cohorts of Batavian infantry and two large mixed units of Illyrians. General Plautius had also promised his legate use of the British fleet based at Gesoriacum in Gaul, as soon as Vespasian had finished off Caratacus and could move on to subdue the remaining southern tribes still intent on defying Rome. But Caratacus had gone to ground and Vespasian was consumed with frustration at the prospect of digging the wily British commander out of his hole. It was already late summer and soon the leaves would begin to brown and fall. There would be plenty of rain and the native tracks would turn into glutinous rivers of mud that would slow down the heavy wagons of the baggage train to an exhausting and filthy crawl. Removing the threat of Caratacus might be the last operation Vespasian would be able to carry out before the campaigning season came to an end.

He had been in command of the legion for nearly three years already, and he doubted whether he had distinguished himself enough for his tenure of command to be extended much longer. The cordial relationship he had established with his general over the last two years was dead. Both men regarded each other with open hostility now, and Vespasian was convinced that Aulus Plautius would have him replaced at the earliest opportunity. Under normal circumstances legates were left to command a legion for three to five years, before returning to Rome to further their political careers. But Vespasian had little taste for such ambitions any more. What was the point of high political office in the senate when the real power in Rome was wielded from the imperial palace? Worse still, promotion to any position of real significance depended on currying favour with the Emperor's Imperial Secretary, Narcissus. The thought of toadying up to a freedman, a decadent Greek at that, made Vespasian feel sick. But he was realist enough to know that the old Republican values his grandfather had set so much faith in were largely irrelevant in the modern world. Where before hundreds of senators had once debated the destiny of Rome, now one emperor ruled. That was the reality he must live with.

From the moment of taking up his appointment to command the Second Legion Vespasian had felt at home. Army life was free of the endless deception and obsequious grovelling that characterised political life in the capital. Serving with the Eagles a man was largely in charge of his own destiny and most men rose through the ranks on merit. There was no intricate weaving of self-interested schemes, and schemes within schemes. Instead, a soldier was given a clear-cut task and left to improvise the best method of carrying out his orders. To be sure, there was a distressing amount of paperwork involved, and Vespasian had never had so little time for rest before in his life. Yet, after the few hours of sleep he managed to snatch, he awoke with a fresh sense of purpose, and a feeling that he was doing something with real value, something that genuinely furthered the destiny of his people, and of Rome itself.

Flavia would be delighted when the time came for him to quit the legion, he reflected guiltily. His wife had always regarded the post of legate as an unfortunate formality, to be undergone before her husband rose to high office. The discomforts of life in the fortress on the Rhine had put her off the army for ever, and now she waited impatiently at the family home in Rome. Not alone though, Vespasian smiled. She had little Titus to keep her company, and that boy had become quite a handful, if the tactful sentences in her letters was anything to go by. The lad should keep his wife busy. Too busy for her to be occupied by anything else.

All the quiet joy of the morning faded away as the prospect of a return to the snakepit of politics in Rome loomed in Vespasian's mind. Even here, on the fringe of the known world, surrounded by his soldiers, he felt the tentacles of treachery and peril reaching out from the heart of the Empire to entangle and crush him. There would be no simple life of a soldier for him, Vespasian reflected bitterly. He was a fool to think otherwise. Politics was part of the air that his class breathed and there was nothing he could do to alter that fact.

A movement on the periphery of his vision drew his attention. Vespasian turned and gazed beyond the rampart below, to where the Third Cohort of his legion had finished demolishing their temporary camp and was forming up into a marching column. The vanguard century followed by the colour party, four more centuries, then a small baggage column, and then the rearguard. Less than four hundred men. The cohort looked small after the vast formations he had watched on the other side of the river, and Vespasian regarded it with a peculiar mixture of intense dislike and hope. They had stained the reputation of his legion and only their obliteration would remove the shame. Obliteration, or some great deed that would redeem them in the eyes of their comrades, and the rest of the army. Therein lay the hope. Either way the problem of the uncomfortable presence of the Third Cohort would be solved.

If his plan worked and Caratacus emerged from his hiding place to take the bait, Vespasian knew that it was almost certain that Maximius and his men would be crushed without mercy long before their comrades could close the trap on the enemy.

The legate continued to watch as the centurions called their men to order and then fell into place at the head of each century. The cohort commander made one last inspection of the column and then strode up to the colour party and cupped a hand to his mouth. An instant later the faint sound of the bellowed order to advance carried up to Vespasian, as the column rippled forward.

'Easy does it, sir,' the optio said quietly to Macro, and nodded towards the camp. 'We're being given the once-over by the legate.'

Macro turned to look and saw the distant figure in the watch-tower, taking in the gilded tunic, burnished by the sun's rays, and the red cloak clasped across his shoulders. Even at that distance the broadness of the head and thickness of neck were unmistakable.

'What's he want then?' the optio muttered.

Macro gave a soft, bitter laugh. 'Just making sure he's seen the back of us.'

'Eh?' The optio turned sharply to face Macro and at once the centurion regretted the careless remark. He glanced towards his optio.

'What do you think, Sentius? The old man's so fond of us that he's come to wave goodbye?'

The optio blushed and then shot a look over his shoulder. 'Straighten that front rank! You're bloody legionaries, not a bunch of auxiliary arseholes!'

Macro was not fooled by this attempt by Sentius to cover his embarrassment, but continued to let his optio take it out on the men. There was no harm in keeping the men on their toes. Disgraced they may be, but they were still legionaries, and Macro was determined not to let them forget that for a moment. Still, he was deeply troubled by what lay ahead, and not just because the cohort would be inviting danger. That was part of the job. Maximius had seemed more than a little cold-blooded when he had briefed them the night before. Almost as if this was a chance to wreak a terrible revenge on the distant relatives of those native warriors whom the cohort commander blamed for ruining his reputation.

There would be a terrible reckoning for the natives when the Third Cohort arrived in the peaceful little valley that stretched alongside the marsh. And not just for the men of the cohort, Macro reflected. If Cato and his comrades fell into the hands of the Britons once the cohort had begun its bloody work then the native warriors would be sure to make every Roman captive die a horrible and lingering death.

As the cohort marched stolidly along the native track that led away to the west, Macro glanced back at the fortified camp. He could not help wondering if this was the last time he would ever see the rest of the Second Legion.

He was already certain that he would never see Cato alive again. Pursued by his own side and hiding out from the enemy, the youngster would eventually be found. Cato would then die with a sword in his hand, in the heat of a short bloody skirmish, or be executed in cold blood. He was probably already dead, Macro decided. In which case Macro would soon be joining him in the shadows on the far bank of the Styx.

Chapter Twenty-Seven

'Honorius died during the night,' Figulus muttered as he squatted down beside the smouldering remains of the campfire. Opposite him Cato was sitting on an ancient tree trunk, covered with lichen and bright yellow growths of fungi. Cato clutched one of the Batavian cloaks around his shoulders and tried not to shiver.

'That's the last of them, then.'

'Yes, sir.' Figulus nodded, and then stretched his hands over the grey ashes, smiling faintly as the warmth flowed over his fingers.

'Twenty-eight of us left.' Cato raised his head and looked round the clearing at the huddled forms of his men. A few were already stirring as the thin light shafted through the boughs of the stunted trees. Some coughed and two men talked in low tones, that dropped even further when they noticed the centurion glancing in their direction. The clearing stood in a leafy dell that was surrounded by low hummocks of land on every side. Beyond that lay the marsh, wreathed with mist that rose every night. The fugitives had been lucky enough to stumble on this place the day after their skirmish with the Batavian horsemen. They had left six of their dead with the other bodies and carried the seriously wounded with them, picking their way along meandering trails deep into the marsh. Cato helped his injured as best he could, but one by one they had weakened and died. Honorius had taken a spear deep in the guts. He was strong and had fought grimly to hang on to life, gritting his teeth against the agony of his mortal wound, face glistening with sweat. Now he was still, and Cato could see his body lying stretched out, arms by his sides, as Figulus had left him.

Cato rose to his feet, face contorting for a moment as he tensed his stiff muscles. Then he looked down at his optio.

'We need to find more food. We haven't eaten for days.'

Figulus nodded.

With the dell established as their camp, Cato had led a small party in search of supplies. He had ventured far down the track that wound past the dell, and two miles on they had come across a small island where four sheep had been penned together beside a small daubed hut. The body of an old man lay within. He had been dead some time and they smelled his decay before they found his wizened body. The old man who must have fallen ill and died in his hut, Cato reasoned. The Romans grabbed the pathetic bundle of rags that had been all that he had, and then tried to drive the sheep back towards the dell. Three of the depressingly stupid animals had bolted and disappeared into the marsh, leaving the fading sounds of their bleating and splashing to carry back to the Romans before the oppressive silence closed in once again. The last beast had been slaughtered and roasted over the fire that Cato allowed his men to start only after the last light had faded from the sky. The animal had been a skinny and miserable beast, which explained her refusal to escape with the others. The lean cuts of meat had lasted two days, and now hunger gnawed at the stomachs of his men again and they looked to Cato to solve the problem.

To be sure, there were animals living around them, but so far they had not been able to catch any of the birds, and only once had they seen anything bigger: the hind quarters of a small deer, swiftly disappearing through a tangle of gorse bushes the moment it scented the men. The spears that Cato's men had taken from the bodies of the Batavians remained unbloodied, and the pained gurglings from the stomachs of Romans threatened to drown out the almost constant booming of a bittern some distance away.

'I'll take a party out as soon as there's enough light,' Cato said. 'I'm sure we'll find something to eat.'

'What if you don't, sir?'

Cato looked carefully at the expression on the face of his optio, but sensed no challenge to his authority there, and felt a moment of shame. Figulus had nothing to prove. Not after he had risked his life to help Cato and the others escape. The optio's current peril was a poor return for the loyalty he had shown his centurion, a fact that only made Cato feel more wretched and guilty. It was a debt he would probably never be able to repay.

But if the loyalty of Figulus was not in doubt, the loyalty of the rest of this sorry band of outcasts most definitely was. Since they had entered the marsh four days earlier Cato had been acutely aware that the distance between them and the legion was more than geographical. The men were only just beginning to realise the true desperation of their situation, and in time they would no longer respond to his rank. When that happened, only Figulus would stand between the centurion and a complete breakdown in authority. If he ever lost the loyalty of his optio Cato was finished. They all were, unless they stuck together and functioned as a unit.

How would Macro have handled things? Cato felt sure his friend would have a much surer grasp of the situation were he here, and he lowered his head to hide his despair before he responded to Figulus' question.

'Then I'll keep taking men out until we do find something to eat. If we find nothing we starve.'

170

'That's it?'

'That's it, Optio. That's all there is for us now.'

'What happens when winter comes, sir?'

Cato shrugged. 'I doubt that we'll last that long . . .'

'That depends on you, sir.' Figulus glanced round, then shuffled round the fading embers so that he was close enough to his centurion not to be overheard. 'But you had better come up with a plan. The men need something to keep them occupied. To keep them from thinking about what happens next. You'd better come up with something soon, sir.'

Cato opened his hands despairingly. 'Like what? There's no kit for them to maintain, no barracks to be ready for inspection, no drilling, no marching and we daren't get into any fight armed as we are. There's nothing for us to do but lay low.' He felt his stomach turn over and a faint gurgling rumble sounded from beneath his filthy tunic. 'And find something to eat.'

Figulus shook his head. 'That's not good enough, sir. You've got to do better than that. The men are looking to you.'

'Do what then?'

'I don't know. You're the centurion. That's your job. Thing is, whatever we do, we must do it quickly . . . sir.'

Cato looked up at his optio and gave a faint nod. 'I need to think. While I'm out hunting, start the men on the shelters.'

'Shelters, sir?'

'Yes. We're staying put for the moment. Might as well make ourselves as comfortable as possible. Besides,' Cato nodded to the men, 'it'll keep them occupied.'

Figulus rose to his feet with a sigh of frustration and turned away, walking over to the side of the clearing where he drew his short sword and slumped back down on the ground. He fished about for the small rock he had tucked in the torn strip of cloth he used as a waistband and began to run it along the edge of the blade in a slow deliberate, grating rhythm. Cato watched for a moment, terribly tempted to shout at him and order him to stop making that irritating noise, but managed with difficulty to restrain himself. Figulus had been right, he realised at once. Soldiers without duties to occupy them were without purpose. And with no purpose it was only a matter of time before they degenerated into brigands.

But what could he achieve with twenty-eight men, armed only with swords, and the few shields and spears they had recovered from the Batavian dead? Mere survival seemed to be the limit of their capacity for action, and Cato sank further into the dark mire of depression.

Before the sun had burned off the mist hanging over the marsh, Cato picked four men to go with him to scout for food. He chose Proculus among them. The man had taken to holding his knees and rocking back and forth the moment he was without any task to do. It was wearing badly on the nerves of the other legionaries and Cato judged that it would be best for all of them if Proculus was out of the camp for several hours. They took the best of the Batavian spears and tucked daggers into the backs of their waistbands. Cato left Figulus with orders to get on with the shelters and led his small party out of the clearing, along the track that wound between two drumlins and down into the marsh. Dark still water, pierced by tall reeds, closed in around the broken track, and the air quickly became thick with the smell of decay and the drowsy whine of insects.

The track was one they had used several times before and they were familiar with its twisting course for the first few miles. Although clearly man-made, it was seldom used and almost disappeared from time to time as grassy tussocks struggled to reclaim it. With Cato in front, and Proculus immediately behind him, the Romans picked their way along, eyes and ears straining for signs of life. From time to time the track dipped down, and was covered with oily water or a soft layer of black mud, which the legionaries had to wade through with soft curses and a great many squelching and sucking sounds that Cato imagined could be heard from miles off. Once it crossed over a far larger track that stretched north and south and seemed to be the native tribes' main route across the desolate marshland. The Romans scurried across the track, nervously glancing both ways to make sure they had not been seen by anyone passing through the marsh.

For the best part of two hours, by Cato's estimation, they continued along the path, eventually coming to the furthest point they had yet explored. Here the path opened on to a strip of firm land covered with dense thickets of gorse. The mist had lifted and only a few patches still spread over the depressing landscape. The sun beat down on the marsh and the air was thick and suffocating. Cato's tunic was stuck to his back with sweat and the prickling effect on his skin was maddening.

'We'll rest and then go back,' he decided.

One of the men shook his head. 'But we haven't found anything to eat yet, sir.'

'Then we'll try again later, Metellus.' Cato forced himself to smile. Struggling through the marsh was a dispiriting business, but it least it kept his men occupied. 'This evening, perhaps.'

The legionary opened his mouth to protest further but he swallowed his words as Cato's smile fell and a gaunt, threatening determination glinted in the centurion's eyes. They stared at each other for an instant, and the other men watched, tense and expectant. Then Metellus looked down and nodded.

'Whatever you say, sir,' he muttered.

'Yes, that's right. Whatever I say . . . Now find some shade and get some rest. I'll keep watch. Then we'll head back to the camp. If we're lucky we might find something on the way.'

The others looked at him with doubtful and bitter expressions, and Cato shrugged wearily. 'Just get some rest then.'

Leaving his men to find some shelter from the sun Cato eased through some bushes, down to where the marsh began. He kneeled down, bent over the water and cupped some of the water in his palm. It had a brown tinge and a brackish smell. Some of the men back in camp had drunk from the marshes close to the dell and had had loose bowels ever since and were steadily weakening. Cato sniffed the water suspiciously, but his throat was parched and he ran a tacky tongue over his dry lips as he weighed up the risk. Then, feeling that death by thirst was no worse than anything else, Cato drank the water and cupped his hand down for more, several times, until he was sated. He stood up and went back to join the others, slipping quietly through the gorse thicket. Three of his men were already asleep, one of them snoring loudly, and Proculus was sitting in the dappled shade of a bush, rocking gently.

Cato was about to offer him some words of comfort when Proculus froze, staring intently back down the path they had come along. Cato turned to look and saw a small deer craning its neck, delicate muzzle twitching in the air. As the centurion stood quite still and stared, the deer ambled on to the path and lowered its head, snuffling from side to side in the long grass. Proculus reached out towards Metellus but Cato raised a finger in warning. The instant Metellus awoke from sleep he was bound to scare the deer off.

So the two men remained quite still, staring wide-eyed and ravenous at the deer as it casually approached. Now Cato could hear the soft thud of its small hoofs on the dry earth and he tightened his grip on the shaft of the cavalry spear, taking up the full weight. The deer paused when it reached the open area, ears twitching at the snoring sound. It stamped one of its front hoofs, waited and stamped again. When nothing moved it waited a little longer and stepped into the space between Cato and Proculus. Then the deer stopped again and turned its finely profiled face away from Cato to stare intently at the frozen Proculus.

Cato eased his throwing arm up and back and sighted along the iron spearhead towards the tan body of the deer. Over the ridge of the animal's back he could see Proculus' face. With a sick feeling of suppressed rage Cato realised that the man was directly in the path of the spear. If the animal moved then Proculus would take the weapon right in the chest.

'Shit . . .' Cato mouthed.

The deer represented a few days of meat for his men. Without it they would starve, and soon be too weak to hunt. Then there would just be a slow lingering death. But if he threw and missed he would surely kill Proculus. Cato prayed to Diana to move the deer on. Just a couple of steps, that was all. But the deer was still as a statue. Only its flanks swelled and fell slightly as it breathed. Cato caught Proculus' despairing expression opposite him and the legionary nodded faintly.

With a grunt Cato hurled the spear forward in a swift flat trajectory. The explosive sound of his effort startled the deer and it jumped nervously into the air. There was a dull whack as the spear bit home, bursting through the hide, through muscle and lodging in the heavy bone beneath the animal's rump. With a shrill bleat of agony and terror the deer crashed down, but almost immediately started to struggle back to its feet.

'Get him!' Cato shouted, rushing forwards.

Proculus scrambled towards the deer with clawing outstretched hands. The other legionaries stirred from their sleep in alarm and snatched for their weapons.

'Get him!' Cato shouted again. 'Before he gets away!'

The deer had regained its feet and turned aside from Proculus and then crashed through the nearest gorse, trailing the spear from its rear end as blood, bright and hot, welled up from the wound. The shaft caught in the thicket and spun the animal's back legs round so that it nearly rolled over. But the deer managed to right itself and stumbled on in a desperate blind panic. Proculus was on his feet and threw himself after the beast, with Cato only a few paces behind. The other men were up now and eagerly joined the chase.

'Proculus! Don't let it get away, man!'

With a loud chorus of snapping and rustling the wounded deer thrust itself away from its pursuers, but the spear shaft snagged and held it back at every turn so that Proculus, scratched and bleeding, closed on the beast. Then the gorse parted, there was a short patch of grass and the ground gave way to a flat expanse of dark, cracked earth. The deer braced itself and leaped forward, arcing up and then crashing down with a soft thud ten feet away. Its hoofs sank through the cracked mud and it struggled forward another step and was stuck. Proculus saw his chance and leaped after the deer, landing in the mud, breaking through the crust and sinking almost knee-deep in the mire beneath. Grunting with effort he dragged one foot out, threw it forward and tried to lift the other, but the suction was too much for him. Ahead of him the deer flailed in a widening circle of foul-smelling mud and the shaft of the spear momentarily swung back, within reach of Proculus. At once he grabbed the shaft, held it firmly and wrenched it free, just as Cato and the others stumbled on to the grassy bank.

'Shit!' Metellus shouted. 'Shit, we've got it!'

The legionary started forward but Cato slapped his arm across the man's chest, stopping him. 'Wait!'

Metellus made to sweep his centurion's arm aside when Cato jabbed his other hand towards Proculus, floundering in the mud as he tried to steady himself for a spearthrust.

'Look!' Cato shouted. 'It's not safe. Just wait!'

Proculus, up to his knees in the glutinous filth, reached forward and thrust the spear into the deer's throat, wrenched the blade free and struck again. With one final terrified squeal the deer's head slumped down into the mud, its tongue lolled out. The tanned chest heaved a few more times and was still. Blood coursed from its wounds and spread brilliantly across the disturbed mud.

Proculus raised the spear over his head and whooped with triumph and delight, then turned towards his comrades with a wide grin, and then frowned as he saw their intent expressions.

'He's sinking,' Metellus said quietly.

Proculus looked down and saw that the black mud had now engulfed his thighs and dark water oozed around the bottom of his ragged tunic. With a huge effort he tried to lift one of his legs, but the effort only led to him sinking a little further into the mud. He turned to his comrades, the first trace of fear etched into his expression.

'Help me.'

'Your spear!' Cato gestured towards him. 'Reach out for us.'

Proculus grasped the shaft, just behind the iron head and stretched out, offering the base of the weapon towards his comrades. Cato extended his arm as far as it would go, fingers straining to reach the end of the shaft, but there was still a small gap.

He turned back to Metellus. 'Take my arm, and hold it tight.'

With Metellus anchoring him to the bank Cato took a tentative step onto the cracked surface of the mud and at once his foot sank in several inches. He leaned forward again, fingers in contact with the wavering end of the spear shaft. He clenched his fingers around the hard wood and began to pull. Along the length of the spear he could see Proculus' knuckles, white with the strain of clutching on to this slender lifeline. Beyond that the wide terrified eyes fixed on the centurion.

'Hold on!' Cato grunted through his teeth. 'Hold on, man!'

For a moment he felt the spear shift towards him, and then there was no more movement, no matter how hard he strained to pull Proculus back to the bank. He closed his eyes and made one last, intense effort, to no avail, and relaxed his muscles.

'This isn't working.' Cato glanced round quickly and snapped out some fresh orders. 'We need some matting. Cut some branches. Toss them on the mud. Do it!'

As he and the others pulled their daggers out and began to saw at the slender branches of the gorse, Proculus looked about him with a growing sense of horror. The mud sucked him down steadily and was now oozing around his waist. Beyond him the deer, still in death, was sinking more slowly, and already the head was hidden from sight, only a stiff ear breaking the surface of the oily water on the surface of the mud.

'Get me out of here!' Proculus pushed down at the mud, then tried to sweep it away from his waist.

'Keep still, you fool!' Cato hissed. 'You're only making yourself sink faster. Keep still!'

The gorse branches were tougher than Cato had expected and still not one bit had been cut free. He drew his knife arm back and stamped down on the sinewy white pulp he had tried to saw through, but the branch just gave way beneath him and did not snap.

'Shit!'

Cato resumed sawing, with increased desperation as he glanced over at Proculus, now up to his chest.

'There!' One of the men grunted, and threw a branch down on to the mud by the bank, and immediately began to saw at another.

'For fuck's sake!' Proculus cried out. 'Faster, you bastards! Faster!'

The dagger cut through the branch by Cato's hand and he turned and tossed it down on top of the first one, glancing across towards the trapped legionary.

'Oh no . . .' Cato whispered. Only the man's head and shoulders were above the surface now, his arms stretched out across the mud towards his comrades. Proculus still held the spear tightly in his right hand. With a gurgle he sank a little further and some of the oily water spilt into his mouth.

'Oh, shit!' Proculus gurgled. 'Save me!'

Cato dropped his knife and took a step towards the branches lying on the mud.

'No!' Metellus grabbed his arm. 'It's too late . . .'

Cato shook the arm free and turned back towards Proculus, and saw that the man's head tipped back, eyes wide with terror as the mud slid remorselessly up the bridge of his nose. Then there was just the top of his head, and his arm raised up, fingers clawing at the air. The head sank out of sight, leaving a dim pool of dark water that bubbled for a few moments and was then still. To one side Proculus' hand rose above the mud, fingers tightly clenched. Then, slowly, they relaxed and the hand gradually flopped forward from the wrist.

For a moment all was still and silent as the men on the bank gazed at the spot where their comrade's head had been.

'Fuck . . .' one of the men breathed.

Cato slumped on to the grass, and the others slowly sat down each side of him. As they stared, the mud slowly, almost imperceptibly, began to swallow up the carcass of the deer, and all they could do was watch with a mixture of shocked grief for Proculus, and a gnawing hunger at the sight of the gradually disappearing deer. Eventually it too was swallowed up as the foul water closed over the bloodied hide, and then there was nothing.

At length Cato stood up and tucked his dagger back into his waistband. 'Let's go.'

'Go?' Metellus frowned as he looked up at his centurion. 'Go where, sir?'

'Back to the camp.'

'What's the point?'

'We have to get moving,' Cato said patiently. 'The mist has lifted. We might be seen.'

'Doesn't matter, sir,' Metellus replied with a despairing weariness. 'Sooner or later, this fucking marsh is going to kill us all.'

Chapter Twenty-Eight

The Third Cohort reached the valley two days after leaving the camp by the Tamesis. Maximius gave the order to pitch tents and dig a defensive rampart as the light faded to the west. Before them lay a shallow vale no more than two miles across and perhaps eight miles in length. Beyond a low line of foothills, the marsh stretched out as far as the eye could see – a dismal patchwork of stunted trees and reeds, broken only by dark expanses of water and the occasional copse atop hummocks of ground that rose above the marsh like the backs of great sea creatures.

From the small watch-tower erected over the camp gate Centurion Macro had a good view down the valley and could see dozens of faint trails of smoke rising up above the gentle slopes. Closer to the camp he could pick out the small clusters of round huts, and a dim haze hanging over a small forest halfway down the valley indicated a settlement of some size. All very peaceful, he mused. In the next few days that would change.

There was a rattle of iron studs on wood and a moment later Maximius' head appeared above the planking of the watch-tower. He hauled himself up and mopped his glistening brow on the back of a forearm.

'Hot work!'

'Yes, sir.'

'But it was worth pushing the men on so we got here before nightfall.'

'Yes, sir,' Macro replied, casting a glance at the legionaries still labouring to finish the last section of ditch and rampart on one side of the camp. The men of the picket line stood in a thin screen a hundred paces out from the ditch. Most were leaning on their shields in postures of absolute exhaustion. If the enemy were to attack now, or this night, the men of the cohort would be too weary to mount a good defence of their camp. To be fair to Maximius, it was the kind of decision that plagued most commanders: a trade-off between a good position and the fighting readiness of the men. At least, when the morning came, the Third Cohort would only have a short distance left to march and would be fit and ready to meet any threat that emerged from the marshes.

Centurion Maximius was staring down the valley in the direction of the hidden settlement. He raised his arm and pointed. 'See that small hill there, to one side of the forest, over that stream?'

Macro followed his direction and nodded.

'That looks like the best spot to set up a more permanent camp. Good views on all sides and a supply of water to hand. Should suit us well, don't you think?'

'Yes, sir.' Macro was getting tired of the rhetorical attempts to instigate a conversation. If Maximius wanted to talk then he was better off seeking the company of the ever-eager-to-please Centurion Felix. Besides, Macro was not sure that he trusted himself to speak with Maximius, burdened as he was with the knowledge that he had been the one to free Cato and the others. Maximius was still looking for the one responsible and so Macro was naturally wary of any attempt to trick him into even the smallest admission of complicity or guilt.

The cohort commander turned to face his subordinate and scrutinised his expression silently for a moment. Macro was uncomfortably aware of Maximius' gaze but was unsure how to respond, and simply kept his mouth shut and stared ahead, as if taking in the lie of the land the cohort would have to march through the next morning.

'You don't like me very much, do you?'

Macro had to face the man now and affected a puzzled frown. 'Sir?'

'Oh, come now!' the cohort commander smiled. 'You've made little secret of your disapproval of me since your appointment to the unit.'

Macro was startled. Had he really been that transparent? That was very worrying. What else had Maximius seen in him? For an instant he felt a chill of fear spread across the back of his neck. Maximius must be trying to play some trick on him, to test him, maybe to trap him, and Macro's mind reeled in panic.

'Sir, I meant no disrespect! It's just my way. I'm . . . I'm not very good with people.'

'Bollocks. That's not what I've been told. You're a natural leader. Anyone can see that.' Maximius' eyes narrowed. 'Maybe that's it. You think you're better than me.'

Macro shook his head.

'What's this? Too afraid to speak?'

Macro was furious and snapped back his reply. 'I'm not afraid, sir! What do you really want? What do you want me to say, sir?'

'Easy, Centurion! Easy . . .' Maximius gave a light laugh. 'Just wondered what you were thinking, that's all. No harm intended.'

No harm . . . Macro felt a bitter contempt for his superior. Good soldiers never played these kinds of games. Only madmen and politicians, and he wasn't sure there was much difference between the two.

'Anyway, I wanted a little talk with you. You've known Cato for a while, haven't you?'

'Ever since he joined the Second, sir.'

'I know. I've looked at the records. So then, you would be the best person to consult about his plans.'

'I wouldn't know about that, sir.'

Maximius nodded thoughtfully. 'But you knew the man. I'd value your thoughts on the matter. What do you think Cato will do? He may be dead already. But let's suppose he's still alive. What would he do now? Well?'

'I . . . I really have no idea, sir.'

'Come on, Macro! Think about it. If I didn't know better, I'd say you were trying to cover for him.'

Macro almost forced himself to laugh, then knew at once that the laughter would sound hollow and fool no one, least of all his nervous commander. 'Sir, you must know my record. You must know that I play by the rules and have no sympathy for any man who breaks them, let alone one who dumps me and the rest of my comrades in the shit. In my book, Cato's got it coming to him. As for what he might do now, I can only guess. I never got to know him well enough to anticipate his actions.' Macro knew that was true enough, and he resisted the urge to smile as he continued. 'He could do anything. Cato might try and make a play for Caratacus himself.'

'That's absurd. He'd never stand a chance.'

'He knows that, sir. But the army is the only family Cato has got. Without us, he's nothing. He'd do anything to earn his place back in the legion. That's why I'm sure he's out there in the marsh somewhere, biding his time and waiting for the right opportunity. Why, he's probably watching us right now . . . And he wouldn't be the only one, sir. Look there!'

Macro nodded down towards the nearest farmstead. A small number of figures were looking towards the fort from behind some low hayricks barely a quarter of a mile away. The distant figures just watched and made no movement.

'Want me to send out a patrol to scare 'em off, sir?'

'No.' Maximius stared hard at the farmers. 'That can wait until tomorrow. In the meantime let the locals spread word of our arrival, and let them sweat. We want to generate all the fear and anxiety we can.'

The next morning the cohort broke camp and marched down the valley. Macro was aware of being watched every step of the way. Occasionally he would glance round and catch sight of a face disappearing behind a tree, or dropping out of sight amid one of the fields of crops they passed by. His long years of experience had given him a good eye for the ground and he scrutinised any good sites for an ambush as they marched along. But there was no ambush, not one act of defiant hostility as the legionaries tramped along through the peaceful valley.

After an hour's steady marching the column followed the track around the forest and turned up the slope of the small hillock Maximius had chosen for their camp. To their left, across the stream, on a gentle rise, sprawled a large village comprised of the usual round huts, together with smaller structures for stables and storage. Smoke eddied gently from the vents of a number of the huts. A few figures moved on the palisade that surrounded the village and Macro noted that the gates were closed.

'Officers on me!' Maximius bellowed.

When all his centurions and optios had gathered the cohort commander removed his helmet, mopped his brow with the felt liner and began his briefing. The rest of the men began work on the area marked out for the camp by the surveyors. A screen of sentries spread out around the crown of the hill, while their comrades began to swing their pickaxes, breaking up the ground for the ditch and rampart.

'Tullius!'

'Sir?'

'I want an extra ditch dug around the camp. Make sure that the ground between the ditches is sown with caltrops. Have some Lilies dug into the ground as well.'

Tullius nodded approvingly. The small pits with sharpened stakes at their centre would be a useful additional defence.

'Yes, sir. I'll pass the word to the surveyor.'

'No. You'll see to it yourself. I want it done properly. I also want a fortified gateway thrown across the main track where it comes out of that marsh. See that it's taken care of the moment our camp is erected.'

'Yes, sir.'

'Now then,' Maximius cleared his throat, and focused his attention on the optios. 'You know why we're here. The general and the legate want those men brought back. They're out there in the marsh, as far as we know. You optios will be running regular patrols into the marsh. We don't know the tracks and paths through the marsh, but,' Maximius smiled, 'we should be able to persuade some of the locals to act as guides a little bit later. In the meantime, despite the fact it looks quiet round here, we should be prepared at all times for an attack in strength.'

Some of the officers exchanged looks of surprise. There had been no indication of trouble as they marched down the valley, and the farmers that lived here probably wielded nothing more deadly than a scythe.

Maximius smirked at their expressions. 'I can see that some of you think I'm being over cautious. Maybe, but don't forget that Caratacus still has a few men left, wherever he is . . .'

Quite enough men, thought Macro. At least enough to wipe out the cohort.

'You don't have to worry about the locals. And you don't have to worry about creating any good relations with them. In fact,' Maximius paused to lend weight to his next words, 'I want you to treat them in a way that makes it painfully clear that Rome is here to stay, and that they are absolutely beholden to our will and at our mercy. You will punish any sign of resistance as harshly as you can . . . Do you understand?'

Heads nodded, and there was a murmur of assent.

'Good. Because if I see any of you going soft on the natives, or showing one shred of compassion or sympathy, then that man will have me to answer to, directly. And I will personally kick his balls through the top of his skull. Clear? Now then, all we need to do is set the tone . . .'

Half an hour later the First Century set off down the slope with Maximius at the head of the column, accompanied by all the optios and Centurions Macro, Antonius and Felix. Tullius, the most senior officer after Maximius, was left to oversee the construction of the camp, and watched anxiously as the small column tramped towards the native village on the far side of the stream. A trampled and churned funnel of earth on each side of the gentle current indicated the presence of a crossing point, and Maximius and his men splashed through the shallows with a loud churning of spray before they emerged dripping on the far bank and started up a worn track towards the flimsy palisade that surrounded the village.

As they approached Macro could see several faces peering at them either side of the gate, and for a moment he wondered if the villagers would make any attempt at resisting the heavily armed Roman column. He raised his hand and let it rest on the pommel of his short sword, ready to draw the weapon the instant there was any sign of trouble. Around him, Macro sensed the growing tension amongst the other officers, and as they came within slingshot range of the gate Maximius gave the order to halt. For a moment he glanced over the defences, then turned to Macro.

'What do you think?'

Macro saw that there was still only a handful of natives watching them, and none of them appeared to be armed.

'Seems safe enough, sir.'

Maximius scratched his neck. 'Then why's the gate still shut, I wonder?' He turned towards the front rank of the column. 'I'll send some men forward, just in case . . .'

'No need, sir.' Macro nodded past him. 'Look.'

The gates were swinging inwards, and a short distance inside the village stood a group of men. At their head stood a tall, thin figure with flowing white hair. He leaned on a staff and remained quite still.

Centurion Felix leaned closer to Macro. 'Welcoming committee, do you think?'

'If it is, then it won't be for long,' Macro replied quietly.

Satisfied that there was no sign of danger Maximius gave the order for the column to approach. As he fell under the shadow of the palisade the man with the staff finally moved, striding purposefully forward to meet his visitors at the threshold of his village. He started to make a speech in a rich deep voice.

'Stop!' Maximius raised a hand and called back over his shoulder. 'Interpreter! On me!'

A legionary doubled forward, one of the recent replacements from Gaul. Macro saw that he had the same Celtic features as the villagers he was about to question. The legionary stood to attention between Centurion Maximius and the elderly native.

'Find out what he wants to say, and tell him to keep it brief,' Maximius snapped.

As the legionary translated the terse request the village chief looked confused at first, and then frowned. When he replied, there was no mistaking the bitter tone of his words.

'Sir,' the legionary turned to Maximius, 'he merely wanted to welcome you to the valley and assure you that he, and his people, will offer you no harm. He had wanted to offer you the hospitality of his hut, and a chance to buy supplies from his farmers. But he says he is surprised. He had heard that Rome was a great civilisation, yet her representatives are so lacking in civility . . .'

'He said that, did he?'

'Yes, sir. Exactly that.'

'Right then.' Maximius pressed his lips together for a moment as he fixed the native with a look of utter contempt. 'That's enough of this bollocks. Tell him that if I want his bloody hospitality then I'll take it, as and when I like. Tell him he and the rest of his people will do exactly what I say, if they want to live.'

Once the legionary had finished, the locals looked at each other in shock.

Then the cohort commander pointed at the small crowd behind the chief.

'That woman, and those brats. They his family?'

The chief nodded after the translation.

'Macro, seize them! Take five sections and prepare to escort 'em back to our camp. There'll be a few more in a moment.'

'Seize them?' Macro was almost as shocked as the villagers. 'Why, sir?'

'Hostages. I want these savages to co-operate.'

Macro felt torn between his distaste for what Maximius was doing and his duty to obey orders. 'Surely . . . surely there's other ways we can win them round, sir?'

'Win them round?' Maximius snorted. 'I don't give a steaming shit about them. Got that? Now carry out your orders, Centurion!'

'Yes . . . sir.' Macro summoned forty men from the head of the column and strode briskly up to the chief's family. He hesitated a moment and then pulled a woman and her three children out from the rest and firmly steered them in between the two lines of legionaries. At once there was a chorus of angry shouts from the villagers. The woman twisted in Macro's grip and looked back at the chief. The old man took a pace forward, stopped and clenched and unclenched his fists helplessly, and as she cried something to him, he grimaced and shook his head. Once there was a screen of legionaries between the woman and the rest of the villagers Macro released her arm, looked her in the eyes and pointed to the ground. 'Stay!'

Centurion Maximius turned to his translator. 'Tell him, I want one child from each family in the village brought here to me right now. If anyone tries to conceal their children, then I'll crucify the entire family. Make sure he understands that.'

The angry grumbling from the villagers turned to a groan of horror and despair as the words were translated. Some of the men started to shout at the Romans, faces wild with rage and hatred. The chief dared not let the confrontation develop a moment longer and hastily stepped into the narrowing space between the villagers and the edgy legionaries. He raised his arms and tried to calm his people down. A while later the noise had subsided to a low undercurrent of bitterness mixed with the sobbing of many of the women and children.

'Tell him to get a move on!' Maximius snapped. 'Before I have to make an example to prove I mean what I say!'

The villagers moved to carry out his orders and as Macro watched with a growing sense of disgust and pity, the families brought out their children and handed them into the rough grasp of the legionaries. Nearly thirty of them stood cowering between the lines of Romans, hemmed in by their broad shields and cowed by their humourless expressions. Some of the children screamed and wailed, writhing in the iron grasp of the soldiers.

'Shut them up!' Maximius bawled out.

One of the optios raised his fist and punched a young boy, no more than five, in the side of the head. At once his screaming sobs ceased as he collapsed, stunned. A woman shrieked and leaped forward, ducking between two legionaries, and making for the child lying sprawled on the ground.

'Leave that brat alone!' Centurion Maximius stormed over to her. The woman, crouched over her son, turned her head to look up at the Roman officer. Macro saw that she was young, no more than twenty, and had piercing dark brown eyes and rich golden blonde hair in two plaits. Her face contorted into a look of contempt and she spat on Maximius' boot. There was a rasp of steel, a glint of a blade biting through the air, a wet crunch and then a thud as the woman's head hit the earth and rolled towards the chief. Her child, recovering from the blow, was drenched with jets of his mother's blood and screamed.

'Oh shit . . .' Macro muttered. Then he felt a warm spurt on his shin and he stepped back quickly.

For a moment there was only the sound of the boy's shrieks, until Maximius kicked the corpse over, away from the child and leaned down to wipe his blade on her tunic. He sheathed it and stood erect, glaring round at the villagers. A man stumbled forward through the crowd, hands balled into fists, teeth-clenched, but was instantly restrained by several of his people, holding him back as he writhed in their hands. Maximius sneered at him, then pointed a finger at the small crowd.

'Tell them, that's what will happen to anyone who defies me. There will be no warning, just death. Tell the chief he's to come with us when we leave. I will give him a list of our needs back at the camp.'

The First Century turned about and, with a terrified mob of screaming children pressed together between the legionaries, the column marched away from the village, back down the slope towards the stream. The villagers followed them through the gate, and a short distance down the slope, numbed into silence by their despair. Macro felt sick, and tore his gaze away from them as he glanced around the valley. Was this the same valley that had been so easy on his eyes as he marched down its length only a brief while before? The age-long serenity of this valley of farmers had been bloodily shattered in the space of a few hours by the men of Rome. Nothing would be the same here ever again.

Chapter Twenty-Nine

The men were beginning to be openly resentful of him, and Cato wondered how long it would be before the sentiment turned into something far more deadly. They had been hiding in the marsh for ten days now, and the lack of food left a gnawing agony in their bellies that preoccupied their minds above all else. The last meal they had eaten had been some days earlier – a small pig that they had found wandering along a narrow path. When the animal had been speared and killed, Cato had heard someone calling out nearby and, creeping forwards with Figulus, he discovered a small farm on a patch of arable ground that barely rose above the level of the surrounding marsh. There were two or three families working the land from a huddle of small huts. Outside the nearest hut sat a young man and his plump wife, playing with two small children, one of them not yet on his feet. To one side of the hut there were two pens, one with chickens and the other contained a large sow and several suckling pigs. There was a small opening in the side of the pig-pen.

'That explains our find,' the optio whispered. 'Now, if only one or two more get it into their heads to go and explore the wide world, we can eat like kings.'

'Don't get your hopes up. They'll miss that pig soon. We'd better get out of here.'

As Cato made to shuffle back his optio grasped him on the shoulder.

'Wait . . . sir.'

Cato turned to give his companion a cold look. 'Get your hand off me.'

'Yes, sir.'

'That's better. What is it?'

Figulus nodded towards the farmer and his family, just as the eldest child's laughter shrilled out in the warm afternoon air. 'There's only one man there.'

'Only the one we can see,' Cato agreed cautiously.

'All right then, sir. Even if there's another inside the hut, we can still take 'em.'

'No.'

'Kill them, hide the bodies and take our pick of the animals.' The optio fixed his gaze on the sow, grunting contentedly in her pen. 'That lot could feed us for a week, sir.'

'I said no. We can't risk it. Now let's go.'

'What risk?'

'The moment anyone comes visiting and finds the place deserted, they'll raise the alarm. The locals will be all over us. So, we don't take the risk. Understand me, Optio?'

There was no mistaking the centurion's tone, and Figulus nodded and carefully crawled back, away from the small farmstead into the reeds. When they rejoined the small party of hunters Cato had brought along, the piglet had already been gutted and impaled on one of the spears for the march back to the camp. At the sound of their approach Cato was glad to see them stop gloating over their kill and snatch up their weapons. The tense expressions relaxed as their officers emerged from the marsh and stood, dripping, on the narrow track. Metellus looked at him hopefully.

'Any sign of more of these, sir?'

'More than you can imagine,' Figulus smiled. 'There's a nice little—'

Cato instantly whirled round on his subordinate. 'Shut your mouth! There's nothing there that concerns us. Got it? Nothing . . . Now let's get this back and eat.'

The men looked on curiously until Cato snapped at them to pick up their kill and sent one man forward and left one behind to make sure they were not followed. They marched back to the camp in silence, stopping only to cover up any blood that dripped from the swaying carcass of the piglet that might lead the farmer after them, once he discovered that one of his pigs had slipped out of its pen.

As soon as the last skeins of pink light had faded from the horizon, Cato gave permission for Metellus to light a small fire. The rest of his band sat in wide-eyed hunger, impatiently waiting for the fire to die down enough to allow them to roast the splayed pig over the red and grey glow of the embers. Soon the rich aroma of cooking meat and the sharper tang of the fat fizzing down into the fire filled the men's nostrils, and they moistened their lips in expectation. At the earliest possible moment Cato ordered Metellus to remove the meat from the fire and start cutting portions for the men. The legionary eagerly sawed away at the tough skin and then sliced through the meat, which oozed red juices as the blade cut it away from the bones underneath. Then, one by one, the men sat round the fire, hot meat cupped in their filthy hands as they tore at it with their teeth. Only now and then would they meet each other's gaze and exchange a contented smile or wink as the warm pork quickly filled their stomachs.

Cato waited until the last man had taken his share, then nodded to Metellus. 'You first.'

The legionary nodded and hacked off a length of loin he had been saving for himself and then moved aside for his centurion. As he pulled out his knife Cato saw that the best cuts had gone and he had to content himself with a chunk of flesh sawn off from around the back of the piglet's neck. Then he sat with the others and lifted the meat to his mouth.

At once, the aroma was irresistible and he sank his teeth in with all the eagerness of a street beggar tearing at the scraps fallen from a rich man's feast. He smiled at the thought. Right now Cato would be more than happy to change places with the meanest pauper on the streets of Rome. They at least were not living in perpetual fear of being hunted down and killed like dogs.

As the fire slowly died down the men finished their first hunks of meat and returned to the rapidly cooling carcass to pick at what was left. For a moment Cato considered ordering them to leave the meat alone. There was no telling when the next meal would come their way, and once the effects of gorging themselves had worn off, the men would soon return to the bitter agony of hunger clawing at their guts. But there was an expression of desperation in the faces of the men crouched around the body of the pig, worrying away at it with the points of their knives and the scrabbling tips of their fingers. Looking at them Cato decided that any order to restrain their appetite might be the last order he would ever give. It made good sense to save the food, to make it last a few more days at least. But hunger had driven the men beyond good sense and he must handle them more carefully than ever if they were to have any hope of survival. So the last of the small pig was greedily consumed and next morning all that was left below the faintly grinning jaws was bone and gristle. The head and trotters they cooked the next night, and Cato refused to take his share in order that the scraps went as far as possible. Then there was nothing, and hunger crept back upon them like a thief.

That was two days ago, Cato thought as he woke up, and winced at the ache in his empty belly. He was lying on his side in the shade of one of the trees that ringed their spartan camp. He turned on to his back and glanced up, squinting as the sun shimmered through the softly rustling leaves above. It was well past noon, and Cato wished that he had slept for longer, having spent the night on watch. After all, there was not much to be awake for. Just the long wait for the scout patrols to come back, and the brief moment of eager anticipation, once they were sighted, that they might have found some food. Followed swiftly by the despairing knowledge that their bellies would remain empty for another night.

Besides being empty-handed, the scouts brought no news of Caratacus and his warriors, also concealed in this marsh. It was as if the depressing miasma had simply swallowed up the remnants of the native army, as it had Proculus.

Cato hastily put aside that memory and turned his thoughts back to the plan he had hoped might win them a reprieve and send them back to their comrades in the Second Legion. He had clearly envisaged the scene: the motley column of bedraggled legionaries marching proudly back towards their astonished legate, who would listen in rapt attention as Cato told him where to find Caratacus and his warriors, pinpointed on one of the maps spread across Vespasian's campaign desk. A sweet fantasy, that. He smiled bitterly to himself. Any comfort that vision had once offered him now seemed quite hollow, and the vision mocked him as he lay on his back staring unfocused at the sky above.

At length he could bear to torment himself no longer, and eased himself up into a sitting position. Looking round the camp he could see the other men, squatting in small groups, talking quietly. One or two glanced back at him as they saw that he was awake, and Cato wondered what they were really discussing as they refused to meet his eyes and looked away. Then he reminded himself that he had given orders that they were to make no unnecessary noise. He was looking for signs of danger all the time now, and if he were not careful it would drive him mad.

Something was not right . . .

Cato looked round the camp again and fixed his gaze on Figulus, sitting under a low bough a short distance away, whittling a fine point on the tip of a slim, relatively straight, shaft of wood. The centurion quickly rose to his feet and strode over towards Figulus.

'What are you doing here? You're supposed to be on patrol.'

'Yes, sir.' Figulus nodded. 'Someone volunteered to take the patrol instead.'

'Someone?' Cato glanced round and then stared down at the optio. 'Metellus?'

'Yes . . .'

'Where did he go?' Cato asked with a sickening realisation that he could already guess the answer.

'Out past that farm we found a few days back. He reckoned that there might be a track leading from the farm towards some larger settlement in the swamp.'

'That's what he reckoned?' Cato said with bitter irony.

'Yes, sir.'

'And you believed him?'

'Why not?' Figulus shrugged. 'He might find something useful, sir.'

'Oh, he'll find something, all right. You can count on it.' Cato smacked his palm against his thigh. 'Right . . . get up! You're coming with me. Get us some spears.'

While his optio quickly rose to his feet and walked over to the weapons stacked in the centre of the camp Cato rubbed his eyes and decided what they must do.

'Sir?'

Cato glanced round. Figulus was holding a spear shaft out towards him. He took it, leaned it against his shoulder and then checked that his dagger was securely fastened by the sash tied around his waist.

'I'm sorry, sir,' Figulus said quietly. 'I didn't think he'd do anything stupid.'

'Really?' Cato muttered. 'We'll find out soon enough. Come on.'

He turned and led his optio towards the exit from the camp. As he reached the edge of the small clearing Cato turned to call out to the others over his shoulder.

'No one leaves the camp. Stay alert.'

Cato strode down the track into the swamp, mentally mapping the tracks he had used since they had found the camp. If Metellus was making for the farm then he would most likely take the track they had followed the day they killed the pig. It had been one of the few patrols Metellus had been out on. Cato had worried that the man's disrespectful attitude might have caused problems, and had confined him to the camp as often as possible. There was a quicker way to the farm, a narrow track that almost disappeared into the marsh in places. It was hard to follow, but if Cato and Figulus hurried they might yet reach the farm before Metellus, and stop him from doing anything foolish.

So he hurried on, sacrificing the usual wary caution with which he had moved through this dismal landscape to the need for speed. The sun shone from a clear sky overhead and the swirling clouds of insects that hovered amongst the reeds closed round the sweating Romans as they waded through small stretches of the thick foul-smelling mud between stretches of the track that snaked through the marsh.

'What do they eat when Roman's off the menu?' Figulus muttered as he angrily swatted a horsefly that was gorging itself on his neck.

Cato glanced back. 'If we don't stop Metellus in time, then there'll be a lot more Romans on the menu. Come on!'

They had been going for nearly two hours, when Cato realised that the landscape around him was wholly unfamiliar. By the arc of the sun, he knew they must be headed in roughly the right direction, but they should have come across the farm long before now. They must have missed it, passed it by, and failed to find Metellus. It was with a sinking heart that Cato was helping his optio out of a deep patch of mud when he glanced back the way they had come and froze.

'What is it, sir?'

Cato just stared for a moment longer and then pointed. 'Look there . . .'

Figulus stepped up on to the earth bank and straightened, following the direction indicated by his centurion. At first he didn't see anything unusual, then a faint smudge blossomed in the distance.

'I see it.'

As they watched the smoke thickened into a thin grey column that trailed up into the clear sky. The base of the column pointed unerringly to its source.

Cato glanced round at the sun, still well above the horizon. 'There's still an hour or two of light left. Too much. We have to get back, quick as we can.'

He plunged back into the mud they had just extricated themselves from and with a sigh of exhaustion and resignation Figulus turned and followed his centurion. The march back was twice as hard, as Cato forced them on as fast as he could manage, heedless of the burning weariness in his weakening limbs, all the while staring anxiously at the thin haze of smoke that, in the fading light, seemed never to get any closer.

They could hear the squealing of the pigs long before they emerged from the track through the marsh and ran the final distance through the trees towards the camp, breathless and leaden-limbed. The sun was now no more than a burnished disc of coppery fire low on the horizon behind them, and they pursued their long distorted shadows into the small clearing that formed their camp. There, beside the smoking remains of the fire, lay two spitted piglets. Tethered to one of the trees the sow looked on in terror, squealing for its young with shrill relentless cries. The surviving piglets clustered round her trotters, pink snouts nuzzling their mother for comfort.

The men were bent over the roast pigs, eating, and one by one they gazed up guiltily as they became aware of the officers' return. One of them nudged Metellus and he slowly rose to his feet as Cato and Figulus came panting up towards the fire. The legionary forced a smile on to his face, bent down and picked up a hunk of meat from the small pile he had carved. He straightened up and held it out towards his centurion.

'There, sir. Lovely strip of belly. Try it.'

Cato stopped several feet short of the fireplace, and stood leaning on the shaft of his spear, chest heaving as he struggled to regain his breath.

'You . . . bloody fool.' He glared round at his men. 'All of you . . . fools. That fire can be seen . . . for miles.'

'No.' Metellus shook his head. 'There's no one near enough to see it. No one, sir. Not any more.'

Cato looked at the legionary. 'Where did you get the meat?'

'That farm we found the other day, sir.'

'Those people . . .?' Cato felt sick. 'What happened?'

Metellus grinned. 'Don't worry, sir. They'll be telling no tales. I took care of that.'

'All of them?'

'Yes, sir.' Metellus' brow creased into a frown. 'Of course.'

One of the other men chuckled. 'Only after we'd had a bit of fun with the women first, sir.'

Cato bit his lip and lowered his head so that the men would not see his expression. He swallowed and fought to regain control over his breathing, even though his heart still pounded in his chest and his limbs were trembling from exhaustion and rage. It was all too much for Cato, and for a moment the temptation to renounce the last vestiges of his authority over these men was overwhelming. If they wanted to destroy themselves, then let them draw the attention of every enemy warrior for miles. What did he care? He had done his best to win them an extra measure of life,

191

against all the odds. And this was how they repaid him. Then there was the smell of the meat, wafting down into the empty pit of his stomach so that it groaned and rumbled in keen anticipation of the feast. Cato felt a cold wave of self-contempt and anger as his weakness washed across him. He was a centurion. A centurion of the Second Legion at that. He'd be damned if he was going to let all that stand for nothing.

'Sir?'

Cato raised his head and looked down on Metellus. The legionary was holding out some meat to him, and nodded at it with a placating smile. It was that sense of being treated as a petulant child that made Cato decide what he must do. He forced himself to look beyond the meat to the legionary who had so selfishly endangered them all.

'You fool! What good is that if we're dead tomorrow – the moment they find us?'

Metellus did not reply, just stared back – in surprise at first, but then his expression changed to one of sullen insubordination, and he dropped the hunk of pork back on to the ground.

'Please yourself, sir.'

Cato swiftly swung the butt of his spear and thrust it into Metellus' chest, knocking the legionary back, into the arms of the men squatting behind him, still eating. Immediately a chorus of angry complaints rent the tense atmosphere.

'Silence!' Cato shouted, his voice cracking with anger. 'Shut your bloody mouths!' He glared at them, daring them to defy him, and then turned his gaze back on Metellus. 'And you – you piss-poor excuse for a soldier . . . you're on a charge!'

Metellus' eyebrows rose for an instant, then he suddenly laughed. 'A charge! You're putting me on a charge, are you, sir?'

'Shut up!' Cato roared back at him, drawing the butt of the spear back to strike another blow. 'Shut up! I'm in command here!'

Metellus was still laughing. 'That's priceless, that is! And what punishment would you have me do, sir? Empty the latrines? Pull an extra guard duty on the main gate?' He waved a hand at the clearing. 'Look around you. There's no camp here. No ramparts to defend. No barracks to clean. No latrine to empty . . . nothing. Nothing left for you to command. Except us. Face up to it, boy.'

Cato shifted his grip on the spear shaft and spun it round, so that its point hovered no more than a foot away from the legionary's throat. Around him the others stopped eating and reached for the handles to their knives and swords, watching the centurion intently.

For a moment everyone was still, muscles tensed and hearts pounding as the sow continued her high-pitched shrieking from the side of the clearing.

Then Figulus slowly stepped forward and gently pushed the tip of Cato's spear down. 'I'll deal with this piece of shit, sir.'

Cato glanced towards him, brows clenched together, and then he lowered his spear as he looked back at Metellus, and spat on the ground beside the legionary. 'All right then, Optio. He's yours. See to it at once.'

As soon as he had uttered the words Cato turned away, in case the glimmer of tears at the corner of his eyes betrayed his strained emotions. He strode off to the side of the clearing and made his way to a small grassy mound that looked out across the marsh.

Behind him Figulus hauled Metellus to his feet. 'Time to teach you a lesson, I think.'

The optio pulled his sword out of his waistband and tossed it to one side, and raised his fists. Metellus eyed him warily and then smiled. The optio was tall and broad, typical traits of the Celtic blood that flowed through him. Metellus was leaner, but had been ruthlessly hardened by the years he had served with the Eagles. The contest would pit brawn against experience, and Figulus could see that Metellus fancied his chances as he lowered his body into a crouch and waved the optio towards him.

Metellus took a pace forwards and with a wild roar the legionary launched himself into the attack. He never made it. Figulus threw his right fist forward in a blur and there was a soft crunch as it slammed into the legionary's face. Metellus dropped heavily to the ground, motionless, knocked out in one blow. Figulus delivered a swift kick to the prone figure, then rounded on the other legionaries.

He smiled, and said softly, 'Anyone else here want to fuck with authority?'

The night passed quietly. Cato took an early watch, sitting in the dark shadows under a tree and keeping watch over the milky wet sheen of the surrounding marsh, bathed in the silvery glow of a bright crescent moon. Down in the camp all was silent, the men having quietly gone to rest under the brooding menace of the optio's gaze. The confrontation had ended for now, but Cato knew that the officers and men would be at each other's throats at the slightest provocation from now on. The ties of training and tradition that still bound them together were unravelling far faster than he had anticipated, and soon all that would remain would be a band of wild men desperate to survive each other, as much as survive the hostile territory that surrounded them.

He had failed, Cato judged himself. He had failed his men, and there was no shame greater than that. And as a result of his failure they would all die in this forsaken wasteland at the heart of a barbarian island.

Despite his tortured reflections on his failure, Cato shut his eyes almost as soon as he had curled up on the ground. He was far too tired to be afflicted by those edgy dreams that usually plague troubled minds, and fell into a deep, dark sleep.

* * *

A hand shook him awake and, after a moment's disorientation, Cato sat up and squinted into the face that loomed over him. 'Figulus. What is it?'

'Shhh!' the optio whispered. 'I think we've got company.'

The shroud of sleep slipped from Cato at once and instinctively he reached for his sword. Around them a thin mist wreathed the camp, and obscured any detail beyond twenty or thirty paces away. A light dew beaded Cato's filthy tunic and the air smelled of damp earth. 'What's happening?'

'Sentries say they can hear men moving close by. Sent for me at once.'

'And?'

'I heard it too. Lots of men.'

'Right. Wake the others. Quietly.'

'Yes, sir.'

As the hulking mass of the optio glided away into the mist, Cato rose to his feet and padded softly across to the path that led up from the clearing to the small hummock where the sentries kept watch. When he reached them, Cato crouched down. He didn't have to ask them to report; the air was filled with the faint clinking of equipment and muffled voices softly passing on instructions that Cato could not quite make out. Even as he crouched, straining his ears, the sounds came closer, all around them.

'We're surrounded,' whispered one of the legionaries, turning to Cato. 'What do we do, sir?'

Cato recognised the man: Nepos, one of Metellus' cronies from the night before. It was tempting to point out to the man that this situation was the consequence of his lack of self-control the day before. But there was no time or point in dwelling on the blame for their perilous situation.

'Fall back. We get back to the camp . . . and hope they pass us by. Whoever they are.'

He led the sentries back down the track and when they reached the clearing Cato saw that the rest of his men were assembled, weapons in hand and waiting for his orders.

'There's nowhere to hide,' Cato said quietly, 'and there's only one way into this clearing. If we try and break out across the marsh, we'll just get stuck and hunted down. Best to stand ready, keep silent, and hope that they can't see us in this mist.'

The legionaries stood in a small ring, facing out, ears and eyes straining to discern the slightest sight or sound through the grey veil that surrounded them. Soon they could all hear the sounds of men moving a short distance away, the rustling of bushes and snapping of twigs under careless footfalls.

'What are we standing here for?' Metellus hissed. 'I say we make a run for it.'

Cato turned on him. 'And I say I'll cut your throat if you make another sound. Got that?'

Metellus looked at him, then nodded and turned back towards the growing sounds of the approaching men, spreading out all around them.

Cato's eyes flickered from the grey outline of one tree to the next, and soon he thought he caught fleeting glimpses of the wraithlike forms of men moving through the trees. Gradually the sounds subsided and then there was silence, broken only by the rustling of the piglets, stirring beside the slumbering form of the sow.

'Romans!' a voice called out of the mist in Latin, and Cato quickly turned towards the sound. 'Romans! Throw down your arms and surrender!'

Cato drew a breath and called out 'Who's there?'

The voice answered at once, 'I speak for Caratacus! He demands you drop your weapons and surrender. Or else, you die.'

'Who's he trying to fool?' Figulus muttered. 'We're dead either way. At least it'll be quick and less painful if we fight. Might take a few of them bastards with us as well.'

Cato could only nod at the prospect of the imminence of his death. It had come to this at last, and he felt his spine and neck clenched in the grasp of an icy fist. He was afraid, he reflected in some small rational part of his mind. At the very end he was afraid to die when it came down to it. But Figulus was right. Die he must, and right here and now, if he were to spare himself the lingering torment of a death at the hands of barbarians.

'Romans! Surrender. You have the word of Caratacus that you will not be harmed!'

'Bollocks!' Figulus shouted back.

Suddenly there was movement all around them and at once figures drifted forward out of the mist, and solidified into the forms of native warriors, hundreds of them, hemming the small knot of Romans in on each side. They slowly closed in and shuffled to a stop no more than ten feet from the points of the Roman spears. Again the voice called out to them, much nearer now, but still invisible.

'This is the last time Caratacus deigns to make his offer. Surrender now and you will live. You have ten heartbeats to decide . . .'

Cato glanced round at the fierce faces of the warriors, woad-patterned beneath jagged crests of lime-washed hair. They stood, poised and ready to rush forward and cut the handful of legionaries to pieces. There was a thud, and Cato glanced round to see that Metellus had dropped his sword. Several more of his men immediately followed suit. For a moment Cato felt nothing but contempt and rage for Metellus. He was on the verge of charging into the enemy line . . . Then he regained control of himself and realised that it would be a futile death. Quite futile. And while he lived there was always hope.

Cato took a deep breath as he straightened up. 'Drop your weapons . . .'

Chapter Thirty

'What do you think they'll do with us?' Figulus muttered. They were sitting inside a cattle byre. The previous occupants had been moved, but not the soiled straw they had lived in, and the faecal filth caked on to the mud and grime that had become a second skin for the Romans.

Cato rested his forearms on his knees and was staring down at his boots.

'I've no idea. No idea at all . . . I'm not even sure why they let us live. They've not taken many of us prisoner before.'

'What happened to the ones they did take prisoner?'

Cato shrugged. 'Who knows? All we've found is bodies – and bits of bodies. I wouldn't get your hopes up.'

Figulus craned his neck round and squinted through a small gap in the willow-weave that formed the wall of the byre. Beyond the wall the rest of the enemy's camp stretched out across the island: hundreds of round huts, enclosed by a low palisade. There was only one approach to the camp, along a slender causeway that crossed the shallow waters surrounding the island. The causeway was defended by two formidable redoubts that projected from the island, either side of the main gate, which itself was made of thick timbers of oak. Inside the gate the survivors of Caratacus' army rested and licked their wounds, while they waited for their commander to decide what to do next.

When the small column of Roman prisoners had been led into the camp a large crowd of warriors and a few women and children had turned out to pour scorn and ridicule on the half-starved and filthy representatives of their vaunted enemy. While keeping his head protected as best he could from the shower of mud, shit and stones, Cato had looked round the camp with a professional interest. The warriors had kept their equipment clean and many still sweated from the training they had been doing before the prisoners had arrived. Cato had expected them to be demoralised and beaten after the almost complete disaster at the crossing of the Tamesis fifteen days before. But these men were clearly fit and eager to return to the fight.

The prisoners had been paraded round the camp and forced to suffer the usual indignities of capture before being led to this byre, where they had remained for three days, fed on scraps and tied up around the wrists

196

and ankles. The existing stench of the small space had been made worse by the urine, shit, vomit and sweat of the prisoners, unable to move far from their position, without disturbing their comrades bound on either side. By day the sun beat down on them, cooking the thick fetid air that filled the byre so that every breath made Cato and his men feel nauseous. Outside, the Britons trained hard, with the monotonous clash and clatter of weapons, punctuated by the grunts and war cries of men determined to fight on against the legions with every fibre of their being.

'Not much chance of finding a way out through that lot,' Figulus said, as he turned round and leaned back against the wicker wall. The optio reached down and tried to ease the leather collar around his ankle into a more comfortable angle. 'Even if we could get out of these.'

Cato shrugged. He had long since given up any thought of escape, after thoroughly assessing the situation. The byre was guarded by three warriors, day and night. While the wall did not represent a serious obstacle to a man determined to find a way through or over it, the long chain that bound all the prisoners made it impossible to get out of the byre.

With all consideration of escape banished from his mind, Cato concentrated on the reason for their being spared in the first place. It seemed to make no sense. They would be useless as hostages. What were the lives of a score of legionaries to General Plautius? And the fact that they were fugitives from Roman justice made them even less valuable as a bargaining counter. So, if not hostages, then what? The alternative purpose of their captivity filled Cato with a horror that clenched its icy grip around his spine.

Human sacrifice.

Caratacus, like all Celt leaders, bowed to an authority placed even above the kings who ruled the tribes of this island – the druids. Cato had encountered them before and carried the scar of a terrible injury given to him by a sickle-wielding druid. Worse, he had seen evidence of what the druids did to the men, women and children they offered up as sacrifices to their gods. The image of himself being slaughtered on a stone altar, or being burned alive in a wooden cage haunted every long hour he spent tethered to his men in their prison.

Most of the others shared his foreboding and sat in silence, only shifting when their position had been endured long enough to become unbearably uncomfortable. Even Metellus and his cronies held their tongues and sat waiting for the inevitable end. Only Figulus seemed to have any fight left in him, and watched and listened intently to the daily routine in the surrounding camp. Cato admired his optio's resolve, irrelevant as it was, and made no attempt to persuade Figulus to stop fretting and accept his fate.

At the end of the third day Cato was woken from a light sleep by a sudden deafening chorus of cheering. Even the guards outside the byre joined in, thrusting their spears up in the air with each shout.

197

'What's all the noise?' asked Cato.

Figulus listened a moment before replying. 'Caratacus. It's Caratacus – they're calling out his name.'

'Must have been away from his camp for a few days. Wonder where he's been.'

'No doubt trying to stir up some more resistance to our legions, sir. He'll soon be running out of allies, I'm thinking.'

'Maybe,' Cato replied grudgingly. 'But it's not going to do us much good, is it?'

'No . . .'

The cheering and acclamation went on for a long time before the native warriors had had their fill and returned to their training and other duties.

The sun dipped down below the top of the wall and threw the prisoners into shadow. This was the time their guards entered the byre and gave them a basket of scraps. The men slowly stirred in anticipation of the chance to try to stave off the aching agony of their hunger. Cato found himself licking his lips and watching the gate that opened into the byre. They were kept waiting a little longer than usual and for a moment Cato feared that there would be no food this evening. Then there was the gentle clink from the chain that fastened the door and it was shoved open. A pale shaft of light stretched across the stinking heap of ordure in the byre, then a shadow passed over it and Cato looked up to see a large warrior looming over them, glaring round at the grimy creatures chained to each other.

'Which of you has the highest rank?'

Even if the accent was thick the Latin was good enough to understand, and Cato made to raise his arm. At once Figulus restrained him with a warning shake of the head and prepared to volunteer himself. But Cato spoke first.

'Me!'

The warrior looked round at Cato and raised his eyebrows. 'You? I asked for your commander, not your goat-herder. Now which of you is it?'

Cato flushed angrily and cleared his throat to reply as clearly as possible. 'I am Centurion Quintus Licinius Cato, commanding the Sixth Century, Third Cohort of the Second Legion Augusta. I hold the senior rank here!'

The warrior could not help smiling at the umbrage he had provoked. He looked Cato up and down and laughed, before he continued in his own tongue.

'I had no idea the men of your legions were led by little boys. Why, you look barely old enough to shave.'

'Maybe,' Cato replied in Celtic. 'But I'm old enough to know you Britons are full of shit. How else could I have cut so many of you down?'

The warrior's smile faded and he fixed the young centurion with a cold glare. 'I'd watch your tongue, boy. While you still have one. You're the one who's up to his neck in shit, not me. You'd do well to remember that.'

Cato shrugged. 'What did you want me for anyway?'

The warrior bent down, undid the shackle around Cato's ankle and slipped the collar off the centurion's leg. Then he hauled Cato roughly to his feet and snarled into his face, 'Someone wants to see you, Roman.'

Cato wanted to recoil from the bared teeth and wide-eyes of the barbarian, and he knew that the man wanted him to flinch, to show some sign of fear. Cato was equally aware that his men were watching him closely; in fear, yes, but also to see if he could face up to the enemy.

'Fuck you.' Cato spoke in Latin. A smile flickered across his lips and then he spat into the warrior's face. His mouth had been dry and it was more air than spittle that struck the warrior. Even so, it had the desired effect and Cato doubled up as the man slammed a fist into his stomach. He sank to his knees, doubled over and gasping for breath, but Cato's ears rang with the cries of support and defiance from the legionaries. The warrior grabbed the centurion by the hair and yanked him back to his feet.

'How funny was that, Roman? Next time I'll crush your balls like eggs. Then you'll never get to speak like a man again. Let's go.'

He threw Cato out of the byre and as he followed he noticed a guard approaching with the basket of food for the prisoners. As the guard neared the entrance to the byre the warrior suddenly lashed out with his fist and knocked the basket flying, scattering the scraps all around. At once a handful of chickens scurried over from beside the nearest hut and began to peck at the stale morsels. The warrior nodded in satisfaction before he turned back to the startled guard. 'No food for the Romans today.'

The guard nodded and warily bent down to retrieve the basket as the warrior clamped a hand round Cato's arm and dragged him away into the heart of the camp. The evening meal was being prepared and the smells of cooking filled the air, tormenting Cato even as he slowly caught his breath. Despite the agony in his stomach he was still aware enough to keep looking around as he was hauled through the camp. There were many warriors here, tough-looking men who looked up as the warrior passed through them with his prisoner. Cured meat hung from racks, and grain pits were filled almost to the brim. These men clearly had the will and supplies to continue the fight and act as a cadre around which further resistance to Rome could be built. If the legions were ever to bring this island under the control of the Emperor then these men had to be utterly destroyed, Cato realised. Not that it was his problem any more. He was no longer a Roman soldier. Indeed, it was almost certain that he would not be anything in the near future. Perhaps he was even now being dragged to his execution – a sacrifice for some druid ritual of the night.

At length, as darkness closed round the camp, Cato was shoved through the opening of one of the larger huts, and with his hands still tied together, he fell awkwardly on to the rushes strewn across the floor. Rolling on to his side, Cato saw a small fire crackling at the centre of the hut. Sitting on a stool behind the fire was a large man with sandy hair tied back from his face. He was wearing a simple tunic and leggings that emphasised the bulk of muscle they covered. Solid arms, ending in long interlaced fingers, supported a bearded jaw. A thick moustache curved down either side of compressed lips. The glow of the fire revealed the face of a man in his late thirties with a prominent brow and broad forehead. A gold torc glinted around his neck, and Cato recognised the design at once. He felt a wave of terrible apprehension.

'Where did you get that torc?' he snapped in Celtic.

The man's eyebrows rose in surprise and he tilted his head with a look of bemusement.

'Roman, I don't think I had you brought here to discuss your taste in jewellery.'

Cato struggled to his knees and forced himself to calm down. 'No, I don't imagine you did.'

The binding around his wrists was uncomfortable, and Cato eased his backside on to the ground, sitting cross-legged, so that he could rest his arms. Then he examined the other man more closely. He was clearly a warrior, and had about him the composed aura of a natural commander of men. The torc was identical to the one that Macro wore about his thick neck. Macro had taken it from the body of Togodumnus, a prince of the powerful Catuvellaunian tribe and brother of Caratacus. Cato gave a brief bow of his head.

'I assume you are Caratacus, King of the Catuvellaunians?'

'At your service.' The man bowed his head with mock modesty. 'I had that honour, until your Emperor Claudius decided our island would make a nice addition to his collection of other people's lands. Yes, I was a king – once. Still am, although my kingdom has shrunk to this small island in the marsh, and my army is made up of those few warriors who survived our last encounter with the legions. And you are?'

'Quintus Licinius Cato.'

The king nodded. 'I gather your people prefer to be known by the last of the names they list.'

'Amongst our friends.'

'I see.' A faint smiled flickered across Caratacus' face. 'Very well, since the last name's the easiest to use, you'll have to consider me a friend, for now.'

Cato did not reply, and kept his face clear of expression as he sensed some kind of trap.

'Cato it is then,' the king decided.

'Why have you sent for me?'

'Because I willed it,' Caratacus replied imperiously, stiffening his back and staring down his nose at Cato. Then he relaxed and smiled. 'Are you Romans so accustomed to asking impertinent questions?'

'No.'

'I thought not. From what I've heard, your emperors don't take kindly to being addressed directly by the common folk.'

'No.'

'But we're not in Rome now, Cato. So speak freely. More freely than you might amongst your own.'

Cato bowed his head. 'I will try to.'

'Good. I'm curious to know exactly what you and your comrades were doing camped in the marsh. If you had been armed legionaries I would have had you killed at once. But for your appalling appearance and handful of weapons you would be dead. So tell me, Roman, who are you? Deserters?' He looked at Cato hopefully.

Cato shook his head. 'No. We are condemned men. Unjustly condemned.'

'Condemned for what?'

'For letting you and your men here fight their way over the river crossing.'

Caratacus' eyebrows rose a fraction. 'You were with those men on the far bank?'

'Yes.'

'Then it was you who trapped my army. By Lud! Those men on the island fought us like devils. So few, but so deadly. Hundreds of my warriors fell to them. Were you there, Roman?'

'Not on the island. That unit was commanded by a friend of mine. I was with the main body on the far bank.'

Caratacus seemed to stare right through Cato as he recalled the battle. 'You almost had us. If you had held your ground a little longer we'd have been caught and crushed.'

'Yes.'

'But how could you hold against an army? You held us for as long as you could. No commander could ask for more of his men. Surely your General Plautius did not condemn you for failing to achieve the impossible?'

Cato shrugged. 'The legions will brook no failure. Someone had to be called to account.'

'You and those others then? That's bad luck. What was your fate?'

'We were condemned to be beaten to death.'

'Beaten? That's harsh . . . though perhaps no harsher than the fate in store for you as my prisoner.'

Cato swallowed. 'And what fate would that be?'

'I haven't decided. My druids need to prepare a blood sacrifice before we return to the fight. A few of your men should appease our gods of war nicely. But, as I said, I haven't decided yet. Right now, I just wanted to see what you men of the legions are like. To understand my enemy better.'

'I'll tell you nothing,' Cato said firmly. 'You must know that.'

'Peace, Roman! I do not mean to torture you. I merely wish to discover more about the manner of the men who fill your ranks. I have tried to speak to your gentlemen officers, the handful of tribunes who have fallen into our hands. But two killed themselves before I could question them. The third was cold, haughty and contemptuous, and told me I was a barbarian pig, and that he would die rather than suffer the indignity of talking with me.' Caratacus smiled. 'He had his wish. We burned him alive. He kept control of himself almost to the end. Then he screamed and wailed like a baby. But I got nothing out of him, except for contempt of the deepest and most vile kind. I doubt I will learn much from your betters, Cato. In any case, it is the men in your legions I want to know about – to understand them; to know a little more about the men against whom my warriors were dashed to pieces, like waves on a rock.' He paused, then stared directly at Cato. 'I want to know more about you. What is your rank, Cato?'

'I'm a centurion.'

'A centurion?' Caratacus chuckled. 'Aren't you a little on the young side to hold such a rank?'

Cato felt himself blush at the casual dismissal. 'I'm old enough to have seen you defeated time and again this last year.'

'That will change.'

'Will it?'

'Of course. I just need more men. I grow in strength every day. Time is on my side, and we will have our revenge on Rome. We cannot lose for ever, Centurion. Even you must see that.'

'You must be tired of fighting us, after so many defeats,' Cato said quietly.

Caratacus stared at him across the glow of the fire. For a moment Cato feared that his defiance had been overdone. But then the king nodded. 'Indeed, I am tired. However, I swore an oath to protect my people from all comers, and I will fight Rome until my last breath.'

'You can't win,' Cato said gently. 'You must realise that.'

'Can't win?' Caratacus smiled. 'It's been a long year for all of us, Roman. Your legionaries must be weary after so much marching, and fighting.'

Cato shrugged. 'That's our way of life. It's all we know. Even when my people are not at war we train for the next one, every day. Every bloodless training battle our men fight increases their appetite for the real thing. Your people have fought bravely, but they are mainly farmers ... amateurs.'

'Amateurs? Maybe,' the king conceded. 'Yet we have come within a hair's breadth of defeating you. Even a proud Roman must concede that. And we're not beaten yet. My scouts report that your Second Legion is camped to the north of the marsh. Your legate has posted one of his cohorts to the south. Imagine, one cohort! Is he really so arrogant as to think that one cohort will contain me?' Caratacus smiled. 'Your legate needs to be taught a lesson, I think. Maybe soon. We'll show him – and the rest of you Romans – that this war is far from over.'

Cato shrugged. 'I'll admit that there were times when the success of our campaign looked in doubt. But now . . .?' He shook his head. 'Now, there can be only defeat for you.'

Caratacus frowned and looked pained for a moment before he replied. 'I'm old enough to be your father and yet you speak as if to a child. Be careful, Roman. The arrogance of youth is not tolerable for very long.'

Cato looked down. 'I'm sorry. I meant no offence. But with all my heart I know you cannot win, and there must be an end to the needless sacrifice of the people of these lands. They would beg it of you.'

Caratacus raised his fist and jabbed a finger at the centurion. 'Do not presume to speak for my people, Roman!'

Cato swallowed nervously. 'And who exactly do you speak for? Only a handful of tribes remain loyal to your cause. The rest have accepted their fate, and come to terms with Rome. They are now our allies, not yours.'

'Allies!' The king spat into the fire in contempt. 'Slaves is what they are. They are less than the dogs who feed on the scraps from my table. To be allied to Rome is to condemn your kingdom to a living death. Look at that fool, Cogidumnus. I hear that your emperor has promised to build him a palace. One worthy of a client king. So he'll condemn his people to become the property of Rome when he dies, just so that he can live out his life in a gilded cage, despised by your emperor and by his own people. That is no way for a king to live.' He gazed sadly into the glowing heart of the fire. 'That's no way for a king to rule . . . How can he live with such shame?'

Cato kept silent. He knew what Caratacus said about client kings was true. The story of the growth of the empire was littered with tales of kings who had welcomed client status, and had been so besotted with the baubles laid before them that they became blind to the ultimate fate of their people. Yet what was the alternative, thought Cato. If not a client king, then what? A futile attempt at resistance and then the cold comfort of a mass grave for those kings and their peoples who prized liberty from Rome over life itself. Cato knew he must try to make the king see reason, to end the senseless slaughter that had already drenched these lands in blood.

'How many of your armies has Rome defeated? How many of your men have died? How many hillforts and villages are now no more than piles of ashes? You must sue for peace, for your people. For their sake . . .'

Caratacus shook his head and continued to stare into the fire. For a long time neither man spoke. They had reached an impasse, Cato realised. Caratacus was consumed by the spirit of resistance. The weight of tradition and the warrior codes with which he had been imbued from the cradle unswervingly bore him down the path to tragic self-destruction. Yet he was sensible to the suffering that his course of action implied to others. Cato could see that his point about their needless suffering had struck home with the king. Caratacus was imaginative and empathetic enough for that, Cato realised. If only the king would accept that defeat must be inevitable, then the impasse would be broken.

At length Caratacus looked up, and rubbed his face. 'Centurion, I'm tired. I cannot think. I must talk with you another time.'

He called out for the guard and the man who had escorted Cato from the pen ducked into the hut. The king indicated, with a brief nod of his head, that he had finished with the Roman, and Cato was roughly hauled to his feet and shoved out into the darkness. He glanced back, and before the leather curtain slipped back across the entrance he had one final sight of the king: leaning forward, his head cradled in his hands, locked in a posture of solitude and despair.

Chapter Thirty-One

'He'll get us all killed.' Centurion Tullius nodded towards the cohort commander. Maximius was briefing the optios in charge of the day's patrols. Each officer commanded twenty men and had a native assigned to them to act as a guide. Every one of them was a prisoner, iron collars chained to the belt of legionary guards. Since their children were being held hostage it was unlikely that they would offer any resistance, or attempt to escape or betray their Roman masters. But Maximius was taking no chances. He had few enough men as it was. Centurion Tullius tapped his vine cane against the side of his greave, making a dull clattering noise. Macro glanced down irritably.

'Do you mind?'

'What? Oh, sorry!' Tullius lifted the cane, tucked it under his arm and glanced back towards the cohort commander. 'I thought we were here to find Cato and the others. Had no idea we were going to try and stir up a bloody revolt as well. Couldn't have done a better job if he had tried . . . the bastard.'

'Perhaps that's just what he's been ordered to do,' Macro wondered aloud.

'What do you mean?'

Macro shrugged. 'I'm not really sure. Not yet. Just seems to be an odd way to get the locals to help us.'

'Odd?' The old centurion shook his head. 'You weren't there when we ran those natives down by the river. He really lost his head.' Tullius lowered his voice. 'He was like a man possessed – wild, dangerous and cruel. He should never have been given a command. As long as he's running the Third Cohort, we're in deep trouble. He's already disgraced us. My service is nearly up, Macro. Two more years to my discharge. I've earned it – spotless record – until now. Even if he doesn't get us killed, the decimation is going to ruin our careers. You and the other centurions are still on the young side, still got years to go. What chance of promotion do you think you'll have with that on your records? I'm telling you, as long as that bastard's in command we're in the deepest of shit.' He looked away from Macro, towards the distant cohort commander and continued softly, 'If only something would happen to him.'

Macro swallowed nervously and stiffened his back. 'I'd be careful what

I said if I was you. He's dangerous, all right, but so is that kind of talk.'

Tullius looked closely at the other centurion. 'You do think he's dangerous then?'

'He might be. But *you* really scare me. What are you suggesting, Tullius? A sharp dagger in his back on a dark night?'

Tullius gave a short, unconvincing, laugh. 'It's happened before.'

'Oh, yes,' Macro snorted, 'I know. And I also know what can happen to the men of those units that are held responsible. I don't fancy ending my days in some imperial mine. And what if he was killed? You'd be in command.' Macro gave the other man a hard stare. 'Frankly, I don't think you're up to the job.'

Tullius looked down before Macro could see the pained expression in his eyes. 'You're probably right . . . I could have done it once, years ago. But I was never given the chance.'

Quite, thought Macro, and his lips curled in contempt.

Tullius looked up. 'Macro, you could take command.'

'No.'

'Why not? I'm sure the men would follow you. I'd follow you.'

'I said no.'

'All we need to do is make sure that Maximius' death doesn't look suspicious.'

Macro's hand shot out and grabbed the older man by the shoulder. He shook Tullius to emphasise his words. 'I said no. Got that? One more word out of you and I'll hand you over to Maximius myself. I'll even volunteer for the job of executioner.' He let his hand slip back to his side. 'Don't ever talk to me about this again.'

'But why?'

'Because he's our commander. It's not our job to question him, just obey his orders.'

'And if he gives us orders that'll get us killed? What then?'

'Then . . .' Macro shrugged, 'then we die.'

Tullius looked at him with a startled expression. 'You're as mad as he is.'

'Maybe. But we're soldiers, not senators. We're here to do as we're told and fight – there's no debating the issue. That's what we signed up to when we joined the Eagles. We swore an oath, you and me. That's all there is to it.'

Tullius stared at him, then jabbed a finger into Macro's chest. 'Then you are mad.'

'Gentlemen!'

They both turned round in alarm at the sound of Maximius' voice. He had finished his briefing and started towards them without the two officers being aware of their superior's approach. At the sight of their surprised and alarmed expressions a frown flitted over Maximius' face before he smiled genially.

'You two look like you're about to knock seven shades out of each other!'

Tullius forced out a weak laugh, and Macro made himself smile as the older centurion replied, 'A minor disagreement, sir. No more than that.'

'Good. What were you disagreeing about?'

'Nothing really, sir. Nothing worth mentioning.'

'I'll be the judge of that.' Maximius smiled again. 'So tell me.'

Tullius glanced at Macro and flapped a hand in the air between them. 'A difference of opinion, sir, a professional difference of opinion. I was saying that we'd have finished the enemy off a lot sooner if we'd had some of the Praetorian Guard units fighting alongside us.'

'I see.' Maximius looked searchingly at his subordinate's expression before turning to look at Macro. 'And what does Centurion Macro think?'

'He thinks the Guard are a bunch of idle wasters, sir,' Tullius chipped in before Macro could respond.

Maximius raised a hand. 'Quiet. I think Macro can speak for himself. Well, what do you think?'

Macro shot Tullius a withering glance before he replied, acutely bitter at the situation Tullius had forced on him. 'They're good men, sir. Good men, but, er, they must go soft after spending too long in Rome . . . sir.'

'And you think the men of the legions are a tougher proposition then?'

Macro shrugged his shoulders helplessly. 'Well, yes, sir. I suppose so . . . yes.'

'Bollocks!' Maximius spat back. 'There's no comparison. Your Guardsman is the finest soldier in the Empire, bar none. I should know. I served with them long enough. Tullius is right. If Claudius had left a few of 'em behind when he buggered off back to Rome last year, it'd all be over by now. The Guard would have sorted Caratacus out in double time.' He glared at Macro, breathing hard through flared nostrils. 'I thought an officer with your experience would have known that. There's no comparison between a Guardsman and your bog-standard legionary.'

'Yes, sir.' Macro coloured. He was tempted to defend himself. To answer back and justify the words Tullius had put in his mouth. To tell Maximius about the balls-up at the battle outside Camulodunum a year earlier that had nearly cost his vaunted Guards their lives. But Macro could not trust himself to continue the discussion: once his spirit of defiance was up there was no telling how indiscreet he would become. Best to let the cohort commander's umbrage wash over him like one of the flotsam-bloated waves that rolled over the shore back in his childhood home just outside Ostia. Macro stiffened his back and stared back into his superior's face. 'As you say, sir. There's no comparison.'

Maximius sensed the ironic tone straight away and dismissed Tullius with a curt word of command. As soon as there was no one near enough to overhear their conversation he turned back to Macro.

'What exactly were you and Tullius talking about?'

'Like he said, sir, it was a professional disagreement.'

'I see.' Maximius stared hard at Macro and chewed on his bottom lip. 'Nothing to do with that traitor we're looking for, then?'

Macro felt his pulse quicken and prayed that there was no sign of guilt written into the expression on his face as he replied, 'No, sir.'

'We're not getting very far with that line of inquiry, are we, Macro?'

'We, sir?'

'Of course.' Maximius glanced round suspiciously and then lowered his voice so that it was barely more than a whisper. 'Who else can I trust in this matter, Macro? Tullius is an old woman. Felix and Antonius are too young to be trusted with secrets, and uncovering secrets. You're the only one of my officers I can rely on. I want this traitor identified and brought to me in chains. You're the perfect man for the job, Macro.'

'Yes, sir.' Macro nodded. 'What exactly do you want me to do?'

'Just talk to the men. Nice and easy. Don't push for information. Say as much as you need to, nothing more, and just listen. Then report back to me.'

'Yes, sir.'

'Right then.' Maximius turned round and nodded towards the last patrol standing at ease by the gate. 'I want you to take them out today. The guide says there's a few small farms to the east. They might be worth checking out. After all, Cato's lot will need food. If there's any sign that the locals have been harbouring them, you know what to do. Make an example of them.'

'Yes, sir.'

'The optio there, Cordus, is from Felix's century. He's a good man, you can rely on him. Now you understand your orders?'

'Yes, sir.'

The cohort commander paused a moment to look intently at Macro. 'Report everything to me when you return – everything.'

Macro saluted. 'I understand, sir.'

'Good luck, then.'

At noon Macro gave the order for the patrol to halt. Sentries were posted at each end of the track and the rest of the men gratefully slumped down on to the ground and reached for their canteens. The sky was a piercing blue, except for a scattering of puffy clouds drifting slowly away to the south of the marsh. Macro craved some shadow and looked at them longingly. The sunshine beat down on the still air that hung over the marshland and every man in the patrol was sweating heavily. The felt liner inside his helmet was drenched and Macro could feel beads of sweat running down his forehead, and dripping on to his cheeks. The heat was exhausting and the men had grumbled about their lot all morning, until Macro had lost his patience and ordered them to shut up. Thereafter they had marched along in silence, growing steadily more surly as the guide led them along the narrow winding paths, through rank-smelling shallows and thickets of gorse without encountering any sign of habitation.

'Cordus!' Macro waved him over. 'Ask him how much further we have to go.'

The optio nodded and strolled over to the native guide. He was a short man, thickset and clad in a rough woollen tunic and leggings. He was barefoot, and bare-headed and the length of leather tied loosely as a collar had chafed his skin and left a weeping red welt around his fat neck. The guide was a metalsmith and depended for his livelihood on the strength in his arms, not his legs, and had suffered even more than the armour-clad legionaries from the morning's march. Although he had claimed to know the route to the farms scattered amid the marsh, Macro suspected that he had nearly lost the way on several occasions. The fact that his family were held hostage in a small cage in the Roman camp had been more than an adequate incentive for him to find the right trail again as speedily as possible. But now he looked spent, squatting on the ground, chest heaving for breath and looking longingly at the canteen his Roman guard was drinking from.

The man started with a small cry of alarm as Cordus poked him with the tip of his boot. With a cringe he looked over his shoulder, squinting up at the optio as Cordus gave a little jerk of the man's lead and forced him to struggle to his feet.

Cordus spoke to him in the smattering of Celtic he had picked up in Camulodunum while the Second Legion had been quartered there the previous winter. Between Cordus' accent and the native's unfamiliarity with the dialect it took a while for the question to be understood, and then the guide was pointing down the track and gabbling away in his own tongue until Cordus snapped irritably at him, yanking the leather lead to cut off the man's anxious stream of speech. He let the Briton drop down on to the ground and tossed the leash back to the legionary in charge of the guide before turning round and heading back to Macro.

'Well?'

'He reckons we should be there within the hour, sir.'

'Shit . . .' Macro mopped his brow as he tried to work out the timing. An hour there, say two hours looking over the small cluster of farms and then six hours' march back to the fort. It would be dusk before they made it back – if they were lucky. Blundering about in the marsh after dark was a pretty dire prospect. Macro took a quick swig from his canteen and wearily rose to his feet. 'Get 'em up, Optio! We're on the move again.'

There was a chorus of groans and angry muttering from all sides.

'Shut your fuckin' mouths!' Cordus shouted, 'or I will personally kick your teeth out the back of your arses! Up! Up!'

Macro made a mental note of approval as the optio strode up and down the path, lashing out at any man who was slow to stir. Cordus was exactly the kind of optio Macro approved of. Not perhaps as bright as Cato had been, but a firm advocate of the kind of harsh discipline that pushed the men on. The thought of Cato was an unwelcome reminder of the purpose of the patrol. Macro compressed his lips and unconsciously started drumming the tip of his vine cane on the hard earth of the path. If they did find Cato and the others, what then? The orders were to take them alive, if possible. But alive they posed a threat to Macro. He would not put it past some of those legionaries to try to strike a deal to reveal the name of the man who set them free in exchange for a more lenient sentence. Some bloody fool was bound to try it on, and the moment Maximius was aware that such a deal was on offer he'd either agree and then, renege on the deal later, or bring in the torturers and get the information out of the hapless prisoner one way or another.

On the other hand, if Macro gave the orders to have them disposed of here in the marsh, questions would be asked. And it wouldn't take a genius to guess at the reasons behind his desire to have them silenced quickly.

Besides, Macro was not sure that he cared to have Cato and Figulus killed if they fell into his hands. It was a wretched situation in every way and he had yet to carry out the subtle orders Maximius had issued him with before he set out.

As the patrol continued along the path behind the overweight guide Macro fell into step beside Cordus.

'Hot work.'

The optio raised his eyebrows. 'Er, yes, sir.'

'Could do with a swim when we get back,' Macro said thoughtfully, as his subordinate tried to work out if this was a statement or an invitation.

'A swim, sir. Right . . . that's just what we all need.'

Macro nodded. 'Especially after a day beating a path through this shitty marsh. If we ever find those bastards, I'll make 'em regret the day they ever decided to go on the run.'

'Yes, sir.' Cordus spat on the ground to clear his throat. 'Them, and that bastard who helped 'em escape in the first place.'

Macro glanced at him quickly. 'Whoever he is.'

'Yes, sir. He's got a lot to answer for all right.' Cordus swatted away a large wasp that had been hovering in front of his eyes.

'Yes, he has.' Macro paused for a moment. 'I suppose you can see why the general had to do it. Order the decimation, I mean.'

'Can you, sir?' Cordus frowned, seemed to think about it a moment, and then shrugged. 'Maybe. But ain't decimation taking it a bit too far?'

'You think so?'

Cordus pursed his lips and nodded. 'Course it is, sir. We fought 'em tooth and nail at the river. There was just too many of them, and we got pushed back. That's the way it goes. Some fights you just can't win. You don't bloody go and throw away forty-odd men to punish a cohort for not achieving the impossible. That's just mental, that is.'

'I suppose. But that doesn't excuse our man from going and setting them free, does it?'

'No. But it makes it understandable.' Cordus looked straight at him. 'Wouldn't you agree, sir?'

'I suppose so. Would you have done it?'

Cordus looked away. 'I don't know. I might have done . . . if someone hadn't beaten me to it. How about you, sir?'

Macro paused a while before he replied. 'It ain't an option for a centurion. It's our job to enforce the discipline, no matter how unfairly it's applied.'

'And if you weren't a centurion, sir?'

'I don't know.' Macro looked away with a pained, guilty expression. 'I don't want to talk about it.'

Cordus glanced at him quickly and then dropped back a pace in deference to Macro's rank. As the patrol wearily continued its march Macro considered Cordus' attitude to the fugitives. If the hardened optio had sympathy for the condemned men, then how many more men in the cohort felt the same way? And Cordus had gone beyond mere sympathy. The optio had hinted at a willingness to have helped the men escape. If that was the common feeling among the men, then the pool of suspects was sufficiently broad to offer Macro some hope of concealment. He felt a momentary lessening of the burden of his complicity in the escape. At least until the fugitives were tracked down.

'That's it?' Macro nodded down the track towards the silent round huts. A faint heat haze wavered across the track and made it look as if the nearest of the huts was floating on a sheet of water.

'Sa!' The guide nodded.

The two men were lying down and peering cautiously through some tufts of grass that grew either side of the track. Ahead of them the track opened out on to a wide area that rose up from the surrounding marsh. The space was covered with barley crops, interspersed with a few penned areas where sheep stretched out in whatever shade they could find, fat flanks rising and sinking as the beasts rested. It was a good place to have settled, Macro realised. Hidden away from the rest of the world, and from the eyes of any raiding parties from hostile tribes. If it became necessary, the narrow track leading into the farmland could be barricaded to discourage any raiders. But there had been no one left to watch the track, and there was no sign of life from the huts.

Macro ran a hand over the sweaty dark curls plastered to his head. He had taken off his crested helmet and left it with Cordus before creeping ahead with the guide. It had been a huge relief to free his head from the tight, confining discomfort of the helmet and the felt liner that was prone to itch when drenched in perspiration.

211

He jabbed a finger back down the track, away from the farm. 'Come on!'

Cordus and the others were tense and impatient and looked up expectantly when Macro and the guide returned. Cordus held out the centurion's helmet and Macro pulled on the liner, then the helmet, as he reported what he had seen.

'Nothing's moving. No sign of anyone at all.'

'Think it's a trap, sir?'

'No. If it was a trap, they'd want to lure us in; make it look peaceful and harmless before they sprung their surprise. It just looks deserted.'

'Or abandoned?'

Macro shook his head. 'There are crops, and I saw some animals. We'll enter the farm in close order and stay formed up until it looks safe.'

As the patrol marched between the nearest round huts the legionaries kept their heavy shields up and darted anxious glances at the entrances and towards any place that might conceal an enemy. But the silence persisted and added to the oppressive atmosphere of heat and stillness that smothered the landscape.

Macro raised his hand. 'Halt!'

The patrol shuffled their boots for a moment and then all was quiet. Macro indicated the largest huts. 'Search them! Two men each!'

As the legionaries peeled away and began to approach the structures cautiously Macro slumped down on a heavily scored tree stump that served the farmers as a base for log-splitting. He reached for his canteen and was about to pull out the stopper when there was a shout from the nearest hut.

'Over here! Over here!'

A legionary backed out of the dark entrance to the hut, his arm raised to cover his nose and mouth. Macro let go of his canteen, sprang up, and ran over to the man. As he reached the hut a foul stench of decay assaulted his nostrils and he slowed down involuntarily. The legionary turned round as he sensed the centurion's approach.

'Report!'

'Bodies, sir. The hut's full of them.'

Macro eased the legionary to one side, swallowed and then, grimacing at the smell, he ducked his head inside the hut, keeping to one side to let the light penetrate the shadows within. The place was alive with the buzzing of flies and Macro saw perhaps ten bodies heaped like discarded dolls in the centre of the hut. Propping his shield up against the door frame, Macro squeezed inside, stepped over to the corpses and kneeled down, fighting back the urge to vomit. There were three men, one old and wrinkled, and the rest were children, twisted grotesquely and staring sightlessly from unblemished faces beneath the usual tousled hair of Celtic youngsters.

A shadow fell across the faces of the dead and Macro looked back towards the entrance to see Cordus hovering at the threshold.

'Come here, Optio.'

Cordus reluctantly advanced, hand over his mouth, and squatted down beside Macro. 'What happened, sir? Who did this? Caratacus?'

'No. Not him,' Macro shook his head sadly. 'Look at the wounds.'

Each of the dead had been killed with a thrust, or a series of thrusts, the classic killing blow of a legionary's sword. 'Celtic warriors tend to use slashing blows. They let the impact of their heavy blades do the killing.'

Cordus looked at him with a frown. 'So who did this? One of our patrols?'

'No. I don't think so. But it was Romans all the same.'

The two officers exchanged looks filled with sad understanding, then Cordus looked at the bodies again. 'Where are the women?'

Before Macro could reply there was another shout. They rose up and hurried from the foul atmosphere of the hut, greatly relieved to burst back into the cleaner air outside. Macro gulped down several breaths to purge the odour of death from his lungs. A short distance away one of the legionaries was beckoning to Macro with his javelin.

'More bodies, sir. In here!'

Cordus was several paces ahead of him by the time they reached the hut and he glanced quickly inside and, after a short pause, withdrew his head and turned to face the centurion.

'It's the women, sir.'

'Dead?'

Cordus stepped to one side. 'See for yourself, sir.'

With a soul-wearying sense of sadness Macro peered into the hut. In the gloom he saw three naked bodies, one little more than a girl. The older women had bruised faces and all had been killed with the same thrusts. One of them was missing a breast, and a congealed mass of dry blood and butchered tissue sat alongside the mottled skin of the remaining breast. Macro felt a dreadful weight bear down on his heart as he stared at the scene. What had happened here? Only Cato's men could have done this. But surely Cato would not have allowed this? Not the Cato he knew. But that would mean that Cato no longer contolled his men. Or – a dark thought crossed Macro's mind – perhaps the reason for Cato's men being out of control was because Cato was no longer around to command them.

Chapter Thirty-Two

Over the following days Caratacus sent for Cato almost every evening, and continued with his curious interrogation. On the second night he offered Cato some food, and before the centurion could help it he had snatched up a leg of lamb and was about to sink his teeth into the meat when he paused. The scent of it wafted up to his nose and tormented him for a moment, before he lowered his arm and set the meat down on the wooden platter Caratacus had pushed across the floor towards him.

'What's the matter, Roman? Afraid I'd poison you?'

That thought had never occurred to Cato as the gnawing hunger had taken over his senses an instant before.

'No. If my men go hungry, then so must I.'

'Really?' Caratacus looked amused. 'Why?'

Cato shrugged. 'A centurion has to share the privations of his men, or he'll never earn their respect.'

'How would they ever find out? You're hungry. Eat it.'

Cato looked at the leg of lamb again and felt his gums moisten in anticipation. His imagination of the flavour of the meat was almost overpowering in its intensity and the power of the temptation to yield suddenly filled him with shocking self-knowledge. He was weak, a man without control over his own body. How quickly his will began to crumble against the urge to indulge himself. He clenched his fists tightly behind his back and shook his head.

'Not while my men go hungry . . .'

'Suit yourself, Centurion.' Caratacus reached down, grasped the shank and tossed the leg towards a hunting dog curled up against the side of the hut. The joint deflected off the ground and struck the animal on the muzzle. The yelp of surprise was quickly stifled as the dog seized the joint in its huge maw and, holding the end down with a shaggy paw, it began to chew. Cato felt sick with hunger and despair at the sight of the long pink tongue slathering over the meat. He tore his gaze away and turned back towards the enemy commander. Caratacus was watching him closely, with wry amusement.

'I wonder how many of your centurions would have turned that down.'

'All of them,' Cato replied quickly, and Caratacus laughed.

'I find that hard to believe. I think you are not as typical of your kind as you make out, Roman.'

Cato assumed that this was some kind of compliment, and that realisation made him feel like even more of a sham.

'I'm not typical. Most centurions are far better soldiers than me.'

'If you say so,' Caratacus smirked. 'But if you are the worst of them, then I must fear for my cause.' He tore off a small strip of meat from another joint and began to chew slowly, gazing abstractedly into the shadows between the roof supports of the hut. 'I find myself wondering if we will ever be able to better such men. I have seen thousands upon thousands of my best warriors die on your swords. The cream of a generation. We shall never see their like again. The great muster of the tribes will soon be no more than a memory of the few who still live and fight at my side. As for the rest . . . the lamentation of their wives and mothers fills the land and yet their deaths have bought no victory, only honour. If our fight is futile, then what is the value of an honourable death? No more than a gesture.'

He stopped chewing and spat out a small piece of gristle.

Cato cleared his throat softly, and spoke. 'Then send a message to General Plautius. Tell him you wish to seek terms. Honourable terms. You don't have to be our enemy. Embrace peace, and find a place for your people in our Empire.'

Caratacus shook his head sadly. 'No. We've talked that over already, Roman. Peace at any price? That is a licence for enslavement.'

'The choice before your people is peace, or death.'

Caratacus stared at him, still and silent as he pondered Cato's words. Then he frowned and lowered his forehead on to the palm of one hand and ran his fingers slowly through his hair.

'Leave me, Cato. Leave me be. I must . . . I must think.'

To his surprise Cato felt a great swell of sympathy rise up within him. Caratacus, so long the ruthless and tireless enemy, was in the end a man. A man tired of war, yet so versed in its lore, from the very first moment that he was old enough to bear a weapon, that he did not know how to make peace. Cato watched him for a moment, almost tempted to offer his enemy some word of encouragement, or even sympathy. Then Caratacus stirred, aware that the Roman was still in his presence. He blinked, then straightened up on his chair.

'What are you waiting for, Roman? Get out.'

As he was escorted back to the foul-smelling pen where the prisoners were still being held Cato felt his spirits rise for the first time in many days. No, even longer than that, he reflected. After two long and bloody campaign seasons it seemed that the enemy was close to accepting defeat. The more he thought about the words and demeanour of his captor the more Cato was certain that the man wanted to have peace for his people.

After a most desperate and determined attempt to defeat the legions, even he had recognised that Rome's resolve to make the island a part of the Empire was unshakeable.

In truth, Cato knew he had been deceitful in his responses to Caratacus. The charge that the natives' resistance to Rome was futile rang hollow in Cato's mind. The legions had been forced to fight almost every mile of the distance they had advanced across this island. Always watching their flanks, glancing anxiously over their shoulders, tensely waiting for the enemy to charge in, kill quickly, and then disappear and look for the next chance to whittle down the invaders.

The legionaries who were still awake in the pen barely looked up when Cato was shoved through the gap in the fence and chained back to the others. Figulus at once shuffled closer to his centurion.

'You all right, sir?'

'Yes . . . fine.'

'What did he want this time?'

It was the same question Figulus asked each time that the officer returned from his interrogation and Cato smiled at the routine they had settled into.

'I think we might get out of this alive after all.'

Cato quietly related what Caratacus had said, and what he had observed. 'But keep it to yourself. No point in building up the men's hopes if I'm wrong.'

Figulus nodded. 'But you think he's going to do it? Surrender?'

'Not surrender. He's too proud for that. He'll never surrender. But he might do something just short of that.'

'That'll do me, sir.' Figulus smiled. 'That'll do nicely for us all.'

'Yes.' Cato leaned his head back against the fence and looked up at the stars. Scattered across the black depths of the night sky they shone like tiny beacons. The air was quite clear and there was almost none of the agitated shimmering and twinkling that the heavens were usually prone to. The stars looked still and serene, at peace. Cato smiled at the thought. The signs were good. If a Celtic king and the stars were in some kind of harmony of spirit, then anything might happen. Even peace.

Figulus leaned closer to whisper. 'What happens then?'

'Then?' Cato thought for a moment. He really hadn't any idea. Almost since the time he had joined the Second Legion it had been embroiled in action with an enemy. First that tribe on the Rhine, and then the great invasion of Britain. Always fighting. But once it was over, they would return to the ordered routine of training and patrols. But what that would feel like, he could not imagine. 'I don't know. But it'll be different. It'll be good. Now let me rest.'

'Yes, sir.'

Figulus shuffled a short distance away and Cato settled back against the fence, face still raised towards the stars. For a while he simply stared, only conscious that a great burden had been lifted from his spirit. Slowly his eyes began to close and the stars drifted out of focus and before long he had fallen into a deep sleep.

Rough hands wrenched him from his slumber, hauling him to his feet in one savage movement. Cato blinked and shook his head, momentarily confused and alarmed. The warrior who had tasked to escort him into the presence of Caratacus was busy freeing the peg that bound him to the rest of the prisoners. Close by, some more men had detached six others and shoved them out of the pen. Most of the legionaries were awake and muttered anxiously to one another.

'What's going on?' Cato asked. 'Where are they being taken?'

Without replying the warrior suddenly struck Cato across the face with the back of his hand. The shock and the stinging pain jolted Cato into full consciousness and he staggered back a pace.

'What—'

'Shut up,' the man grunted. 'Open your mouth and I'll hit you again.'

He turned Cato towards the entrance to the pen and thrust him through the gap, sending the centurion sprawling on the ground outside. The wicker gate was closed and a guard rammed the locking peg back into its bracket.

'Get up, Roman!'

Hands still bound, Cato rolled on to his knees and struggled to his feet. Immediately he was thrust forward, away from the pen, towards a group of horsemen mounting up a short distance away, a handful of shadowy figures in the pre-dawn twilight. As they got closer Cato recognised Caratacus sitting silently in his saddle. Their eyes met briefly and before Caratacus glanced away Cato saw the cold, bitter hatred in the man's expression and felt a chilling tremor of fear trickle up his spine. Something had happened. Something dreadful, and now any hope he might have had that Caratacus was considering coming to terms with Rome had been swept away. There was pure murder in the eyes of the enemy commander now. Cato looked round, and saw the other six men who had been dragged from the pen being herded away into the shadows at spearpoint. He turned back to Caratacus.

'Where are they being taken?'

There was no reply, no sign that he had even been heard.

'Where are—'

'Silence!' his guard roared, slamming his fist into Cato's stomach. The breath was driven from him and he bent double, gasping for air.

'Get him on a horse,' Caratacus said quietly. 'Tie him over the saddle. I don't want him escaping.'

As Cato wheezed painfully, strong arms raised him and tossed him across a woollen saddle, face down. A rope was bound tightly around his ankles and then secured to the bindings between his wrists and secured with a knot. Cato was looking down the side of the horse towards the dark ground beneath. He twisted his head and tried to catch Caratacus' eye, but there was no sight of him from this angle and Cato let his head hang down, resting his cheek against the coarse, bitter-smelling, saddle-cloth. At once someone clicked their tongue and the horse lurched forward, at the tail end of the small party of horsemen.

They trotted out of the camp, across the narrow causeway and on to a trail whose details slowly became clearer as the light strengthened. Cato's mind raced as he tried to work out the reason for this sudden shift in the mood of Caratacus. Where was he being taken, and what had happened to the other prisoners? But there were no ready answers, only a growing fear that he was being delivered to his death, and that soon the rest of the Roman prisoners would be following him to theirs. From the chilling hatred he sensed in the men around him, Cato was sure that death, when it came, would be a welcome escape from the torments these warriors had planned for their captives.

Some hours later, after a long uncomfortable ride through the hot humid air of the marsh, they came to a small farmstead. Raising his head Cato could see a loose settlement of round huts, surrounded by farmland. Two more warriors were waiting for them and respectfully rose to their feet at their commander's approach. Caratacus halted his men and gave the order to dismount. Then he disappeared inside one of the huts and for a while all was still. Cato sensed an awful tension in the air as the warriors waited for Caratacus to reappear, and he felt afraid to move for fear of drawing any attention to himself. Instead he hung limply across the horse's back and waited.

How long it was, he could not say. At last the men stiffened in expectation, and Caratacus was standing beside Cato, knife in hand. The Roman twisted his head and looked up at an awkward angle, trying to gauge the other man's expression and wondering if this was the last view he would ever have of this life.

Caratacus glared back, eyes narrowed in disgust and hatred. He raised the knife hand towards Cato, and the centurion flinched and shut his eyes tightly.

There was a rasping tear and the length of rope that tied his hands to his ankles beneath the belly of the horse parted and fell away. Cato started to slide forward and just had time to duck his head between his arms before he toppled off and landed heavily on the ground.

'Get up!' Caratacus growled.

Cato was winded, but still managed to roll on to his knees and rise awkwardly to his feet. At once Caratacus grabbed him by the arm and dragged him towards the hut he had entered earlier. The loud buzz and whine of insects filled Cato's ears and the warm sickly stench of decay hit him like a blow. A powerful shove propelled him through the small doorway and Cato fell into the dim interior. He pitched forward and landed on something cold and soft and yielding. His eyes adjusted quickly to the darkness and as he raised his head Cato saw that he had landed, face first on the bare stomach of a woman, a fringe of pubic hair rasped against his cheek.

'Shit!' he cried out, scrambling away from the body. A small pile of sharp flints lay to one side and he stumbled on to them, painfully grazing the palms of his hands as he spread his fingers to cushion the landing, and then tightly clenched his fingers around one of the sharp-edged stones. There were more bodies in the hut, also naked, sprawled amid wide tacky patches of dry blood. It was then that Cato realised where he was, and who had done this terrible deed. 'Oh shit . . .'

The shock and the stench finally overwhelmed any last vestige of self-control and Cato vomited, spewing acrid gouts of sick on to his knees, until there was nothing left inside him, and the acid fumes wafted up to him and made him retch more. Slowly, he recovered and saw that Caratacus was staring at him from the far side of the hut, staring over the bodies that lay between them.

'Proud of yourself, Roman?'

'I – I don't understand.'

'Liar!' The king spat the word out. 'You know who did this well enough. This is the work of Rome. This and another hut, filled with bodies of defenceless farmers and their families. This is the work of an empire you said would befriend us.'

'This is not the work of Rome.' Cato tried to make himself sound as calm as possible, even though his heart was beating like a drum roll in its mortal terror. 'It is the work of madmen.'

'Roman madmen! Who else would have done this?' Caratacus raised his fist and stabbed a finger at Cato. 'Are you accusing my men?'

'No.'

'Then who else but your people could . . . would have done this? This is the work of Romans.' He dared Cato to disagree, and the centurion was aware that denial would cost him his life.

Cato swallowed nervously. 'Yes, but . . . but they must have been acting outside their orders.'

'You expect me to believe that? I've been receiving reports for days now about the punitive actions your legionaries have been conducting against the people who live in the valley. Flogging women and children, the firing of farms, and scores of killings . . . and now this. When we spoke last night you promised an end to war. I . . . I nearly believed you. Until now, until I have seen what the Roman peace is truly like. Now I can see it all clearly, and I know what I must do. There will be no peace between us. There can never be peace. So . . . I must fight your people with every fibre of my being while I still draw breath.'

Cato saw the wild expression, the fists clenched so tightly that knuckles stuck out like bare bones, and the tight line about Caratacus' jaw, and knew that there was now no hope of peace while Caratacus lived. His own life was forfeit, and so were those of the men still being held in the pen back at the enemy camp. All because Metellus could not control his desire for a decent meal. For an instant Cato hoped that Metellus would be amongst the first to die, and that his death would be long and lingering to compensate for all the suffering his appetite had brought to the world. It was sad that this bitter thought should be his last, Cato smiled, but there was no helping it. He looked up at Caratacus and resigned himself to death.

Before the enemy commander could act the sound of voices – anxious and alarmed – reached the ears of the two men in the hut and both turned towards the small entrance. Caratacus ducked and hurried outside, momentarily darkening the hut as he squeezed under the lintel. Then Cato rose up, took a last glimpse at the corpses, and followed his captor.

'What is it?' Caratacus called out to his men. 'What's happening?'

'Roman patrol, sire.' One of the warriors thrust an arm out, pointing down the track that led into the farmstead. 'Maybe twenty men, on foot.'

'How far away?'

'Half a mile, no more than that.'

'They'll have cut us off before we can ride out of here,' Caratacus said. 'Does anyone know if there's another way off this farm?'

'Sire,' one of his bodyguards cut in, 'I know this land. It's almost entirely surrounded by mud flats and marches. We'd never get the horses through it.'

Caratacus smacked his hand against his thigh in frustration. 'All right then. Get the horses. Take 'em to the far side of the farm and keep them out of sight. They mustn't make a sound, understand?'

'Yes, sire.'

'Then go!'

The warrior shoved a companion ahead of him and both men ran towards the horses tethered to a rail in the middle of the ground between the huts. Caratacus beckoned the other three men. 'Take the prisoner, and follow me.'

Cato was grasped by the shoulder and pulled along in the wake of the enemy leader. Caratacus led the small party across the farm buildings, ducked between two animal pens and ran towards the only part of the farmland that seemed to rise any appreciable height above the surrounding landscape. A stunted copse grew on the low crown of the slope just over a hundred paces away and Caratacus led them towards the trees at a brisk pace. Cato knew this was a chance to wrench himself free and try to escape. He felt his pulse quicken and his muscles tensed. He tried to brace himself for the decisive moment and he briefly imagined how it would happen, and just as briefly saw himself cut down by a sword as he tried to make for the safety of his comrades. He might be under sentence of death, but he might yet redeem himself by passing on the information about the location of the enemy camp.

By the time these thoughts had raced through his mind it was already too late. They were close to the trees and the man holding Cato's shoulder tightened his grip painfully and thrust the centurion towards the shadows beneath the low boughs of the nearest tree. Cato tripped over a root and thudded down on the ground, knocking the wind from his lungs. With a sickening rage of self-loathing he knew he had missed his chance to escape.

As if reading the Roman's mind the man who had been tasked with guarding him rolled Cato on to his front and, wrenching his hair back the Briton slapped the flat of his dagger blade against the throat of his captive.

'Shhh!' the warrior hissed. 'Or I'll slit you from ear to ear. Got it?'

'Yes,' Cato quietly replied through gritted teeth.

'Good. Keep still.'

They lay still, peering through the long grass that grew under the outermost branches of the trees, and waited. Not for long. Cato saw the red of a legionary shield emerge round a bend in the track. For a moment he felt a desperate longing for the company of his own people. The scout trotted forward, glancing round at the huts as he reached the centre of the farm. The legionary stopped, looked round cautiously, head cocked to one side as if listening, then he backed away, turned, and ran off.

Shortly afterwards the patrol marched into the village, and Cato picked out the crests of a centurion's helmet, and that of an optio. The two officers led their men into the loose circle of huts and halted the patrol. Then the centurion barked out a few orders, sending men running to search the nearest huts. He unbuckled the strap beneath his helmet and lifted it from his head. Cato took a sharp intake of breath as the dark hair and high forehead of Macro came into view. What the hell was Macro doing with such a small patrol? Cato's heart rose at the sight of his friend and he lifted his head to see better. The blade at his throat slid round so that the edge rested on his skin and rasped painfully.

His guard thrust his face close to Cato's and whispered fiercely. 'One more move, Roman, and you die.'

Cato could only watch from afar, in an agony of despair and helplessness as the Romans searched the huts, and Macro glanced round, his gaze sweeping right over Cato and the other men still and hidden just inside the fringe of the copse. There was a muffled shout and Macro turned and hurried inside a large hut. He emerged shortly afterwards, in response to another shout and made his way to the very hut that Cato had been kneeling in shortly before. This time it was longer before he emerged, and Macro walked slowly from the dark entrance, a knuckled fist held to his mouth. For a moment all was quite still, as Macro paused and stared at the ground, shoulders slumped wearily. Then, as Cato and the warriors either side of him watched silently, Macro looked up, stiffened his back and shouted out a string of orders. The men of the patrol trotted over to him, closed ranks and stood facing the copse, waiting for the command to move.

'Patrol!' Macro's parade-ground shout carried clearly to Cato, and the men either side of him tensed up, sword hands immediately reaching for their weapons. Macro's mouth opened wide and the sound reached them an instant later. 'Advance!'

The patrol tramped forward towards the concealed men, and Caratacus glanced towards the man still holding the knife at Cato's throat.

'When I say . . . kill him.'

The patrol marched up to a small hut, turned round it and began to head off down the track that led away from the farmstead. Caratacus let out a sibilant breath of relief and the warriors' tension eased off as the Roman patrol marched away. Cato could only stare at the backs of the legionaries with a terrible longing.

As they reached the edge of the farm, Macro stopped out of line and let his men file past as he gazed back towards the silent huts one last time. Then he turned away, and moments later the scarlet horse-hair crest of his helmet dipped out of sight behind a line of gorse thicket. Cato lowered his head on to his arms and shut his eyes, fighting back waves of black emotions that threatened to engulf him and shame him in front of these barbarians.

A shadow came between him and the sunlit farmland beyond the copse.

'Get up!' Caratacus snapped. 'Back to the camp. I've got something special in mind for you and your men.'

Chapter Thirty-Three

'So they're still around, then?' mused Centurion Maximius. He looked past Macro, through the tent flap and into the dusk beyond. The sun had just set and he pulled one of the parchment maps across the desk and smoothed it out between himself and Macro. 'This farmstead you were taken to was about . . . here.'

Macro looked down at the spot the cohort commander indicated and nodded.

'Right. Then we can assume they're somewhere close by. No more than half a day's march, I'd say.'

'Why's that, sir?' asked Macro. He waved his hand across the map in a broad sweep around the tiny sketch that marked the farm's location. 'They could be anywhere.'

'That's true, but not likely.' Maximius smiled. 'Think about it. They're hiding. They won't venture too far simply because they want to avoid natives and Romans alike. They have no access to guides, so they won't be familiar with the paths, and will fear getting themselves lost, or cut off from each other. They'll return to their lair each night, so we can narrow the search to the area around this farm. Assuming it was them who massacred the farmers.'

'Had to be, sir. Injuries were almost certainly caused by short swords. In any case, it's hardly likely that Caratacus and his men would go round bumping off their own people.'

'No . . .' Maximius tapped his finger on the simple sketch of the farm. 'But it seems a little strange. I didn't have much time to get to know Cato, but massacre, and rape? Doesn't seem like his style.'

'No, it doesn't,' Macro added quietly. 'I don't think he can be responsible for this.'

'Well, somebody was.' The cohort commander looked up. 'I thought you knew him well?'

'I thought I did, sir.'

'Could Cato really have done this?'

'No . . . I don't know . . . I really don't know. Might have been raiding for food, raised the alarm and then had to mix it with the locals. They got into a fight, and had to put them all to the sword.'

'Is that what it looked like?'

Macro paused a moment to reflect, but after what he had seen at the farm, there was little doubt in his mind. 'No.'

'So Cato, or some of his men, have gone native. Or at least they're pretty desperate. That's good. Should make them easier to deal with, when the time comes.'

Macro raised an eyebrow. 'When the time comes, sir? I thought that was the reason we were here.'

'And so it is!' Maximius laughed lightly. 'Although it has been a good opportunity to teach the locals how to behave.'

Macro stared at him. If the brutality of the last few days was a lesson to the natives, then what exactly had they learned about their new masters? That Rome was as cruel and brutal as any horde of barbarians. That, Macro reflected cynically, was hardly likely to foster good relationships with the locals over that vital period when Roman laws and Roman rule were being established in the new province. The local tribe was getting brutalised by Maximius on the one hand and raided and massacred by Cato and his fugitives on the other. All of which could only strengthen their resolve to aid Caratacus and his warriors. Maximius had done a blinding job of bolstering support for the enemy all right.

And as for Cato . . . for a moment Macro could not think. He was sure that he had known Cato well, but the massacre at the farm was the work of another kind of man. The two memories did not sit well together. But then again, not much made sense to him at the moment. The decimation of the cohort as punishment for being pushed aside by overwhelming odds. The perverseness of fate for selecting the blameless Cato for execution when it was Maximius who bore the responsibility for the escape of Caratacus. Now this unaccountable cruelty of Maximius towards the natives of this valley, matched only by Cato's heartless slaughter of the farmers and their families. It was as if reason itself had been driven from the world. With a chilling sense of foreboding it occurred to Macro that he lived at the whim of maniacs.

Maniacs like Centurion Maximius, who was grinning at him now. 'I tell you, Macro, it's all working out very nicely indeed. Soon the locals won't even be able to take a shit without wondering how we'll react. They'll hate us more than they've hated anything before in their miserable lives. If they find Cato and the others before we do, then you can be sure they'll show those bastards even less mercy than we will.'

'Yes, sir.' Macro cleared his throat uneasily. 'As you say, it's working out well.'

'And once Cato's been seen to, we can attend to Caratacus.'

Macro struggled to hide his astonishment. Tracking down a few pathetic fugitives was one thing. Taking on the likes of Caratacus was just this side of lunacy. A nasty thought abruptly intruded on his surprise, and he looked more closely at his commander and attended his words with a heightened concentration.

Maximius smiled. 'If we can deliver Caratacus to the general, then we'll be allowed to rejoin the legion. We'll be the legate's blue-eyed boys. You and me.'

'What about the others? Tullius, Felix and Antonius?'

'Tullius is an old woman,' Maximius sneered. 'And the others are young fools. Thank the gods they lacked the guile and treachery of that bastard Cato. You're the only one I ever had any confidence in, Macro. Only you.'

'Uh . . .' Macro flushed. 'Thank you, sir. I'm sure your confidence in me has not been misplaced. But I think you judge the other officers too harshly. They're good men.'

'You think so?' Maximius frowned. 'I doubt it. I'm surprised you can't see their faults too, unless . . . unless you're on their side.'

Macro made himself laugh. 'We're all on the same side, sir.'

Maximius did not respond, and there was a tense pause as the cohort commander scrutinised his subordinate. Then he relaxed a little. 'Of course you're right, Macro. Pardon me. I just had to be sure of your loyalty. Now then, on to other business, the real reason you were assigned to lead that patrol. Did you speak to anybody? Did you discover anything about the traitor who freed Cato?'

'Not really, sir. From what I heard it could have been any of the men. No one is particularly happy to be hunting down their comrades, especially when they don't believe they should have been condemned in the first place. Sorry, sir.' Macro shrugged. 'That's all.'

'That's all,' Maximius repeated mockingly. 'That is not all, Centurion. Not by a long way.'

Macro felt the familiar chill of anxiety, and tried not to let his guilt show. 'Sir?'

'If that's how the men feel, then they're as good as traitors themselves.' Maximius grasped his jaw in the palm of a hand and stroked the bristles on his chin nervously, gazing down into his lap. 'If they think they can get away with that, they're in for a great big bloody surprise. I'll show them . . . It's not the first time I've had to deal with their kind. Oh no, but I showed 'em what I was made of then, and I'll do the same again now. No one's going to make a fool out of me and get away with it.'

Macro kept quite still during and after this outburst, trying not to draw any attention to himself while Maximius perceived threats in every corner. Then the cohort commander glanced up with a small start as he became aware of Macro's presence again. He shook off the spell and smiled warmly.

'You'd best get some rest, Macro. You're going to need it over the next few days if we're going to show those scum we mean business.'

Macro was uncomfortably aware that he was not sure which scum Maximius was referring to and he nodded in response as the cohort commander waved a hand towards the flap of his tent.

Macro quickly rose from his seat, anxious to quit the scene. 'Good night, sir.'

He turned and strode away, ducking outside into the cool evening air, breathing its freshness in eagerly. Two clerks were working on trestle tables to one side of the entrance to the tent. One was filling a lamp with oil, to provide illumination when the last glow from the western horizon had died away. Macro made for the tent lines of his century and as he did so a figure passed him in the twilight. Optio Cordus saluted as he marched by. A few paces further on Macro glanced back over his shoulder, just in time to see the optio enter the cohort commander's tent.

'Curious,' Macro said softly to himself.

Why should Maximius want to debrief Cordus as well? Didn't he trust Macro enough to let him recount the details of the patrol?

Then it hit him, and Macro gave a bitter smile. Of course he was not trusted. Macro had not been sent on the patrol to sound out the men. He had been sent on the patrol to be sounded out by Cordus. Which meant that Maximius trusted him enough to suspect that he was the traitor. Plots within plots, Macro sighed. It was clear that during his service with the Praetorian Guard Maximius had spent far too much time in close proximity to the endless intrigue of the Imperial Palace. Well, if he saw plotters on every side, then let him. That was to Macro's advantage: safety in numbers. With this vaguely comforting thought Macro returned to his tent, checked that his optio had nothing to report, undressed and then collapsed on to his bed and quickly fell asleep.

The following morning the enemy sent the Roman occupiers of the valley a clear message of defiance. As the dawn mist cleared it revealed six frames that had been set up a short distance from the fort. On each frame a man had been tied, spread-eagled in the tattered remains of their army tunics. Each was gagged securely so that their death agonies had not been overheard by the Roman sentries on watch during the night. Every one of them had been gutted; skin and muscle peeled back and pegged to their sides to expose the raw, red meat and bone of the chest cavity. Their guts lay beneath their feet, where they had fallen, and glistened in dull grey and purple heaps. Each man had been castrated and his genitals hung from a thong around his neck.

A horseman was waiting beside the frames. He remained, still and silent, as the alarm was raised inside the fort. The palisade above the rampart was quickly lined by fully armed troops. Still he waited, until a cluster of red crests appeared amongst the gleaming bronze and iron helmets on the wall. Then with a quiet word to his beast he edged closer so that all might hear his words.

'Romans! Romans! I bring you a warning from my king, Caratacus.' He swept his arm out, round and back towards the bodies in a dramatic gesture. 'He offers you this example of what will happen to any Romans who fall into our hands if you dare to harm any more of the people of this valley, or those who dwell in the marsh beyond.' The messenger paused, and continued in a voice that dripped with contempt. 'My king wonders what kind of men wage war on women and children. If there are real warriors amongst you, then let them seek us out and fight us man to man. We grow weary of waiting for you to come and face us in battle. We had heard that the men of the Second Legion were the very best in General Plautius' army. Prove it, or forever wither before the scorn and pity of better men!'

The horseman turned his beast around and trotted casually away from the fort, not once looking back over his shoulder. On the gatehouse tower of the fort the officers of the Third Cohort watched him until he disappeared into a copse of trees that grew close to the edge of the marsh.

Macro, with a wry smile, admired the man's composure. 'Now that one had style.'

Centurion Felix snorted. 'Style? Let me down there and I'll teach that bastard about style.'

'Oh, really?' said Tullius. 'You'd just charge in there and teach the natives a lesson, would you?'

'Too bloody right I would!' Felix turned to the cohort commander. 'Sir? Let me take my century in there. Find that bastard and take the skin off him, nice and slow.' He thrust his finger towards the six bodies outside the fort. 'Just like they did to those men.'

'Don't be such a fool, boy.' Centurion Maximius sneered at him. 'You'd really fall for such obvious bait? How the fuck did you ever make it to centurion?'

Felix coloured, then opened his mouth to protest, but no words emerged. He glanced away from his superior and stared again at the bodies in mute protest.

Maximius laughed. 'Who do you suppose those men are? All our patrols are in and none of our men has gone missing.'

Felix took a moment to work it out. 'Cato's lot?'

Maximius patted him on the shoulder. 'See? The boy can learn! That's right. Cato's men.'

'Oh . . .' Felix looked again at the bodies, with a less fraught expression.

'And how much do you suppose I care what Caratacus has done to them? In fact, he's saving me the job.' Maximius shook his head and smiled. 'It's rather funny when you think about it. He seriously thinks that we might be provoked into action by his little display. Or that we might go easy on the locals.'

Macro watched him silently, noting the sudden gleam that sparked in Maximius' eyes. The cohort commander turned to his officers with a smile.

'We can turn this one round rather neatly. We're not going to go after them and rush into a trap. Even Caratacus must know we're not that foolish. And we're not going to go easy on the locals either. Why should we? The more of Cato's men he kills to make his point the better, as far as we're concerned. So let's make an example of that village. Let's kill ten of them for every one of Cato's men.' He nodded to himself. 'Caratacus and his men will be forced to react. If we're lucky, we might even draw them out of the marsh and get them to have a go at the fort. We'll just let them come on, and then slaughter them like dogs, right in front of our ramparts. Let 'em fill up the ditch with their dead. If any of them are stupid enough to surrender, then they'll be screaming for mercy before I let the bastards die. They'll never make a fool of Gaius Maximius again. Never!'

Macro was filled with astonishment at the relish with which his commander spoke the last words. Maximius was suddenly self-conscious, and glanced round at his officers with a quick smile, flashing his stained teeth at them. 'Come, lads, we've got work to do.' He glanced over his centurions, then his gaze settled on Macro. 'You've got the best job of all, Macro.'

'Sir?'

'Get your men formed up. I want you to take them into the village. Round the locals up and select sixty of them – men, women and children. Then take 'em over to that lot,' he nodded towards the Roman dead. 'Then kill them. Make it last. I want to hear them scream. Better still, I want Caratacus to hear them scream. When you're done make sure all the heads are put on poles. Understand?'

Macro gave a sharp shake of his head.

'What's so difficult to grasp? You're not Centurion Felix here . . .'

'No, sir.' Macro shook his head again. 'I can't do it.'

'Can't do it?' Maximius looked astonished. 'Bloody hell, man! It's the easiest thing in the world. What do you think all the bloody training has been about for the last fifteen years of your life? Kill them.'

'No . . . sir.'

'Kill them. That's an order.'

'No. I won't. Like the man said, real soldiers fight men. They don't massacre women and children.'

Maximius glared at him, mouth tightly shut and nostrils flared. The other officers and the nearest legionaries stirred uneasily. Macro drew himself up to his full height and stared calmly back. He had said his piece, and braced himself for the counterblast. He was surprised at the calmness that suffused his body. He had felt this way a few times before, when death in battle seemed inevitable. Calmness. Or was it merely resignation? Macro didn't know, and he didn't really care. It was simply a moment of curiosity about himself and his motives. Cato would have known the answer, he thought, and could not help smiling at the introspection he normally did not tolerate in his young friend. It was almost as if he had to fill in for the lad when Cato was not there, so used to his company had Macro become.

'What's so funny?' Maximius asked softly.

'Nothing, sir. Really.'

'I see . . .' The cohort commander narrowed his eyes. 'I had hoped that you, of all my officers, would be loyal to me. I can see now that my trust in you was misplaced. I wonder how deep your treachery runs.'

'Sir, I am no traitor. I'm loyal to the oath I've sworn every year since I joined the Eagles.'

Maximius leaned closer. 'Is it not part of your oath to obey the orders of a superior officer?'

'Yes, sir,' Macro replied evenly. 'But I question your fitness to command this cohort.'

Maximius took a sharp breath, then spat out his reply. 'You dare to question my fitness?'

'I do. If the other centurions have any sense, and the guts to own up to their feelings, they'd say the same.'

'Silence!' Maximius roared and struck Macro across the face with the back of his fist. The blow was sharp and hard, and Macro saw an explosion of white as he staggered back under the impact. As his vision cleared he tasted blood in his mouth and, raising a hand to his lip he discovered it was split. Blood dripped steadily from his chin as he steadied himself and faced the cohort commander again.

'Centurion Macro is confined to his tent.' Maximius looked round and sought out a face in the press of men who had drifted closer to witness the extraordinary confrontation. 'Optio Cordus! Step forward! I'm making you acting centurion in command of Macro's century.'

'Yes, sir!' Cordus smiled.

'You will carry out my orders concerning the villagers. To the letter, understand?'

'Yes, sir.'

'You will show no mercy, and none of your predecessor's lack of backbone.'

'No, sir.' Cordus flashed a smug sidelong glance at Macro.

'Now escort Macro to his tent, and post a guard outside. He is to speak to no one. Get on with it.'

Cordus turned to Macro, and the latter, with lips curled in contempt, gave a shrug and turned away from the cohort commander, striding towards the ramp that led down into the fort.

Chapter Thirty-Four

'He's killed the men who were taken out of here earlier,' said Cato, once the warriors had chained him back into position and left the pen.

Figulus nodded. 'That's what I thought. Where did they take you, sir?'

'To that farm. The one our friend Metellus visited. Caratacus wanted me to see the bodies.'

'Why?'

Cato shrugged. 'He thinks the Third Cohort is responsible for the massacre. I daren't tell him the truth.'

'I should fucking hope not.'

Cato smiled briefly. 'Anyway. I had hoped that I might still talk him round. But I don't think there's any real chance of peace any more. He'll fight us to the end now – however many of his own people and ours have to die in the process.'

'Did you really think he'd ever give in?' Figulus asked.

'I hoped he would.'

Figulus shook his head sadly. 'You don't know the Celts very well, sir. Do you? Fighting is in their blood.' He smiled. 'Maybe in my blood too. My grandfather was a warrior of the Aedui tribe. The last time they rose in revolt against Rome was shortly before I was born. Even though the tribe had been beaten, he never gave in. Him and the other warriors who survived the last battle. They hid in the forests and continued the fight until they were too old to wield a sword. Then they just starved to death. I can remember finding their bodies, once in a while, when I was a kid and we went hunting in the woods. My grandfather crawled into our village one day, starving and sick. My mother barely recognised him. It's the first time I ever met him. Anyway, he died. But the last words on his lips – the last thing he ever said – was to utter a curse on Rome and her legions. Caratacus is cut from the same cloth. He'd never have surrendered, sir.'

'Seemed close enough to it the other night.'

'Don't fool yourself, sir. It was just a lapse, the faintest shadow of a doubt and nothing more. And now he'll fight on until he dies.'

Cato stared at his optio for a moment, before shrugging and looking away. 'Maybe. But you joined the Eagles. Perhaps he could be persuaded to as well.'

230

Figulus laughed softly. 'My father had seen enough of Rome to know that she would never be beaten. So he served in the auxiliaries and raised me to be as Roman as possible. Perhaps more Roman than most Romans. I doubt my mother's family would even recognise me any more, let alone consider me one of their own. I joined the Eagles, and I fight for Rome, but I still understand the Celtic mind, and I know Caratacus will never give in to Rome. Never. Mark my words.'

'Then that's a shame. A man should know when he's beaten. He should face the facts.'

'Oh, really?' Figulus turned to look at his centurion. 'Then how about you, sir? Doesn't look like we've any hope of getting out of this place. Are you ready to give in and die?'

'That's different.'

'Oh?'

Cato nodded. 'He's got responsibilities. Caratacus holds the fate of many in his hands. I'm just fighting for me. For my survival. I'll do anything I can to survive.'

Figulus looked at him a moment, then said, 'You're not so different as you'd like to think, sir. He has his people to care about, and you have yours.' Figulus nodded at the other men in the pen.

Cato look round at the remaining men squatting against the wicker walls. Most were just staring blankly at the ground between their feet. None of them was talking, and Cato realised they had resigned themselves to death. And there was nothing be could do about it.

It was different for Caratacus. He could make a difference. That was why he owed it to his people to make peace, while they still respected his will. While they were still prepared to follow him. Unlike these poor men, Cato reflected. They were beyond the boundaries of the normal discipline that bound them to his will. Only Metellus seemed to have any sense of purpose left, however futile the situation seemed. He sat hunched over the chain where it joined his ankle collar, worrying away at it with the edge of a small stone. Cato wondered what the legionary thought he would do if he managed to break the chain. There were still three guards outside the pen, and the pen itself was in the middle of an enemy camp packed with thousands of Celt warriors. Cato shook his head, turned his gaze towards Figulus and spoke very quietly.

'We'll be joining the others in the near future. Once Caratacus has finished off the Third Cohort.'

'They're nearby?'

'Yes. I saw Macro and a patrol earlier. Caratacus says they're camped just outside the marsh. Seems that Maximius is laying into the local villagers with more than usual relish. Caratacus won't stand by and let it happen. Besides, I get the feeling that his warriors need a victory badly.'

Figulus was silent for a moment before he responded. 'From what I

231

saw on our way in here, our lads are going to be outnumbered five or six to one, sir.'

'About that,' Cato agreed. 'If they're caught by surprise it'll be over very quickly.'

'Yes . . . there's not much we can do about it, sir.'

'No.' Cato was tired, and the powerlessness of their situation bore down on him like a great weight. Even conversation was too much effort. Looking round he sensed the same despondency and despair in the rest of his men. They too knew the end was coming and were contemplating their deaths with the same quiet desperation as their centurion.

As the night fell over the enemy camp, fires flared up in the open spaces between huts. Soon the smell of roasting pork wafted through the palisade to add to the torment of those chained inside.

'I could murder a pig,' Metellus grumbled, and a few of the men raised an ironic laugh.

Cato frowned and snapped back at the legionary, 'That's the reason why we're here in the first place. You and your bloody stomach . . .'

As the evening wore on the enemy camp took on the spirit of celebration. The warriors feasted, and from the sounds of their revelry it soon became evident that they were drinking themselves into a raging frenzy. The air was thick with slurred singing, punctuated by roars of laughter. The prisoners in the pen listened sullenly to the drunken din, and Cato wondered if they were being saved to provide some bloody entertainment later on. The hairs on the back of his neck tingled with icy terror at the recollection of the men he had once seen thrown alive to hunting dogs at the court of King Verica of the Atrebatan tribe. Was that preferable to being imprisoned in a wicker cage and roasted over a fire? That had been the fate, so Cato had heard, of some other prisoners who had fallen into enemy hands. There would be little mercy for Romans amongst the tribesmen who had suffered such grievous losses against the legions in battle.

'Bastard Romans . . .' A voice muttered in Celtic just the other side of the wicker wall. 'Why have we got to guard them all night?'

'Yes,' someone else chimed in. 'Why us?'

'Why us?' a voice mimicked him. An older man from the sound of it, Cato decided. 'Because you're little boys, and I'm stuck here to make sure that you don't create any mischief, when I should be over there with the rest of the lads getting a skinful.'

There was clear resentment in the man's tone. Cato felt a racing light-headedness as his mind grasped at a plan that formed even as the older guard finished his grumbling and fell silent.

He drew a breath and called out in Celtic, 'Hey, guard! Guard!'

'Shut your mouth, Roman!' the older man snapped back.

'What's the party for?'

There was a low chuckle. 'The party? Why, that's being held in honour of all the Roman heads our warriors are going to take tomorrow!'

'Oh, right . . . So only your warriors are feasting then. Not your women, or your children . . . not you.'

'Shut your mouth, Roman!' the older guard shouted. 'Before I come in there and shut it for you. For ever!'

There was a pause before one of the youths continued, 'Why can't we have a drink?'

'You want a drink, eh?' the older warrior replied. 'You really want a drink?'

'Yes.'

'Think you can handle it?'

'Of course I can!' the youth shot back indignantly.

'Me too,' his friend added.

'Well then,' the warrior lowered his voice into a conspiratorial tone. 'You two stay here, and I'll go over and see what I can find for us.'

'What about the prisoners?'

'Them? They're quiet enough. Just keep a close eye on them until I get back.'

'How long'll you be?'

'Long as it takes,' the warrior chuckled, as he turned and strode away towards the raucous festivities.

Inside the pen Cato felt his pulse quicken, and twisted round, groping with his tied hands for a small gap in the wicker weave behind his head. He thrust his fingers in and gently prised two thick lengths apart, just wide enough for him to see outside. A short distance away the warrior was just disappearing behind a hut. Beyond him the gently sloping thatched roofs of the surrounding huts were rimmed with a bright glow from the fires, and here and there sparks swirled up into the night. Cato strained his neck and pressed his face closer to the gap. To one side he could just see the two boys who had been left on guard. They were armed with war spears and stood close to the pen, their features sketched in by soft strokes of light from the loom of the fires. Boys they may be, but they looked quite capable of killing a man if they needed to. Cato turned back and grasped his optio's arm.

Figulus had not been asleep, but lost in thought and he stirred anxiously. 'What? What is it?'

'Shhh!' Cato tightened his grip. 'Be quiet. One of the guards has gone.'

'So?'

'Now's our chance. Now, or never.'

'What you going to do about these?' Figulus raised his hands and nodded at the leather thongs binding his wrists.

Cato ignored him and, reaching down, he pulled up the hem of his tunic and started groping around inside his soiled loincloth. Figulus looked at him and shrugged. 'Well, I suppose there's always time for one last—'

'Quiet!' Cato struggled for a moment and then withdrew his hands, and opened one palm to reveal a small flint with a sharp edge chipped on to one side. 'Give me your hands.'

Figulus reached over and Cato at once started to saw on the tough leather thongs.

'Where did you get that, sir?'

'The farm. Thought it might come in useful. Now, keep still.'

'You had it hidden there all the way back?' Figulus grinned. 'Must have been uncomfortable.'

'You can't imagine . . . Now shut up and hold still.'

Cato concentrated on cutting through the optio's bonds, fingers gripped tightly round the smooth side of the flint as the sharp edge snagged and tore at the twisted strips of leather. He worked fast, conscious that the older warrior might return at any moment, despite the lure of drink and food. The first thong parted and Cato concentrated on the remaining two. The second went soon after, with a sharp cry of pain from Figulus as the flint slipped and cut into his skin.

'What's that?' Cato heard one of the guards say.

'What?'

'Sounded like someone in there, in pain.'

His companion gave a nasty chuckle. 'If that's what they sound like now, I can hardly wait to hear them once the druid gets his hands on them. Sit down, get some rest. You'll need it tomorrow.'

'Right.'

Cato breathed deeply and continued, taking care this time not to hurt his comrade as he worked away at the last strip. As the flint bit into the leather, Figulus strained his muscles to part the thong, and the bone-hard tension in the strip of leather made Cato's work far easier. A moment later the optio's wrists flew apart as the thong snapped.

'Now me,' Cato whispered, passing him the flint. 'Be quick!'

Figulus worked at the bonds in a frenzied blur of movement and soon Cato's hands and feet were free. As he rubbed at his sore wrists Cato nodded to the others and the optio crept round the pen to the next man and began work. Once the circulation had eased and he felt his hands would not betray him when he went into action, Cato turned round and peered through the gap in the wicker wall again. The two remaining guards were squatting on the ground just outside the entrance to the pen, staring wistfully towards the sounds of the distant revelry.

When the last of the men was free Cato beckoned to them. There were only twelve of them left, and one of those was so racked and weakened by diarrhoea that he could barely stand up.

'There's no time for details, men,' Cato whispered urgently. 'We must have a go at the two sentries outside. As soon as we get the gate open we rush 'em. After that, we'll make for the edge of the village.'

'And go where?' Metellus interrupted. 'Place is surrounded by water. There's only one way out.'

'There's a few boats over that way.' Cato pointed to the southern side of the camp. 'I saw them when we approached the entrance to this place. We'll take those.'

'Then what, sir?'

Cato looked at him directly. 'We have to warn the cohort, and get a message to Vespasian.'

For a moment Cato feared that Metellus would protest, but the legionary gave a faint nod of acceptance.

'Right then, let's move. When the gate opens, you move – fast.'

Cato turned, and worked his way over the puddles and heaps of filth towards the inside of the gate. It was fastened by a stout wooden bolt on the outside, a short distance from the top. While the others crouched down, silent and tense and ready to spring, Cato slowly rose up to the full extent of his height, peering over the gate at the dark backs of the two guards. He reached a hand over the top of the wooden frame and groped down for the peg that fastened the gate. While his eyes remained fixed on the guards Cato's fingers crept down the rough surface of the wood until his arm was fully extended. Then he took a breath and rose up on the tips of his toes. This time the very tips of his fingers brushed the top of the peg. Cato strained to reach further but could gain no purchase on the wood shaft, and finally he withdrew and slumped back behind the gate with a sharp intake of breath.

'Shite,' he mouthed. 'Can't reach it.'

'Try again,' Figulus urged him. 'On my back.'

The optio dropped on to his hands and knees and leaned gently against the inside of the gate. Cato placed a boot on the optio's shoulder and gently raised himself up again, ignoring the grunt of pain from Figulus as the iron studs of Cato's boot bit into his flesh. This time Cato could see clearly over the top of the gate and he carefully reached down to the peg and gently took up the strain. It had been firmly jammed into the receiver and he gritted his teeth and strained to pull it free. Then, at last, it shifted a little, then a little more. But this time it turned slightly with a faint squeak. Cato's hand froze and his eyes flickered up towards the guards, just in time to see a head turn towards him.

There was an instant of terrible stillness as the boy looked at the gate in puzzlement. Then he snatched up his spear, scrabbled round and shouted at this comrade, 'They're escaping! Up! Stop 'em!'

Cato threw both arms over the gate, grasped the peg and wrenched it free with all his strength. The peg shot out of its receiver and the gate crashed open as the legionaries behind it surged forward, clambering over Figulus and sending Cato flying forwards. He crashed to the ground at the feet of the guard who had spotted him, and rolled on to his side, arm raised, ready to protect himself. He saw the young warrior towering above, dark against the starry sky, and saw him draw back his spear to strike at his helpless enemy. Before the iron tip began to thrust down a dark shape flew over Cato, crashed into the boy and knocked him to the ground. More dark shapes fell upon the guard and there was a horrible gurgling choking sound, a brief thrashing of limbs and then silence. As Cato regained his feet he saw the other guard running away, towards the glow that rimmed the nearest huts.

'Stop him!' Cato hissed.

Close by, Metellus snatched up the first guard's spear and sprinted forward. Then he realised the boy would reach his comrades before he could catch him. The legionary stopped, threw back his spear arm, sighted the back of the guard twenty paces ahead, and hurled it forward. Cato missed the flight of the spear in the darkness, but a moment later there was a thud, and explosive gasp of breath, and the native boy pitched forward. Metellus ran forward to make sure that his enemy was finished, and wrenched the spearshaft from the back of the dead boy.

The men gathered around Cato in the darkness, breathing hard and eagerly waiting for his orders, flushed with exultation at their escape and the prospect that they might yet live. They looked to him, and for a moment Cato felt paralysed by the responsibility for these men's lives. Then the moment passed and he looked round.

'Get their weapons. Then put the bodies in the pen.'

Figulus took the other spear and after a brief rummage over the corpses two men had spears and one held a dagger. The guards were then bundled into the pen and then Cato shut the gate, found the peg, and quickly jammed it back into place.

'Good. Now let's go.' Cato turned away from the pen and was about to lead his men off, when a voice called towards them. He spun round, eyes darting from hut to hut until they fixed on a shadow walking uncertainly towards them from the direction of the feast.

'You're in luck boys!' The voice was slurred but Cato still recognised it as that of the older man who had left his young charges alone earlier on. 'I got you some drink!'

He held up a stoppered jar as he walked unsteadily towards the pen. Then he stopped, lowered the jar and stared. 'Boys?'

'Get him!' Cato called out, starting forward. 'Before the bastard brings 'em running.'

The warrior threw his jar towards Cato and turned to sprint away, screaming out as he ran. He had sufficient head start that Cato knew it was futile to go after him.

'Shit!' he breathed.

'Now what?' Figulus muttered. 'We fight our way out?'

'No chance,' said Metellus. 'They'll be all over us any moment.'

Cato turned to his men. 'We split up. Go like hell, and no heroics, whatever you see or hear. Someone has to warn Maximius. Metellus, take your friends that way. Figulus and the others will come with me. Best of luck.'

Cato made a quick salute to Metellus and the four men who stood with him and then turned and ran, crouching low, towards the southern side of the enemy camp. Already the sounds of revelry had died away and now the faint clatter of equipment and urgent shouts revealed that the enemy were alerted.

Metellus shouted from the direction of the pen, 'They're on to us! Let's go lads, this way!'

As Cato ran in the opposite direction, weaving between the huts, he heard the cries of Metellus and his men become more distant and then drowned out by the shouts of the warriors who hunted them down. The narrow ways that twisted between the huts soon disorientated Cato and he had to stop a moment to try to get his bearings, while Figulus and the others glanced round anxiously.

'Where's Lucius?' someone whispered. 'And Severus? They were behind me just now.'

A figure rose up and took a pace back the way they had come.

'Stay where you are!' Cato hissed. 'They'll have to take their own chances now. Like Metellus and the others.'

'But, sir—'

'Quiet man!' Cato glanced round at the huts, then up at the pattern of stars in the night sky. 'It's this way . . . I think.'

'You think?' one of the men muttered.

Cato felt a wave of rage well up inside him. 'Shut up. This way, then. Let's go.'

Shortly afterwards they were through the last of the huts and racing down a low bank towards the edge of the water. The stars shone brilliantly in the night sky and their reflections shimmered off the oily smooth surface of the water that surrounded the camp.

Figulus grasped his arm. 'Over there!'

Cato followed the direction the optio indicated and saw the dark shapes of small boats drawn up on the shore fifty paces away.

'That'll do us. Come on.'

They ran down along the edge of the water until they came to the boats, over a dozen of them. From one came the unmistakable sounds of lovemaking, and Figulus looked towards Cato and drew a finger across his throat. Cato shook his head. There'd already been enough killing and it seemed abhorrent to slaughter a pair of lovers into the bargain. As it was, the moans and groans and cries of passion were sufficiently loud to cover any sounds made by Cato and his men as they eased two of the craft into the water and pushed them out until the cold water reached their thighs.

'Optio,' Cato whispered.

'Sir?'

'Take that man. Get away from here any way you can. Then go north. Find Vespasian and tell him where this camp is, and tell him that Caratacus is about to move against the Third Cohort.'

'What about you, sir?'

'I'm going to warn Maximius.'

Figulus shook his head wearily. 'It's your funeral.'

'Maybe. But there's far more lives at stake than his. Just make sure you find Vespasian. If he's quick he might just save the Third Cohort, and force Caratacus to fight.'

'Yes, sir.'

'Then go.' Cato reached out his hand and the two men exchanged a forearm grasp. 'Good luck, Optio.'

'You too, sir. I'll see you back at the legion.'

'Yes . . . go.'

There was a good deal of splashing as the Romans clambered aboard the two boats. A dark shape rose from one of the craft on the river bank and a string of foul Celtic oaths followed them into the darkness as the four men paddled away. Once they had put some distance between them and the island camp Cato glanced back over his shoulder. There was a faint glimmer that silhouetted the roofs of some of the huts, and the wavering spark of torches being carried amongst the huts. But no sign of pursuit.

'We did it, sir!' the legionary with Cato laughed. 'We escaped from those bastards.'

Cato strained his eyes. 'It's Nepos, isn't it?'

'Yes, sir.'

'Well, Nepos, we're not out of trouble yet. So do me the favour of keeping your damn mouth shut, and paddle for all for you're worth.'

'Yes, sir.'

Cato took one last look back, and wondered briefly if Metellus had found a way out. Of all the condemned men who had escaped with him, only a handful now remained. And on their shoulders rested the lives of hundreds of comrades, who were completely unaware of the attack that Caratacus was about to unleash on them.

Chapter Thirty-Five

'Are you sure about this, sir?' Nepos muttered as they crouched down in some long grass scarcely a hundred paces from the main gate of the fort. The ramparts loomed grey and forbidding in the thin mist of dawn. The brooding, menacing atmosphere in the valley had been present the moment the two men had emerged from the track leading through the marsh and seen the stakes lining the route ahead, each one bearing an impaled head. Nepos looked round at the centurion.

'Sir, if we go in there and give ourselves up, we're dead men. Might as well save them the bother of clubbing us and just bash our brains out on the nearest rock.'

'They have to be warned,' Cato replied firmly.

'Can't we just shout the details out to them, then bugger off sharpish?'

'No. Now shut up.'

Cato took a deep breath and then rose to his feet. Cupping his hands to his mouth he faced the gate and shouted the warning given to sentries by returning patrols.

'Approaching the fort!'

There was a moment's silence and then came the response. 'Advance and give the password!'

Cato looked down at Nepos. 'Right then, let's go.'

The legionary reluctantly stood up beside his superior, then Cato advanced slowly towards the gate. He could already hear the sentry shouting for the duty officer, and could imagine the duty century being roused from their slumber by rough kicks from the centurion and optio. They would scramble into their armour, snatch up their weapons and rush up on to the ramparts under a barrage of abuse from their officers. As the two filthy, bearded fugitives walked steadily out of the mist, through the dew-drenched grass, helmeted heads began to appear along the wall. Javelins wavered above them like tall rushes in a light breeze.

'Shit . . .' Nepos whispered. 'This was a bad idea. We're dead.'

'Shut up!' Cato snarled. 'Not one more word.'

They stopped just before they reached the defence ditch, which stretched out along the ramparts either side of the gate.

'Who the hell are you?' a voice called down from the gatehouse.

Cato drew a breath before he replied, struggling to sound as authoritative as possible. 'Centurion Cato, legionary Nepos, of the Sixth Century, Third Cohort, Second Legion.'

Cato could see heads craning over the wooden rail of the palisade for a better look. Excited muttering rippled down the length of the wall.

'Silence there!' a voice roared out, and Cato saw the transverse crest of a centurion's helmet appear above the gate. The face was indistinct in the dim light but the voice was unmistakable. As soon as the men had fallen silent Tullius looked down on the wretched figures standing outside the fort, then fixed his gaze on the taller and thinner man. For a moment neither officer spoke and Cato was consumed by a sudden terrible doubt and wondered if it had been a foolish mistake to have presented himself before the fort. Perhaps Nepos had been right. They should have stood off, shouted the warning, and then fled for safety. The dread was over in a moment, as Cato reminded himself that his only future lay with the army, whatever the outcome.

'Centurion,' Tullius called out, 'what the hell are you doing here?'

The formality of his tone was not lost on Cato and he knew that Tullius was trying to give him one last chance to run.

'I have to speak to Maximius. At once.'

Tullius stared at him a moment, then shrugged before he turned away to give his orders to the men waiting below by the gate. 'Open her up. Optio of the watch! Send a squad out to arrest those men.'

With a deep groan from the hinges the gates swung inwards and at once eight men with drawn swords doubled out and surrounded Cato and Nepos. There was no hiding the surprise in their expressions as they beheld the two fugitives. Surprise, and distaste, Cato realised, and he was suddenly very conscious of their filthy and ragged appearance and felt ashamed. Even so, he drew himself up and, with as much dignity as he could scrape together, he marched in through the gate, flanked by his guards. Out of one prison and straight into another, he mused bitterly, and could not suppress a rueful grin.

The guards halted once the party had entered the fort and the gate was shut behind them. Cato turned to look up at the gatehouse and saw Tullius swing himself on to the ladder and climb down. There was no expression on the veteran's face, and Cato felt the spontaneous smile of greeting fade from his lips. Tullius stopped, a few feet from Cato and shook his head.

'What the fuck do you think you're doing?'

Cato cleared his throat. 'I must speak to Centurion Maximius, sir.'

Tullius stared at him a moment and then, without looking away, he gave an order. 'Optio of the watch.'

'Sir?'

'My compliments to the cohort commander. Tell him he's wanted at the main gate.'

240

Once the optio had trotted away Tullius stepped right up to Cato and spoke softly.

'What are you playing at, lad? The moment Maximius claps eyes on you you're a dead man.'

'If I don't warn him, then we're all dead men.'

'Warn him?' Tullius frowned. 'Warn him about what?'

'Caratacus. He's on his way here with what's left of his forces. He intends to wipe you –' Cato smiled – 'us – he intends to wipe us out.'

Beyond Tullius, Cato caught sight of the optio scrabbling to a halt as a figure strode round the corner of a line of tents. Maximius thrust the man to one side and bellowed down to the men at the gate.

'What the hell is going on? Centurion Tullius! What are those bloody beggars doing in my fort? We're not a hostel for vagrants!'

Tullius turned round and snapped to attention. 'Beg to report, sir. It's Centurion Cato, and one of his men.'

'Cato?' Maximius faltered a moment, and then continued forward as he stared at Cato in frank astonishment. Then as he confirmed the centurion's identity for himself Maximius smiled with cruel relish. He stood before Cato, hands on hips and head slightly cocked as he appraised the pair of men before him. His nose wrinkled.

'You stink.'

'Sir, I have to tell you—'

'Shut up!' Maximius screamed back. 'Shut your mouth, you disgusting piece of shit! One more word and I'll cut your throat.'

He turned to Tullius. 'Throw 'em in the latrine ditch and post a guard!'

Tullius' eyebrows rose. 'Sir?'

'You heard me! Carry out my order.'

'But, sir, Centurion Cato came here to warn us.'

'Centurion Cato?' Maximius stabbed his finger into Tullius' chest. 'He's no centurion. Got that? He's a condemned man. A dead man. Don't ever refer to him by that rank again. Do I make myself clear?'

'Yes, sir,' Tullius replied quietly. 'But the warning?'

Maximius clenched his fists as the blood drained from his face. 'Carry out my orders! If you don't want to end up like Macro, then fucking move yourself!'

Tullius shrank back. 'Yes, sir. At once, sir.'

The old centurion turned and snapped out his orders to the section that had escorted Cato and Nepos inside the fort, and now stood at attention to one side. At once the two fugitives were grasped by the arms and rapidly marched away from the gate towards the far corner of the fort. Cato twisted his head round.

'Sir, for pity's sake, hear me out!'

'Centurion!' Maximius spat. 'Silence that prisoner!'

'Caratacus is coming!' Cato managed to get out before Tullius jumped towards him and slapped him hard across the jaw. For a moment Cato was dazed by the blow, then he tasted blood and felt his mouth fill up with a thick gout. He dropped his head to one side and spat it out, before he shouted out one last warning.

'Don't—'

Tullius raised his fist.

'All right,' Cato mumbled. 'All right. What did he mean about Macro?'

Tullius looked over his shoulder, and saw that Maximius was taking the sentries to task, bawling out a diatribe against sloppy watch-keeping. Tullius turned back to Cato.

'Macro's under arrest.'

'Arrest?' For a moment Cato was struck by the dreadful thought that his friend's role in the prisoners' escape had been discovered, and, for what it was worth, he tried to bluff it out. 'What's he been arrested for?'

'Macro refused an order to carry out reprisals on the natives.'

'Reprisals?'

'Yesterday six of your men were butchered, right in front of us. Maximius ordered Macro to kill sixty villagers in return. He refused. So, Maximius placed him under arrest and handed his century over to an optio, Cordus, a right nasty piece of work, who was only too happy to carry out the order.'

Cato looked at him. 'You're serious?'

'Deadly. But quiet now!' For an instant Tullius leaned closer to whisper. 'We'll talk later. Too many ears close by.'

They marched on in silence, until they reached the lean-to shack that sat over the fort's latrine channel. The odour, as they approached, was overpowering – even after the stench of the pen in which the Britons had held them prisoner. Tullius made for the wooden trapdoor that covered the channel between the latrine and the grate through which the sewage trickled out into the drainage ditch that led directly down the slope away from the walls of the fort. Grimacing, he lifted the hatch and threw it back against the wall of the latrine.

'Get in.'

Cato looked down into the disgusting dark sludge below and shook his head. 'No.'

Tullius sighed, and turned to the escort, but Cato grasped him by the arm.

'We saw the heads down by the track leading into the marsh. What's been going on here?' Cato could see the older man was wavering. 'Tell me.'

Tullius glanced round nervously before he replied. 'All right. He's like a madman – Maximius. He's been slaughtering the natives like he was on piece work.' Tullius rubbed his chin. 'Never seen anything like it. It's as if the man's possessed . . . mad. That's what Macro reckoned. Like Maximius was taking revenge on the locals for all the shit that's happened to the Third Cohort.'

'Maybe,' Cato replied, and paused a moment in thought. 'But I wonder why the legate sent the cohort here. Has to be more to it than just hunting us down.'

'What are you saying?'

'Think about it. We lost contact with Caratacus. The general had to find some way to lure him out into the open. Now it's happening.'

'But how could the general know that Maximius would go crazy and provoke Caratacus into an attack? He couldn't have known.'

'Yes he could . . . if he ordered Maximius to start slaughtering the locals.'

Tullius shook his head. 'No. There's no method in what he's been doing. Just madness.'

'He is mad,' Cato affirmed, 'if he doesn't get ready to prepare for the attack. By the end of the day, Caratacus and thousands of his men will arrive in front of the ramparts. They're bent on revenge, and they'll take this place by storm and slaughter everyone in it. We won't stand a chance.'

Tullius stared at Cato, struggling to hide his fear, and the young officer pushed home his advantage.

'There is only one way out of this for the cohort. Only one way I can see. But it's no good unless I, we, can persuade Maximius.'

'No!' Centurion Tullius shook his head. 'He won't listen. And he'll make sure I suffer for even talking to you like this. Get in the hole!'

'For fuck's sake!' Cato tightened his grip and pulled the older man round to face him. The legionaries reached for their swords. 'Listen to me!'

Tullius raised his spare hand. 'Easy, lads!'

Cato nodded his thanks, and continued in a desperate whisper. 'You're a bloody veteran, Tullius, and those medallions on your harness weren't given to you for book-keeping, or covering your arse. If you haven't got the balls to stand up to Maximius, then at least let me have a go.' Still staring into the older man's eyes, Cato relaxed his grip and gave the arm a gentle, reassuring squeeze. 'We're talking about more than one man's life here. If Maximius doesn't listen, we're all dead. You can make a difference, right now.'

'How?'

'Dismiss this escort. Then take me to his tent. Send someone for Macro. He can meet us there. We have to talk Maximius round. Before it's too late. Now, dismiss these men and hear me out.'

Cato could see the hesitation in the other man's expression and leaned closer. 'We can survive this. Better still, we can come out of it with honour. Best of all, we should be able to finish Caratacus off once and for all.'

'How?' Tullius asked. 'Tell me how.'

Chapter Thirty-Six

Half an hour later, Cato eased himself under the back of Maximius' tent. He glanced round and was relieved to see that the place was empty; the clerks were on the morning inspection with the cohort commander. Cato held the leather flap up and beckoned to Nepos. The legionary scrambled under and moved over so that his centurion could still see Tullius.

'All's clear. I'll wait for you in here, sir. You'd better get Macro now.'

It felt odd to be giving the veteran orders, and Cato realised that it would be best to preserve some sense of the proper code of behaviour if he were to keep Tullius on his side. The old centurion might be well past his prime, and his nerves were clearly worn down, but he still had the sense to see what needed to be done. Cato knew he must have every ally he could win over before he dared to confront Centurion Maximius.

Tullius nodded. 'Right. Just you stay out of sight, young Cato.'

Cato nodded and let the leather drop back to the ground. Glancing round he saw the cohort commander's personal chest. A red cloak was folded over the side and leaning against it was a sword. It was not the finely crafted sword he habitually wore, just the standard issue, with a handle worn glassy and smooth with age. Cato smiled. It must be a relic from Maximius' days as a legionary, now just a keepsake. A most useful keepsake. Cato quietly drew the blade and then flipped the corner of the cloak over the top of the scabbard to conceal the sword's absence.

He passed the sword to Nepos. 'Take this, and then hide yourself over there, just inside his sleeping quarters. You stay there, and keep silent. Only come out if I call for you. Understand?'

'Yes, sir.'

'Good. Now go.'

As Nepos padded away Cato glanced round for a hiding place for himself and then turned back to the chest. It had high sides and had been positioned out of the way at the rear of the tent. Treading softly round the chest he lowered himself behind it and settled down to wait for Maximius to return with his officers. It was fortunate, Cato reflected, that the routine of the Roman legions was immutable. The cohort commander would return to his tent for the morning briefing of his officers just as certainly as night followed day.

Outside the tent the sounds of the legionaries going about their duties was familiar and reassuring after the anxious days Cato had spent hiding in the marsh. Not for the first time he felt that the legion had become his home, and for as long as he lived he would only ever feel safe and secure while he was in its embrace.

There was little chance of a long life now, he decided bitterly. Even if Maximius didn't try to kill him on the spot, then the enemy warriors bearing down on the fort would succeed where the centurion had failed. For a moment Cato was tempted to call for Nepos and make a break for it, and get out of the fort, before the cohort commander returned to his tent. Cato clenched his teeth and punched his thigh furiously. He had committed himself now, and he must confront Maximius if there was any chance to avert disaster.

Time passed with frustrating slowness, and Cato sat in tense anticipation as his ears strained for the first sound of the cohort commander's approach. A few times he heard Maximius bellow out an order, or an angry curse, as he did his inspection of the fort. Each time Cato prepared himself for the job he must do, and each time it was a false alarm his resolve crumbled a little more and he felt he was one step closer to succumbing to his fears and running away.

Then, at last, he heard Maximius again, close at hand and clearly approaching the tent.

'Tullius!'

'Sir?'

'Have you briefed the optios about today's patrols?'

'Yes, sir. Before the inspection.'

'Good. Just the centurions, then. Ah, there they are. Get to the briefing! Move yourselves!'

Cato shrank down behind the chest and hardly dared to breathe as blood pounded in his ears. The leather sides of the tent shimmered as Maximius brushed through the flaps into his quarters. There was a grunt as the cohort commander eased himself into a chair, then the tent shimmered again as the other centurions, breathing hard, joined him and Tullius.

There was no preamble as Maximius barked out an order. 'Take a seat gentlemen, we're running late.'

There was a short shuffling as the officers sat down.

'Where's Acting Centurion Cordus?' Maximius snapped. 'Tullius?'

'Sorry, sir. I sent him to the village to get some natives. The fort's run-off channel is backing up and needs to be dug deeper.'

'Hardly requires the personal attention of a centurion, does it?'

'He was available, sir. And more than keen to do the job.'

'No doubt,' Maximius chuckled. 'Fine lad, that. If only all my officers were as eager to treat these barbarians like the vermin they are ... You told him to go, Tullius, so you can go and fetch him.'

'Yes, sir . . . By your leave?'

'Just go.'

For a moment no one talked, until Tullius had left the tent, then Maximius laughed again. 'Just make sure that you don't end up like that one, lads.'

Cato heard Centurion Felix echo his commander's mirth. Then Maximius abruptly stopped.

'What's the matter, Antonius? Cat got your tongue?'

'No, sir.'

'So why the long face?'

'Sir . . .'

'Spit it out, man!'

'I was thinking about what Cato said earlier. His warning.'

'A warning, indeed!' Maximius snorted. 'He's just had enough of the marsh. You saw the state he was in. That crap about a warning was just some pathetic attempt to wheedle his way back into the cohort. Anyway, now that the bastard's back in our hands, and the rest of them are no doubt dead, we can finish our business here and take him to Vespasian and rejoin the legion. You should be celebrating, Antonius, not worrying like an old woman.'

Cato heard Felix snort his derision, before Centurion Antonius muttered his reply: 'Yes, sir . . .'

'What the hell's that smell?' Maximius sniffed. 'Smells like something crept in here, had a shit and died. What is that stench?'

There was a flicker of light on the back of the tent as the flap was opened again.

'Tullius?' Maximius sounded surprised. 'Already? Then where's— What is the meaning of this? What the hell is Macro doing here? Why is he armed?'

Taking a last breath to try to calm his nerves, Cato stood up. 'Sir, you have to listen.'

'What the . . .?' Maximius twisted round at the sound of his voice. 'Cato? What the hell is going on here? Guards!'

Tullius shook his head. 'No use, sir. I sent them to fetch Cordus, on your authority.'

'My authority?' Maximius looked from Tullius to Macro, then round at Cato. His eyes suddenly widened. 'What is this? A mutiny?'

'No, sir,' Tullius raised a hand and advanced. 'You have to listen to us. Listen to Cato.'

'I'll see you in hell first!' Maximius spat, and bolted to his feet. 'Antonius! Felix! Draw your swords!'

'Stay where you are.' Macro leaped forward and raised the tip of his sword, close to Felix's throat. 'Don't even think about moving. Tullius! You watch him.' Macro nodded at the cohort commander. But it was too late. Maximius was on his feet, sword drawn, almost as soon as Macro

246

had spoken. Tullius faltered, looking from Maximius to Macro with a helpless expression.

Cato turned to the flap leading to the cohort commander's sleeping quarters. 'Nepos! Get in here!'

The legionary rushed in, and stood poised with Maximius' sword raised and ready to strike. For a moment Cato stared nervously as the cohort commander's muscles trembled in readiness to spring. Maximius' eyes narrowed briefly and he concentrated his piercing gaze on the legionary.

'Drop that weapon! That's an order!'

The tip of Nepos' sword dipped slightly and Cato stepped in between them, breaking Maximius' line of sight to the legionary.

'Obey him, and you're a dead man. Understand?'

Nepos slowly nodded and Cato turned round to face the cohort commander. 'Put your sword down, sir.'

Maximius was still for an instant, then the tension around his eyes eased off and he managed a smile. 'You have the advantage, Cato. For now.'

'The sword, sir . . . put it down.'

Maximius relaxed his arm and let his blade fall to his side.

'Drop the sword, sir,' Cato said firmly. 'I won't warn you again.'

'And let your man strike me down? I don't think so.'

No one spoke as Cato reached out his hand towards the cohort commander. Cato felt his heart pounding in his chest, and his throat tightened as he tried to conquer his fear. For a moment it seemed that Maximius had seen through him, and a contemptuous smile slowly formed on the older man's lips. Cato tilted his head forward and refused to let his gaze waver.

Eventually Maximius nodded and sheathed his sword. 'All right, boy. Let's hear you out.' Maximius casually turned his back on Cato and stepped towards his desk, 'Tell me about this attack.'

Cato saw Tullius' cheeks puff out as he breathed in relief. But Cato knew it wasn't over yet. He quickly moved up behind Maximius, shot out a hand and snatched the cohort commander's sword from its scabbard with a sharp rasping noise. He stepped back and raised the blade towards the spine of his superior. Maximius froze.

'You'd better replace that, before it's too late,' he said.

'It's already too late,' Cato replied.

Tullius started forwards. 'What the hell are you doing, Cato?'

'Sir, we can't trust him. He'll pretend to hear us out and the moment we leave this tent he'd have us arrested, or killed on the spot. Nepos?'

'Sir?'

'Tie him up.'

'What about him?' Macro prodded his sword at Centurion Felix. 'This one won't rise against his master.'

'Yes, Felix as well. We have to be quick.'

247

While the two officers were held at the point of a sword, Nepos hurriedly undid their bootlaces and used the tough leather thongs to bind their wrists and ankles. Tullius and Antonius looked on in mounting horror.

'You can't do this,' Tullius muttered. 'This is mutiny. Shit, you'll get us killed.'

'It's too late now, sir,' Cato said gently. 'We're all involved. Me, Macro, you and Antonius. If we let them go now, we'll all be executed.'

Maximius shook his head. 'It's not too late for you, Tullius. Or you, Antonius. Stop these madmen and you have my word, you'll not stand trial.'

Cato glanced at Tullius and saw that the old man was wavering. 'Tullius! You set me free. You arranged for Macro to be armed and brought here. There'll be no mercy for you now, sir. There's more at stake than our lives. He's not fit to command this cohort. Not when we're about to be attacked by Caratacus. Sir, hold your nerve. Your men need you.'

Tullius looked from Cato to Maximius and back again and rubbed his face. 'Damn you, Cato! You'll be the death of me.'

'We're all dead in the end, sir. All that matters is to make certain your death isn't pointless. If we release him now, Maximius will have us killed like dogs. If he saves us for trial, then we'll just die in chains when Caratacus gets here. But if we – you – take command, then there's a chance some of us will survive the attack. Better still, we might even be able to finish Caratacus off for good. If that happens then it's possible General Plautius will overlook this.'

'Fucking fat chance of that!' Maximius snorted.

Cato ignored him, concentrating his attention on Tullius. 'Sir, you change your mind now and you're dead. Stick with our plan, and we may live. That's all the choice there is.'

Tullius bit his lip, caught in an agony of indecision. At last he nodded his assent.

'Good!' Macro clapped him on the shoulder, then turned to Antonius. 'And you? Are you with us?'

'Yes . . . but if it comes to a trial I want it understood that I was obeying your orders.'

Macro snorted. 'Thanks for the loyal support.'

'Loyalty?' Antonius arched an eyebrow. 'That's in rather short supply at present. I just want to live. If the choice is as Cato has described it, then going along with you is simply the best bet.'

'Fine by me,' said Cato. 'Nepos, take these two through to Maximius' sleeping quarters and tie them to the bed. Gag them as well. They have to be kept silent.'

'There's a better way of keeping 'em quiet,' Macro added.

'No, sir. That's not necessary. Not yet.'

248

While Nepos dragged the two bound officers away, the rest gathered round the large desk in the centre of the tent. For a moment there was an uneasy silence before Cato cleared his throat and turned to Tullius.

'Sir, what are your orders?'

'Orders?' The veteran looked confused.

'You're the senior officer present,' Cato prompted. 'We have to make sure the cohort is ready to defend itself. The plan, sir?'

'The plan? Oh, yes.' Tullius gathered his thoughts, looked over the desk for the map of the surrounding marsh that Maximius had drafted, based on reports from the patrols, and any information the local villagers had been persuaded to divulge. The sketched marks of small tracks crisscrossed the outline of the marsh. A broader line marked the main route through the marsh, leading north towards the upper reaches of the Tamesis. Tullius placed his finger on the map.

'If Cato is right, that's where Caratacus and his force will be coming from. There are a handful of other tracks that could be used to enter the valley, but they're not suitable for large bodies of men. So, we're counting on him coming down the main track. That's where we'll have to hold him. Build up the existing gateway and hope we can hold it.'

Antonius looked up. 'Leave the fort? But that's madness, sir. If he outnumbers us why not fight him from proper defences? It's our best chance.'

'No, it's not,' Cato interrupted. 'Centurion Tullius is right. We have to try and hold him back, stop him breaking out of the marsh and into the valley.'

'Why?'

'When I escaped from his camp—'

'His camp?' Antonius looked astonished. 'How on earth—'

Cato raised a hand to silence him. 'I'll explain it to you later, sir. The thing is, I sent my optio north with a message for Vespasian. He should have reached him by now. So Vespasian will know about the location of Caratacus' camp. He'll also know that he intends to attack the Third Cohort and which route he is likely to take. If I know the legate, he'll see this as an opportunity to finish Caratacus off. If he takes the legion and advances down that track, he'll be able to fall upon the rear of the enemy force. Caratacus will be caught between Vespasian and the Third Cohort and cut to pieces, provided we can contain him in the marsh. And that means leaving the fort and taking up position across the track. If we stay in the fort, then Caratacus will be able to escape south the moment he spots Vespasian's forces.'

'That's a lot of ifs,' Antonius remarked quietly. 'I'll add a few of my own: what if Figulus doesn't make it? What if Vespasian doesn't believe him? What if you're wrong? What if Vespasian doesn't act?'

'It's true, Figulus might not reach the legion,' Cato admitted. 'We have to hope that he did. The fact that he's risking execution by returning to the legion must carry some weight. We have to count on the legate seeing the opportunity to end this campaign once and for all.'

'And if he doesn't?'

'Then we'll hold Caratacus off, for a while at least. If we cause enough damage then maybe they'll pull back long enough for us to try and get back to the fort. Otherwise,' Cato shrugged, 'otherwise they'll eventually roll over us and cut the cohort to pieces.'

'Thanks.' Antonius clicked his tongue. 'Most inspiring briefing I've ever had.'

'The thing is,' Cato continued. 'We have to get into position as fast as we can, and prepare the defences. Sir?' He turned to Tullius. 'We're ready for your orders.'

'Just a moment,' Antonius interrupted and jabbed his thumb towards the cohort commander's sleeping quarters. 'But what are we going to do about those two?'

'I suggest we leave them here, sir.'

'And how are we going to explain Maximius' absence to the men? Him and Felix?'

'We're not. Tullius can give all the orders as if they're from Maximius. He's the adjutant. Who would question him?'

'If Maximius fails to put in an appearance, they might.'

Cato smiled. 'By then, they'll have other things on their minds.'

Then he heard the rhythmic tramp of marching boots, approaching the tent. He glanced at Tullius.

'Someone's coming.'

The older centurion hurried to the tent flap, looked outside briefly, then turned to the others.

'It's Cordus, and he's got Maximius' guards with him.'

Chapter Thirty-Seven

Macro grabbed Tullius by the shoulder. 'Get out there and deal with him.'

'What shall I say?'

'Anything. Just don't let him get inside the tent. If he does, it's all over for us.'

Tullius swallowed nervously, then steadied himself for an instant and ducked outside.

'Cordus! There you are. What the hell kept you?'

'I-I was in the village, sir.' The tone was aggrieved, verging on insolent. 'Like you ordered. The natives have started on the ditch, sir.'

'Good job. Well done. Now we've got work to do. The cohort's on the move. Your orders are to pass the word for all units to assemble, fully equipped.'

'All the men, sir?'

'That's what Maximius said.'

'Who's going to oversee the natives?'

'Send them back to the village, and release all the hostages.'

'Release the—' Cordus' voice started to rise, before he took control of his frustration. 'Yes, sir. I'll see to it.'

'Good. Once that's done, take your century down to the track that leads into the marsh. Start work on strengthening the existing gateway. We need to prepare it for an attack in strength. I want the rampart higher and the ditch dug deeper, and wider. We have to be able to defend it.'

'Defend it from who, sir?'

'The enemy. Who else? It seems that Caratacus plans to attack after all. Now carry out your orders.'

'Yes, sir . . . But first, I must report to Centurion Maximius. Excuse me, sir.'

Inside the tent Macro and Cato exchanged anxious glances, and Cato tightened his grip on the cohort commander's sword.

'Make your report later!' Tullius snapped. 'Carry out your orders, or I'll have you on a bloody charge.'

'I don't think so, sir,' Cordus replied quietly. 'We'll see what Maximius has to say about this.'

'On whose authority do you think I give these orders?' Tullius shouted

251

back. 'Get out of my sight, you jumped-up little prick! Go, before I have you for gross insubordination.'

There was a pause, during which Cato and Macro stood quite still, tense and strained. Then Cordus gave way.

'Yes, sir.'

'And take these guards with you. Maximius wants every man at work on the defences as soon as they're kitted up. Better find a cart and take all the entrenching tools you can carry with you.'

'Yes, sir . . . as Centurion Maximius commands.'

'That's right. Now get moving.'

Cordus called the guards to attention, ordered them to turn about, and then marched towards the main gate. The leather flaps were swept aside and Centurion Tullius walked unsteadily into the headquarters tent. He slumped down in a chair to one side of the desk.

'Well done, sir,' Cato said with a smile. 'A fine performance. He'll be out of the way when we make our move. Are there any other officers who might give us problems?'

'No.' Tullius puffed out his cheeks. 'Maximius has really pissed most of them off. He's been playing up to the men for weeks now, and undermining our authority over them. The officers would be glad to see the back of him. But they'd never support a mutiny.'

'Then we won't give them one, sir,' Cato smiled encouragingly. 'If we can keep them busy, it'll all be over, one way or another, before they ever know the cohort is under a new commander.'

Trumpets began to sound the assembly across the fort and from outside the tent came the muffled sounds of the men gathering their equipment and bundling out of their tents to run to the assembly point just inside the main gate.

Cato leaned towards Tullius. 'You'd better go and take charge, sir.'

'Yes, yes, of course. Antonius, come with me.' The old centurion looked up at Cato. 'I'll send for you and Macro as soon as Cordus has left the fort.'

Macro shifted uneasily. 'If anyone asks, and they will, then you'd better have a good reason for reinstating us. At least, you'd better be able to convince the men that it was Maximius' idea.'

'Tell them the truth, sir,' Cato added. 'Tell them that Caratacus is coming and that the cohort requires every available man under arms to fight the enemy. And that's the only reason Maximius has agreed to release us, temporarily.'

'Right . . .' Tullius looked doubtful. 'Come on, Antonius.'

Macro waited until the two centurions had left the tent before he turned to Cato. 'Doesn't exactly make you feel hopeful, does it?'

Cato shrugged. 'With the odds that I've faced in recent days, right now I feel like I'm well ahead of the game.'

'Ever the bloody optimist,' Macro grunted.

'All the same, there's one last thing I need to sort out before Tullius sends for us.'

'What's that?'

'We need Nepos to stay here and keep an eye on Maximius and Felix. If you keep watch for a moment, sir, I'll give him his orders.'

'All right.' Macro crept over to the tent flap and peered cautiously outside. There was no one close at hand, just distant figures visible through the gaps in the lines of tents. They were forming up, making ready to march out of the fort. Macro glanced back towards Cato and saw his young friend talking earnestly with Nepos, speaking quietly. Macro could not catch what was being said. The legionary seemed to be listening intently and shook his head.

'You have to!' Cato snapped at him, then glanced quickly at Macro. He turned back to the legionary and dropped his voice as he continued. Eventually Nepos nodded slowly when Cato had finished issuing his orders. The centurion patted Nepos on the arm and gave him a few last words of encouragement before he turned and made his way quietly across the tent to join Macro.

'Nepos doesn't look happy.'

Cato shot him a searching glance and then shrugged. 'He's not keen on staying behind.'

'So I noticed.'

'Hardly surprising,' Cato smiled. 'Being left alone when the rest of the cohort is leaving the fort.

'Frankly,' Macro muttered, 'I'm not sure who's going to have the better deal. Any possibility that Nepos might want to swap duties?'

Cato gave a dry laugh as he glanced back towards Nepos, ducking quietly back into the cohort commander's sleeping quarters. 'Oh, I should think there's every possibility of that.'

Once the cohort had formed up behind the main gate, Centurion Tullius passed on the orders from the cohort commander and told the men that Centurion Felix had volunteered to find the legate and inform him of the Third Cohort's situation. Tullius explained that since the cohort was well under strength, Maximius had decided that every available man should be readied for the coming fight. Accordingly, Macro had been given command of the Fourth Century, Felix's unit, and Cato would be once again marching at the head of the Sixth Century. On cue, the two officers emerged from between the lines of tents behind Tullius and were presented to the men of the cohort. The astonishment of the legionaries was short-lived as Tullius gave the order to march at once and, century by century, the men of the cohort tramped out of the fort and headed towards the track leading into the marsh.

Optio Septimus, who Maximius had appointed to replace Figulus, kept pace alongside Cato. From time to time he glanced at his centurion with a surly and hostile expression that Cato could well understand. He had been enjoying his first taste of command, and had relinquished it with a barely tolerable show of bad feeling. Cato decided that the best way of dealing with the resentment was to keep the man occupied.

'The men are straggling, Septimus! Close 'em up!'

The optio dropped out of line and started to scream abuse at the men marching past him, striking out with his staff at any legionary who permitted a gap to open up between himself and the man ahead of him. The blows were unnecessarily savage, but Cato forced himself not to intervene. The last thing the century needed now was a confrontation between its officers. He would have to let Septimus vent his frustration and anger on the men for now. As long as they hated Septimus, they might be inclined towards a better relationship with their newly reappointed centurion.

It felt strange to Cato to be once again commanding the men he had led into battle at the crossing on the Tamesis. Last time they had failed to hold the enemy back and Cato had suffered decimation as a result. This time failure would lead to the death of them all. And if they survived the coming hours? Cato smiled grimly to himself. However things turned out, he was still a condemned man and faced execution, or, if he was spared, it was most likely that he would still be disgraced and dismissed from the army. With a stab of anger he cast thought of the future aside. He must keep his mind on the present.

The men's surprise at Cato's temporary reprieve was all the more heightened because it had been on the orders of the cohort commander, so ruthless and fanatic in his hunt for the condemned men in recent days. As Cato had appeared at the assembly area, most had looked at him in wonder, but a few faces conveyed resentment and – worse – suspicion. Certainly, his grimy visage, matted hair and straggly beard sat poorly upon the face of a man with the rank of centurion. He had recovered his scaled armour and harness from the cohort's quartermaster, a source of yet more resentment, since the man had been hoping to sell the equipment for a tidy sum. But the ill feeling of others was no more than a faint shadow cast across the sense of contentment that Cato felt. To be back in his armour, with a good sword at his side and a stout shield on his arm felt natural and comforting. Almost as if the previous weeks of misery, hardship and peril had been washed away like a layer of dust in a summer shower.

Almost.

'Sir!'

Cato looked up and saw a runner approaching from the head of the column, which had just started to cross the crest of a small hill. The centurion stepped out to one side as the runner drew up by the Sixth Century.

'Sir, Centurion Tullius sends his compliments, and says that Cordus and his men are in sight.'

Cato could not help smiling at the thinly veiled warning, and then he nodded to the messenger. 'Thank him for me, and let Tullius know I am aware of the situation.'

The messenger frowned at the oddness of Cato's reply. 'Sir?'

'Just tell him exactly what I said.'

'Yes, sir.' The legionary saluted and turned away, running alongside the cohort back towards Centurion Tullius at the head of the column. Cato felt a stab of anxiety over the need to leave the cohort in the hands of the old officer. There had been no other way of handling things. It was risky enough removing Maximius from the scene. Any attempt by Macro or Cato to take charge of the cohort was doomed to failure, so Tullius it must be, if the men were not to have their credulity stretched too far.

As the tail end of the cohort crossed the brow of the hill Cato glanced ahead and saw the distant figures of Cordus and his men toiling away as they widened the ditch across the path that led right through the heart of the marsh. The acting centurion was wearing a red cloak to distinguish himself from his men, and Cato idly wondered if he had pilfered it from Macro's stores, slipping into the centurion's clothes as readily as he had assumed Macro's command. It was an unworthy thought and Cato was angry at himself for giving it expression. Cordus was merely obeying orders. The fact that he took great satisfaction in obeying the cohort commander was immaterial, Cato told himself.

The newly arrived centuries were deployed either side of the track before they were ordered to down shields and javelins and head over to the cart to be issued with picks and shovels. Their officers set them to work at once on the ditch and rampart.

'Not your men, Cato,' Tullius called out as the Sixth Century marched up. 'I want you to advance ahead of the cohort. Take up position half a mile along the track. You may need to buy us time to finish the defences. As soon as you see the enemy, send a runner back to let me know.'

'Yes, sir. How long should we hold them for?'

'As long as you can. If we complete the work before Caratacus arrives I'll send a runner to recall you. Then just leave a small picket and fall back here with the rest of your men. No heroics, understand?'

Cato nodded. Behind Tullius' shoulder he saw Cordus striding over towards them. As soon as the acting centurion recognised Cato he faltered for an instant.

'What the hell is he doing here?'

Tullius glanced round angrily. 'Is that question addressed to me?'

Cordus tore his gaze away from Cato and then noticed Macro beyond, as his former centurion began to bellow orders to the legionaries of the Fourth Century. Eyes narrowing suspiciously, Cordus turned back to Tullius. 'What's going on here? Where's Centurion Maximius, sir?'

Tullius nodded back in the direction of the fort. 'He sent us ahead. Said he'd be along directly.'

'Oh really?' Cordus looked round at the other officers and caught the eye of Antonius. 'Where's Maximius?'

Antonius glanced at Tullius, for reassurance, before he replied. 'Like he said, back at the fort.'

'The fort . . . I see. So while we're about to take on a force many times our size, the commander of the cohort is attending to a few details back in the fort. Is that about it . . . sir?'

Cato could see that Antonius would help them no further, and that Tullius could not carry it off for much longer. So he stepped in front of Cordus, one hand resting on the pommel of his sword.

'You've got your orders, Cordus. Get back to work.'

The acting centurion eyed him with open contempt. 'I don't take orders from condemned men, let alone condemned boys.'

Cato stepped closer, drawing his sword at the same time, pressing the point into the armpit of the other man – all of it hidden from the surrounding legionaries by the folds of the two officers' capes. Cato's face was no more than a few inches from the pockmarked flesh of Cordus, and he could smell the rank acid smell of cheap wine on the older man's breath.

'Never speak that way to a superior officer again,' Cato said softly through clenched teeth, and prodded with the point of his sword. Cordus flinched and bit down on his pain as the blade pierced his flesh. Cato smiled, and whispered, 'Next time you give me, or any of the other centurions, one word of insolence, I swear by all the gods, that I will gut you. Do you understand me? Don't talk, just nod.'

Cordus stared back, eyes burning with cold fury, then he dipped his head, once.

'Good.' Cato slowly withdrew his blade and gently pushed the other man back with his spare hand. 'Now get back to your unit, and carry out your orders.'

Cordus reached under his armpit and winced as he glared at the young centurion. Cato stared back, then nodded his head towards the defences. Cordus took the hint.

'Very well, sir.'

'That's better. Now go.'

Cordus retreated a few paces before he turned and strode quickly towards the men of the Third Century. He did not look back, and Cato watched him long enough to make sure that Cordus did as he was told. Tense and trembling Cato turned towards Tullius and Antonius.

'Well done, lad.' A smile flickered across Tullius' worn features. 'That's him dealt with.'

'Only for now, sir,' Cato replied. 'We'll have to keep an eye on him. He could cause us problems. Which reminds me, where are Maximius' guards?'

'By the supply cart.'

Cato glanced over to the cart and saw the six men standing beside it, shields grounded and spears leaning against their shoulders. 'I'll take them with me, if you don't mind, sir.'

'What for?' Tullius frowned. 'We need every man here.'

'They've sworn an oath to protect the cohort commander. If Cordus gets close to them, he might persuade them to back him, next time he tries to confront us.'

'You think he will?' Antonius asked.

'If Caratacus doesn't arrive by the time we've finished our defences, then the men will have time on their hands, and they'll do what they normally do in such circumstances: talk. Given the presence of me and Macro, and the absence of Maximius, I should think we've given them plenty to talk about.'

Antonius looked down at his boots. 'We're fucked.'

'Any way you look at it,' Cato smiled. 'Now, sir, the guards?'

'You can't have them,' Tullius said. 'I need them. I'll put them to work here, and keep Cordus away from them. Now you and your men had better get down that track.'

The Sixth Century trudged through the posts of the gateway. On either side legionaries paused to watch them as they passed, and then hurriedly returned to work as their officers screamed at them for stopping. Macro was standing on top of the rampart and waved briefly to Cato as he directed his men to start pounding in the stakes of wood they had brought from the fort to act as a makeshift palisade. The gateway was set back from the rest of the rampart, which angled in towards it, so that any attackers would be subjected to fire from three sides if they made any attempt to assault the gate. As his century marched out from the lines of defence, the ground on either side of the track gave way to patches of mud, then still expanses of dark water from which the pale yellow stalks of clumps of rushes rose up, their feathered heads hanging motionless in the hot still air.

When they reached the first bend in the track Cato stopped to look back at the rest of the cohort and marked the distance to the gateway. It was essential that he was familiar with the topography. If the enemy came upon them before they were recalled by Tullius, then Cato and his men would be making a fighting withdrawal. The weight of their armour and equipment made it impossible for them to outpace the enemy, who would be thirsting for Roman blood in any case. They would have a short head start on Caratacus and the Britons, and then the Sixth Century would have to fight nearly every step of the way back to the cohort frantically struggling to complete the defences. It would be a close thing – if they made it. But if their sacrifice bought Tullius and the others enough time to complete the defences, the Third Cohort might be able to hold off Caratacus and his force. Long enough, at least, for

Vespasian to march across the marsh and close the trap on the enemy and crush them.

Cato smiled at the thought. That would be the end of any meaningful resistance to Roman rule, and both sides could get on with the task of turning this barbaric backwater into a civilised province. He had had his fill of killing the native warriors, who had far more courage than sense. They were good men and, given the right kind of leadership, they would become firm and valuable allies of Rome. All this was possible once Caratacus was defeated . . . Then the smile faded from Cato's lips.

The enemy would only be defeated if Vespasian arrived in time to crush them against the Third Cohort's defences. It was possible that Vespasian would not arrive in time. Indeed it was possible that the legate was not even marching towards them. It was even possible that Figulus might not have reached the Second Legion, let alone managed to persuade Vespasian to lead his men along a narrow track through the heart of an enemy-controlled marsh.

Cato realised that all along he had been counting on the legate's willingness to take calculated risks to achieve significant results. Then Cato wished he had gone north to find the legate himself, not trusting his optio to make the case for him. But that would have meant sending Figulus back to the cohort and the much harder task of persuading Maximius to take on the enemy, or finding a way of replacing the cohort commander, if he proved obdurate. Cato could not be in two places at once and did not trust anyone else to do either job for him. It was just the kind of intractable problem that made being an officer such a nightmare. Indecision was bad enough, but endless hypothesising after the event was pure torture. If only he could accept the consequences of his decisions, thought Cato, and just get on with it. Like Macro.

He tried to push further thought aside. He trotted to the front of his century, and continued a hundred paces beyond, to scan the route ahead. The track followed the high ground, such as it was, and skirted round the dismal pools and mires that stretched out on both sides. Where the land was dry, stunted trees and clumps of gorse clustered together. Beyond that, sweeping expanses of rushes restricted the view, so that there would be little warning of the enemy's approach. Cato irritably slapped his thigh with a clenched fist. The tense frustration simmered in his breast as he led his men deeper into the marsh, all the while expecting the next turn of the track to bring them face to face with Caratacus and his warriors.

As soon as Cato estimated they had marched half a mile, he ordered the Sixth Century to halt. The unit changed from column to line, six deep with a front of twelve men across the width of the track, their flanks covered by dense growths of prickly gorse that would tear the skin off any man who tried to force his way through. Two men were sent two hundred paces further along the track to keep watch.

Cato turned to his men, briefly recalling the first time he had stood before them as their newly appointed centurion. He remembered many of the hard-bitten faces before him and felt a new sense of confidence that they would acquit themselves well when they confronted the enemy.

'Stand down!' he ordered. 'But stay in place.'

Cato squinted up at the bright sky and felt the sweat pricking out under his heavy military tunic, which in turn was weighed down by his scale armour. His throat felt thick and his lips were dry and rough to the tip of his tongue.

'You can take a good drink from your canteens. Chances are we'll be too busy later on for you to use them.'

Some of the men chuckled at that, but most stared ahead steadfast until Septimus had bellowed the order to fall out. The men laid down their shields and javelins and squatted down on the hard dry earth of the track. Some reached for their canteens at once, while others undid their neck cloths and wiped away the sweat that was streaming down their faces.

Septimus approached Cato. 'Can the lads take their helmets off, sir?'

Cato glanced up the track. All seemed quiet enough and there was no sign of any alarm from the two lookouts.

'Very well.'

Septimus saluted and turned back to the resting men. 'Right lads, the centurion says you can remove helmets. Just keep 'em handy.'

There were groans of relief all round as the men fumbled with the leather ties and lifted the heavy, cumbersome helmets from their heads. The felt linings were so soaked with perspiration that they stuck to the heads of the legionaries and had to be peeled off separately. Underneath, drenched hair stuck to their scalps as if they had just emerged from a steam room at the baths.

Cato took a last look towards the lookouts and then slumped down on the track a short distance in front of his men. His fingers worked at the straps of his helmet and then he lifted it off and lowered it into his lap, brushing his fingers over the thin layer of dust that coated the top of the helmet. He set it down beside him and reached for the canteen slung from his sword belt. Cato had just eased the stopper out of the neck of the canteen and had raised it halfway to his lips when there was a distant shout. At once he turned to stare up the track, along with several of his men. One of the lookouts was running down the track towards them. Cato could see that the other man was still watching something further off. A moment later, he turned and sprinted hard after his companion.

The nearest lookout jabbed his javelin back over his shoulder as he ran and now his warning was clearly audible to every man in the Sixth Century. 'They're coming!'

Chapter Thirty-Eight

Cato dropped his canteen and scrambled to his feet, shouting out orders. 'To arms! To arms! Move yourselves!'

All around him legionaries heaved themselves up and grabbed at their liners and helmets, jamming them on and fumbling desperately with the straps they had untied just moments earlier. All the discomforts of heat and thirst fled from their thoughts as the men rushed to arm themselves. From the track came the continual cries of the lookout as he raced back to join his comrades: 'They're coming!'

Shields and spears were snatched up from the dusty track and held ready as the legionaries shuffled into position. Cato drew his sword and punched it into the air to gain his men's attention.

'Sixth Century! Sixth Century, prepare javelins!'

Some of the men had instinctively reached for their short swords and now released the handles and hefted the shafts of their javelins, staring anxiously down the track. Cato turned to watch with them, willing the lookouts to run faster. The first of them came jogging up, blown by the effort of sprinting back to the century under the weight of armour and weapons. He stopped in front of Cato and bent forward, gasping for breath.

'Make your report, man!' Cato snapped.

'Yes . . . sir.' The lookout forced himself to stand erect and swallowed to clear his mouth of phlegm. 'Beg to report . . . the enemy's approaching, sir. A quarter, perhaps a third of a mile down the track.'

'What's their composition?'

'Cavalry and infantry, sir. There's eight or ten scouts out front. They saw us and rode back to the main force.'

'They'll make their report,' Cato mused. 'Then Caratacus will send them back in strength to beat us up while the main body deploys.'

Septimus gave a contemptuous snort. 'Then they're wasting their time. There's nowhere they can deploy here. They'll have to fight us on a narrow front. It's going to hurt them more than it's going to hurt us.'

Cato smiled faintly as he turned to look down the track. There was no point in reminding the optio that even a few thousand Britons might have an outside chance of besting a few score of legionaries.

'I want you to run back to Centurion Tullius. My compliments to him, and tell him the enemy is in sight. We'll fall back slowly and delay Caratacus for as long as we can. Got that?'

The legionary nodded. Cato raised a hand to shade his eyes as he stared down the track. 'Where's the other lookout?'

The legionary turned to follow the centurion's gaze. 'Decimus was trying to estimate their strength before he followed on. Look, sir, here he comes.'

A distant figure came scurrying round the bend, head down and heavy shield bobbing as he ran. His comrades began to shout encouragement as Decimus sprinted for all he was worth. Every so often his helmet glinted as he turned to glance back. The first of the enemy horsemen appeared round the bend when Decimus was still a hundred and fifty paces from the rest of the century. Cato cupped a hand to his mouth, shouting alongside the rest of his men as the optio looked on disapprovingly. Cato guessed that a veteran like Septimus thoroughly disapproved of officers who refused to comport themselves with a cool detachment. Sod him, thought Cato. There was a time and a place for a stiff and unyielding demeanour, and this was not it.

'Run, man! Run! The bastards are right on you!'

Decimus threw down his javelin, but kept hold of his shield and ran on. Behind him the enemy warriors, more than thirty of them, urged their mounts on, determined to ride the Roman down before he could reach the safety of the tight line of red shields that stretched across the track. The tips of their lances glittered as they dipped and were lined up on the back of the man fleeing from them.

'He's not going to make it,' Septimus decided. 'They'll have him.'

'No,' Cato replied instantly. 'Come on, Decimus! Run!'

There was not much further for the legionary to cover, but there was even less between him and his pursuers.

'I told you . . .' There was no mistaking the trace of smugness in the optio's voice, and Cato burned with cold fury at the man's callousness. The horsemen would not have Decimus if there was anything he could do about it. The centurion turned away from the desperate spectacle, towards the rest of his men.

'Front rank! Ready javelins!'

It took a moment for the men to respond, so rapt were they in the fate of their comrade.

'Ready your bloody javelins!' Cato roared at them.

This time his men hefted their weapons, stepped forward two paces and swung their throwing arms back. Decimus saw the movement and faltered briefly before he hurled himself towards the line of shields. Right behind him the Britons whooped with cruel glee as they realised that there was no chance now that their prey would escape them, still thirty paces from his comrades.

'Decimus!' Cato shouted to him. 'Drop down!'

261

Realisation of the centurion's intention suddenly dawned in the legionary's terrified expression and he threw himself forward on to the track, rolled a short distance to one side and covered his body with his shield as best he could as Cato shouted an order to the front rank.

'Javelins . . . loose!'

There was a chorus of explosive grunts and ten dark shafts curved through the air, passing over Decimus and striking the horsemen immediately behind him with a series of dull thuds as the sharp points punched into the flesh of men and beasts alike. At once the air was split by the agonised whinnies of two mounts and the snorts from the others as they tried to swerve away from the stricken horses. One man was down, pierced clean through his breast, and he crashed down on top of Decimus, splintering the javelin shaft with a loud crack. He quivered for an instant, then died.

The impetus of the charge had been broken, and the enemy milled round the stricken tangle of the writhing, wounded horses. Decimus saw his chance at once, heaved the body off his shield, scrambled to his feet and threw himself towards the front rank of the century, abandoning his shield.

'Come on!' Cato desperately beckoned to him. 'Make a gap!'

Two of the men shuffled aside and Decimus made for the space that had appeared between their shields. Just as he reached his comrades, Cato glimpsed something blur through the air behind Decimus and then the legionary tumbled forward into the Roman ranks with a cry of pain. Cato pushed his way over to Decimus and kneeled down. The shaft of a light javelin pierced through the back of his leg, just above the top of his boot, and blood welled up where the thin iron head had entered the flesh.

'Shit! That hurts!' Decimus hissed through clenched teeth.

Glancing up, Cato saw that the horsemen had withdrawn a short distance down the track and were re-forming, ready to charge again.

Septimus loomed over them, glanced at the javelin and nodded to Cato. 'Hold him!'

Taking a firm grasp of the shaft, and ensuring that the angle was right he suddenly pulled the javelin out as Decimus howled with agony. The point came free and there was a rush of blood from the puncture. The optio examined it quickly, then wrenched the legionary's neck cloth away and bound the wound tightly.

'Serves you bloody well right!' Septimus snapped. 'Shouldn't have dropped your shield. How many times have you been told that in training?'

Decimus winced. 'Sorry, sir.'

'Now get up. You're useless to us with that leg. Get back to the cohort.'

The legionary looked to Cato, who nodded his assent. With gritted teeth Decimus struggled to his feet and limped through the lines of his comrades. He started down the track, leaving a trail of small splashes of blood from the sodden dressing.

A voice shouted, 'Here they come again!'

Cato raised his shield and pushed forward into the front rank. Septimus hurriedly took up position to the extreme right of the century. Cato glanced round, saw that his men were grimly prepared for the next charge by the enemy horsemen. Just behind him the century's standard-bearer had drawn his sword and was leaning forward expectantly.

'Standard to the rear!' Cato snapped at him. The bearer frowned, sheathed his sword and pushed his way to the rear of the small formation. Cato shook his head angrily. The man should know better. His first duty was to guard the standard, not to get stuck into the enemy. He'd have to have words with the bearer, if they were still alive tomorrow.

With a wild cry the horsemen surged forward, the hoofs of their mounts drumming deafeningly on the dry track. For a moment Cato was about to order another volley of javelins, but then realised that the century would need to conserve every advantage in the ordeal of arms they would have to endure.

'Shields up!' Cato shouted. 'Second rank! Pass javelins forward!'

The iron heads of the javelins rippled forward to the men in the front rank. Cato snatched at one and lowered the point towards the swiftly approaching horsemen. On either side, his men thrust their points out between the shields. Cato hunched his neck down so that his face was protected by the rim of his shield, and stared into the oncoming charge. The Britons were screaming their war cries with maddened exultant expressions in the last instant before their mounts slammed into the Romans. There was a thud of bodies on shields, and the grunts of legionaries driven back. Cato felt his arm jerk as the flank of a horse thrust itself upon the iron head of his javelin. The animal reared, threatening to tear the weapon from his grasp, and Cato yanked it savagely, gouging a bloody hole in the animal's sleek hide. Something flashed above his head and he just had time to duck down as a spear tip slashed forward, narrowly missing his head and glancing off the neck guard with a sharp clatter. Cato's head snapped back painfully and he found himself staring up into the horseman's face, frozen in a feral grin of stained teeth under a dark drooping moustache. Instinctively, Cato swung his javelin round and thrust at the man's eyes. Before the thrust landed the rider yanked sharply on his reins and wheeled his horse away, knocking the tip of the javelin to one side.

For a moment Cato was not engaged, and he glanced round. A horse was down on its back, lashing the air with its hoofs as its screaming rider was crushed beneath it. Two more of the enemy were down on the track, mortally injured, one of them writhing as he clasped his hands over a terrible injury that had ripped open his stomach. But not one Roman had been cut down. After the impact, they had recovered and maintained the shield wall in good order, while above them spears and shields clattered uselessly against the large curved surfaces of the Roman shields.

263

The enemy horsemen kept the attack up for a little while longer, then their leader bellowed an order and they abruptly disengaged and trotted back a short distance, just out of javelin range. Beyond them Cato glimpsed the head of the enemy column marching round the corner where the two Roman lookouts had been posted shortly before. It was time to start the withdrawal.

'Fall back! Optio!'

'Sir?'

'Take half the men. Retire a hundred paces and form a new line. Leave a gap for us to pass through when we reach you.'

'Yes, sir!'

Septimus gathered his men and they trotted up the track until they reached a point where the space either side of the track was again hemmed in by clumps of gorse. The optio halted the men and formed them up.

Cato nodded his satisfaction then turned back to assess his situation. The horsemen were preparing to charge again; tightening the grip on their reins and weapons. As soon as the first man urged his mount forward Cato shouted an order to ready javelins. The horsemen faltered at the sight of the dark, deadly shafts being prepared for them, and then reined in and drew up, still out of range.

'Good,' Cato muttered. 'Port javelins! Sixth Century will prepare to retire . . . march!'

The legionaries started to retreat in good order, keeping their faces to the enemy, as they stepped back carefully to avoid any stumbling. The horsemen stared at the Romans for a moment and then a chorus of jeers and catcalls pursued the legionaries up the track. One of Cato's men started to shout some abuse back.

'Silence!' Cato shouted. 'Ignore them. We've got nothing to prove. It's not our men who are lying dead on the track!'

The five sections under Cato's command steadily withdrew towards Septimus and his men. Even so, the gap between the Romans and the head of Caratacus' column had narrowed considerably by the time Cato passed through the gap Septimus had left for him.

'My turn to fall back,' said Cato. 'Their infantry might well be on you before you get to us.'

'Looks that way, sir.' Septimus nodded. 'Don't get too far ahead of us.'

'I won't. Good luck.'

'Fuck that,' muttered Septimus. 'We're going to need bloody divine intervention to see us through this lot.'

'You're not wrong,' Cato smiled. 'Stick it to them, Optio.'

Septimus saluted and turned away to make sure that his thin line was tightly closed up and ready to resist the coming onslaught. Cato led his men further up the track and as they reached a bend he halted and formed them up. In the distance, above the low-lying expanse of rushes and stunted trees and clumps of gorse he could see the distant figures of the rest of the cohort toiling away at the contruction of the rampart and palisade.

'Not so far to go, lads!'

'Far enough,' someone muttered.

Cato spun round. 'Silence there! We'll make it back. I swear it.'

He turned back to see how the Optio was faring. Septimus was already on the move and the rearmost rank trudged slowly backwards. Only a short distance beyond them the horsemen had edged off the track and the main column of enemy infantry was marching swiftly forward, eager to close with the hated Romans and cut them to pieces.

Towards the front of the column was a chariot. Standing on the platform, behind the driver, was Caratacus, bare-headed and bare-chested, with the huge gold torc around his muscular neck. One hand grasped the shaft of a great war spear, nearly twice as tall as the man himself. The other rested easily on the side rail of the chariot and despite the rutted surface of the track the native commander rode his vehicle with a superb sense of balance and self-confidence.

Caratacus raised his spear and thrust it towards the retreating Romans in a savage gesture of command. At once his warriors let out a huge roar and surged forward, swords and spears raised up and ready to strike. Septimus halted his men, closed up and shouted an order for them to unleash their javelins. It was a desperate measure and Cato wondered if the optio had let desperation overcome good sense. The effect of the collective volley in the confined space of the track would be devastating, but there would be no javelins left after that, only swords.

Septimus' shouted commands were just audible above the din of the enemy. 'Javelins . . . loose!'

A tattered dark veil lifted up from the legionaries, arced into the air and then lashed down on the natives. Their war cries faded for a moment, then the sound of the impact carried to Cato and his men: a rattling, thudding chorus that was quickly swallowed up by cries of pain and shouted curses. Septimus yelled at his men to continue falling back.

There was a brief respite while the Britons picked their way through their dead and injured littering the ground from which the dark shafts of javelins protruded at every angle. Then the battle cries picked up once again and the enemy raced forward. But the full impact of their mass charge had been broken by the volley and they hurled themselves individually upon the broad shields and glinting blades of the legionaries. The first few were cut down without difficulty and the men did not even break step as they continued towards Cato. Then, as warriors charged home as a mass, Septimus and his men slowed to a halt and were forced to fight to stay in formation. To fight for survival.

As more and more of the enemy piled into the mêlée the legionaries began to move towards Cato again, only this time they were not giving ground, they were being driven back. Watching them draw closer Cato knew that it was only a matter of time before Septimus lost enough men that the survivors would no longer be able to hold their formation. Then they would be broken and cut down. The leap-frog withdrawal of the sixth century would no longer be possible, Cato realised. Their only chance was to stay together now.

As Septimus' men began to pass through the gap left open for them, Cato called out to the optio, 'Form your men up behind me. We can't afford to divide the century any more.'

Septimus nodded and turned to deploy his men as the five fresh sections under Cato's command took over the fight.

Tightening the grip on his sword and hefting the shield forwards and up, Cato stepped forward and pushed into the front line. At once a heavy blow from an axe drove his shield back into him. But this dense fighting at close quarters was what the Roman legions trained for, and Cato rode back with the blow. Then, transferring his weight on to his back foot he launched himself against the enemy and felt his shield smash into a body with a loud thud. There was a grunt of pain and surprise, and Cato rammed his short sword forward, round the edge of the shield, and was rewarded by the shock of an impact that ran up his arm. He withdrew the blade, noting the blood dripping six inches from the point. A fatal injury in all probability and, he realised with surprise, he had never even seen the man who had suffered it.

Another impact on his shield, and this time fingers curled over the top of it, inches from his face, and wrenched it back. Cato held on with all his strength, then swung his helmet forward, crushing the enemy's knuckles with the solid iron cross brace above his brow. The fingers were snatched back and Cato thrust his shield forward, into space this time, and then stepped back to draw a breath.

'Sixth Century! Sixth Century, give ground! Optio?'

'Sir!'

'Call the time!'

'Yes, sir . . . One! . . . Two! . . . One! . . . Two!'

At every command the men in each rank carefully retreated a pace in the face of the enemy, and then resumed the fight. Cato was content to yield control of the pace to the optio. Once the fighting started in earnest the world of the men engaged in a deadly contest became a whirling chaos of weapons clashing, men grunting, cursing and screaming their defiance and agony. Instinct, honed by relentless years of training, took over, and any sense of the passage of time was lost in the savage intensity of surviving the moment.

There were few chances for lucid thought as Cato fought to stay alive, but he snatched glimpses of Caratacus, only fifteen or twenty feet away, urging his warriors on, bellowing a war cry that carried clearly over the cacophony of battle and drove his men to new heights of ferocity.

'One!' Septimus called out.

If only Caratacus could be killed, Cato managed to think, as he drew back another step. He chopped at a bare foot raised to kick at his shield.

'Two!'

If Caratacus fell, then maybe the fight would go out of these demons, who seemed to know no fear as they threw themselves at the line of Roman shields. The legionaries in the front rank were starting to tire and the first two men to die were cut down and killed in quick succession. Their places were instantly filled by men from the second rank, and the retreat continued under the relentless attack. One by one, more legionaries fell, to join the native dead and wounded trampled down by the wave of warriors that flowed down the track.

Cato thrust his shield into the face of an older warrior, no less savage than his younger comrades, and backed out of the front line.

'Take my place!' he shouted into the ear of a legionary in the second rank, and the man pressed forward, shield out and sword ready to thrust into the mêlée. The centurion pushed his way through the dense pack of Romans, until he found Septimus, standing beside the century's standard-bearer.

The optio nodded a greeting. 'Hot work, sir.'

'Hot as it gets.' Cato made himself smile, desperate to give the impression of calm professional detachment that Macro seemed to achieve so effortlessly. He looked up the track towards the cohort's fortifications, now just beyond the final bend in their return journey.

Septimus followed the direction of his centurion's glance. 'Shall I send a runner back for more men, sir?'

The thought of more legionaries hurrying forward to support their retreat was a comforting, tempting prospect. But Cato realised that such a request, even if Tullius agreed to it, would only place more men in danger and weaken the cohort where its soldiers were most necessary: on the rampart, denying Caratacus and his warriors any escape from the marsh.

He shook his head. 'No. We're on our own.'

The optio nodded slowly. 'Fair enough, sir. But we're not going to be able to hold them back for much longer. If they break the line, we're finished.'

The line was now no more than five deep and Cato knew that if they could not reach the fortifications soon, then the enemy would be able simply to brush aside the few remaining legionaries. He had to act now, and gamble his remaining javelins on one last cast of the dice.

Cato turned to his optio. 'I'm going to give the order to use the last javelins in one volley. When it strikes, we fall back. If we're lucky we can make it most of the way back to the cohort before the enemy come on again. Understood?'

'Yes, sir. Is that wise – to use them all up?'

'Maybe not. But we'd better use the javelins while we still can, eh?'

Septimus nodded.

'Rear ranks!' Cato shouted, his voice rough and grating in his dry throat. 'Ready javelins. Aim long. Aim for that big bastard on the chariot!'

The retreat had stopped and while the men in the front rank fought off the enemy, those behind, still carrying their javelins, quickly opened their ranks and swung back their throwing arms.

'Remember, aim long! Javelins, loose!'

This time the thin spread of dark shafts arced up high, gleaming as they reached the top of their trajectory, then dipped down sharply to plunge into the tight mass of men around Caratacus and his chariot. Cato was watching this final volley with an intense stare and saw a javelin strike through Caratacus' shoulder, carrying the enemy commander down on to the bed of his chariot and out of sight. Above the cries of the injured a deep groan sounded from the throats of the British warriors as they realised that their leader had been struck. The column wavered as those at the front turned to see what had happened, then they began to ebb back towards the chariot, disengaging from the Romans. Cato saw his chance and took it.

'Fall back! Fall back!'

The remnants of the Sixth Century started to march away from the enemy, the rearmost men keeping a close watch behind them as they made best speed towards the safety of the distant cohort. Cato led them round the final corner and ahead of them the track led straight towards the hastily erected fortifications, no more than two hundred paces away. The temptation to run for it was overwhelming but Cato knew that he and his men must retire in good order.

'Don't run, lads! Keep in formation!'

Behind them, there was a shout, an order, and Cato recognised the voice of Caratacus, bellowing at his men to renew the assault. They took up his cry with a roar.

Cato glanced at his optio. 'That didn't last long.'

'No, sir,' Septimus smiled ruefully. 'Not much gets between your average Celt and the prospect of a good fight.'

Ahead of them, Cato could see figures rushing to man the rampart that stretched across the track and a short distance into the marsh on either side, ending in a small redoubt on each flank. A hundred and fifty paces to go, and there was a glimmer of light from the gate as it was heaved open. Cato glanced back and saw the first of the enemy warriors burst round the bend, weapons raised and mouths gaping as they screamed out their war cries. With a pounding of hoofs and a rumble of wheels, Caratacus' chariot lurched round the corner. The enemy commander stood over the axle, one hand clasped to his injured shoulder, the other jabbing his war spear towards the enemy. Cato could only admire his ruthless sense of purpose that spared him no agony.

When the Sixth Century had halved the distance to the fortifications Cato glanced back again and was shocked to see that the enemy were almost upon them. Ahead, on either side of the track, lay the defensive ditch, strewn with sharpened stakes. Then the earth rampart, where the rest of the cohort leaned over the palisade, shouting desperate encouragement to their comrades. Cato realised that he and his men weren't going to make the gate before the enemy crashed into them.

'Halt! Form up to the rear!'

Even with the open gate tantalisingly close to them the men of the Sixth Century readily obeyed the order. They quickly turned, raised their shields and closed ranks into a compact defensive formation. But this time, when the enemy charged home, the legionaries reeled under the impact. The line of shields was driven in, sending one of the men sprawling back. Before anyone could step into his place a huge Celtic warrior burst in amongst them, whirling an axe over his head. An instant later it swept down towards the legionary who had been thrown back on to the ground. He saw the blade coming and threw up an arm to protect his face. The axe barely shuddered as it cut clean through the man's forearm, shattered his helmet and buried itself deep in his skull.

'Take him down!' Cato screamed hoarsely. 'Kill him!'

Three swords thrust into the warrior and he gave an explosive grunt and sagged to his knees, the deadly axe dropping from his nerveless fingers as he died. But before the gap he had forced in the Roman line could be filled, another warrior leaped forward and landed astride his fallen comrade, slashing at the nearest legionary with his long sword. The Roman just managed to turn enough for the blow to land on the shoulder of his segmented armour and there was a loud crack as his collarbone shattered under the impact.

More enemy warriors burst in amongst the men of the Sixth Century, and Cato knew that any formation was no longer possible. He thrust himself forward into the dense brawl, pushed up against the back of one of his men and braced his legs to help heave the man forwards. But the pressure from the enemy warriors was irresistible, urged on by Caratacus, roaring his encouragement. Cato felt himself being forced back, step by step, until the century was astride the ditch and the ramparts loomed up behind him. The man in front of him shuddered, convulsed and then fell to the side, into the ditch and was impaled on the sharpened stakes lining the bottom. Then Cato was in the middle of the fight, crouching low, shield close and sword held horizontal, ready to thrust.

On either side of him legionaries and Celts were locked in a bitter and merciless struggle. The collapse of the Roman formation meant that both sides were pressed together in a tight pack where slashing weapons were useless and the short swords of the legions came into their own. The Britons knew they were outclassed and now punched and clawed at the Romans, fingers and fists scrabbling for purchase on any unprotected Roman flesh. With a shrill scream a young warrior hurled himself upon Cato, one hand clenched round the wrist of his sword arm, the other groping for his throat. For an instant Cato panicked, his muscles frozen in

269

helpess terror, then the instinct for self-preservation made him release his grip on the shield, ball his spare hand into a fist and smash it into the cheek of the enemy warrior. The man just blinked and continued in his fanatical effort to throttle the Roman centurion. Cato tried once more, with no effect, then dropped his hand to the dagger at his waist. Snatching it out, he thrust it up and forwards, into the stomach of his attacker. The young man's look of hatred turned into one of surprise and pain. Cato thrust again with all his remaining strength, and felt his dagger rip sideways, and a sudden warm gush over his hand and forearm as the enemy went limp and slid away, but was still held up by the press of bodies around him.

'Run for it!' Cato shouted to the surviving men of his century. 'Run!'

There was a loosening of the mêlée as the legionaries backed away, or simply turned and dashed for the small opening in the crudely constructed gateway. It was now a running battle, with Romans slashing around them as they ran for safety and the Britons worrying them like hunting dogs trying to bring down their prey. Cato made for the standard-bearer and was relieved to see Septimus already at the bearer's side, hacking away at any Britons that dared to venture too close. Then the three of them, back to back, shuffled towards the gate, up the last few feet of the narrow ramp leading between the enfilading defences. Above them their comrades dare not shower the attackers with their javelins for fear of hitting their own men.

Cato sensed the gatepost at his shoulder and shoved the bearer inside. 'You too, Optio!'

'Sir!' Septimus began to protest, but Cato cut him short. 'That's an order.'

With his back to the gatepost, Cato wrenched up a fallen shield and faced the enemy. One by one his men fought their way past him, while the centurion thrust and hacked with his short sword to keep Caratacus' men at bay. At last, there seemed to be no more Romans alive in front of the defences, but Cato felt compelled to take a last look to be certain. A strong hand grabbed him by the shoulder and hauled him inside the gate.

'Close it!' Macro shouted, and two squads of legionaries threw their weight behind the rough timber as the enemy warriors thrust against the far side, struggling to push it open. But the legionaries were better organised and quickly closed the gate and fastened the locking bar in place as the timbers shook under the impact.

'Let 'em have it!' Tullius shouted from the rampart, and Cato saw the legionaries throw volley after volley of javelins down into the tightly packed bodies on the far side of the gate. Screams rent the air and then the pounding on the gate stopped, and the shouts and cries of the enemy drew away.

Cato squatted on the ground, one hand resting on his shield, the other in

270

a fist about the handle of his short sword which he used to support his exhausted body.

'You all right, lad?'

Cato looked up, and shook his head at Macro. 'Could use a drink.'

'Sorry,' Macro smiled as he reached for his canteen. 'All I've got is water.'

'That'll have to do.'

Cato gulped down several lukewarm mouthfuls, and passed the canteen back to Macro. Then he slowly rose to his feet and stared over Macro's shoulder.

'What's up?'

'Look.' Cato pointed. A thin trail of smoke was rising up from the direction of the fort.

Chapter Thirty-Nine

'Now what?' Macro growled. 'They can't have got round us, surely?'

'No. That's not possible.'

'Why not?'

Cato nodded his head towards the marsh. 'That's Caratacus' vanguard out there; the first of his men to reach us.'

'So who's that over at the fort?'

Before Cato could reply Centurion Tullius came running over to them, an anxious expression on his face. 'You've seen it, then?'

'Yes, sir,' Macro replied evenly. 'That's why we're facing in that direction.'

'They've got behind us. Right behind us.' Tullius' mind raced ahead. 'We've had it. Once they've finished at the fort, they'll attack here. We'll be caught between them and cut to pieces. We should never have left the fort. Maximius was right.' Tullius turned to face Cato. 'It's all your fault. Your plan, and now it's a bloody disaster. I should never had listened to you.'

Cato kept his mouth shut, feeling first anger and then contempt for his superior, but conscious that he must let none of this show. Now was not the time to defend himself against such spineless accusations. He had to handle the situation carefully, before the old centurion panicked and made a rash, genuinely disastrous decision. Besides, Cato knew that Tullius was wrong.

'I must have been mad to listen to you,' Tullius continued bitterly. 'Mad. I should never have set you free. In fact, I think you should be relieved of your command.'

'Now hold on a moment, sir.' Macro stepped forward. 'That ain't fair. We all agreed to the plan. The lad's not to blame.'

Tullius turned his bitter gaze to Macro. 'Perhaps I should have you both put in irons.'

'Sir,' Cato interrupted quietly, 'we shouldn't be doing this. Not in front of the men.'

Tullius glanced round, and saw that the nearest legionaries were looking at them curiously. 'Get back to your stations! Keep your bloody eyes on the enemy!'

The men glanced away and tried to look as if they had never been interested in the officers' confrontation in the first place. Tullius made sure that none of them was eavesdropping before he turned back to Cato and Macro.

'I'll deal with you two later. Right now I need every man who can hold a weapon. But I promise you, if by some miracle we get out of this alive, there will be a full accounting for this balls-up.'

Macro's nostrils flared as he took a deep breath and leaned forward to respond in kind. But Cato grasped his forearm and spoke before his friend could make a bad situation any worse.

'Yes, sir. We agree. But let's deal with the attack first. You can do what you like with us later.'

Centurion Tullius nodded. 'Very well. We have to get out of this trap.'

'If we quit the rampart,' said Macro, 'while that lot are licking their wounds and working themselves up for another attempt, we might make it back to the fort before they can catch us. We'd stand a better chance there.'

'Assuming that the force sacking the fort is small enough for us to overcome,' Tullius replied. He stared at the smoke billowing up in the distance. 'In any case, we don't know how badly they've damaged the defences.'

'Sir?'

'What now, Cato? Another brilliant plan?'

'No, sir. I just think there's no point in returning to the fort. We don't know what we might find there. The defences could still be standing; they might not. In which case we're better off staying here. Besides, I don't think whoever's having a go at the fort need concern us.'

'Oh, really? And what makes you think that?'

Cato ignored the sarcasm. 'It's not Caratacus' men. It's more likely to be the natives from the village. A chance for them to have their revenge. They'll just take what they can and destroy the rest. Then, my guess is, they'll panic and run for cover.'

'Your guess . . .'

'If Cato's right,' Macro looked anxiously back towards the smoke, 'what about Maximius and Felix? And that Nepos? We have to send someone back to save them. Let me go, sir. I'll take half a century and—'

'There's no point,' Cato cut in. 'They're already dead. Whoever's there – villagers or the enemy – won't have spared them. Besides, as the cohort commander says, we need every man here to hold off Caratacus. Hold him off long enough for Vespasian to arrive.'

'If he arrives,' Macro replied.

'All right then,' Cato nodded, 'if he arrives. But that's what everything hangs on now. If the legion's not coming then nothing we can do will make a difference. We'll be overwhelmed and wiped out. But if the legate is coming, then we must hold on here for as long as possible. That's all that matters now.' Cato stared determinedly at Centurion Tullius. 'Sir, we've no choice. We have to make a stand.'

273

Tullius was silent for a moment as he struggled to come up with an alternative to Cato's bleak outline of their predicament. But the more he thought about it, the less choice there was, and in the end he slapped his thigh with frustration.

'All right, then. We stay and fight. Macro?'

'Sir?'

'I want a man posted on that hilltop, to keep watch for any force coming at us from the fort. See to it.'

'Yes, sir.'

Tullius nodded and then strode over towards the gate and clambered up the steps on to the rampart.

Macro turned towards Cato, his cheeks puffing as he blew a sigh of relief. 'That was close. For a moment there I thought he was going to slap us in chains. You really think it's the villagers having a go at the fort?'

Cato shrugged. 'It doesn't matter.'

'We shouldn't have left the others behind,' Macro reflected guiltily. 'Do you think there's any chance—'

'No. None.' Cato turned to him with a deadpan expression.

Macro frowned. 'What do you mean?'

A shout echoed from the rampart. 'Enemy's on the move!'

The two centurions scrambled up on to the rampart and pushed their way through the legionaries packed along the palisade, until they reached Tullius. Antonius and Cordus were with him, staring out over the palisade towards the enemy warriors streaming along the track towards the fortifications. Cato noted a number of bodies sprawled in the ditch either side of the gate, some still writhing feebly on the sharpened stakes that lined the bottom of the ditch.

Tullius turned to give his orders. 'You know your positions. Go to them.'

Cordus headed towards the right-hand redoubt where his men clustered, ready to hurl their javelins into the flank of the approaching enemy. Macro had been assigned the redoubt at the other end of the defences, and the centuries of Antonius and Tullius were to hold the length of wall in between.

'What about my men, sir?' Cato asked.

'Take what's left and form them up behind the gate. You're the reserve. If they force the gate, you must keep them out, at all cost.'

'Yes, sir.'

Tullius drew his sword and picked up his shield, then snarled at Cato. 'Go. Get out of my sight.'

Cato saluted and quickly climbed down from the rampart. The survivors of the Sixth Century were already rising wearily to their feet at his approach. He did a quick head count and found that he had forty-six men left.

'Septimus!'

'Yes, sir.' The optio snapped smartly to attention.

'Get 'em formed up behind the gate. Swords drawn and shields up. We may be needed in a hurry.'

While the optio quickly marshalled the legionaries into position Cato went over to examine the gateway. A few timbers had already started from their rope fixings after the impact of the first assault.

He turned back to his men. 'First section! On me.'

Two men stepped out of formation and came trotting over to him.

Cato frowned. 'Where are the rest?'

'Dead and missing, sir,' one of the legionaries replied. 'We were pretty badly carved up out there on the track.'

'Right,' Cato responded tersely, and looked beyond the man to the rest of his unit. 'Second section, on me.'

Five more men came over and Cato indicated the gate. 'We won't need to open that again. I want it strengthened. Use the cart, turn it on its side and push it hard up against the gate. Once you've done that, start digging and get the earth piled up behind. Leave your shields at the foot of the rampart. Now, move!'

They ran off to do his bidding and Cato went over to join Septimus in front of his men, standing ready to reinforce any weak point in the defences. From the far side of the rampart came the roar of the enemy, charging home. A handful of arrows and light javelins arced over the palisade. With a sharp metallic ring the helmet of one of Tullius' men snapped back and he fell from the wall, tumbling down the reverse slope of the rampart to lie still on the ground.

'Raise shields!' Cato ordered, and the men hefted them up to cover their bodies as a steady shower of missiles struck at the defenders on the rampart, or zipped past them, occasionally clattering off the shields of the survivors of the Sixth Century. Cato continued to scan the ramparts, noting the enemy must have quickly scaled the ditch and mounted the far slope, since he could see men clearly engaged with the enemy on the far side of the palisade. The defenders were holding their own for the moment. Not one enemy head could be seen struggling to climb over the palisade. But the fight was not entirely one-sided. Already at least a dozen Roman bodies were scattered across the slope leading down from the rampart. There were more along the palisade itself. Those who were wounded tried to struggle clear of the mêlée to avoid any further injury, as well as not hindering their comrades still locked in combat with the enemy.

In front of Cato the men he had assigned to bolster the gate had succeeded in overturning the cart and shoving it tight against the loose timbers. Now they were at work breaking up the hard ground a short distance back from the cart and shovelling the spoil against the cart. The gate shimmered under the impact of swords and axes thudding into the far side. Already, small splinters were flying through the air this side of the gate.

Cato was racked with frustration at having to remain behind the gate, unable to see how the fight was progressing. It seemed to him that unless the enemy broke off soon they must surely overwhelm the men on the palisade.

The fight went on and on. Up in the flanking redoubts the legionaries had expended their remaining javelins. The men who had been issued with slings were whirling the leather thongs about their heads before releasing the deadly missiles into the dense ranks massed before the defences. The rest of the legionaries were hurling rocks and larger stones in a desperate bid to break the resolve of Caratacus and his men. Cato saw Macro bend, snatch up a rock from the dwindling stockpile and turn to hurl it with all his strength across the palisade. Macro watched the fall of the shot, and then thrust his fist into the air in a gesture of triumph. The next instant he threw himself flat as an arrow slashed through the space he had been standing in just before.

'Cato!' Tullius shouted from the palisade, just above the gate. 'Battering ram coming up! Get your men up against the gate. Bolster it up!'

'Yes, sir! Sixth Century, sheathe swords! Follow me!'

Cato led them over the loose earth to the cart, then pressed his shield against the side of the cart and leaned into it. Men followed suit on either side, and when the surface was covered, the rest pushed up against the backs of their comrades. The hacking sounds from the far side abruptly ceased and a rising roar of cheers filled Cato's ears.

'Brace yourselves!' he called out, and gritted his teeth.

The next moment there was a massive crash from the far side of the gate and Cato reeled back from it as if he had been kicked by a maddened mule. As soon as he recovered his balance he threw his weight forwards again, and felt the reasurring pressure from behind as his men struggled back into position.

'Here it comes again!' someone shouted, and again the men of the Sixth Century were hurled back. But the gate still held.

Overhead Cato heard Tullius bellowing above the din, 'Use everything you've got! Hit them! Kill the bastards!'

The ram struck the gate five more times, and on the last blow Cato saw a timber splintered inwards. One of his men screamed as a long splinter shot into his cheek, just below the eye and tore open the flesh. The legionary reached for the splinter and tugged it out, gritting his teeth. Blood gushed down his face and spattered across his armour, and he threw himself back against the gate. Brave, thought Cato, wondering for an instant how he would have reacted to such an injury. Then he focused on the gate and realised, with a sinking feeling of horror, that it would withstand only a few more blows from the battering ram before it burst apart.

Another blow came, further splintering the damaged timber, but Cato sensed that the blow had not been as forceful. Then he thought that the enemy cheers from the track had died down, though it was hard to be sure since his heart pounded in his chest and his head rang with the heavy throb of the blood pulsing through him. There was more cheering now, and it took Cato a moment to realise that those were Roman cheers. Cheers, catcalls and shouts of contempt.

'They must have pulled back!' one of Cato's men shouted.

'Quiet there!' Septimus shouted. 'Stay in position!'

The cheering continued, and there were no more blows from the battering ram. Cato waited a moment longer until he was satisfied that it was safe, then ordered his men to fall back to their reserve position. They stood panting and tired, but desperately relieved that the defences held, and that they themselves were still alive.

'Centurion Cato!' Tullius called down from the rampart.

Cato took a quick breath and forced himself to stand erect before he replied. 'Sir?'

'Your men have had their rest. You're relieving Antonius. Get your men up here as soon as the Fifth Century get off the wall.'

'Yes, sir.'

'Rest?' one of Cato's men muttered. 'Who's he fucking kidding?'

Some of the other legionaries started grumbling and Septimus wheeled round on them. 'Shut your mouths! Save it for the bloody natives!'

The grumbling stopped, but the air of sullen resentment hung over them like a shroud. As the men of the Fifth Century filed down from the rampart and passed Cato, he saw that many of them were wounded, some barely able to stay on their feet.

'Bad up there?' one of Cato's men asked.

'They're bloody crazy,' came the reply from the dazed optio of the Fifth Century. 'Never seen anything like it. Just threw themselves at the wall like they wanted to die . . . bloody madmen.'

'Optio!' Cato beckoned him closer. 'Where's Centurion Antonius?'

'Dead . . .'

'Dead, *sir*!' Cato snapped at him. 'It's "sir" when you're addressing a superior officer!'

The optio stiffened to attention. 'Yes, sir. Sorry, sir.'

Cato nodded, then leaned closer and continued softly, 'You're in command now, Optio. You set the standard. Don't let your men down.'

'No, sir.'

Cato stared at him for a moment, to make sure that his nerve had steadied. 'Carry on.'

'Yes, sir.'

'Cato!' Tullius bellowed. 'What are you waiting for! Get your arse up here!'

'At once, sir!'

The men of the Sixth Century hefted their shields and followed Cato up on to the rampart. He was not prepared for the sight that met his eyes

277

when he looked over the palisade. The optio's comment about the madness of the enemy was fully borne out. They lay heaped before the palisade. A great tangle of bloodied limbs, shields and weapons stretched from the rampart in a rough triangle, with its apex on the track that led into the marsh. Here and there the injured still moved. Cato watched a man with a javelin in his spine claw his way back to his comrades re-forming for the next assault a hundred paces down the track. He dragged his nerveless legs a short distance from the mound of bodies before his strength gave out and he collapsed on the hard earth of the track, his gleaming torso heaving from the effort.

'A welcome sight.'

Cato tore his gaze away from the crippled enemy warrior. Tullius had thrust his way through the defenders and had observed the young centurion's shock at the bloody vista before the defences.

Cato stared at him, and nodded dumbly. Tullius looked down the track and shook his head in wonder. 'Looks like they'll be having another go any moment now. You'd better get your men ready.'

'Yes, sir.' Cato saluted and glanced along the palisade towards the thin line of men that stretched out towards the redoubt where he could see Macro smiling as he did the rounds of his men, giving them a slap of encouragement on the shoulder as he passed by. He caught sight of Cato and flashed him a brief thumbs-up. Cato nodded, and turned his mind to his immediate duty. He saw a number of legionaries sprawled along the line of the palisade. They would be a hazard to have underfoot when the next attack came.

'Get those bodies off the rampart!'

There was no sense of ceremony as his men heaved their comrades' corpses down the slope, limbs flopping loosely as they tumbled. As soon as the task was complete Cato ordered them to stand to and his men faced the enemy, swords drawn. As he walked down the line Cato was pleased to see that there was no sign of fear in their expressions, just the resigned determination of seasoned veterans. They would hold their position and fight until they were cut down, or the enemy gave way. Cato was pleased by their composure, but the pleasure was tinged with regret. If only Vespasian and General Plautius could see them now. The shame of decimation was behind them, and they would sell their lives like heroes. Unless the legate arrived in time the only witnesses to their valour would be the enemy. And the native warriors were so insanely intent on obliterating the cohort that they be insensible to the courage of the Romans. Cato smiled to himself. It was a strange thing, this life in the legions. Two years he had served under the Eagles, and yet each battle always felt like the first and last. He wondered if he would ever become accustomed to the peculiar intensity of sensation that went with every battle.

'Man approaching!'

The voice was distant, and Cato could not place the direction at first. Then, as he saw heads turn to glance back behind the wall, he followed suit and saw the lookout Macro had posted waving his arm to attract attention and then point back towards the column of smoke that marked the site of the fort. No one moved. One man represented no threat, just a source of curiosity, and they waited for further information about the approaching figure.

The lookout turned his back to them for a while and then called out, 'One of ours!'

An icy tingle of dread rippled up Cato's spine. Supposing it was Maximius? Or Felix? Their arrival would result in his death just as surely as an enemy sword-thrust. Then he angrily told himself that such a fear was wholly baseless. He already knew who that man must be, long before he ran over the brow of the hill and staggered down towards the rampart.

'Sir!' the lookout shouted towards the defenders. 'It's Nepos.'

Tullius turned to seek Cato out. 'Centurion Cato, come with me.'

They climbed down and marched towards Nepos as the legionary covered the last stretch of the slope leading down from the hill.

Tullius drew up in front of him. 'Make your report! What happened at the fort?'

Nepos struggled for breath and, licking his lips, he glanced quickly at Cato.

'Tell him what happened,' said Cato.

'The villagers, sir, they ransacked the place . . . set it on fire . . . I left the tent to see . . . to see what was happening. They saw me; gave chase . . . I tried to get back to the headquarters tent . . . but some of 'em had got there before me.'

Tullius shot a horrified look at Cato before turning back to the legionary. 'And Maximius? Felix?'

Nepos lowered his head, struggling for breath.

'What happened?' Tullius grabbed his arm. 'Tell me!'

'They're dead, sir. Nothing I could do to save them. The villagers went after me. I had to run . . .'

The man was spent and had nothing further to add. Tullius released his grip and stared back towards the diffuse column of smoke hanging over the valley.

'Poor bastards.'

'Yes, sir.' Cato nodded. 'But how could we know the villagers would attack the fort?'

'We should never have left them there.'

'Sir, we weren't to know. And we had to deal with the threat from Caratacus.' Cato spoke calmly, and with direct emphasis. 'No one is to blame. Fortunes of war. Nothing we can do about it now, sir.'

Centurion Tullius looked at him, and was silent for a moment. 'No. Nothing.'

'And now, sir,' Cato continued, 'the enemy's building up for another attack. We should get back on the wall. Nepos?'

'Yes, sir.'

'Take some equipment from one of the casualties, then join me on the rampart.'

'Yes, sir.'

Tullius watched the man trot across to one of the bodies and help himself to a sword, helmet and shield. 'I hope he's telling the truth.'

'Of course he is, sir. After what Maximius has been doing to the locals recently, I'd be surprised if they didn't take the chance to get their revenge at the first opportunity. Wouldn't you? Wouldn't anyone else?'

Tullius turned to look at Cato, fixing him with a searching stare. 'There's nothing you want to tell me?'

Cato raised his eyebrows. 'I'm afraid I don't understand, sir.'

'What did you—'

Before Centurion Tullius could ask his question there was a cry from the palisade.

'Enemy's on the move!'

Chapter Forty

This time the enemy was more cautious. Caratacus had managed to rein his warriors in, and the head of the column approaching along the narrow track was composed of men carrying shields. Instead of the usual Celtic rush, the enemy advanced slowly, struggling to keep in the unfamiliar formation as a number of them held shields overhead. It was crudely handled but clearly based on the model they had deployed when Caratacus had forced the crossing of the Tamesis. If barbarians continued picking up more tricks of the trade from the legions, Cato reflected, Rome was going to have its hands full in a few more years.

Septimus gave his centurion a wry look. 'Much more of this and we might as well sign them on as an auxiliary cohort.'

'Give me an ally rather than an enemy every time,' Cato muttered. He glanced beyond the approaching shield wall and saw Caratacus directing the operation from further down the track, well out of javelin and slingshot range. The enemy leader stood on his chariot, while an attendant was busy tying a rough dressing around his shoulder. When the front rank of the enemy column was no more than fifty paces from the Roman defences Caratacus cupped a hand to his mouth and shouted an order for them to halt. The warriors shuffled to a stop, adjusted their line, and began to spread out each side of the track, to the very fringes of the marsh. When the line was ready the men holding the upper tier of shields moved forward, into position, and then all fell still. Caratacus turned to a compact group of men standing beside his chariot and waved them up the track. Cato saw that they carried no swords or shields, just heavy haversacks hanging across their chests, and something that flickered like thin snakes drooping from their hands.

'Slingers . . .' He drew a deep breath and called a warning out to his men. 'Prepare to receive slingshot! Shields up.'

All along the palisade the men lifted the rims of their shields and hunched down behind them as they braced for the fusillade of missiles that were far more deadly than arrows, and the supply of which would take a lot longer to exhaust than javelins. Cato, poised to duck down as soon as the enemy loosed the first volley, kept watch over his shield. The slingers ran down to the shield wall, then spread out to give themselves room to swing the leather cords that stretched out to the pouches containing the shot. A low whirring began to build up as the first slingers prepared to unleash their missiles.

'Here it comes!' Septimus bellowed. 'Heads down!'

The whirring peaked and then suddenly the air was filled with a thwipping noise an instant before the shot struck home with a series of sharp cracks all along the palisade. With a loud ringing one clattered against Cato's shield boss, knocking it in so that as Cato loosened his grip he felt the dented metal brush against the back of his knuckles. A lucky shot, Cato smiled ruefully, and of course it had to strike his shield. An instant later one of the slingers was even more lucky. A heavy round stone passed clear through a gap in the crude palisade and smashed into the ankle of a legionary just to one side of Cato. The man cried out as his bones were pulverised by the impact and he crumpled to one side, clutching at his ankle, and starting to howl in agony.

Cato turned towards his optio. 'Septimus! Get him off the rampart!'

Under the cover of his shield the optio clambered over to the injured man, grabbed him by the forearm and dragged him bodily down the rear of the rampart to where the rest of the injured lay along the base of the defences. No one could be spared to attend to their wounds while the cohort was under attack, and they lay in the hot afternoon sun, some crying out, but most of them still, biting back on their pain. Those who could, saw to their own injuries and then tried to help the men around them. Septimus hauled his casualty over to the end of the row of injured and then scurried back into position on the palisade.

As the rattling fusillade continued, more shots found their targets and took a slow steady toll of dead and wounded, even as they continued to batter and splinter the broad shields that lined the top of the rampart. Time was on the Romans' side, Cato comforted himself as he hunched down and gritted his teeth as another slingshot cracked against the surface of his shield. The longer Caratacus kept this up, the closer Vespasian came to closing the trap. But there was no sense in the Third Cohort exposing themselves to more damage than necessary.

'Stay down!' Cato called to his men as he dropped back out of line and scrambled along the rampart to where Tullius sheltered behind his shield.

'Sir!' Cato called. Tullius glanced round.

'Sir, shouldn't we pull the men back on to the reverse slope, out of the line of fire?'

Tullius shook his head. 'They can take it. Besides, we don't want the enemy thinking we'll duck a fight.'

'This isn't a fight, sir.' Cato waved his hand to the growing line of casualties below the rampart. 'It's just a waste of good men.'

'I'll be the judge of that, Centurion!' Tullius snapped at him. 'Now return to your position.'

Cato considered protesting, but the glint in Tullius' eyes showed that the veteran was in no mood to listen. He'd clearly had enough of Cato's advice and it would be dangerous to push him any further.

'Yes, sir.' Cato saluted and made his way back to his men, still suffering the intense bombardment of slingshot in resigned silence. There was no let-up, no diminishing of the volume of missiles smashing and cracking the palisade and the men who defended it, and Cato wondered how many of them would be left by the time dusk gathered over the marshes. By then, the legate would surely have arrived.

'There's movement down the track!' Septimus called out, and Cato risked a glimpse round the edge of his shield. Behind the slingers, streaming past Caratacus on his chariot, came a dense body of men, many of whom were carrying bundles of wood and crudely constructed ladders.

Cato ducked his head back and shouted to his men, 'Sixth Century! Draw swords!'

There was a drawn-out chorus of rasping noises as the men drew their weapons, and then the legionaries of the other centuries followed suit. The Romans tensed their muscles, anxiously waiting for the order to rise up and confront the fresh wave of attackers. Cato took another look. A gap had opened up in the enemy shield wall, and beyond that the slingers parted each side of the track as the assault party rushed through, running the remaining distance to the Roman defences. Over their heads the slingers resumed their bombardment of the Third Cohort. There was none of the usual shouting of war cries as the native warriors reached the edge of the ditch and started to pick their way across the bodies of their comrades who had died in the earlier assaults. With Romans waiting ahead of them, and their own men flinging slingshot from behind them, they just wanted to get the attack over with as quickly as possible. The bundles of wood were cast down where the ditch still yawned before the low rampart and the warriors streamed across, throwing themselves up the steep slope on the far side.

'Stand up!' Tullius roared out, and the other officers echoed the call along the rampart. The legionaries rose to their feet, moved up to the palisade and raised their blades, ready to meet the attack. The last few slingshot zipped through the air, bringing down one more Roman before the natives were forced to stop their bombardment for fear of hitting their own men. There was almost no interlude between the last of the shot flying overhead and the first clashes of weapons along the rampart. The makeshift ladders were thrust up against the palisade and the Celt warriors swarmed up and attempted to swing themselves over the rampart and engulf the defenders. From the flanking redoubts Cordus and Macro urged their men on, hurling and throwing whatever missiles they had left into the flanks of the attacking force.

Cato tightened his grip on his sword and shield, and pressed forward. The roughly hewn top of a ladder slapped up against the palisade immediately to his left and an instant later a burly warrior clambered up, reached an arm over the palisade and began to pull himself up. Cato thrust the point of his sword at the side of the man's head and felt the thud and crunch of bone jar down his arm. The man dropped away and Cato turned to the nearest legionary.

'Here! Help me!'

Pushing the guard of his sword hand against the top of the ladder Cato tried to heave it back on top of the attackers. But there was already a man on the lowest rung, and the Briton swung himself up as fast as he could, meeting Cato's terrified gaze with a mad glint of triumph in his eyes.

'No you fucking don't, mate!' The legionary cut with ferocious strength, his sword cleaving the man's skull and splattering himself and his centurion with blood and brains. As the man fell Cato thrust the ladder away from the palisade and nodded his thanks to the legionary.

Cato glanced round and saw that so far not one of the enemy had secured a foothold on the rampart. But even as he watched, a short distance to his right a section of the palisade was wrenched away from the rampart, showering the attackers with rubble as the loosened earth behind it collapsed. With a cry, the legionary who had been fighting immediately above them, tumbled forward into the mass of warriors below and was butchered as he sprawled on the slope.

'Watch it!' Cato shouted to his men. 'They're pulling up the palisade!'

While their comrades had been keeping the legionaries occupied with their ladder assault, small groups of the enemy had been digging away at the foundations of the palisade and working the timbers loose. Already, as Cato looked along the line of the rampart he saw other sections being pulled away. As soon as a gap had opened up in the palisade Celt warriors swarmed up and heaved themselves on to the rampart.

'Shit!' Septimus cried out angrily. 'We should have dug them in deeper!'

'Too late for that now.' Cato turned back to the enemy, and hacked his sword down at a man being hoisted up by his companions. The warrior was armed with a long-handled axe and managed to block the centurion's blow, but in doing so overbalanced and tumbled back on to the slope.

Elsewhere the Sixth Century was not doing so well. In two places where the palisade had been ripped down a handful of warriors had won a foothold on the rampart and were bodily heaving the defenders back to create more space for their comrades to climb up after them.

'Septimus!'

'Sir?'

Cato indicated the nearest breach in the palisade. 'Take six men. Push them out, before it's too late. Move!'

The optio recognised the danger at once, and made for the breach, pulling men out of the line as he made his way along the rampart. As the legionaries approached the breach they formed up into a compact battering ram of flesh and metal, and charged home on a two-shield front, all that the narrow walkway permitted. They crashed into the enemy warriors and cut them down before the Celts recovered from the shock of the impact. The dead and injured were thrown down on top of the enemy still struggling to squeeze through the gap and up on to the rampart. Septimus and his men hunched round the crumbling earth and hacked at any enemy foolhardy enough to make another attempt at breaking into the Roman line. But beyond them Cato saw that the situation at the second breach was far more serious. The enemy had won some space on the rampart and were quickly feeding men into the gap. Turning round Cato shouted at the nearest man not engaged in the fight along the palisade.

'Run round that lot to Centurion Macro. Tell him he needs to drive them off the wall and plug the gap. I can't spare any men. Go!'

As the legionary half ran, half slithered down the slope Cato felt a dull vibration under his feet and, realising what it must be, he glanced towards the gate. Behind the rampart the reserves were hurrying forward to counter the impact as best as they could. In front of the rampart the enemy warriors had retrieved the battering ram, from where it lay amongst the bodies on the track, and were renewing their attack on the gate.

Cato realised that the cohort was losing control of the fight. The timbers of the gate had been designed to control the movement of natives into and out of the marsh, not to withstand a determined assault. The enemy would burst through them soon enough. If that failed then they must eventually create enough gaps in the palisade that the legionaries couldn't defend them all. In either event, the cohort was doomed.

Overcome by bloodlust, some of the enemy who had hauled them-selves up on to the rampart now spied the line of casualties along the base of the rampart and charged down upon them with whooping cries of triumph. Wounded and almost defenceless, the Roman casualties could do little to protect themselves as the Britons butchered them on the ground. But the temptation of an easy kill was their undoing, as it diverted them away from ensuring that they held on to the opening they had torn in the Roman defences. With as loud a roar as they could muster, Macro and half of his men were sweeping along the rampart from the direction of the redoubt, charging down and cutting through the knot of warriors who were desperately trying to hold the way open for the men struggling to feed into the gap. A moment's delay and the Celts would have had more than enough men through the gap to hold off Macro's relief force. As it was, they were steadily killed, or pushed back, until the last of them was ejected from the rampart. Their comrades slaughtering the Roman wounded realised the danger, and struggled up the slope to fight for the precious stretch of bloody earth around the gap in the palisade. But they were too late and too few to make a difference, and they died before they even reached the top of the slope, tumbling back down to sprawl amongst the bodies of the men they had so mercilessly killed only moments earlier.

As soon as the rampart was secured Cato looked round to see what progress the enemy warriors were making on the gate. The slow pounding rhythm continued relentlessly, and then there was a splintering crash as the first of the timbers gave way. That was it then, Cato decided, with a heavy sinking feeling in his chest. A few more blows, then the gate would be shattered enough for the attackers to wrench the remnants aside, pour through the opening and tear the surviving men of the Third Cohort to pieces.

Then he was aware that the pounding had stopped, and looking both ways along the rampart he saw that more and more of his men were standing back, disengaged. They lowered their shields and leaned on the rims, exhausted and gasping for breath. Before them the Celts were falling back from the ramparts, streaming away towards Caratacus, still standing, feet astride, atop his chariot. Only, now, he was looking down the track, in the opposite direction to the Third Cohort.

'Sir!' Septimus pushed his way through the defenders towards Cato. 'Can you hear it?'

'Hear what?'

'Listen.'

Cato strained his ears, but all he could hear, above the pounding of blood through his weary body, was the panicked cries of the enemy warriors retreating from the ramparts, and jamming into a dense, immovable mass around their commander's chariot. Cato shook his head and Septimus thumped his fist down on the palisade.

'Just listen, sir!'

Cato tried again, and this time, there was something else, over and above the rising cries of despair and panic from the enemy: a distant clash and clatter of weapons and the thin tinny blare of a trumpet. And only one army on this island used trumpets that sounded like that. Cato grinned as a wave of pure relief washed over him and filled his heart with joy.

'It's the legate. It has to be.'

'Of course it bloody is, sir!' the optio laughed, and slapped him on the shoulder. 'Bastard had to leave it until the last moment, didn't he?'

As more of the legionaries became aware of the noise they looked round at each other in delight, and then started cheering and making obscene gestures at the fleeing enemy. The ferocious arrogance with which the native warriors had attacked the cohort earlier in the afternoon had evaporated the moment word spread through their ranks that a powerful enemy force had appeared behind them. Now their only thought was for escape and survival. Only Caratacus' bodyguard held firm – a small tight-knit unit of aristocrats and elite warriors that struggled to maintain a tight cordon around their king, contemptuously thrusting aside the frightened masses that streamed past them. Already, some of the enemy had realised that the marsh was their only hope of salvation, and they struck out from the track, wading out amongst the rushes, and struggling when they reached the expanse of mud beyond, stumbling through the ooze that clung to their legs and made every pace a test of strength and ultimately endurance.

'Not a pretty sight, is it?'

Cato turned to see Macro at his shoulder. The older centurion was staring sadly at the spectacle on the track. 'A broken army is a bloody pitiful thing.'

'As sights go, that one will do me nicely.'

'Heads up,' Macro said quietly, looking past Cato's shoulder. 'Here's Tullius . . . Congratulations, sir!'

'Eh?' Tullius looked anything but pleased, and Cato saw that his stare was fixed beyond the broken native force, towards the distant standards of the Second Legion, twinkling in the late afternoon sunlight. 'I wonder if Vespasian will be so quick to offer his congratulations.'

Tullius gave Macro and Cato a meaningful look before he turned towards the nearest troops. 'Get out of here!'

As soon as the legionaries had shuffled out of earshot Centurion Tullius faced his subordinates and spoke in a low, urgent tone.

'What are we going to tell the legate?'

Cato raised his eyebrows. 'Tell him? Sorry, sir, I don't understand.'

Tullius leaned closer and stabbed Cato's chest with his finger. 'Don't be fucking cute with me, lad. I'm talking about Maximius. How are we going to explain that one away?'

'Pardon me, sir, but there's nothing to explain away, provided we stick to our story. With Antonius dead, there's only you, Macro, me and Nepos who know what really happened.'

'Scratch Nepos from the list,' said Macro, jerking his thumb along the rampart. 'He's back there. Spearthrust went right through him. He didn't have time to find himself any armour before he got into the fight. Shame.'

'Yes, a shame,' Cato repeated slowly. 'So only three of us left now, sir. All we have to do is stick with the story we gave out to Cordus. It's not perfect, but it's all we've got, and there's nothing anybody can prove beyond what we tell them.'

'What if Nepos was wrong? What if Maximius is still alive. Or Felix?'

'They're dead,' Cato said firmly.

'What if they're not? We should tell the truth. Tell Vespasian that Maximius was endangering the cohort. That we had to restrain him in order to save the men, and to catch Caratacus in this trap.' A sudden gleam of inspiration burned in the old centurion's eyes. 'We won this victory. We made it possible. That's got to count for something.'

'No.' Macro shook his head. 'No, it won't. If we tell the truth then we're admitting mutiny. You know what the general's like. Even if Vespasian spares us, Plautius bloody well won't. It'll be a nice chance to demonstrate what a fine disciplinarian he is. I won't be put to death for that bastard Maximius. The lad's right. We have to stick to our story if we want to come out of this alive, and hope that Maximius and Felix are dead.'

Tullius turned his gaze towards Cato and frowned. 'You seem pretty confident that they are dead.'

Cato returned his stare without any expression on his face, then replied, 'I don't see how they could have survived the villagers' attack. Nepos was sure they'd been killed. That's good enough for me.'

'Let's pray it's good enough for Vespasian,' Macro added softly.

Tullius stared over the rampart towards the approaching legion, still hidden from view by the bend in the track. He chewed his lip for a moment and then nodded. 'All right then . . . we stick by the story. But there's one last thing we can do to help our cause.'

Macro looked at him suspiciously. 'Oh? What's that then, sir?'

'Give Caratacus to the legate.' Centurion Tullius had shifted his gaze to the enemy commander still beleaguered by the crush of men around his chariot and bodyguards. Tullius issued his orders without once turning to look at the other officers. 'I want you to take two sections down there and capture him.'

Macro laughed. 'You what?'

'I said, take two sections down there and take him prisoner. You and Cato.'

'That's madness. You trying to get us killed or something? . . . Oh.' Macro's surprised expression turned to a sneer. 'That's it, isn't it?'

Still Tullius refused to look at them as he spoke with an icy formality. 'You have your orders. Now be so good as to carry them out. At once.'

Macro glanced round to make sure he would not be overheard. 'Now listen here, you bastard—'

'Sir!' Cato grasped his arm and held him back. 'Let's go.'

'What?' Macro glared at his friend. 'Are you mad?'

'The cohort commander is right, sir. If we can give Caratacus to the legate, then we should be in the clear. Please, sir, let's get moving before he gets away.'

Macro felt himself being dragged back, and was sure that the world had gone mad. What other explanation could there be for Cato's connivance with Tullius' absurd order? As Cato summoned the men that Tullius had allowed for the task, Macro looked at his companion with a deeply concerned expression. 'What the hell are you playing at?'

'We have to do it, sir.'

'Why?'

'How would it look if we had a blazing row in front of the men? They're already suspicious enough as it is.'

'But he's trying to get us killed.'

'Of course he is.' Cato turned to face his friend directly. 'It makes sense. If we're dead he can blame the whole thing on us, and never have to worry that his part in Maximius' death will be revealed. But if we live, and take Caratacus prisoner, then at least he's got something impressive to throw in front of the legate. Either way, he's better off than if we all sit and wait for Vespasian to arrive and pass judgement.'

'What about us?'

'If we capture Caratacus, then we're in a better situation too.' Cato shrugged. 'If we stay and face the legate empty-handed, then I'd say our chances are less than even.'

Macro stared at him a moment, before replying, 'I'd hate to come across you on a gambling table.'

Cato frowned. 'This isn't a throw of the dice, sir. It's the logical thing to do under present conditions. It makes most sense.'

'If you say so, lad. If we're going, we might as well get on with it.'

The battered gates were thrown open and the two sections, with Macro and Cato at their head, marched out in a tight formation. They trod carefully over the tangle of bodies, dead and living, that sprawled before the Roman defences. A few of the enemy injured still attempted to resist, and Macro had to dodge to one side to avoid a feeble slash at his leg. He swivelled round, sword drawn back ready to strike and saw his assailant, a little boy, lying propped up against the corpse of a huge warrior. The boy held a dagger in one hand and the hand of the dead giant in the other. A javelin head had ripped a gaping hole in the boy's chest and his torso was covered in a glistening coating of blood. Macro shook his head, lowered his sword and rejoined the formation.

As they picked their way towards the enemy commander the bodies began to thin out, the footing became more reliable and they increased their pace towards Caratacus and his bodyguard.

'Halt!' Macro bellowed. 'Form wedge on me!'

Cato took up position at his friend's shoulder and the rest of the men fanned out on each side with a small reserve of six men inside the wedge to give body to its initial penetration of the enemy line. The enemy scattered ahead of them, no longer willing to fight, even though they outnumbered the small Roman formation. Only Caratacus and his bodyguard stood firm. The enemy commander raised his arm and shouted an order. His bodyguard moved forward and formed up across the track. Cato counted twenty-two of them. An almost even contest then, and a true test of each side's élite fighting men. The contrasts in size, equipment and appearance could not have been more marked. The bodyguards were all huge men, tattooed with ornate swirling patterns. Each carried a long sword or spear, an oval shield and most had helmets and chain-mail armour. As the Romans approached the Celts roared out their battle cries, insults and cries of defiance. Beyond them Caratacus looked on with a haughty expression of pride in his men.

Macro caught the expression as well and raised the point of his sword towards the enemy commander.

'That's right, mate!' he called out. 'We're coming for you!'

Caratacus sneered. Macro laughed and glanced back at his men. 'Be ready to charge the moment I give the word. Go in hard and stick it to 'em!'

The two sides were no more than twenty paces apart and Cato felt sure that Macro must order them to charge now, while there was still time, but the veteran centurion continued the approach at a measured pace for a moment longer. The tension shattered as Caratacus screamed an order and his men launched themselves forwards.

'Charge!' Macro roared, and Cato broke into a run.

An instant later the two small bands collided with a chorus of thuds and grunts and a sharp ringing of clashing blades. The Roman formation cleaved a passage through the loose enemy line and the legionaries turned outwards to fight the enemy warriors. The impact had borne a handful to the ground and they were killed before they could recover their breath and climb back on their feet. The Roman formation disintegrated after the charge, and around him Cato saw Romans and warriors locked in a series of duels.

With a savage cry one of the enemy, a dark-haired brute with a blue tattoo of a horse across his chest, charged at Cato, swinging his sword down towards the crest of the centurion's helmet. Cato swung his sword up at an angle and parried the blow away from his head, letting it rattle and scrape its way down his shield. The wild strike had exposed the enemy's side and Cato slammed his sword home into the man's ribs, breaking two apart as the point of the sword drove through flesh and muscle to pierce the man's heart. Blood pumped from the wound after Cato wrenched the blade back. He poised for another strike, but the man was finished, and slumped to his knees, muttered a curse and then toppled on to his back.

Cato turned and saw the back of a man fighting one of his legionaries. This was no formal fencing match, but a fight to the death, and he plunged his sword into the man's spine without a moment's hesitation.

'Watch it!' Cato shouted as the legionary nodded his thanks, then his face turned to an agonised expression of surprise as a spearhead erupted through his throat, tearing a metal plate free from the leather straps that bound the segmented armour together. The legionary lurched forward and over, wrenching the spear from the grip of the man behind him. Dodging round his mortally wounded comrade, Cato leaped at the unarmed man and slashed at his eyes, blinding him and almost severing his nose. The warrior screamed as his hands clutched at his face. Cato quickly turned and looked for another foe.

The fight was going their way. Most of the bodyguard were down, and the survivors were having to take more than one man at a time. Macro finished his man off and, glancing round, he caught Cato's eye.

'Let's get him.'

Cato nodded and they edged away from the last act of the unequal mêlée, then turned towards the chariot. Caratacus shouted an order to his driver and stepped back off the platform. With a crack of the reins the two horses reared and plunged forwards. Cato felt a blow to his side as Macro thrust him out of the path of the chariot and he rolled off the track into the crushed grass along the edge.

'Macro!'

Cato glanced round just into time to see his friend throw himself down, covering his stocky frame with his shield as the horses' hoofs pounded on the dry rutted earth of the track. Instinctively the animals tried to avoid the scarlet shield, and shied to one side, swinging the chariot round. The finely crafted wheel banged up on to Macro's shield, canting the platform over. With a cry the driver pitched forward into the traces as the chariot began to overturn, then the whole lot, horses, driver and chariot, crashed into the small knot of men still fighting it out.

'Shit . . .' Cato muttered in horror, before he clambered to his feet, snatched up his sword and rushed over to Macro. 'Sir!'

'I'm all right.' Macro shook his head and let Cato help him to his feet. 'Shield arm's gone numb, though. Where's Caratacus?'

Cato glanced round, and saw the enemy commander running into the marsh, his shoulder still swathed in a bloody bandage. 'There!'

'Come on.' Macro punched him on the arm. 'After him!'

They crossed the track, ran down the small bank and plunged into the rushes growing at the edge of the solid ground. Brackish water splashed up round their boots, and Cato could clearly see the muddy rippling patches ahead that marked Caratacus' route. 'This way!'

The rushes closed in on each side, dense pale stalks giving a dry rustle as the two men splashed forward. The water deepened, rising up to Cato's knees, and it was no longer possible to see where Caratacus had run.

Cato held up his arm. 'Stop!'

'What the . . .?'

'Quiet! Listen!'

They stood there, straining to hear any sound from their prey. In the distance the sounds of the legion cutting the remnants of Caratacus' army to pieces drifted through the still air. Individual cries of terror or defiance echoed faintly from afar, but there was no sound close at hand.

'What'll we do?' Macro whispered.

'Split up.' Cato jabbed his sword to the left where there appeared to be a gap in the rushes that might have been made by the passage of a fugitive. 'I'll go that way. You sweep round to the other side. We'll close up on each other if we don't find anything. All right?'

Macro nodded, not even thinking to question the fact that it was his young friend who was giving the orders. The young centurion began to wade off.

'Cato . . . no foolishness.'

Cato flashed him a quick smile. 'Who? Me?'

Macro watched him disappear amongst the tall stalks and shook his head wearily. Whatever fate was looking after the lad's welfare was working overtime. One day Cato was going to catch her on the hop . . .

Cato waded forward, the oily water swirling away from his thighs as the centurion eased himself between the rushes. As he approached a patch where they grew more densely his eye caught a flash of red and he looked closer. A smear of blood gleamed on one of the stalks. Cato tightened his grip on his sword and pushed on, carefully feeling his way through the tangle of soft vegetation hidden beneath the dark surface of the water. Behind him the sounds of the battle gradually faded, muffled by the marsh plants stretching out around him. Cato proceeded cautiously, eyes and ears straining to detect the faintest sign or sound of his prey. But there was nothing, just the unnaturally loud buzz and whine of the insects that swirled lethargically around him.

The rushes began to thin and the water became deeper as Cato emerged into a small open expanse of water. Close to him was a small hummock of earth. The remains of an uprooted tree lay across the tiny island, now covered with a luxuriant growth of emerald moss. The island presented a good point to try to get a better sense of the lie of the land, and Cato slowly waded over to it. As he emerged from the water he saw that his boots were covered with a thick black slime that weighed them down as if they were made of lead. He sat down on the tree trunk and reached for a slimy length of branch to help clean the muck from his boots. A bittern boomed from nearby, causing Cato to jump in alarm.

'Bastard bird,' he muttered softly.

An arm shot round his throat and yanked him backwards off the tree trunk. He tumbled back, flailing his hands and letting go of the sword. There was a grunt as he landed on top of someone. Someone built like a brick shit-house. The arm round his throat clenched tighter and behind his head Cato could hear the rasping breath as the man strained with the effort. Cato writhed frantically, trying to free himself, and clawing at the arm, struggling to loosen the grip, in vain.

'Goodbye, Centurion,' a Celt voice whispered hoarsely in his ear.

Cato jammed his jaw down against his chest and bit down on the tattooed flesh of the forearm. His teeth crunched through skin and muscle, as the man behind suppressed a howl of pain deep in his chest, and tightened his grip. Cato felt the first wave of light-headedness and bit as hard as he could, until his teeth met and his mouth was filled with blood and a warm lump of flesh.

The man gasped in agony but didn't loosen his grip.

Unless he could do something else, Cato knew he was as good as dead. He let one of his hands fall way, and groped behind his back, fingers scrabbling across the fine cloth of the man's leggings. He found the soft yielding package of the man's groin and dug his fingers into the scrotum and squeezed for all he was worth. At the same time he slammed his helmet back and heard the bone in his enemy's nose crunch. With a deep groan the man relaxed his grip for a moment. But that was enough. Cato wrenched the arm away from his neck, thrashed his way to one side and rolled off. He was on his feet in an instant, crouched and ready to fight. Six feet away, beside the tree trunk, was Caratacus, doubled up and groaning as he reached between his legs. Blood was streaming from his nose and arm, and he abruptly threw up when he could bear the agony no longer. He presented no danger to Cato in that state, and the centurion rose to his feet, tenderly massaging his throat as he looked round, saw his sword and went to retrieve it.

When Caratacus had finished being sick he painfully heaved himself round so that his back rested against the tree trunk. He glared at Cato, eyes filled with bitter hatred, until recognition dawned in his expression.

'I know you.'

Cato nodded, and undid the leather ties, heaving the heavy metal helmet from his sweat-drenched scalp. Caratacus grunted.

'The boy centurion . . . I should have had you killed.'

'Yes. I suppose so.'

'Funny, isn't it,' the king grimaced as he fought off another wave of agony, 'the way things turn out?'

'Funny?' Cato shrugged. 'No, it's not funny. Not even close to it.'

'So much for the Roman sense of humour.'

'There's been too much death for me, my lord. I'm sick of it.'

'Only one more to go then, before it's all over.'

Cato shook his head. 'No. You're my prisoner now. I'm taking you back to my legate.'

'Ah,' Caratacus grinned weakly. 'Roman mercy. Finally. I think I'd rather die here than as a sacrifice at your emperor's victory parade.'

'No one's going to sacrifice you.'

'Think I'm stupid?' Caratacus snarled. 'You think my people have ever forgotten what your Caesar did to Vercingetorix? I'll not be paraded through your forum, then strangled like some common criminal.'

'It won't happen, my lord.'

'You're sure?'

Cato shrugged. 'Not my decision. Come on, let me help you up. But no tricks, understand?'

Cato moved behind him and, gently lifting the king under his good shoulder, raised Caratacus up on to the log. A wave of pain swept through the Briton, and he gritted his teeth until it had passed.

'I'm not moving any further. Let me die here . . . please Roman.'

Cato stood over him, and stared down at the ruin of the man who had caused Rome so much frustration and fear over the last two years of campaigning. There was no question that he would be treated as a trophy. A quaint bauble for Claudius to dangle in chains for the entertainment of foreign potentates. Until the day that the Emperor tired of him and used him one last time to entertain the mob with some cheap death at the games.

'I spared you, Roman.' Caratacus' eyes were pleading. 'I let you live. So let me choose how I die.'

'You were going to burn me alive.'

'A mere detail.' He raised his hand and gestured towards Cato's sword. 'Please . . .'

Cato looked down at him. Once the most powerful of kings amongst the tribes of this island, he was now defeated and broken. Quite pitiful . . . Pity? Cato was surprised at himself. Why should he feel pity for this man who had proved such a pitiless enemy? And yet there was already a peculiar, aching sense of loss in his heart now that the enemy had been brought low. It was tempting to allow him one last dignity, to let him die in peace, and Cato looked down at his sword.

The Briton followed his gaze and nodded.

'Make it quick, Roman.'

Caratacus turned his head away, and clenched his eyes shut. For a moment all was still: the native king waiting silently for his end, and Cato holding the sword tightly in his hand. In the distance the sounds of battle had ended, aside from the shrill screams of the wounded. The insects buzzed in a cloud around the two men, drawn to the warm scent of the bloodied bandage wrapped around Caratacus' shoulder. Then Cato abruptly shook his head and smiled. He relaxed his grip on the sword handle, and with a dextrous twirl he rammed the blade back into its scabbard. Caratacus opened one eye and squinted up at him.

'No?'

'Sorry. Not this time. You're worth more to me alive.'

Caratacus opened the other eye, looked hard at Cato, and then shrugged. 'Fair enough. It would have been a nice end. Still, you might live to regret sparing me.'

'Don't get your hopes up.' Cato stepped away from him, cupped his hands to his mouth, drew a deep breath and called out, 'Macro! Macro! Over here!'

When they emerged from the marsh, the sun was low on the horizon, and washing some low puffs of clouds in a brilliant red. They carried Caratacus between them, one arm over each of their shoulders. Gasping for breath under his weight they splashed out of the rushes, struggled up the grassy banks and deposited the Briton by his upturned chariot, before slumping down to rest beside him. Behind them a column of legionaries was trudging towards the gate.

'Here.' Macro pulled the stopper out of his canteen and passed it to Cato. The young centurion raised it to his lips, and then noticed that Caratacus was watching him closely. Cato lowered the canteen and passed it to his prisoner, who tipped it up and eagerly swallowed several mouthfuls.

Macro was angry. 'What did you do that for? Letting some hairy-arsed barbarian clap his lips on my canteen. You're going soft, lad.'

'We want him in good condition.'

'A bit of thirst won't kill him.'

'No.'

Macro turned to look at him. 'Bit full of yourself, aren't you?'

'Just tired, sir.'

'Well, you'd better perk yourself up, lad. We'll need our wits about us when we report to the legate.' Macro looked more searchingly at Cato and saw that his friend was close to exhaustion, covered in filth, and still sporting the straggly growth of beard that he picked up as a fugitive hiding in this stinking marsh. Cato's tunic was little more than a rag and the harness and belts hung loosely on his gaunt frame.

Macro clicked his tongue.

'What?'

'Just thinking. The legate's going to have a hard time working out which one of you is the barbarian.'

'Very fucking funny.'

'Heads up! Here he comes now.'

The two centurions wearily clambered to their feet at the sound of approaching horses. The legate, with his tribunes, approached along the side of the track. At sight of the two bloodied and mud-stained officers standing to attention Vespasian reined in. Macro he recognised at once, but the thin, bearded youth caused him to frown for a moment, before his eyes widened in astonishment.

'Centurion Cato . . .? Bloody hell, it is you.'

'Yes, sir.'

'Your optio told me you were still alive. He turned up, with a few others, at the camp. Told me quite a story.' The legate shook his head. 'It's hard to believe.'

'I know, sir.' Cato smiled, and stepped aside to reveal the sullen-faced prisoner sitting by the remains of his chariot. 'We've got something for you, sir. May I present Caratacus, King of the Catuvellaunians.'

'Caratacus?' Vespasian stared down at the man for a moment. Then he dropped his reins, swung himself down from his mount and approached his enemy. 'This is Caratacus?'

The native king looked up and nodded faintly.

'Then it's over,' Vespasian said quietly. 'It's all over at last.'

The legate stared in wonder at his defeated enemy: the man who had fought the legions every step of the way, almost from the moment Claudius' Eagles had first landed on these shores. Then he looked to the two officers who had captured the enemy commander. For once, adequate words failed him.

'Good job.'

'Good job?' Macro looked astonished. 'Is that it?'

'Thank you, sir.' Cato interrupted him. 'We're just doing our duty.'

'Of course you were. I wouldn't expect any less of the two of you.' Vespasian smiled. 'And believe me, Centurion Cato, I'll try to make damn sure that everyone knows it.'

Chapter Forty-One

'This makes for very difficult reading.' Vespasian tapped a thick finger on the parchment roll on the desk in front of him. 'I assume you gentlemen know what this is?'

Cato resisted the impulse to glance sideways at Macro and nodded. 'Centurion Tullius' report, sir?'

'Exactly.' Vespasian looked out over the camp of the Second Legion. Neat rows of goatskin tents stretched out all around, and beyond that the comforting sight of the ramparts of a camp constructed in the face of the enemy. Even though Caratacus and the remainder of his army had been obliterated the legate was not a complacent man. He was aware that some of his peers might accuse him of being overcautious. Ironic, given the mad dash he had led through the heart of the marsh that day. But on the whole Vespasian was very content to be cautious. Careful even. Particularly with his men's lives.

Outside, a crescent moon bathed the world in pale silver-blue light and stars twinkled benignly in the heavens. Their distant diamond coldness was contrasted here on earth by the campfires glittering like living rubies. Despite having fought an engagement earlier in the day, his men were happy enough, and the lilt of their conversation, punctuated by bouts of hard laughter, drifted over the camp. It occurred to him that this was what peace felt like. After the best part of two seasons of the bloodiest campaigning his men could remember.

The only immediate reminder of the day's conflict was the sharp odour from the smouldering remains of fires. The smell wafted over from the silent outline of the Third Cohort's abandoned camp, a short distance away. The palisade had been repaired by the legate's engineers, and an internal ditch added to secure Caratacus and hundreds of his men, being held prisoner. Vespasian would have liked to have made an example of the villagers who had sacked the camp, but the natives had run off at the sight of the legion, though only after they had torched the headquarters and a few of the men's tent lines. Little enough damage considering the opportunity that an abandoned camp had presented to the vengeful natives.

Abandoned, that is apart from the cohort commander and one of his centurions. They had paid the price for lingering in the camp to complete an urgent dispatch, or so the report of the senior surviving officer claimed

– corroborated by the two men who stood to attention in front of the legate's campaign table.

Vespasian picked up the scroll and tapped it against his chin as he regarded the two centurions, and thought the matter over. The fact that Tullius had submitted his report written on a scroll, rather than the usual wax tablets, indicated that he wanted a permanent record of events kept in the archive. That in itself was suspicious; the preferred option of men out to cover their backs.

Vespasian tossed the report on the desk. 'I'm afraid I don't believe a word of it, gentlemen. So tell me, what really happened?'

Cato answered for them. 'It's as Tullius says, sir. We were offered the chance to fight.'

'With no prospect of remission of punishment?'

'With respect, sir,' Macro bowed his head, 'when your mates' lives are on the line, you don't stop to argue the terms. You just fight.'

'That I can accept. But this business about Maximius staying behind to finish some paperwork . . . What was it? Ah yes, a dispatch to me.'

Cato shrugged. 'That's how it happened, sir. Permission to speak freely, sir?'

'That would be a most refreshing change, Centurion. Go on.'

'I suspect the cohort commander knew we were heading into a pretty hopeless fight. I think he was looking for a way out.'

'I see. And Centurion Felix?'

'Maybe he was trying to save Felix. Maximius had his favourites, sir.'

Vespasian smiled. 'And then there's you two. A fugitive on the run from military justice, and an officer who refused to obey an order. I'd say he was within his rights not to bestow any favours on the pair of you. Wouldn't you agree?'

'That's how it looks from the outside,' Macro admitted. 'But you had to be there, sir. You had to see the way he ran the cohort. He just wasn't up to the job. First that balls-up at the Tamesis, for which Cato and others were punished. That wasn't justice, sir. Then there's the way he treated the locals. You'd think he was trying to stir 'em up deliberately. Force them to react. I'd say the man was mad.'

Vespasian shifted in his chair and cleared his throat. 'That's not relevant, Macro, and you know it. Sometimes an officer has to be a harsh disciplinarian. Perhaps Maximius did what he thought was necessary.'

Cato was staring hard at the legate. 'Unless, of course, he was ordered to give the locals a hard time . . .' His eyes narrowed. 'That's why the legion was camped at the end of the track on the other side of the marsh. That's why you marched so quickly to relieve us. You were expecting Caratacus to come out and fight, sir.'

'Silence!' Vespasian snapped, then continued in a cold, threatening tone, 'What the legate of this legion thinks is not the concern of his centurions. Do I make myself clear?'

'Yes, sir!' Cato said stiffly.

'Good. Then all that matters is what I decide to do with you two.' Vespasian leaned back in his chair and regarded them without expression for a moment. Cato felt the sweat break out on the palms of his hands as he balled them into tight fists behind his back.

'Once again, you have performed a valuable service for your comrades, and the Emperor,' Vespasian began. 'I think it's fair to say that your action in blocking the enemy's route from the marsh sealed the fate of Caratacus. And your capture of their commander alone is enough to win the highest of military decorations. Not to mention a promotion.'

Macro beamed at Cato, but Cato sensed this was merely the preamble to something a lot less laudatory.

Vespasian paused briefly before he continued. 'However, I have to say that you, Cato, are still under sentence of death, and you, Macro, are guilty of insubordination and mutiny, which also means a death sentence. If the testimony of one of the other surviving officers of the Third Cohort is to be believed, the pair of you might have a hand in the killing of Centurion Maximius.'

'Cordus!' Macro spat. 'It's that bastard, Cordus. If he—'

'Wait!' Vespasian snapped. He raised a hand as Macro opened his mouth to continue his protest. An unaccustomed moment of discretion forestalled any further protest from passing Macro's lips.

'As you know, there's no proof to back up his evidence. That aside, I cannot ignore the fact that rumours about the death of Maximius are rife throughout the legion. So you two present me with something of a quandary. I can't hold you to account for the murder of another officer, not without solid evidence of your involvement. Of course, I'm sure I could get the general's authority for a summary punishment . . .'

He paused to let the threat sink in.

'The problem is that you two have become heroes to the men of this legion. If you're executed after all that you have achieved, the morale of this unit would be severely damaged for some time to come. The commander of this legion cannot afford to have that additional burden placed on his shoulders. Equally, I cannot allow you to continue to serve in this legion with the other men aware of your possible complicity in the murder of another officer. That would be an appalling threat to the discipline needed to run the legion. I can't have my senior centurions going around watching their backs all the time in case some disgruntled legionary, or gods forbid, another officer, takes it into their head to settle an old score. You cannot be allowed to set such a precedent. You see my difficulty?'

Macro responded first. 'What are you suggesting, sir? Are you going to discharge us?'

There was a look of horror on the face of the older centurion as the full implication of such a possibility struck home. No more life in the legions.

No more chance of booty, no fat gratuity and a comfortable and honourable retirement in some provincial colony. All Macro had known was soldiering. Without the army, and without any income what could he do? Beg? Become a bodyguard for some spoiled brat of a senator's son? The fleeting images that poured through his mind promised only misery. The destruction of his being by a slow, remorseless process of degradation.

Cato was in a more reflective frame of mind. He was young. He had seen rather more of life and death than he had ever imagined, and bore the scars to prove it. Perhaps he had had enough of this life and might find something better. Something more peaceful, more rewarding, something less likely to see him in an early grave.

'Discharge?' Vespasian raised his eyebrows. 'No. You're far too valuable to Rome to throw away in such a manner. Far too valuable. If I've learned one thing as a legate, it's this. While good officers might be in short supply, outstanding officers are a genuinely rare commodity. Rome can't afford to waste them. But, I'm afraid, your life in the Second Legion is over. You'll hope to be transferred to another legion.'

'Which one, sir?' asked Cato.

'None of the units in General Plautius' army, that's for sure. Rumours about your past will follow you wherever you go in this province. So, you'll have to be reassigned. You're leaving Britain. I'm taking you back to Rome with me. I'll see what I can arrange for you with the imperial general staff. Narcissus owes me a favour or two.'

Cato could not hide his surprise. 'You're leaving Britain, sir? Why?'

'My tour of duty's over,' Vespasian replied simply. 'I was notified shortly after your escape. In a few days I'll no longer be legate of the Second. My replacement is due to arrive any day now.'

'Why, sir? Surely after all you've achieved . . .?'

'It seems I've lost the confidence of the general.' Vespasian gave a weary smile. 'Besides, there are plenty of senators who are queuing up for the chance to win a little glory. I don't have much influence at the court of Claudius. They do. Do I really have to spell it out to you?'

'No, sir.'

'Good.' Vespasian nodded. 'Now, I've other work to attend to. Plenty of things to get sorted out before my replacement arrives. You have a few days to settle your affairs in the Second Legion. Pay your debts. Get your savings refunded, and make your farewells. You're dismissed.'

Chapter Forty-Two

Ten days later, Cato and Macro were sitting on a rough wooden bench opposite the merchant ship that would carry them, and the legate, across the sea to the port of Gesoriacum on the Gaulish coast. The *Ajax* was tied alongside the wharf at Rutupiae. Dressed in simple tunics, they sat in the shade and watched the captain shouting at the stevedores that were unloading his cargo of wine from the hold. The slaves had been doing their best to crack one of the amphorae and get a free drink. The captain, however, had carried such cargoes many times before and was threatening to have the skin off the back of the first man who damaged a jar. His voice was hoarse from competing with the shrill cries of the gulls that swirled over the harbour, scavenging.

It had been well over a year since they had last visited the invasion port. Cato had been the optio in Macro's century at the time; a self-conscious and anxious creature who doubted he would live long enough to see the winter. Rutupiae had been a vast supply depot, constantly replenished with food, equipment and men throughout the first season of campaigning. Hundreds of ships had filled the narrow channel leading out to the open sea, waiting their turn to berth at the wharf. There were thousands of slaves labouring to unload the supplies that would keep the voracious Roman war machine grinding forwards.

Since then an advance base had been constructed well up the Tamesis, where Emperor Claudius had joined his army before it swung north and east to defeat Caratacus before the walls of his capital at Camulodunum. Rutupiae was only of minor significance to the military effort now. There was already a large civilian population and a settlement, sprawled back from the wharf. Warehouses had replaced the depot's stockade and they backed on to a makeshift forum where merchants and bankers mixed amongst the stalls of traders, who had arrived from Gaul to take advantage of the new market for the empire's goods.

'It's hard to believe all this has happened so quickly,' said Cato.

'Ain't progress wonderful?' Macro grinned. 'Give it a few more years and it'll look as if Rome has always been here. Might have been a nice place to retire.'

'Seriously?'

Macro thought about it for a moment. 'No. The climate's shit and the

301

drink's piss. Give me a tidy little farm in Campania any day. Got an uncle with a small vineyard near Herculanium. Now that's the kind of retirement for me. Quiet spot by the sea where the biggest danger to life and limb is a bad oyster.'

Cato forced himself to smile. Macro had less than ten years to serve. Cato faced another twenty-three more years with the Eagles, assuming they both survived that long. Not many did on active service. If the enemy didn't get you, the rigours of campaigning almost certainly would. Both men gazed out across the settlement to the rolling farmland beyond, conscious of the fact that they might never see these shores again. Then Cato broke the silence.

'What do you think will happen to us?'

Macro pursed his lips. 'Another legion, I expect. Just pray that we get a nice quiet garrison unit. Preferably in Syria.' Macro's eyes glazed over as he daydreamed about his favourite fantasy posting. 'Yes, Syria would do nicely . . .'

Cato knew that this happy reflection would go on for a good while yet, and beckoned to a passing wine-seller, buying a cup for each of them. The wine-seller, a swarthy fellow with a Greek accent, grunted as he saw the mess tins emerge from their kitbags.

'Soldiers, eh?'

Cato nodded.

'New arrivals?' the wine-seller asked hopefully. 'I could show you the best places to drink. The best places with the best girls.'

'No. We're leaving.' Cato nodded. 'On that ship.'

'Pity. Don't see that many legionaries these days. That's bad for trade.' The wine-seller glanced over them as he poured out the measures from his jar. 'Not medical discharges then?'

'We're being transferred.'

'That's a first. Traffic in healthy soldiers has been one way. You're lucky to be getting off this island in one piece.'

'Tell me about it.'

The wine-seller wished them a safe journey, after one final effort to interest them in a very reasonably priced whorehouse just round the corner.

As soon as the wine had been unloaded the merchant captain began supervising the loading of the return cargo – mostly bales of fur, and two large cages containing several huge hairy hunting dogs that stared lethargically through the bars as they were swayed across and down into the hold. It was mid September, and the air had a chilly edge to it, though the captain's face was beaded with sweat from his efforts. He caught sight of the two Romans and beckoned to them impatiently.

'Heads up,' said Cato. 'We're wanted.'

They heaved their kitbags on to their shoulders and crossed the wharf, carefully negotiating the narrow gangplank and jumping down on to the deck.

'Take all the time you want,' the captain said irritably. 'It's not as if I've got to catch the tide or anything.'

'I think he's in a hurry.' Macro winked at Cato as he slowly set his kitbag down and stretched his back. 'Anyway, you're not going anywhere until the other passenger arrives.'

The captain crossed his thick arms. 'No?'

'Not if you know what's good for you.'

'No one threatens me on the deck of my own ship, least of all a pair of squaddies. If he's not here by the next watch bell, we're leaving.'

'No we're not,' Macro said firmly. 'I doubt the legate would be very amused.'

'Legate?' The captain's eyebrows rose.

'Titus Flavius Vespasian. Late of the Second Legion Augusta. Oh, and we're not squaddies, mate. We're centurions.'

'Centurions?' The captain eyed Cato curiously. 'Both of you?'

'Oh, yes. So don't give us any trouble, friend.'

The captain did not reply. He just glared at them, and turned away quickly, shouting a string of orders to his crew.

'What a prick,' Macro muttered.

'Wonder what's keeping the legate.' Cato stared along the wharf. 'He's only supposed to be paying his respects to the garrison commander.'

Macro shrugged. 'You know what his class are like. Very clubbable. Probably swapping their addresses back in Rome right now.'

Cato suddenly craned his neck. 'There he is!'

'So much for that theory,' Macro grumbled. 'At least we can set sail before that bloody captain has a stroke.'

The legate, like his centurions, was travelling light. All his baggage would follow on later and eventually catch up with him in Rome. His travelling chest had already been carried aboard and he wore a silk tunic with a gold weave in the hems – a simple design, but one that clearly indicated his social status – and people cleared the way ahead of him as he strolled along the wharf, looking for the *Ajax*. Cato waved his arm and caught the legate's attention, and a moment later his iron-studded boots thudded down on the deck. Cato and Macro automatically stood to attention.

'At ease.' Vespasian looked troubled. 'I've just heard some news that may be of interest to you. An army dispatch rider arrived this morning.'

Macro scratched his chin. 'What's that then, sir?'

'Caratacus has escaped.'

'Escaped?' Macro shook his head in disbelief. 'How?'

'It seems there was a riot over the prisoners' food rations. Some men were sent in to quieten them down. Turns out the riot was staged, and the prisoners rushed the stockade gate the moment it was opened. Apparently they just threw themselves at the guards bare-handed. Hundreds of them were killed, but they made sure Caratacus got away. How's that for loyalty?'

Vespasian turned to Cato. 'You know him. What do you think he'll do now?'

Cato shrugged. 'I don't know, sir. I only talked with him a few times.'

'Will he try to continue the fight?'

Cato nodded. 'Yes, sir. I believe he's the kind of man who will never give in. He'd rather die, if he had to.'

'So, it's not over, then.' Vespasian shook his head sadly. 'After everything that's happened, I'd hoped . . .'

He didn't finish the sentence, and just looked away with a weary expression. The legate walked slowly to the front of the vessel and leaned over the bow rail. Macro and Cato watched him for a moment before Macro spoke.

'You have to hand it to Caratacus. Never say die.'

Cato nodded and said quietly, 'At least he was kind enough not to escape before we got full credit for his capture.'

Macro looked at Cato wide-eyed. Then he roared with laughter and slapped his friend on the shoulder. Cato winced.

With the last of his passengers on board, the captain gave the order to cast off and two large sweeps were lowered over the sides. With the crew straining at the long oars the ship was slowly rowed out into the channel, until the *Ajax* was clear of the other vessels. Then the oars were shipped and the sails unfurled. A light breeze carried them out to sea where the wind strengthened, the mainsail filling up like a pot belly. The bow rose and fell as it met the ocean swell. Cato and Macro moved to the back of the ship and leaned on the stern rail, watching the coast gradually slip away until Britain was no more than a vague outline on the horizon. At that point Macro lost interest, and wandered forward to the main mast to try to interest some of the crew in a game of dice.

Cato stayed at the rail, wondering why he suddenly felt so emotional at the disappearance of the land where he had suffered so much pain, so much loss, and seen more than enough cruelty to last him a lifetime. He should feel relieved to be quitting the island, he thought. Instead, he felt a peculiar emptiness, like he was leaving some essential part of himself on those shores. A moment later, the stern of the vessel reared up and Cato had one final sight of the distant land, then the *Ajax* swooped down the far side of the swell and Britain disappeared for good.

A little later Cato sensed a presence at his shoulder and glanced back. Macro was standing there, looking into the creamy wake behind the ship. 'Seems no one on this bloody ship is prepared to gamble with a centurion.'

'Can you blame them?' Cato smiled.

'I don't suppose you—'

'No.'

'Oh, right.' Macro did not hide his disappointment. 'What are you moping about here for?'

Cato stared at his friend for a moment. In truth he had begun to think about the future. About what would happen now that they had left the Second Legion. The legate had promised to act as their patron when they reached Rome. He would try to use what influence he had to secure them appointments in a new legion, but that would depend on vacancies. Right now only the units in Britain were on active service, and the demand for centurions amongst the other legions posted across the Empire would be limited. The prospect of several months kicking his heels in Rome, with an increasingly frustrated Macro for company, was none too appealing. Cato just hoped that when the time came, their new legion would offer his friend a chance to get stuck into some serious soldiering, before he went completely mad.

Cato smiled. 'Just thinking.'

'What about?'

'What comes next. Anything has got to be better than the last two years of campaigning.'

'You think so?' Macro sniffed. 'Believe me, there are worse places. And with our luck, you can be sure we'll be seeing them.'

Cato turned to look back over the stern, his eyes following the diminishing traces of the *Ajax*'s wake, until he was staring at the horizon.

'I wonder if we'll ever see Britain again?'

Macro shrugged his heavy shoulders. 'Frankly, lad, I fear we just might.'

Author's Note

Although Caratacus and his warriors were driven from the battlefield by the legions in the year following the invasion, the indomitable British commander continued a spirited resistance against Roman rule. After his defeats in the south-east of the island Caratacus fled to the tribes that inhabited modern-day Wales. These wild and warlike mountain tribes shared his desire for independence, and were encouraged in their will to resist by the druid cult based in their refuge on the island of Anglesey. Their determination to fight on, coupled with the mountainous terrain, made life very difficult for governors of the new Roman province of Britannia for many more years. Caratacus shared his new-found experience of the most effective kind of warfare to wage against Rome with the mountain tribesmen, and fast-moving raiding columns posed a constant danger to the widely dispersed Roman soldiers and their tenuous lines of supply.

Rome had a long tradition of never admitting defeat, or permitting pockets of resistance to continue in lands it had laid claim to. Eventually Caratacus was driven out of Wales and fled to the north of Britain, in a bid to whip up support amongst the powerful Brigantian confederation. A considerable number of Brigantian nobles were sympathetic to his cause, but their ruler, Queen Cartimandua, was afraid of provoking the wrath of Rome. How that turned out is another story. A story that may well require the return to Britain of two very experienced and talented legionary officers.

Cato and Macro are on their way to Rome. We know from the tombstones of centurions that such men served in a variety of units across the length and breadth of the Empire. Our heroes can expect to travel to new lands and encounter a wide range of enemies in the future. But before Cato and Macro secure appointments in a new legion they must first overcome the rumours and suspicions surrounding their recent actions during the war against Caratacus. They must prove themselves worthy of being reappointed to the ranks of Emperor Claudius' legions. Ahead of them lies a perilous undercover mission to secure a sacred artefact that will determine the destiny of the Empire.

THE FIRST

PHOTOGRAPHS